By the Noble Daring of Her Sons

By the Noble Daring of Her Sons

The Florida Brigade
of the Army of Tennessee

Jonathan C. Sheppard

THE UNIVERSITY OF ALABAMA PRESS

Tuscaloosa

Copyright © 2012
The University of Alabama Press
Tuscaloosa, Alabama 35487-0380
All rights reserved
Manufactured in the United States of America

Typeface: AGaramond

∞

The paper on which this book is printed meets the minimum requirements of American National Standard for Information Sciences—Permanence of Paper for Printed Library Materials, ANSI Z39.48-1984.

Library of Congress Cataloging-in-Publication Data

Sheppard, Jonathan C., 1980–
    By the noble daring of her sons : the Florida Brigade of the Army of Tennessee / Jonathan C. Sheppard.
        pages cm
    Includes bibliographical references and index.
    ISBN 978-0-8173-1707-2 (trade cloth : alk. paper) — ISBN 978-0-8173-8603-0 (ebook) 1. Confederate States of America. Army. Florida Brigade (1863–1865) 2. Florida—History—Civil War, 1861–1865—Regimental histories. 3. United States—History—Civil War, 1861–1865—Regimental histories. 4. United States—History—Civil War, 1861–1865—Campaigns. I. Title.
    E558.5.F55S54 2012
    973.7′3—dc23

                                                                            2011050827

Cover: Hardee pattern battle flag of the 1st Florida Infantry Regiment, ca. late 1862–1863. Inscription: 1st Florida Shiloh and Perryville. Collections of the Museum of Florida History.

To the memory of my Father

Contents

Photographs follow page 148

Maps

Preface

Somewhere in an unmarked grave on the Murfreesboro battlefield lie the remains of George Hartsfield. A soldier in the 3rd Florida Infantry Regiment, Hartsfield had already endured his share of suffering in the service, having been wounded at Perryville that October. Sufficiently recuperated, he rejoined his company in time for what would be his last battle. Hartsfield was representative of the majority of soldiers who fought in General Jesse Johnson Finley's Florida Brigade; a North Carolina–born farmer, he was both illiterate and hailed from a non-slaveholding family.

Perhaps the fact that Hartsfield has lain undisturbed in an unknown location for more than 148 years is also symbolic of Finley's Florida soldiers. Their story, like his grave, remained forgotten, their deeds bypassed in the vastness of Civil War historiography. Between 1861 and 1862, Floridians like Hartsfield flocked to join the six regiments that eventually constituted the Florida Brigade of the West. As the fragile remains of the 1st and 3rd Florida Infantry Regiments' battle flag attests, the brigade's various regiments witnessed action in most major battles of the Western Theater. Until November 1863, the 1st, 3rd, 4th, 6th, and 7th Florida Infantry Regiments, and the 1st Florida Cavalry Regiment, Dismounted, served in separate brigades in different areas of the west. While the 1st, 3rd, and 4th regiments soldiered with the Army of Tennessee, the other regiments protected the important Virginia-Tennessee rail line against East Tennessee Unionists.

Following its organization in November 1863, the Florida Brigade became the epitome of the hard-luck Army of Tennessee. Below strength, shouldering a motley assortment of weapons, and shoddily equipped, the soldiers of the brigade followed their commanders through some of the hardest fighting of the war. From Missionary Ridge to Nashville, attrition whittled away at the already small units. A great many fell in battle, wounds incapacitated others, and still more wasted away in Northern prison camps. At the time of the surrender at Bennett Place on April 26, 1865, just over four hundred veterans remained with the brigade.

This work presents the first full-length study of the Army of Tennessee's Florida Brigade; it is therefore a survey of the battles and the hardships of military life during the American Civil War. While I strove to document as many of the Florida soldiers' own experiences as possible, it became necessary when describing certain events to provide a glimpse of the big picture. Through the existing primary sources of Florida soldiers, their Confederate comrades, and enemies, I set forth to give the most complete account of the western Florida Brigade's role in the Civil War.

Their history is more than just accounts of familiar battles; it is the tale of ordinary citizens who, during extraordinary times, were called to fight their fellow countrymen. It is one of schoolmates going to war and families left behind. Unfortunately, is also the chronicle of a people fighting to maintain a society built upon slavery.

Without mentors, family, and friends, this book could not have been attempted, much less completed. I would like to extend my gratitude and appreciation to those who accompanied me on this journey.

This study began under the guidance of Dr. Jim Jones, and his suggestions and critiques helped mold this book. I consider it an honor to have him as a constant source of inspiration and, most important, my friend. I would also like to thank Professors Michael Creswell, Peter Garretson, Joe M. Richardson, and Tony Stallins, each of whom has helped me forge my academic career.

My research for this topic led me to many archives and libraries in several states; at each the archivists and their staffs were extremely accommodating and provided an excellent environment for research. I would like to thank in paticular Dr. Boyd Murphree and the archivists at the Florida State Archives in Tallahassee. The Florida State Library staff were also extremely helpful in locating various microfilmed newspapers and made available the Washington M. Ives Jr. Papers. I would also like to extend my gratitude to the Interlibrary Loan staff at Strozier Library at Florida State University, as well as to Special Collections; Norwood Kerr at the Alabama Division of Archives and History; Joan D. Linn at the Keystone Genealogical Library at Monticello, Florida; Melissa Smith of the Howard-Tilton Memorial Library at Tulane University; Eric Milenkiewicz of the Special Collections Library at the University of California, Riverside; John Coski at the Museum of the Confederacy; James Cusick, curator at the P. K. Yonge Library of Florida History; and the knowledgeable and helpful archivists at both the National Archives in Washington, D.C., and the Duggan Library at Hanover College. I also must thank Dr. William Hugh Tucker for allowing me permission to cite letters from *The McKenzie Correspondence, 1849–1901,* and the *Florida Historical Quarterly* for their permission to reprint parts of my article, "'This Seems to Be Our Darkest Times': The Florida Brigade in Mississippi, June–July 1863," *Florida Historical Quarterly* 85, no. 1 (Summer 2006): 64–90, which appears in chapter 11. I offer my appreciation to Dan Waterman and all the wonderful staff at The University of Alabama Press, and special thanks go to Jennifer Backer, my excellent and proficient copyeditor.

I am hugely grateful to Zack Waters of Rome, Georgia. A proficient and knowledgeable Florida Civil War historian and fellow Braves fan, Zack generously invited me to Rome and provided me with a stack of his own carefully collected research. Without these letters and unpublished manuscripts, the Florida Brigade's story could not have been adequately told. His suggestions throughout the writing process were extremely helpful.

Lastly, I need to thank the Ramsey Bend crew for putting up with me; my grandparents and other family members for their support; and lastly for Mother and my late father, whose love and guidance I shall never forget.

By the Noble Daring of Her Sons

1   Therefore Let Us Unite
Florida's Secession

The Florida that attracted Americans between 1790 and the early 1800s was a land of natural beauty and promise. Americans probably first arrived in this alluring territory during the 1790s when the Spanish government "invited foreigners to settle in Florida by offering homestead grants." Thereafter, they kept coming, by both legal and illegal means. These foreigners, with their slaves, supplemented the ethnic potpourri that existed in Florida during the Second Spanish Period. Many were well established by 1821, the year Spain bequeathed Florida Territory to the United States.[1]

The American pioneers arrived via widened Indian trails, such as the "Coffee Road" that wound southward from Georgia and allowed access to the virgin pine forests and oak hammocks of northern Florida. Others, from Virginia and North Carolina, "took a more circuitous route, traveling with their families and slaves from the Atlantic ports by boat, and debarked in Florida at the ancient Spanish outpost of St. Marks." They forded the spring-fed rivers and streams that flowed sluggishly to the Gulf of Mexico and the Atlantic, and camped beneath palms and among Spanish Bayonets until they completed their log cabins.[2]

The early American settlers arrived in Florida for various reasons. Unpropertied men sought to escape states that allowed only property owners to hold voting rights. These tenant farmers "hoped, in new states and territories, to establish themselves as independent landowners, and to demand that planters treat them as equals." To these whites, Florida offered two inducements: its land prices, which remained cheap throughout the 1850s, and its "soils suitable for many different crops." Rich soil meant good cotton land, which in turn meant the possibility of one day owning slaves and commanding a vast plantation. As Chandra Manning has appropriately noted of the slave-owning society, "Again and again, southern whites abandoned places of poor soil and disappointing prospects for new locations where land and slave ownership seemed possible." Many who migrated into the state included the parents of soldiers who would fight for Florida during the Civil War.[3]

Early on, Florida Territory's good soil also lured established planters away from their homes in Virginia and North Carolina, as the Upper South had experienced a "shift in clime" that "helped drive planters south and west." In addition to this natural phenomenon, after centuries of use the nutrients of many older fields were depleted, making a search for new lands necessary. When word arrived that Florida's "soil was especially suited for the growth of Sea Island cotton," which was "superior to the short staple" and had a "market price per pound . . . about twice that of short staple," many planters made the move. Some planters correctly assumed that crops other than cotton would prosper in Florida, and experimented with tobacco and sugar.[4]

Many of the planters and small farmers who migrated to Florida to take advantage of the rich soils and the potential to own slaves settled in the fertile regions between the Suwannee and Apalachicola rivers. This area, which came to be called Middle Florida, grew very quickly from "a wilderness" with few inhabitants in 1821 to one with a population of nearly sixteen thousand by 1830. Over the next decade, its population doubled again; in 1840 more than thirty-four thousand persons called Middle Florida home. The majority of these pioneers were slaves.[5]

With its planters utilizing slave labor, Florida quickly became infused with the economic infrastructure of the South. By 1860 slaves working on several thousand plantations within the state harvested an estimated sixty-five thousand bales of cotton per annum, along with both sugar cane and tobacco. There were also thousands of smaller farms scattered throughout the state.[6]

This area, nestled between the older and more established regions of East and West Florida, became the home of the territory's American pedigree. Its early counties were called Franklin, Hamilton, Jefferson, and Madison after the Founding Fathers and presidents. Gadsden gained its title from a territorial politician who later served as ambassador to Mexico. Liberty embodied the nation's freedom, and Leon honored the territory's Spanish discoverer, Ponce de Leon. The United States made a further mark on Middle Florida by overseeing the establishment of a new capital city, Tallahassee, thus moving the government away from the established towns of St. Augustine and Pensacola.[7]

With the conclusion of the Second Seminole Indian War in 1842, Congress passed the Armed Occupation Act, which "permitted settlements from present day Gainesville south to Peace River and the Seminole reservation." The act provided 160 acres to any family head who resided on the granted land for five years. The legislation essentially provided a buffer of armed settlers between the reservation and the populated areas of East and Middle Florida.[8]

Subsidized by the federal government, more than six thousand pioneers pushed into South Florida and settled on more than two hundred thousand acres. Some moved to pursue farming, while others discovered that the prairies inland from Tampa Bay supported cattle, and ranching flourished. While some of the settlers who took advantage of the act already resided in Florida, "it was estimated by June 1843, that well over one-half of the people filing claims" under the Armed Occupation Act "were from outside Florida—most from Georgia and South Carolina."[9]

Generally, Florida's migrants before 1840 were from the Upper South and politically conservative. This was not so of the immigrants of the 1840s and 1850s who poured into the fledgling state from South Carolina and Georgia. On the eve of the Civil War, the number of South Carolinians living in the Land of Flowers had "almost doubled and the number of Georgians" increased by half: "The largest number of nonnative Floridians were from Georgia and South Carolina, in that order, and together they constituted about one-third of the total population by 1860." These settlers moved "into Florida with . . . idiosyncracies developed" and with their numbers could easily influence the ballot box.[10]

Throughout the late 1840s and 1850s, Deep South pioneers added to Florida's already motley population. These new residents not only wished to re-create their societies within Florida but also sought political dominance. What resulted then were communities of Georgians and South Carolinians who maintained close ties with their native states and eventually helped push Florida toward secession.[11]

Deep South planters flooded into Florida, bringing with them their slaves in an attempt to take advantage of the "affordable and inhabitable acreage . . . available only a few hundred miles away" from their old plantations and worn-out soil. "Even those who missed the opportunity for free land under the Armed Occupation Act found that acreage relatively cheap." The South Carolinians and Georgians started new plantations within the state, particularly in Middle Florida and to the southeast in Alachua, Columbia, and Marion counties. By 1860, 78,699 whites lived within the state; 1,888 of them owned the state's 56,000 slaves.[12]

South Carolinians and Georgians seemed to dominate the peninsula, perpetuating Democratic politics within their counties. Because two-thirds of Madison County's large planters hailed from South Carolina, the area became known as the Palmetto County. By 1860 in Alachua County, "native Georgians accounted for 309 of the county's heads of household," and South Carolinians headed 338 families. Combined, residents from these two states represented "74.9 percent of Alachua County's slaveholding population." Georgians also composed the second-largest group of citizens within Leon County.[13]

To be sure, these South Carolinians and Georgians, who brought with them their politics and society, helped tether the ties between the peninsula and its Deep South neighbors. As the decade of the 1850s wore on and the Democrats gained tight control over Florida, South Carolinians began to realize that in the event of a crisis they could count on their kin living to the south.[14]

Many of these new residents adhered to the radical principles of John C. Calhoun and out of their ideals developed the "'South Carolina School' of Florida politics." South Carolinians in Florida practiced this "school's" teachings, which "desired to replicate the Palmetto State in Florida." The "supreme aim" of the Democrats who belonged to this informal clique "was to protect Southern Rights and the institution of slavery" within Florida. This group included Madison Starke Perry, the firebrand and future president of Florida's Secession Convention, and

David Levy Yulee, who served as a U.S. senator through much of the antebellum period.[15]

During the 1840s and early 1850s, the conservative Whigs and radical Democrats, whose parties formed during Florida's Union Bank crisis of the late 1830s, maintained the two-party system in Florida. The latter party gained an upper hand early, as countrymen who wished both to assert their influence in the territory's political affairs and to exact revenge on a bank that was very particular with regard to whom it loaned money joined. Later, the two parties adhered to the ideology of their national namesakes.[16]

Though the Whigs managed to gain power in the election of 1848, because of their portrayal as a party that "expressed concern for the entire nation" and one that "would not be influenced by a section of the party but would rather function as an American body," their fortunes turned with the Compromise of 1850. Florida Whigs supported the Compromise, which among its many provisions allowed California to join the Union as a free state in the hope that it would maintain national party unity. Southerners understood that this addition would upset the balance maintained in the Senate and bar slavery from the shores of the Pacific. Because the Whigs demonstrated a reluctance to fight for what many considered Southern interests during that tumultuous congressional session and "as the perceived threat to the institution of slavery increased," Floridians saw the Democratic Party as the institution's ablest defender.[17]

The Whig Party's decline accelerated with the passage of the Kansas-Nebraska Act in 1854, which opened these two territories for settlement on the grounds of popular sovereignty. Southern Whigs, unwilling to compromise their remaining power to satisfy national unity, voted for the bill and the party soon collapsed. It passed into history for it no longer could claim to "express concern for the whole nation," as its members could not find a middle ground on the vital issue of slavery in the territories.[18]

The Democrats of Florida first advocated disunion during the debates over the Compromise of 1850. Individuals first supported secession; it was not party policy initially. Following the passage of the Compromise Omnibus Bill, some of Florida's Deep South agitators who thought the North had treated the South unjustly formed the Southern Rights Association in Middle Florida. The association members pledged to provide "resistance to the encroachments of the North on the constitutional rights of the South." Members also promised to "vote only for open and zealous advocates of southern rights, to give preference to goods of southern manufacture and boycott northern firms professing abolitionist sentiments."[19]

During the 1850s, the state Democratic Party was influenced by the influx of South Carolinians and Georgians into the Land of Flowers, but the party's radicalism grew due to other outside forces as well. John E. Johns, a historian of Florida's role in the Civil War, identified the "formation of the Republican party" in

1854 as the "primary cause for the vast popular support which aligned itself behind Florida Democrats." Floridians saw the party, which contained abolitionist elements, as a direct threat to their society.[20]

During the latter half of the 1850s, one particular development drew even more of Florida's citizens to stand with the radical Democrats. In October 1859 the abolitionist John Brown and more than a dozen followers attempted to seize the federal arsenal at Harper's Ferry, Virginia, with the purpose of arming a planned slave revolt. Though U.S. Marines quickly captured Brown and quelled the rebellion, Southerners were hasty to lay blame for the attempted insurrection at the feet of the Republicans and were ever watchful for other abolitionist plots.

Within Florida, as elsewhere throughout the South, "Democrats were prominent in this agitation. Local leaders were vigorously at work throughout Florida during the spring and summer of 1860. The state administration was Democratic and the governor used the influence of his position to arouse the state." In December 1859 the Democrat-controlled Florida legislature established Florida's policy toward a Republican presidential victory: in essence, if a Republican were elected, Florida would take action for "self-defense."[21]

Southerners were further roiled by the "publication of [Hinton Rowan] Helper's *Impending Crisis of the South* with the sanction of northern congressmen." This work infuriated Southerners because Helper was a North Carolinian, who, while praising the free labor system of the North, demonstrated, using mounds of statistical data, that the institution of slavery would lead the South to ruin. Fueled by fear that a Republican president would disturb the institution of slavery, the South's economic and social base, the Democrats ensured "Florida was ready to follow South Carolina over the cliff that was secession into the abyss of disunion and defeat in the Civil War."[22]

The strain that the burden of slavery placed on the United States came to a breaking point in November 1860. The upcoming presidential election and its pressing issues were the subject of Florida's major newspapers and journals. The majority of the state's journals endorsed Southern Democrat John C. Breckinridge, the sitting vice president. He hailed from Kentucky and became the choice of Southern Democrats following a divisive schism that rocked the National Democratic Convention in Charleston.

At the convention, when Northern proponents of the party failed to appease their Southern comrades with a pro-slavery platform, delegates of the Deep South stalked angrily from the hall. The two wings of the party tried again in Baltimore, but that turmoil-filled experience ended as well with delegates walking out. Finally, Southern Democrats took it upon themselves to nominate a national candidate, Breckinridge, to defend their interests. Northern Democrats chose as their nominee party stalwart Stephen A. Douglas. The champion of popular sovereignty, the short and stocky Illinois senator had also gained fame for winning passage of the Compromise of 1850, taking over the troubled set of bills from an ailing Henry Clay.

Florida's citizens read numerous editorials vilifying Douglas, one of which claimed that "the principles enunciated by Mr. Douglas, are contrary to all Democratic doctrine." Florida's editors, however, did not reserve all of their harsh criticism for the Illinois senator. Though there was little chance that the Republican candidate, Abraham Lincoln, would receive any votes in Florida, a likely threat existed in the Constitutional Union candidate John Bell.[23]

The Constitutional Union Party arose in May 1860 when "old-line Whigs and [the] Americans [Party], met in convention in Chicago . . . in an effort to allay sectional animosities and in an attempt to save the Union." The leaders of this party hoped to convince voters that they remained the only true national party, pledging to "uphold the Union as it is, . . . oppose the efforts of all sectionalists, North or South, to weaken undermine or destroy it." The party attempted to draw the nation's moderates, arguing in its platform that "the continued agitation of the slavery question, either for the protection or prevention of slavery by Congress, can have no effect, except in tending greatly to . . . sectional divisions merely to promote the ambitious and dangerous views of designing demagogues, while it endangers the safety of the Union, and should therefore be discountenanced, and frowned down, by every friend of his country."[24]

Though Florida's Constitutional Union Party claimed to adhere to the national party platform, many historians have debated the degree to which its members were committed to preserving the Union. Some Florida voters certainly believed in these centrist principles, but at least one historian has argued that because the Democratic rhetoric had so saturated the voting public, "there were now no real Unionists among politicians: all were secessionists of one stripe or another." However, the historian Herbert Doherty Jr. argued that Florida's Constitutional Union Party was simply a facade behind which "did old Whigs bestir themselves to a last effort against the Democrats" in an attempt to reestablish a conservative voice within Florida politics.[25]

Doherty argued that many Constitutional Union Party members remained steadfast to their old Whig principles of preservation of the Union and the old Whigs promised to mute any voices calling for secession. Likewise, another historian agreed that the "Constitutional Union men declared that disunion was the issue of the campaign," and with Governor Madison Starke Perry boasting that "Florida would follow the lead of any single cotton state that might secede," it became difficult to argue with this viewpoint. Despite the Constitutional Union Party's call for cool heads, "on their demand for secession if Lincoln should be elected, the Democrats carried all before them."[26]

The important point is that during the fall of 1860 the Constitutional Union Party presented the people of Florida with a choice at the polls. As the two parties backed Breckinridge and Bell as their respective candidates in the presidential race, Democrat R. B. Hilton contested Constitutional Unionist B. F. Allen for a congressional seat. For the gubernatorial race, the Democrats, following a lengthy balloting process, nominated John Milton, a Jackson County planter, lawyer, and politician. At Quincy in June 1860, the Constitutional Union Party had chosen Duval County planter and former Whig Edward Hopkins as their candidate.[27]

In October, Milton's hard campaigning along with the Democrats' political superiority helped send him to the governor's office with a 1,742-vote majority. The Democrats' cheerfulness quickly disappeared, however, when the nation elected its first Republican president on the first Tuesday in November. Within the state Breckinridge polled 8,534 votes, while Bell managed 5,437. A disappointing 327 Florida voters thought Douglas would make an excellent executive.[28]

Once Abraham Lincoln's election became certain, ex-Whigs in Florida favored disunion. Two facts above all others likely contributed to this change of heart. The first was a fear of the repercussions similar to those that had occurred following the debates over the Compromise of 1850, which the Whigs had supported. Their actions cost them support in the state and eventually came to nil following the passage of the Kansas-Nebraska Act in 1854. The second was Lincoln's unpredictable stance on the slavery question.

Writing from Ocala days after the election, the East Florida lawyer Samuel Darwin McConnell wrote to his fiancée, "The election has caused considerable excitement here for several days past. As the election of Lincoln seems certain, nearly everyone here is in favor of a dissolution of the Union. I think it is almost certain that some of the Southern states will secede."[29]

Floridians responded to the news of Lincoln's election with anger, and citizens prepared to support the Deep South states in taking action against the incoming Republican administration. In the weeks following the election, mass meetings were called in towns throughout the state as Floridians attempted to commit their feelings to paper in the form of resolutions and proclamations, all calling for a secession convention. After years of political infighting within the state, it became ironic that a cause for national disunion required a plea for the state's citizens to stand together.[30]

In St. Augustine, residents asked their fellow citizens to stand together in a declaration: "let us unite, as one man, to the resolution to protect our rights, our families and neighbors, against the insidious wiles of the emissaries of our enemies." The residents of the Ancient City warned that no compromise could patch the nation's fractures in 1860 for "time and experience have taught us that, the majority in the people of the Northern States are resolved not to keep faith with us." A Fernandina editor claimed that in Florida "a stern spirit of resistance to Black Republican domination is every where manifest, and her sons, as one man, will rally round the state banner, whenever its folds are shaken out to the Breeze."[31]

In Jefferson County, situated in the plantation belt of Middle Florida, the towns-people of Waukeenah met to create a petition arguing for secession. The document stated that the citizens were "laying aside all old party prejudices to unite together and carry out whatever plans may be devised as the best to oppose the tyranny of Black Republican sway: and as dearly as we have cherished the Union we will give up even that rather than surrender our rights." William S. Dilworth, a Georgia-born politician and lawyer from the nearby town of Monticello, addressed the citizens in the county newspaper for the secessionists: "We hope in this matter to see Florida stand . . . united as one man. We can say this much at least, if there is any backing out on the part of Florida, it won't be found in old Jefferson."[32]

When the Florida legislature convened in late November at the behest of Governor Perry, the politicians heeded the cries of their constituencies and voted to hold a secession convention in Tallahassee beginning on January 3, 1861. On December 20, 1860, South Carolina seceded, and fervor for disunion within Florida rose; two days later, citizens of the state voted to elect delegates to represent them in the secession convention. The *St. Augustine (FL) Examiner* applauded the election of delegates, exclaiming that "all who engage in it are exercising their rights as FREEMEN and INDEPENDENT citizens. We are FREEMEN, the government has once admitted that we were, now should we submit to those who say we are not?"[33]

During the first week of January the delegates gathered in Tallahassee and set about the business of secession. Though he was not a member of the convention, Western Circuit judge Jesse J. Finley was in town to administer the president-elect's oath of office. The judge, a former Whig, addressed a crowd at the capitol at the height of the proceedings, saying in part that he "thanked God that South Carolina was out of the Union, and hoped that Florida would be so this week."[34]

The deliberations lasted five days, and following a failed effort by conservative ex-Whigs to delay secession until both Georgia and Alabama had quit the Union, the convention voted, 62–7, in favor of disunion on January 10, 1861. The delegates signed the secession ordinance the following day amid celebration. The editor of Tallahassee's *Floridian and Journal* wrote triumphantly, "On the 6th day of November, a sectional minority for sectional purposes, took control of the Government, and now in less than ninety days from that untoward event, three of the Sovereignties composing the Union have separated themselves from it."[35]

Even before Florida's delegates officially announced their decision on secession, they determined to display a show of force against federal forts and the lone arsenal within the state. Urged on by Senator David Yulee and the convention, Governor Perry authorized the Florida militia to act. Companies seized the Apalachicola Arsenal at Chattahoochee on January 6 and the Castillo at St. Augustine the next morning. As the lone ordnance sergeant of the ancient fort handed over the keys to the throng of militiamen, the U.S. flag came down from the flagstaff and one of secession went up in its place.[36]

During the antebellum years, Florida was populated by outsiders, as Georgians and South Carolinians moved into the state by the thousands and seized political power. These radicals, as the conservative element in the state's potency waned, helped to guide Florida toward secession. The question that remained as 1861 dawned was, could the population of a state whose disheveled past exhibited disharmony now put aside its political differences to rally behind a cause for Florida?

2 Like Achilles He Has Girded on His Armor

April–September 1861

Throughout the spring and summer of 1861, Florida armed her sons for war. The basis of the Florida Brigade, the 1st, 3rd, and 4th Florida Infantry Regiments, mustered into service during this initial wave of patriotic fervor. These three regiments, the bulk of their companies from Middle Florida counties, began serving together in Tennessee in 1862 and remained together until the end. Though they could not know that their common destiny lay at Perryville, Missionary Ridge, and Bennett's Place, North Carolina, in 1861 the men grew weary guarding the state's coasts. As Florida's populace grudgingly abided a Federal presence at Key West, they worried about Federal raids on their shores and held their breath as conflict loomed at Pensacola.

By noon on January 10, 1861, the ordeal was over and Lieutenant Adam Slemmer could breathe more easily. That morning he oversaw the transportation of his small garrison of artillerymen from Fort Barrancas, near the Pensacola Navy Yard on the mainland, across Pensacola Bay to unoccupied Fort Pickens. The move placed a mile of water between his troops and the secessionists; moreover, Slemmer now had the Gulf of Mexico at his back. This meant that the Federal Navy could easily reinforce and supply pentagon-shaped Pickens, which sat among sand dunes on the western tip of Santa Rosa Island. The bespectacled lieutenant hoped that Pickens's thick walls and heavy ordnance would suffice to discourage an attack by secessionist soldiers.[1]

The next night Alabama state troops arrived at Pensacola and on January 12, together with Florida militia companies, they seized the navy yard without a fight. Fort Barrancas, whose position commanded the mouth of the bay, and Fort McRae, a small installation just opposite Fort Pickens across the ship channel, also fell into the hands of the secessionists. After Lieutenant Slemmer refused several demands for surrender, a few hotheads among the militia demanded that they be permitted to assault Fort Pickens, but the appointed commander of forces at Pensacola, William Chase, displayed caution. A retired army engineer, Chase had overseen the construction of Fort Pickens, and although the fort was lightly defended, the historian George Pearce has argued that the old engineer understood his fort's potential: "Unquestionably, the possibility of heavy casualties resulting from a direct attack by" his "generally poorly trained and badly equipped volunteers was of the utmost importance in any decision to attack the fort."[2]

Chase's decision was upheld by adopted Pensacola resident and U.S. senator Stephen R. Mallory. The future Confederate Navy secretary, along with David Levy Yulee and numerous other southern senators, including Mississippian Jefferson Davis, telegraphed Governor Madison Starke Perry on January 18, telling the executive, "We think no assault should be made. . . . Bloodshed now may be fatal to our cause." Over the next ten days more troops from Alabama arrived in the Pensacola area; day after day the men, standing on the ramparts of Forts Barrancas and McRae, watched Fort Pickens across the blue sheen of the bay.[3]

On January 28 news surfaced that President James Buchanan had ordered reinforcements to the small garrison on Santa Rosa Island. Southern senators remaining in Washington immediately placed an offer before the lame-duck president, stating that "the inevitable consequence of re-enforcement under present circumstances is instant war, as peace will be preserved if no re-enforcements be attempted." Buchanan folded, and on January 29 orders went out from the secretaries of war and the navy to forces in the Pensacola area, instructing commanders to land the new troops only if Fort Pickens came under attack or if preparations for an attack were under way.[4]

The "Fort Pickens Truce" served to dull the sharp calls for fighting at Pensacola. However, as it was attempting to assert its newfound sovereignty, the Confederacy could not abide the Federal flag flying over its soil. Therefore, in early March, despite the uneasy calm, the Provisional Confederate Government that had formed in Montgomery in February appointed Brigadier General Braxton Bragg to command Confederate forces in West Florida.[5]

In addition, on March 9, 1861, the Confederate secretary of war dispatched telegrams to the governors of seceded states, calling for troops to report to the Confederacy's vulnerable coastline, with five thousand designated for Pensacola. In this number, the Confederate War Department required five hundred Floridians for service within their state. Governor Perry dispatched the order across the peninsula and almost immediately companies formed and applied for active service. In Jefferson County, the governor's order reached James Patton Anderson.[6]

Standing above average height and sporting a dark, wiry beard, thirty-nine-year-old James Patton Anderson lived a full life before migrating to Florida in 1857. Born near Winchester, Tennessee, in February 1822, Anderson, following his father's death in 1831, lived with his mother's family in Kentucky. As a young man he also lived among northerners, as he attended and graduated in 1840 from Jefferson College in Cannonsburg, Pennsylvania. Following graduation, Anderson followed his remarried mother to Hernando, Mississippi, where he served nine months of every year as a deputy sheriff, and spent the summers in Kentucky studying law.[7]

In October 1847, as the Mexican-American War raged, the Mississippi governor cut Anderson's newly established law partnership short when he asked the young man to form a company for service south of the border. Anderson was elected captain, and his unit became part of a five-company battalion that departed for Tampico, Mexico, in early January 1848. Garrisoned at Tampico, the Tennessean rose to the rank of lieutenant colonel, commanded his battalion, and survived a bout of malaria. The Mississippi troops returned home in July 1848 and were mustered out of service. Though Anderson did not see action in the war, he gained invaluable experience in commanding volunteers.[8]

A Democrat, Anderson won election to the Mississippi legislature in 1849 and was seated in January 1850, just as the Compromise crisis was beginning. The new politician allied with another Mexican-American War veteran, Jefferson Davis (now a U.S. senator), in combating the proposed compromise. Both were defeated in 1851, Davis while running for Mississippi's governorship and Anderson for reelection to the state house. Anderson's support of Davis in the fight over the Compromise and during his bid for governor would not go unnoticed by the future Confederate president. In 1853, Davis, newly appointed as secretary of war, arranged for Anderson's appointment as a U.S. marshal in the Washington Territory.[9]

Thirty-one years old and recently married, Anderson boarded a steamer at New Orleans for Washington Territory. Once there, he worked to take an official census and, in his spare time, practiced law. In 1855 the Democrats nominated him to become Washington's non-voting delegate to Congress. Anderson won the election, serving as the territory's delegate until 1857, when newly elected president James Buchanan offered him the position of "Governor and Superintendent of Indian Affairs in Washington." Anderson refused this appointment and instead moved to Jefferson County, Florida, to enjoy the climate and manage Casa Bianca, his aunt's profitable plantation of four hundred acres and fifty-four slaves.[10]

Anderson immersed himself in Florida politics, fitting in well with the proponents of the "South Carolina School." Anderson was a member of Jefferson County's delegation at the Secession Convention in Tallahassee and in February 1861 represented the state in the Provisional Confederate Congress. On March 26, after receiving the Confederacy's request for soldiers, the governor wrote to Anderson, asking the lawyer to raise a company to fulfill a portion of Florida's quota. Across the state, volunteer companies applied to the governor to become part of the 1st Florida Infantry Regiment. Nine companies were chosen to rendezvous at Chattahoochee to form a regiment, elect their officers, and then travel to Pensacola.[11]

Soon after receiving the governor's message, the soldiers of the 10th Florida Militia Regiment received orders to assemble at the courthouse in Monticello. Although the Florida militia had undergone reorganization in 1860, and its men elected officers for the companies and regiments throughout the state, Floridians ignored this establishment as they scrambled to form volunteer units. In Monticello, after the militia formed ranks, Anderson and others gave rousing, patriotic speeches and then called for volunteers. As their members stepped forward to enlist in the company headed to Pensacola, the organized militia units in Jefferson County found themselves gutted.[12]

In Madison on April 2, 1861, "Batchelor," a correspondent traveling in Florida for the *Charleston Daily Courier,* witnessed the ceremony held for Captain Richard Bradford's departing company. The proud Batchelor was happy to report to Charlestonians that "the company from this place numbers 80 men, 24 of whom are native Carolinians." At the occasion, women from the Madison Female Seminary presented the company with a flag requesting that the volunteers "preserve it from all strains of cowardice and treachery." Following the flag presentation, the company marched to the Florida Atlantic & Gulf railroad station where local militia fired salutes as the troops boarded the cars for Chattahoochee. The editor of Madison's *Southern Messenger* wrote of the new soldiers, "A nobler band of youths never graced the armies of Rome or Athens or Carthage in their days of renown." In Apalachicola too, the community treated volunteers of the "Franklin Rifles" to a supper and presented the unit with a flag.[13]

In Tallahassee, Batchelor watched a "Battalion of Volunteers" drill in the streets as they awaited their day of departure. The soldiers of one of the two Leon County companies ordered to report to Chattahoochee formed their company in November 1860 and dubbed themselves the "Leon Artillery." This company, according to member John R. Blocker, met following the state's secession and "voted to offer our services to the Governor. We were accepted." Blocker remembered that his company was made up of "Tallahassee boys, young, healthy, and many of them wealthy." Among those serving in Blocker's company as privates were George M. Edgar, a Virginia Military Institute (VMI) graduate who taught at the West Florida Seminary, and George Troup Maxwell, formerly Professor of Obstetrics and Diseases of Women and Children at Oglethorpe Medical College in Savannah.[14]

The majority of the companies that gathered at Chattahoochee during the first week of April hailed from Middle Florida. Of the ten that eventually formed the 1st Florida Infantry Regiment, two originated from Leon County, and Franklin, Gadsden, Madison, and Jefferson counties each provided one company. This Middle Florida majority became evident when the men elected radical Democrats as field officers. Of the remaining four companies, two formed in Alachua County and one each in Jackson and Escambia. Because the companies were quickly organized, none obtained the number of soldiers officially required under army regulations. As a result, the regiment contained only seven hundred officers and men when it departed for Pensacola. Few of the companies possessed uniforms or adequate arms.[15]

Like the soldiers of most Civil War regiments, the volunteers of the 1st Florida Infantry elected their noncommissioned and commissioned officers at both the company and regimental levels. As James M. McPherson has written, the practice of using the ballot box in the military became an American tradition in the volunteer ranks because "citizen soldiers remained citizens even when they became soldiers." The historian Bell Wiley has noted that the ability to elect officers "was a privilege jealously cherished by the volunteers, and much ado was made of its exercise." These early elections became a kind of popularity contest and the men soon discovered whether their choice had been a wise one. Fortunately for the soldiers, the Conscription Act of 1862 enabled many regiments to reorganize and choose new officers to replace those who proved ineffective.[16]

The 1st Florida chose its officers on April 5, 1861, and to no one's surprise the men elected Anderson as colonel with "no opposition." For lieutenant colonel, the soldiers chose William Kelly Beard, a thirty-year-old North Carolinian. Raised in St. Augustine and Tallahassee, he was the son of John Beard, a prominent Florida Democrat. The younger Beard owned twenty-two slaves in 1860, and prior to the formation of the 1st Florida he operated businesses in both St. Marks and Tallahassee.[17]

Thaddeus A. McDonell of Gainesville became the major. The only field officer native to Florida, the thirty-year-old McDonell was born on Amelia Island but grew up in Savannah. The young major was also unusual in that he owned no slaves. An adventurer, McDonell had traveled to New Orleans in 1851 to join Narciso Lopez's invasion of Cuba. The young man missed the expedition, though, and when word of Lopez's execution reached him in the Crescent City, he returned to Florida. In 1857 McDonell began practicing law in Alachua County and was active in Democratic politics. In the later years of his life, McDonell claimed he had organized the "first company accepted by the Governor of Florida into the Confederate service after the first call for troops had been made." VMI alumnus George M. Edgar was elected to the rank of sergeant major and became the regiment's first drillmaster.[18]

With the elections completed, the Floridians boarded several steamers for their journey up the Chattahoochee River to Columbus. The steamers were necessary because although two railroad companies, the Florida Atlantic & Gulf Railroad and Florida Railroad, had worked during the 1850s to link East and Middle Florida, no rails were laid westward to unite these regions with West Florida. To further complicate matters, the Panhandle's roads remained little more than trails, and marching through would take a significant amount of time. River travel remained the only viable option because no rail connection existed between Middle and East Florida and Georgia. Ironically, the single rail connection that Florida maintained with another state was the Alabama & Florida Railroad, which was built to carry Alabama goods and cotton to Pensacola and help fasten West Florida's economy to that state. However, in 1861, the railroad was still unfinished and "it did not run much farther than the [Florida] state line."[19]

Taken north by the chartered steamers *Time* and *William H. Young,* the 1st Florida Infantry reached Columbus, Georgia, on the morning of April 6, 1861. At the River City, the volunteers would board cars for Pensacola. A member of the Jefferson County company, writing as "W.S.," complained that "a more disagreeable trip can hardly be conceived—the accommodation for the men being particularly objectionable." The *Daily Sun,* a Columbus paper, reported that the new soldiers were "generally a fine looking body and seem to be in excellent health and spirits. They are commanded by intelligent and experienced officers, some of whom, we believe have seen service on the 'tented' field.'" Columbus's other paper, the *Daily Enquirer,* informed its readers that "most of the companies are uniformed and armed, and have beautiful banners; others have yet to be furnished; and they are generally hardy and fine looking men on whom their country can securely rely."[20]

Because of the lack of transportation, the men were delayed in leaving Columbus until April 9, when they embarked at the Opelika Depot and traveled west, passing through Auburn and Montgomery before making the southwest swing toward Pensacola. On April 12, 1861, the 1st Florida Infantry Regiment camped near the town of Evergreen, Alabama. As the volunteers bedded down for the night, activity began on the windward beaches of Santa Rosa Island. Launches, rowed from the USS *Brooklyn,* ferried reinforcements in the form of U.S. Marines and artillerymen ashore, thus breaking the Fort Pickens Truce. Though the landing was detected by Confederates, no shooting occurred; several hundred miles to the east, however, the night sky over Charleston Harbor shone bright with the bursting of projectiles.[21]

From the moment Braxton Bragg arrived at Pensacola until the bombardment of Fort Sumter, the general worked to improve his positions and ready his troops for war. Throughout the late spring, Bragg's soldiers drilled on the parade ground and worked to construct gun emplacements, while the general pondered various ways of seizing Fort Pickens should the need arise. Of the three plans he considered, the general "favored an infantry assault on the fort after its walls had been broken by heavy guns and mortars." His view was not shared by Confederate president Jefferson Davis, who was unsure Bragg's attack would carry the fort and "if it failed, the Confederates would be branded as aggressors and have nothing tangible to show for it." Bragg never received orders to carry out his attack, and Fort Sumter would thus become the spark for the flames of war.[22]

The 1st Florida's soldiers awoke the next morning to find the Confederacy at war. They continued their journey to Pensacola, where on April 19, 1861, they were mustered into Confederate service for twelve months. The regiment was encamped north of the Pensacola Navy Yard, in what twenty-two-year-old Georgia native Augustus O. McDonell described as a "level piece of ground, with dwarf pines, magnolias, and various other shade trees to beautify it." The men dubbed their encampment Camp Magnolia, and amid swarms of annoying mosquitoes the volunteers of the 1st Florida were promptly introduced to the life of a soldier.[23]

William Trimmer recalled that "many of us boys imagined they came for a nice easy pleasant time, the heavy details daily imposed on each company soon learned us differently. . . . The camp detail was daily kept at work cleaning up the timber, digging up roots of pine trees, leveling the soil and in a few days had prepared a fine parade ground of a few acres. Colonel Patton Anderson had the regiment out for drill at 8 AM and again at 10 AM and at 1 PM. Six hours were daily spent in drilling." The men not only worked to create a satisfactory campground and performed drill, but they also built sand fortifications on the shore of Pensacola Bay. A Quincy newspaper reported in June that "the drilling has been rigidly enforced, and the result is Florida has a regiment of well disciplined troops . . . prepared to undergo the severest hardships of war."[24]

Drill became a daily necessity for the Civil War soldier, as it helped instill discipline and instruct the soldiers in military maneuvers. Each moment spent in either company or battalion practice helped prepare the regiment for "marching in step, manoeurving [sic] together on the word of a command and forming a front in unison." Throughout the war, fields near camps were laid bare as the men tramped about, constantly seeking to perfect their ability to move from column to line of battle, maintain their formation during an advance, and dash about as skirmishers. All helped bring a controlled order to the battlefield and enabled the men to stand up to the crashing volleys and bayonets of the enemy.[25]

Roderick "Roddie" G. Shaw was another soldier enduring the rigors of army life. A twenty-year-old Quincy resident who enlisted in the 1st Florida's Gadsden County company, he sarcastically described the hard duty to his sister: "I have a nice time of it now these last hot days working in the sun and especially when digging holes for posts . . . nevertheless I am not one of the Kind to fuss about it. I came for the purpose of making a soldier of myself as long as I was here and lay off the 'Gentleman' and 'Dandy.'"[26] As spring wore on, Pensacola Bay remained quiet. The soldiers continued to drill and construct batteries for the heavy guns that began arriving in May following the completion of the Alabama & Florida Railroad. Though Fort Pickens's garrison numbered nearly one thousand men by mid-May, Bragg continued to plan for an assault. These plans were put on hold indefinitely in late May, however, when the Confederate War Department ordered the general to dispatch three regiments to Virginia.[27]

In June the 1st Florida Infantry Regiment received its tenth company, the Pensacola Guards, of which the *Pensacola Weekly Observer* wrote: "In them are centered the bright hopes of the fathers and mothers of our city. They are with a few exceptions all Pensacolians by birth and lineage, but everyone of them are identified with our city and its interests." Despite this bit of excitement, the inactivity that existed around Pensacola Bay during the summer dampened the spirits of the 1st Florida's soldiers.[28]

Twenty-one-year-old Thomas Eston Randolph, a 1st Florida soldier who hailed from Tallahassee, recognized the problems that an attack on Fort Pickens presented to the Confederates, writing home that "in my opinion this will be a second Sebastopol, unless by some means we get a fleet that can drive the yankee ships away, and starve the fort out." The private also complained, "You cant imagine how bad the fleas are in this sand bed, we are literally overrun with them . . . I don't think any of the plagues which were inflicted on the old Egyptian could have been more terrible than this. I hope we will get through here soon and leave this place." Thomas's younger brother William, also a soldier in the 1st Florida, longed for service in Virginia, "the seat of war, where actions are so fierce and frequent." Loathing the inaction of the spring and summer, yet another 1st Florida soldier, S. H. Harris, argued that the Confederates could have "blowed every" Yankee "off Santa Rosa Island but the mercy goodness of Jefferson Davis would not allow it. I suppose his policy is for a forty year war."[29]

The 1st Florida Infantry Regiment suffered not only from boredom that summer but also, due to the quickness with which the companies answered the governor's call, from a paucity of uniforms, equipment, and weapons. Upon the regiment's formation, the companies shouldered a variety of firearms. As William Trimmer related in his memoirs, his company, the Franklin Rifles, were issued the Model 1855 Rifle Musket, even while the "Jefferson and Bradford [Madison] Companies drilled with the old flintlock musket." Before the fall, the Confederate government, in order to standardize the distribution of ammunition, armed nine 1st Florida companies with .69 Model 1842 Springfield muskets. The Pensacola Guards were armed with the "Minie musket," meaning either the .577 Enfield or .58 Springfield rifled-musket.[30]

Uniforms and accoutrements for the soldiers were a different story. Although the Florida legislature had allotted $100,000 in November 1860 to purchase the necessities of war, little action was taken before Florida's first troops were called up in March 1861. The soldiers did without much of the equipment needed for proper campaigning, including knapsacks, haversacks, and canteens. Not much help was forthcoming from the Confederate government in 1861, and many soldiers had to wait until they encountered Federal soldiers on the battlefield before becoming fully equipped. Captain Alexander Bright of the Pensacola Guards wrote to citizens of that town of the supply difficulties: "It appears from what I can learn from Gen. Bragg that the Confederate States have neither accouterments nor acquipints [sic] for our company at this time . . . we therefore would respectfully ask you as the Committee of relief to procure . . . the following articles: 75 cartridge boxes, 75 knapsacks and canteens and tents for our Company that we may be enabled to march to any point that we may be ordered." Evidently the committee made the purchases, as a Confederate inspection officer reported that he thought the Pensacola Guards were "by far the best company in the Florida Regiment."[31]

With several thousand Confederate troops at Pensacola, the defense of one of the state's most populous cities was ensured. However, more than 1,500 miles of coastline with its countless inlets and bays and numerous rivers allowing access to the interior of the state caused Florida officials to worry. Ex-Whig George T. Ward, who would die commanding the 2nd Florida Infantry at Williamsburg, warned in May 1861 that the forces of "the North . . . will be directed against our sea-coast and its property, and they will endeavor to ravage . . . the coast of Florida. The capital of the last-named State is in close proximity to the Gulf—twenty miles by railroad—and in the midst of the most dense negro population and the largest plantations in the state."[32]

Ward continued in his letter to Secretary of War Leroy Pope Walker, "If the plantations belonging to our Gulf coast are ravaged or deserted, to avoid the plunder of negros (not to speak of insurrection), the capacity of the country to contribute to the war is at an end." The possibility of a Federal invasion was very much on the mind of Governor Madison Starke Perry as well.

In April 1861, soon after Florida responded to meet the first Confederate troop quota, the government called upon the Land of Flowers to raise two thousand more soldiers to fight for the Confederacy. Using this quota, Governor Perry raised a regiment, the 2nd Florida Infantry, to represent Florida in Virginia. However, the governor, also concerned about the defense of the state, wrote on June 1, "We have batteries erected at several points on the coast, requiring at least two regiments to garrison." To defend the population and property of Florida from incursions from the coast, the state formed the 3rd and 4th Florida Infantry Regiments from the April quota and another quota issued in June 1861.[33]

In June, the governor's office began dispatching instructions to volunteer companies throughout the state to report to Fernandina on Amelia Island. There, the companies united to create the 3rd Florida Infantry Regiment and elect its officers. The regiment that formed on Amelia Island derived five companies from East Florida and four from the Middle region, with two companies each from Duval, Columbia, and Jefferson counties. Madison, St. Johns, and Walkulla counties also contributed volunteers to the new regiment. The Hernando County Wildcats provided South Florida's lone representation in the regiment.[34]

An interesting aspect of the 3rd Florida Infantry is that several of its companies were established minutemen organizations. The Florida Independent Blues from St. Augustine formed in May 1860 in response to the Charleston Democratic convention, and its members belonged to "some of the town's best known families." The unit's commander, John Lott Phillips, was born on the island of St. Helena in 1812 and came to the United States as a young man. A captain in the Second Seminole Indian War, the half British, half German Phillips also held numerous public offices in St. Augustine.[35]

The Jacksonville Light Infantry, which became Company A of the regiment, was an even older unit, having been organized in April 1859. The company could also claim the title of best dressed in the regiment, as its members owned uniforms of "blue cloth, with three rows of brass buttons in the front, and high caps with black pompons, also white pants in warm weather, other times blue cloth." The company carried a silk battle flag bearing the slogan "Let Us Alone," which had been presented to them by the ladies of Jacksonville. The Light Infantry were commanded by Dr. Holmes Steele, a newspaper editor and former mayor of the city.[36]

The majority of the regiment's companies, however, were raised following secession and the call for volunteers. One such unit, the Jefferson County Beauregards, organized on April 26, 1861, and the men promptly elected Daniel Butler Bird as their captain. A planter whose holdings included 1,500 acres and 44 slaves, Bird also served as a Florida Militia brigadier general. At the company's organization, a new member of the unit declared his and his comrades' intentions: "We are in for the war, and we must act the man. . . . We'll teach the fanatics, that we are all true men, That our homes, our fire side and freedom we'll defend." Mustered into state service in mid-May, the Beauregards camped near Monticello "for the purpose of daily drill, until ordered to some point by President Davis." Numbering 62 men, the Beauregards reported to Amelia Island in June.[37]

Jefferson County's other company in the 3rd Florida, the Jefferson Rifles, formed late in 1860 and lost many members to Anderson's Pensacola volunteer company. The reduced outfit offered its services to Governor Perry on May 6, 1861, hoping for attachment to the 2nd Florida Infantry. Instead, in July the state government ordered the Jefferson Rifles to report to Fernandina. Because the company numbered but forty-five soldiers, Captain William O. Girardeau, the former headmaster of the Jefferson Academy, began a hasty recruiting drive that included a stop at nearby Waukeenah Academy. Girardeau spoke to the academy's young men during their Summer Examination and seventeen students enlisted. The school's headmaster, Samuel Pasco, had already mustered into the service that May and likely had planned to close the school.[38]

The twenty-seven-year-old principal was not a southerner or a native of the United States. Born in London in 1834, Pasco's ancestors hailed from Cornwall, and his father, John Pasco, worked as a temperance advocate. Young Pasco migrated with his family across the Atlantic to Prince Edward Island in 1841; in 1843, the family moved to Charlestown, Massachusetts. Samuel Pasco was known as "genial and social in disposition, and easy to approach." The young man reached medium height and carried a head of "raven black hair." A pair of dark eyes sat above a protruding nose, wide lips, and sharp chin.[39]

The young Englishman received his education at Charlestown High School and graduated from Harvard in 1858. Pasco did not wait long for employment, for as one of his former students noted at Pasco's funeral, Jefferson County's planters, "ambitious for their sons and reaching out for the very best[,] engaged the services of most excellent Harvard to secure them a young man worthy of the work. Samuel Pasco was Harvard's answer."[40]

Arriving in Jefferson County in 1859, Pasco had "never identified himself with any political party, and had not even voted." However, the "two years spent in the intimacy that the warmhearted Southern hospitality soon established between [Samuel Pasco] and the families of his pupils, completely won him over to the cause of the South." Following the announcement that the Jefferson Rifles were departing for Fernandina, the academy trustees publicly proclaimed of their young teacher, "like Achille[s] he has girded on his armor and [is] ready for the fight" and "that should he at any time during the war need assistance, in any way which can be in our power to tender, we will most cheerfully do it. And we hereby assure our young friend that he will always find a home in our families, and a friend in every member of our households."[41]

The Jefferson Rifles bivouacked at the Jefferson County Courthouse on the evening of July 23 and made ready to march to the depot the following morning. Lemuel Moody, a plantation overseer in the county and member of the company, wrote from Monticello that night: "Give my love to all my young friends and tell them that I am" taking "oup Arms a gainst Ole Abe." As the soldiers boarded the train the next morning, Samuel Pasco, writing behind the pseudonym "INOE," recalled that "the manly words of encouragement and advice, the sea of beautiful faces, the bright eyes striving to smile in the midst of their tears . . . made our part-ing easier."[42]

The journey to Fernandina became a nightmare for the volunteers, as they were confined to two boxcars and exposed to almost constant rain and gnawing hun-ger. Pasco (as INOE) expressed disappointment that the soldiers had to devour food prepared by the ladies of Monticello on the trains rather than savor the home-cooked meals in camp. However, he admitted to the folks back home that many of the companies that set out for Fernandina had no food and arrived hungry and fatigued.[43]

On July 25, upon the rendezvous at Fernandina, the soldiers set about the task of electing their regimental officers, and William Scott Dilworth, then a private in the Jefferson Beauregards, with the backing of the Jefferson County and Middle Florida companies, became colonel. Dilworth's campaign for the position began in May, when the editor of the *Family Friend* wrote a strong piece favoring the lawyer. "We will not pretend to say," wrote the editor, "that he is thoroughly con-versant with military tactics and discipline, but he has the capacity and mind to speedily acquire all necessary information; he is brave and chivalrous, and at the same time, possessed of cool, calculating judgement—all of which is very desir-able in a commanding officer."[44]

A Georgian by birth, Dilworth was a thirty-nine-year-old widower who had long been an advocate of secession. Born in Camden County in May 1822, Dil-worth migrated to Florida in the early 1840s, where he practiced law and became involved in Democratic politics. By 1860 Dilworth, who had amassed 2,200 acres and 42 slaves, was a veteran of the state legislature and that election year his name was mentioned at the state Democratic convention for a possible congressional bid. Though the Democrats chose another candidate for Congress, Jefferson County sent Dilworth to the state Secession Convention in Tallahassee where he voted for disunion.[45]

Less information is available regarding Dilworth's subordinates. While East Floridians elected Arthur J. T. Wright, a Georgian residing in Columbia County, to the lieutenant colonelcy, Madison County's Lucius A. Church won the position of major. Arthur Wright, at age thirty-three, served as a major in a state militia regiment and was a highly prosperous merchant in Lake City. He also gained command experience during brief service in the Third Seminole Indian War. The store owner possessed nine slaves and represented Columbia County at the Secession Convention, where he cast a vote for secession. Lucius Church, a twenty-nine-year-old Georgia native, owned a plantation in Madison County, likely given to him by his father. The elder Church served as postmaster of Madison and owned numerous slaves. The newly minted major spent one term in the state legislature during the 1850s and ran unsuccessfully as a Constitutional Union legislative candidate in 1860.[46]

Following the organizational period at the town of Fernandina, the 3rd Florida Infantry Regiment's companies never again served together during the unit's time in Florida. Instead, the various outfits were dispersed to strategic locations on the Atlantic seaboard. Six companies were stationed around vital Fort Clinch on Amelia Island, where the duty was similar to that of the troops at Pensacola. Of the early days on Amelia Island, nineteen-year-old Benton Ellis of Company C recalled that "we were being drilled, and were engaged in building batteries of sand." Two units went to Jacksonville to man an earthwork at the mouth of the St. John's River, and two others garrisoned the Castillo in St. Augustine. In August, at these various locations, Confederate officers mustered the volunteers into service for twelve months.[47]

While the 3rd Florida's companies deployed to various locations along Florida's Atlantic coast, the 4th Florida Infantry's units were scattered to defend vital ports on the Gulf Coast. The latter regiment's companies traveled to their assigned locales during May and June, and the soldiers selected their regimental officers on July 1. Though officers were elected, Confederate officials did not muster the various companies into the Confederate Army until August and September. Until then, the units remained in the service, and pay, of the state.[48]

The 4th Florida was similar to the 1st and 3rd Florida with regard to its composition. The 4th Florida's West Florida companies hailed from Washington and Jackson counties; its Middle Florida soldiers came from Franklin, Liberty, Madison, Suwannee, and Lafayette counties; and East Florida provided two Columbia County outfits with New River (now Bradford), Marion, and Levy counties contributing as well. South Florida's lone representative in the regiment was a Hillsborough County unit.[49]

Possibly because of a strong conservative element within the regiment, particularly from Columbia County (which gave the majority of its votes to the Constitutional Unionists in the 1860 election), the 4th Florida Infantry selected as its colonel Edward Stephens Hopkins, an ex-Whig and former Constitutional Union gubernatorial candidate. "The plough-boy of old Duval," as his supporters dubbed Hopkins during the 1860 campaign, was, at fifty-one years old, the oldest man to hold a colonelcy in any of the Florida Brigade's regiments during the war. A gaunt-faced gentleman, he possessed long features and a shock of dark hair.[50]

Like William Dilworth, Hopkins possessed little military experience, though he had volunteered during the Second Seminole Indian War, and then as an elected brigadier general in the Florida State Militia during the 1850s. The colonel walked with a limp, a result of an 1837 duel between him and General Charles Floyd. On October 5, the two men, at odds over Floyd's cattle encroaching on Hopkins's land, met on Amelia Island with their choice of weapons: shotguns, pistols, and Bowie knives. Starting with the shotguns, the two would then continue with the pistols and Bowie knives until one, or both, were dead. They did not need the pistols and Bowie knives; after the two antagonists exchanged shotgun blasts neither could continue. While Floyd somehow stayed on his feet, Hopkins collapsed, his body riddled with buckshot.[51]

Born into a wealthy family in McIntosh County, Georgia, in January 1810, the future 4th Florida colonel was, for much of his life, a slave-owning planter. A lifelong conservative, Hopkins gained an appointment from President William Henry Harrison as customs collector for Brunswick, Georgia, a position he kept until 1844, at which time he moved to Florida. A state senator in the 1850s, Hopkins campaigned as the Constitutional Union gubernatorial candidate in 1860. Eager to fight, Hopkins inquired of Secretary of War Walker in May 1861, "If an efficient company is tendered for the war, will they be received and ordered to the frontier on active . . . duty?"[52]

Another conservative, Matthew Whit Smith, became the 4th Florida's lieutenant colonel. Born in Tennessee in 1814, Smith came to Florida as a volunteer during the Second Seminole Indian War and remained. A lawyer in Columbia County, Smith was Lake City's first mayor and also owned a Jacksonville newspaper. An opponent of secession, he made an unsuccessful bid to represent Columbia County in Tallahassee during the convention. However, after the state seceded, Smith, like many other ex-Whigs, joined with the disunionists to protect their interests. As soon as the regiment's companies gained their places at points along the Gulf Coast, Smith took command of the Cedar Keys detachment.[53]

One of Smith's protégés, Wylde Lyde Latham Bowen, won the position of major of the new regiment. The twenty-two-year-old Bowen hailed from Grainger County,

Tennessee, and had graduated from Mossy Creek Baptist College early in 1860. That same year, Bowen read law in the Columbia County law office of M. Whit Smith and Washington Ives Sr. Following the election, Major Bowen commanded the 4th Florida Infantry's three companies at Fort Brooke on Tampa Bay.[54]

By the end of September, the 4th Florida Infantry Regiment remained dispersed, mainly along the Gulf Coast. Three companies remained at Fort Brooke under Bowen's command, and another three defended the inlet at St. Marks. A single company garrisoned Cedar Keys, and two others reinforced the garrison of Fernandina.

As summer gave way to fall, Florida's first volunteers became Confederate soldiers. Drilled in the manual of arms and hardened by the physical labor of clearing ground for camps, constructing batteries, and mounting cannon, the men slowly conformed to military life. While these soldiers remained on the coast, they longed for the war in Virginia and Kentucky and, most of all, battle. The months ahead would answer this wish but also deliver aggravation, as the Floridians fought not only the Federal Army but also disease and their own politicians.

3

The War Trumpet Is Sounding Its Blasts in Every Direction around Us

October–December 1861

Throughout the fall months, Florida's soldiers remained in their tents, attempting to ward off the boredom that threatened to conquer their spirits long before they had a chance to fight the Yankees. During this relatively dull period, the troops experienced only spurts of excitement. Disease claimed its first victims during these months, which, along with inaction, sobered the volunteers' hearts. Meanwhile, their regimental leaders traded partisan jabs with the newly inaugurated governor, John Milton, over the administration of the war in Florida.

On Pensacola Bay, dissatisfaction with the inactivity and constant boredom was not confined to enlisted men. Colonel Anderson and Company I captain Thompson B. Lamar, the brother of the Southern statesman L.C.Q. Lamar, both yearned for action and the chance to serve in units from their home states. Writing to a relative in early October, Anderson praised his men, noting, "I have an excellent Regiment here . . . it is well disciplined and drilled." However, he also expressed his desire to serve at the front. The Kentucky-raised Tennessean confessed, "I am in a perfect fever to get to [Kentucky] in her hour of need. . . . If the [president] insists on keeping me here on a peace establishment all winter, I will resign and join Gen. [Simon Bolivar] Buckner's ranks as a private."[1]

Even before Anderson issued his plea to serve in Kentucky, he and Lamar, a fellow Jefferson County resident, asked permission to raise "strictly a Confederate Regiment—not from any particular state, but from each state." The two men argued that they were "citizens of Florida but have a very general acquaintance in the States of Mississippi, Kentucky, Tennessee, and Georgia" and entertained "no doubt that from these States a Regiment can be promptly organized which will enlist for the war." The two officers intended, as an ad in the *Monticello Family Friend* boasted, that the regiment was meant for "active service" in Kentucky.[2]

Anderson and Lamar attempted to exploit the fact that the 1st Florida Infantry Regiment did not have the correct number of soldiers required by Confederate Army regulations. In both letters Anderson alluded to the fact that "Death, disease and discharges from other causes have reduced it [the 1st Florida] to a mere battalion." Writing from Tallahassee, J. H. Randolph explained to Confederate major George Fairbanks, "I understand there is a plan also on foot to change the

Regt which is not full, into a battalion and thus leave the higher officers free to be transferred to other regiments."[3]

Less than a week after Anderson wrote his request for a transfer to Kentucky, the colonel came under enemy fire for the first time. During September, Union sailors and marines carried out two daring raids within Pensacola Bay, burning both a wooden dry dock and the *Judah,* a privateer fitting out for sea. In retaliation, General Bragg ordered a raid against Santa Rosa Island to take place on the night of October 8–9. By September, the number of Union soldiers and Marines on Santa Rosa Island had grown to such an extent that many pitched their tents outside the protective walls of Fort Pickens. The 6th New York Volunteer Regiment's encampment lay nearly a mile from the fort and was plainly seen through Confederate field glasses. Along with Federal artillery batteries, this encampment became the target for Bragg's forces.[4]

Braxton Bragg's attack plan called for three ad hoc battalions consisting of soldiers from the various regiments under his command. Bragg named Colonel Anderson to lead the second battalion, which included 180 soldiers of the 1st Florida, companies of the 7th Alabama, and Louisiana troops. The other battalions were led by Colonels James R. Chalmers and John K. Jackson, with Brigadier General Richard H. Anderson in overall command. A smaller, fourth group, under a Lieutenant Hallonquist, was designated to carry out the spiking of cannon and destruction of the enemy's camp.[5]

On the evening of October 8, as soldiers of the 1st Florida readied for dismissal from drill, the captains passed through the ranks of their companies, spreading the word of the impending attack. Each captain was to select eighteen men from his unit, and in the Franklin Rifles, "The orderly sergeant, Abbot, called out: 'All who want to go step out two paces!' At the command nearly the entire company stepped forward. Captain [William] Cropp ordered the married men back," selecting only unattached soldiers for the daring mission. Roddie Shaw, on guard duty at the Pensacola Navy Yard with the Gadsden County Young Guards, related that "[t]here were men from 6 companies in the reg. the others being on important detached service could not leave their posts."[6]

Around ten o'clock that night, the raiders from Pensacola, white cloth tied around their right arms to distinguish friend from foe, boarded a motley assortment of vessels for the eight-mile journey to Santa Rosa Island. Reaching their destination just after 2:00 A.M., Confederate troops waded ashore several miles from the 6th New York's camp. The commanders of the battalions gathered their soldiers and immediately began moving silently westward toward their intended targets.[7]

Chalmers's troops moved along the northern shore of the island, while Anderson's column skirted the Gulf beaches. Colonel John Jackson's men moved over the dunes in the center of the island. The objective of these soldiers was, in the words of General Richard Anderson, to "place their commands, if possible, between Fort

Pickens and the camp of the enemy. Lieutenant Hallonquist followed . . . with orders to do whatever damage he could to the batteries, buildings, and camps from which the enemy might be driven."[8]

Not long after the advance began, the columns on the north and south beaches encountered Union pickets, and muzzle flashes were seen in the darkness. The attack might have foundered, but Jackson's column surged over the dunes and shrubs in the middle of the island, taking the Union skirmishers by their flanks and yelling as they entered the New Yorkers' camp. As the Federal volunteers retreated from the surprise attack of Jackson's soldiers, the columns of both Anderson and Chalmers advanced among the tents. Almost immediately the detachment charged with destruction set about their task. Roddie Shaw, watching from the navy yard, wrote that "the whole encampment was on fire."[9]

The Floridians moved forward, led by twenty-four-year-old Captain Richard Bradford of Madison. Bradford, a lawyer who had just returned to Pensacola from a twenty-day furlough, was surprised by a Private Scott, a New York soldier, as he made his way around the camp's hospital tent. Unsure of the identity of the other soldier in the darkness, Bradford inquired, "Who are you?" Scott pointed his firearm at Bradford, replied, "I'll show you who I am," and fired. Bradford, dying as the round tore through his chest, became Florida's first death in the conflict. The deceased captain became an instant martyr, and the legislature soon renamed New River County in his memory. The moment after Bradford's corpse fell onto the sand, several Floridians discharged their own weapons at Scott, killing the unfortunate Federal. Despite the loss of a leader, whom Shaw insisted was "one of the best officers in our reg[iment]," and two enlisted men, several Florida officers stood guard around the hospital to ensure its protection.[10]

As the encampment burned around them, troops looted the New Yorkers' baggage until daylight, when a gun fired from the naval yard signaled the troops to begin withdrawing. As the Confederates departed from the camp, their path was interdicted by United States Regulars, dispatched from Fort Pickens. Possessing rifled-muskets, the Regulars, according to William Trimmer, "passed us in the dark posting themselves in a dense thicket to intercept our men who were returning," and a running fight broke out over the course of the four miles from the camp to the boats. Shaw reported that his "men retreated followed by the regulars. Twice they stood and drove the regulars back." At one point during the retreat, Willie Denham of Jefferson County went down, shot through the jaw. His brother Andrew, "setting his teeth . . . leaped over the fallen form and, with irresistible fury, led his followers against the Federals."[11]

With the boats reached, the men scrambled to climb aboard as rounds struck the water around them. Henry A. Tillinghast, a South Carolina native and Tallahassee clerk who was described as an "excellent and talented young man," fell dead as he gained the boats. Dr. Cary B. Gamble, surgeon of the 1st Florida, had accompanied the expedition to attend to the wounded. As the raiders reached the invasion beach, the doctor "seized a boat and placing five of our wounded in it put off directly across the bay for our camp, drawing the fire of the fort upon his boat."[12]

By 11:00 A.M. on October 9, the assault force regained Pensacola. Of the nearly one thousand men who participated in the attack, seventeen were killed and thirty-two wounded, including General Richard Anderson. Of the former, besides Richard Bradford and Tillinghast, the Florida regiment also lost Sergeant William Routh and Privates William Smith, John J. Thompson, Joseph Hale, and Thomas Bond. Eight Floridians suffered wounds during the engagement and twelve were captured in the confusion, including the officers who prevented the destruction of the hospital. The Federal forces on Santa Rosa saw fourteen killed, twenty-nine wounded, and twenty-four missing. Following the disorganized skirmish, Andrew Denham told his brother Willie, "One of us must go into another regiment; I cannot stand that again." Clearly, the danger posed by battle dawned on these young men, and they wanted to spare their family the burden of mourning two sons killed in the same fight.[13]

Though the small clash jaded the expectations of some of the soldiers, the majority of the Florida regiment did not even participate in the raid. Roddie Shaw, whose Young Guards watched over the navy yard magazine the night of the raid, complained, "The 'Y.G.' wear long faces. It is true they give [us] important posts to guard but they are determined to not let us fight." S. H. Harris also expressed his displeasure in not participating in the attack, writing that General Bragg was "determined that none of us shall ever get in a fight."[14]

The attack hardened the resolve among those who survived. The veterans of Leon County's Company A published a tribute to its fallen members, claiming that "we have sustained great loss by their death, and that we shall do all in our power to avenge their fall." Anderson's desire for a transfer waned after the raid, particularly when Bragg appointed him to command a brigade on October 12.[15]

Throughout the remainder of October most companies of the 1st Florida remained encamped near the navy yard, though some were always on detached service in the vicinity. In mid-November ships ferried eight companies from the navy yard to Deer Point, the westernmost tip of a peninsula that jutted into Pensacola Bay and on which the government grew live oaks. The point gained importance because it lay only a short distance across the bay from Pensacola itself. Bragg, afraid the Federals might emplace cannon on the peninsula, dispatched the 1st Florida to the location to establish a Confederate presence. Choosing a position near the Live Oak Plantation, the Floridians cleared land for a new camp, which lay surrounded on three sides by a "jungle of brambles and marsh that is impassable, and the fourth side . . . protected by entrenchments." The Floridians dubbed their new home Camp Bradford and built huts to shelter themselves from the winter elements.[16]

On Amelia Island, three hundred miles east of Pensacola, and at other scattered locations along the state's Atlantic coast, the neighbors and relatives of the Pensacola volunteers struggled through the fall to become soldiers. Besides the daily routines of drill and manual labor, tedium remained the norm. Samuel Pasco wrote from near Fernandina, "We are still leading a life of comparative inactivity; while the war trumpet is sounding its blasts in every direction around us."[17]

The majority of the 3rd Florida Infantry Regiment was stationed on the sixteen-mile-long Amelia Island, where its soldiers protected the mouth of the St. Mary River from seizure by the Federal Navy. Though Fort Clinch, an unfinished masonry fortification, sat on the northern tip of the island, near the town of Fernandina, the Confederates mounted few guns there. Instead, sand batteries, constructed along the island's northeastern shore, allowed the Confederates to defend themselves against their enemy.[18]

The newly minted 3rd Florida remained plagued by the paucity of trained officers able to lead the volunteers through the manual of arms. Colonel William S. Dilworth, who matured into an able administrator during the months spent on Amelia Island, wrote to Secretary of War Leroy Pope Walker and Florida congressmen just a few days after his election as colonel, pleading, "I have no drill officers. My regiment is comprised entirely of citizens. I would be glad to have two drill officers attached to this regiment immediately."[19]

The drill officers did not arrive quickly enough, and the elected officers had a rough time both learning and teaching maneuvers. Lemuel Moody, the Jefferson County overseer, wrote from Fernandina in August, "We have the poorest set of field officers in the Southern Confederacy." A month later, however, Samuel Pasco related that "Our officers have had little or no assistance in drilling the company, and have had to depend on their books, but in spite of their disadvantages, the company has gradually improved." A visitor to the Jefferson Rifles camp that same week agreed with Pasco's assessment, writing: "On my arrival, Lieut. [Matthew Harvey] Strain was drilling the [Jefferson] Rifles, which he done with military skill. Afterwards I learned that he was an excellent drill officer. I saw this company also drilled by Lieut. [Charles] Johnson, who acquitted with credit, throwing the company into different positions, with ease; but above all, the privates presented the most interesting appearance; the step was regular quick, and every man seemed to pride himself in presenting a soldier-like appearance."[20]

While Amelia Island was recognized as a strategic location, panic mongers, chiefly governor-elect John Milton and ailing Brigadier General John B. Grayson, the newly appointed commander of the Department of Middle and East Florida, made desperate assertions that the Federals were constantly plotting to seize the island. Grayson wrote of Amelia Island soon after his assumption of command, "The batteries are incorrectly put up and not finished. The enemy can land where they please . . . Florida will become a Yankee province unless measures for her relief are promptly made." John Milton complained to Stephen R. Mallory, the Confederate secretary of the navy, "at Fernandina . . . I am informed even the cannon have not been mounted, and dissipation and disorder prevail."[21]

Regardless of the pleas for Floridians to unite behind secession, the first fall of the war demonstrated that the state's citizens could not forget their past political disagreements. John Milton, who was inaugurated on October 7, 1861, became the chief antagonist of the volunteers' efforts. Milton used his position to attack not only political opponents, chiefly Edward Hopkins and other conservatives, but also those who disagreed with his judgment. Milton did not confine his hostility to parlors in Tallahassee but libeled volunteer officers to the Confederate authorities in Richmond. Governor Milton accused fellow Democrats William Dilworth and A.J.T. Wright of "habitual intemperance," and argued this transgression caused demoralization among the soldiers. Later, Governor Milton conceded that Dilworth was "improving, and will, I think, make an efficient officer."[22]

In spite of Milton's criticism of his performance, Colonel Dilworth performed an admirable job for the Confederacy at Fernandina. During September, the colonel divided his soldiers' time between drill and work details that labored to construct sand batteries and mount cannon. Some of the soldiers viewed the manual labor as demeaning; one unnamed officer, in the words of Samuel Pasco, "continually reminded us that we were only a set of ignorant plough boys whom he was trying to make something of." Benjamin W. Partridge, a fifteen-year-old former student in the Jefferson Rifles, wrote, "We have been right hard at work and now I think the meanest place in the S.C. [Southern Confederacy] is safe."[23]

In an attempt to provide his volunteers more time to learn the art of soldiering, Colonel Dilworth issued a plea to East Floridians, asking for "at least sixty able negro men, in order to complete our defences." The colonel wrote that for his soldiers "[t]o carry on this work, drill has been almost entirely neglected. Men who never before have been accustomed to work, have been handling the spade, the shovel and the wheelbarrow, with a hearty good will that would astonish their friends at home. After working night and day for a considerable time . . . they are becoming exhausted."[24]

Nearly 120 slaves, dispatched by owners in Marion and Alachua counties, arrived on Amelia Island soon after. These forced laborers were put to work mounting cannon at both Fort Clinch and the sand batteries. Meanwhile, Colonel Dilworth, in the words of one visitor, spent his days "actively engaged and bending every energy of his mind to the accomplishment of the important work before him." Yet the colonel still had his miscues. On a cool night in mid-October, after seeing what he perceived to be a rocket fired from the blockading vessels, he ordered his soldiers from their tents. The tired men stumbled from their blankets, formed ranks, and prepared to proceed to their batteries. Benjamin Partridge wrote that "in about an hour the Col came back come to find out it was only a meteor."[25]

Besides training his soldiers as infantrymen, Colonel Dilworth, after his proposal to form an artillery battalion fell through, also had to make artillerymen of his Florida volunteers. In November 1861 a Federal squadron under the command of Samuel duPont seized Port Royal, South Carolina, with its excellent anchorage. Confederate positions along the South Atlantic seaboard, fearing they were the next target of this menace, doubled their efforts in preparing for an attack, which they believed was inevitable.[26]

That same month, in order to better coordinate the seacoast defenses, the Confederate War Department created the Department of South Carolina, Georgia, and East Florida, and placed in command a general whose earlier campaign in western Virginia had been less than successful: General Robert E. Lee. To bolster the Fernandina defenses, Lee immediately ordered Confederate Navy lieutenant William A. Webb to Amelia Island to begin training the infantrymen in the art of gunnery. Weeks later Dilworth reported that he was "drilling at the guns as much as possible."[27]

Even as his soldiers picked up the ramrod and sponge for training with artillery, Dilworth continued to try to come up with ways to increase their effectiveness should Federal troops make a landing. He recognized that the island's terrain was perfect for sharpshooting and fighting a delaying action, but his men were armed with "the condemned and imperfect 'U.S.' muskets, utterly unfit" for the type of fighting he intended to pursue. Dilworth requested rifled-muskets for his companies, which Confederate ordnance chief Josiah Gorgas approved and promptly forwarded. By the time winter descended upon Florida and the troops huddled in palmetto shacks for comfort, Colonel Dilworth conceded, "God knows I have worked harder here than I ever did in my life, and that my only motive has been to serve my country."[28]

Though the minor problems on Amelia Island caused John Milton to have sleepless nights, the chief sources of the governor's anger were the 4th Florida Infantry Regiment and the newly instituted 1st Florida Cavalry. Milton thought that both regiments, commanded by ex-Whigs, had been formed illegally or, in the case of the 4th Florida, at least needed to hold new officer elections due to the fact that some companies had not been included in the voting process. That fall, Milton wrote spiteful correspondence to Richmond regarding the two units and their commanders. The conflict Milton waged on paper possibly caused the recipients to question Florida's commitment to the cause.

Milton first directed his vindictiveness toward William George Mackey (W.G.M.) Davis, a forty-nine-year-old Virginian who had settled in Apalachicola during Florida's territorial days. Davis, who had gained a reputation as "a lawyer of eminent legal attainments," practiced in Tallahassee, and despite having never pursued political office, he was selected to represent Leon County in the state's Secession Convention. As a conservative, Davis supported a proposal to delay secession at least until Alabama and Georgia acted, and after this attempt at moderation failed, he submitted to the obvious and cast his vote in favor of secession. In mid-1861 Davis had written to the secretary of war: "I propose to raise a Regiment of mounted men for the service of the Confederate States. The men to be mounted in Virginia if preferred by you and to be enlisted in Florida and the part of Georgia bordering on Florida." Leroy Pope Walker honored Davis's request, and the middle-aged conservative lawyer began mustering cavalry companies into service.[29]

Middle and East Florida communities responded to the call, and citizens would soon hear the tramp of horse hooves in nearby fields as the men practiced various cavalry maneuvers. The majority of companies that constituted the 1st Florida Cavalry Regiment were raised in East Florida; Leon County provided Middle Florida's only representatives. Some of the companies had formed during the spring and had remained in state service while awaiting assignment to a regiment.[30]

The recruiting process took up much of September and October, and it was not until January 1862 that the regiment obtained ten companies. During 1861, the new organization was continually referred to as a battalion, and Judah P. Benjamin, then acting secretary of war, commissioned W.G.M. Davis as the battalion's lieutenant colonel.[31]

The battalion's appointed major, George Troup Maxwell, was a veteran of the 1st Florida Infantry Regiment's early days in Pensacola. A native of Bryan County, Georgia, the thirty-four-year-old Maxwell had attended Chatham Academy in Savannah and then earned his M.D. from the University of the City of New York in 1848. Maxwell practiced in Tallahassee for nine years, where he served as captain of the Tallahassee Guards militia company.[32]

A surgeon at the Key West Marine Hospital from 1857 to 1860, Maxwell returned to Tallahassee early that crucial election year. For a brief time before secession Maxwell taught obstetrics at the Oglethorpe Medical College in Savannah. The *Florida Sentinel* indicated that the people of the state capital held Maxwell in high regard, for when he left Tallahassee for Savannah the editor noted, "He has the warm personal regard of troops of friends here, among all classes, who love him for his elevated character, his many eminently social qualities."[33]

As the 1st Florida Cavalry companies mustered into Confederate service, John Milton went on the offensive against Davis's battalion. The governor wrote to Secretary of War Judah P. Benjamin, assuring the adopted Louisianan that "I venture the prediction that in less than two months, he will be more anxious to get rid of what is known as Davis' Cavalry Regiment. . . . It will prove useless and vastly expensive."[34]

The major reason that John Milton, one of the strongest supporters of Jefferson Davis and the Confederacy, was unwilling to support a cavalry battalion was because of the expense the people of Florida would incur in equipping the mounted soldiers. Furthermore, Milton argued that Davis's recruitment competed with state-raised infantry units, wooing away volunteers who were "now in favor of riding into service." Another argument against the regiment, in Milton's eyes at least, was that it was led by an ex-Whig. He confessed in a January 1862 letter, "Patriotic statesmen who witnessed the untiring, however feeble and unsuccessful, efforts of Mr. W. G. M. Davis to prevent Florida from seceding and vindicating fearlessly and gallantly her rights, cannot appreciate the favor which the Confederate Government . . . have conferred upon Mr. W. G. M. Davis."[35]

However, John Milton was alone in his complaints, at least as far as the Confederate government was concerned. General James Trapier, who commanded in Florida following General Grayson's death, refused to endorse the governor's argument, writing instead that "I need as part of my force to do the duty of scouts and patrol parties ten companies of mounted men." The general also wrote in January 1862 that one debate over the regiment lay in the fear that the horses would "'absorb all the corn in Fla.' It may be so," Trapier continued, "but if Florida is invaded I expect to make good use of this arm; and shall not therefore dispense with it unless specifically ordered to do so." In January 1862 the battalion gained its ninth and tenth companies, and the Confederate War Department designated the unit a regiment. There was little more John Milton could do to prevent its formation.[36]

In the heyday of antebellum Florida, cotton bales lay stacked on Apalachicola's wharves, awaiting shipment to factories in the North or Europe. Cotton brokers at the port, which flourished at the mouth of its namesake river, bought thousands of pounds of the crop grown not just in Middle Florida but in Alabama and Georgia as well. The river provided an avenue of transport for these farmers' cotton bales, but it could just as easily serve as a route for invasion.[37]

The 4th Florida Infantry Regiment, with its assignment to guard vital points on the Gulf Coast, dispatched companies to Apalachicola to prevent such a move by the enemy. During the fall, Milton, who took a special interest in the port because his plantation in Jackson County was near the river, became aggravated by Edward Hopkins's defensive arrangements. The governor had no qualms about attacking the efforts of his former political opponent, and the fiasco at Apalachicola demonstrated the disharmony that remained among Florida's citizens.[38]

Colonel Edward Hopkins accompanied three companies to Apalachicola soon after the regiment mustered that September. At the port, the colonel faced a difficult problem: two channels, flowing between several barrier islands, allowed access to St. George Sound. The citizens of the town had constructed a battery on the mainland which, theoretically, could "command the several approaches to the town."[39]

Determined to prevent Union ships from entering the bay, Hopkins angered Apalachicola citizens when he dismantled the mainland battery and transported the cannon to nearby St. Vincent Island. From that barrier island, the colonel apparently hoped to challenge blockaders and demonstrate a show of force in the area. The plan was sound in theory, as Hopkins probably understood the disaster that would befall the port if Federal vessels brought it under their guns.

The problem with Hopkins's plan, however, was that he proposed to defend only the west pass channel, situated between St. Vincent and St. George islands, leaving the other, between the eastern tip of St. George and Dog Island, open to enemy ships. Therefore, if the east pass fell, Confederates on St. Vincent would suffer the severance of their supply line. Three hundred Confederate soldiers would find themselves stranded on the island, and Apalachicola would fall.

To defend himself against criticism regarding his decision, Hopkins wrote to Judah P. Benjamin: "It would be well for the Department to examine the Coast Survey of 1858, which proves that it [the west pass] is the only inlet worthy of notice." Despite this assurance, Governor Milton continued to believe Apalachicola might succumb to the enemy under Hopkins's plan. He wrote to President Jefferson Davis of the problem: "I regret to say that Colonel Hopkins' military ability is much doubted by many worthy citizens, and unpleasant circumstances have consequently occurred, which I apprehend will result unhappily."[40]

The governor requested that President Davis transfer Hopkins and his companies to St. Marks rather than allow the strained relationship between the 4th Florida and the civilians to continue. Edward Hopkins did not help his cause when he failed to effectively discipline the companies at Apalachicola; one officer complained that "he cannot even drill a squad of men." Hopkins, according to Governor Milton, also went absent without leave in October to visit Tallahassee. The governor, in his personal assaults, whimpered to Davis that Hopkins's election to colonel had been illegal because only eight companies voted and one was "commanded by a nephew of Colonel Hopkins."[41]

Pressing his attack on Hopkins and the 4th Florida, possibly in an attempt to obtain commissions for friends, Milton asked Davis to consider reorganizing not only the 4th Florida but also the 1st Florida Cavalry. The governor asked Davis to "reserve to yourself the appointment of field officers, and appoint such as are known to you, or such as I may recommend." Milton pushed his argument for a shake-up of the 4th Florida by attacking Hopkins's subordinates, writing of Wylde L. L. Bowen that he was a "major of no military education, and if I am informed rightly, on an accidental visit to Florida." He also informed the president that M. Whit Smith was "said to drink to great excess." Milton was mistaken regarding Bowen, but his comments regarding Smith were not far from the truth. Augustus Henry Mathers, one of the 4th Florida's assistant surgeons, wrote from Cedar Keys, "Colo Smith is not here . . . and the post would not be worsted if he never Came back it would have gotten rid of another drunken-no-Count-man, for such he is."[42]

By the end of October, Milton, after failing in his attempts to secure commissions for his appointees, requested that the Confederate War Department assign

Hopkins and the 4th Florida away from Apalachicola. By early November, the colonel complied with his new orders and removed his companies to Amelia Island. The 4th Florida's contingent at St. Marks departed as well, leaving Apalachee Bay under the protection of state troops.[43]

During the final months of 1861, as Florida placed more men in uniform, problems arose over fears that the Federal Navy would exploit the poorly defended coastline and launch raids against the state. Such fears failed to materialize in 1861, but Floridians at least began to prepare for the possibility of an invasion. The various strategies regarding the implementation of these plans created friction between the newly inaugurated John Milton and the elected officers of Florida's regiments. During the fall, Milton quarreled with every colonel in the state, save Anderson, whom he revered.

These disputes, the roots of which could be traced back, in most cases, to prewar political affiliations, created disorganization within the state and interfered with the regiments' assigned tasks. The squabbling also embarrassed the state and made Confederate officials question the ability of the state to contribute to the overall war effort. Only when the regiments departed from the state and left the altercations behind would they free themselves from the disharmony that had plagued Florida's antebellum history.

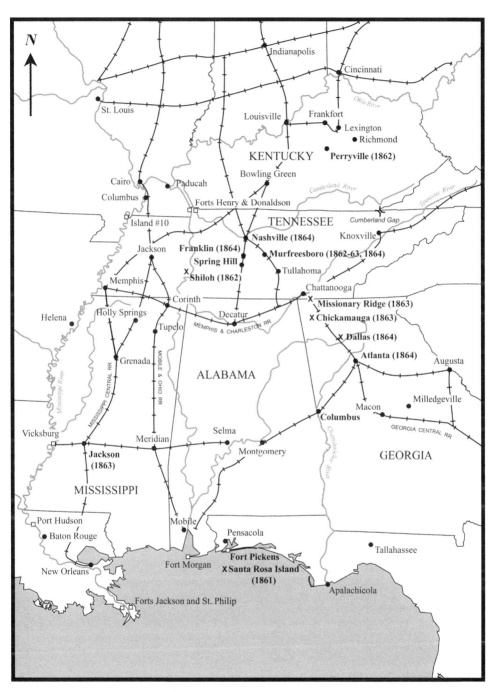

N

Indianapolis

Cincinnati

Ohio River

St. Louis

Louisville   Frankfort

Lexington

Richmond

KENTUCKY   **Perryville (1862)**

Bowling Green

Cairo   Paducah

Cumberland River   *Tennessee River*

Columbus

Island #10   Forts Henry & Donaldson

TENNESSEE   Cumberland Gap

Nashville (1864)   Knoxville

Jackson   **Franklin (1864)**

Spring Hill   **Murfreesboro (1862-63, 1864)**

x **Shiloh (1862)**   Tullahoma

Memphis   Chattanooga

Corinth   Decatur   **Missionary Ridge (1863)**

Helena   Holly Springs   x **Chickamauga (1863)**

Tupelo   MEMPHIS & CHARLESTON RR

x **Dallas (1864)**

Mississippi River   Grenada   **Atlanta (1864)**   Augusta

MOBILE & OHIO RR   ALABAMA   Milledgeville

MISSISSIPPI CENTRAL RR   Macon

Vicksburg   Meridian   Selma   **Columbus**   GEORGIA CENTRAL RR

Jackson   Montgomery   GEORGIA

(1863)   *Chattahoochee River*

MISSISSIPPI

Port Hudson   Mobile

Baton Rouge   Pensacola

Tallahassee

Fort Morgan   **Fort Pickens**

x **Santa Rosa Island**

New Orleans   **(1861)**

Apalachicola

Forts Jackson and St. Philip

The Civil War in the Western Theater

4 Its Flag Will Show Where the Fight Was Hottest

January–April 1862, West Florida and Shiloh

As the Yankee and Rebel armies in the East spent the winter of 1861–62 in relative inactivity, the fighting continued elsewhere. Union offensives, mainly in the form of joint operations, carried the war to the Confederate coastline. Crucial gains were made on the Atlantic and in the Gulf of Mexico, but the most important coordinated attack occurred inland. Here in February, Ulysses S. Grant's bold move up the Tennessee and Cumberland rivers seized the momentum for the Federals in the Western Theater and exposed the heartland of the Confederacy to invasion. This latter offensive rattled the Southern people and then gave way to the carnage of Shiloh, where Floridians learned of the horrors of war. Back home, their kin and neighbors laid down their implements of peace and raised even more regiments, eager still to take part in the conflict.

On the morning of February 15, 1862, Confederate troops smashed into Union picket lines near vital Fort Donelson, situated on the Cumberland River. Donelson, the sole barrier between the Union fleet and the important manufacturing center of Nashville, contained a garrison of twenty-one thousand Confederate soldiers; they now found themselves surrounded by General Ulysses S. Grant's Federal Army. Already, Fort Henry on the Tennessee River had capitulated, opening that waterway to the Federal Navy. In order to maintain their hold over the Cumberland River, and hence Nashville, Fort Donelson became a critical point for the Confederates.[1]

Recognizing that losing both the fort and thousands of troops might have severe repercussions, the Confederates planned an attack to open a route by which the beleaguered garrison might reach safety. That way, if the fort fell, at least the troops might survive to fight again. The morning offensive succeeded in opening the road to Nashville. Yet, owing to the ineffectiveness of the fort's commanders, no breakout took place and Grant's forces soon turned the tide on the attackers, ending any chance of escape. Though the Confederates might still have evacuated some troops from the position, the two ranking generals at the fort fled, leaving General Simon Bolivar Buckner to surrender the garrison the next day.[2]

The threat to Fort Donelson had precipitated a retreat into Tennessee by the Confederate Army occupying Anderson's beloved Kentucky. In early March, Albert

Sidney Johnston's jaded and tired force finally halted at Corinth, Mississippi, where they combined with troops led by P.G.T. Beauregard to form the Army of the Mississippi and prepared to defend West Tennessee and the Mississippi Valley. But the damage was done, as Nashville, along with Middle Tennessee and Kentucky, were lost. Following the Federal forces' stunning successes on the two rivers, the Confederacy scrambled to reverse its ill fortunes.

After the loss of Fort Henry, Confederate District of Florida judge Jesse Johnson Finley sat at his desk in Marianna and put pen to paper. Though the judge had turned forty-nine the previous November, he was determined not to let his age keep him from the army. In fact, Finley's youthful appearance belied his age: he had a tendency to be overweight and it showed in his round face, and this, combined with a full head of dark hair, only enhanced his youthfulness. He addressed the paper to Judah P. Benjamin and announced: "I have been in doubt as to whether it was proper for me to continue my present position (Judge of the District of Florida) or whether it was my duty to enlist a corps of men for the war. . . . Our late reverses at Fishing Creek, at Roanoke Island and on the Tennessee River, have ended this doubt." The judge asked for permission to raise a company of infantry for the war.[3]

Like Anderson, Jesse J. Finley hailed from Tennessee, being born in Wilson County in 1812. Educated in Lebanon, Tennessee, Finley commanded a volunteer company in Florida during the Second Seminole Indian War and then returned to Nashville to read law. Widowed soon after, Finley migrated to Grenada, Mississippi, where he practiced law and toyed with the idea of moving to Texas. He traveled to Arkansas instead, where as a Whig he gained election to the state senate. However, he relinquished this seat soon after to move to Memphis to resume practicing law. Politics intervened once again, and Finley was elected mayor. However, when he became a widower once again, he sought a fresh start in Florida in 1846 following the end of his term.[4]

In Florida, Finley returned to politics and remarried. Whigs of Jackson County elected him to the Florida Senate in 1850, where he introduced and supported a bill that allowed the people of Florida to elect their judges. In 1853 Governor William Mosley appointed him to complete an unfinished term as Western Circuit Judge, a position he occupied until 1861. The judge had, in his own words, remained true to his conservatism in 1860, voting "for John Bell for President and Edward Everett for Vice President." After Lincoln's election, Finley advocated secession, "believing . . . that it was a peaceful remedy."[5]

Finley's proposal to raise a company came in response to yet another Confederate War Department call for troops, this one coming on February 2. Under this newly imposed quota, Florida would furnish two regiments and a battalion to fight for the duration of the war. The troops would rendezvous at preselected locations and there "be clothed, supplied, and armed at the expense of the Confed-

erate States." Furthermore, each enlistee would receive a fifty-dollar bounty for
volunteering. From this request came the 5th and 6th Florida infantry regiments,
and companies such as Finley's applied for service within these new units.[6]

While the 5th Florida soldiered in Robert E. Lee's Army of Northern Virginia,
the 6th's destiny lay in the west. The regiment contained a strong West Florida
flavor, as seven of its companies originated in that region. Gadsden County, just
east of the Apalachicola River, provided three companies as well. In late March
the various units were ordered to bivouac at the Chattahoochee Arsenal, where
the regiment entered a camp of instruction. Because of West Florida's strong conservatism, the soldiers elected ex-Whigs as their officers.[7]

Jesse J. Finley, well known to the new soldiers from his days riding the circuit,
became colonel. Angus D. McLean from Walton County gained the rank of lieutenant colonel thanks to the efforts of his numerous kin and schoolmates. An educated young man, McLean turned twenty-six in 1862 and held a law degree from
Cumberland University in Lebanon, Tennessee.[8]

Daniel Lafayette Kenan, who preferred to be called Lafayette, gained the majority of the votes for major. Though born in North Carolina in 1825, Kenan came
to Florida with his family at the age of six. Thirty-seven years old in 1862, Major
Kenan possessed sharp features and a high forehead, exposed by a receding hairline.
Married with a house full of children, Kenan was a wheelwright and carriage maker
by trade. A devoted Whig, he also represented Gadsden County in four state legislative sessions during the 1850s. Kenan's peers wrote glowingly of his character:
"generous, benevolent, patriotic, and public spirited . . . at all times manifesting a
lively interest in all public enterprises pertaining to the prosperity and happiness
of the community." In their choice, the 6th Florida's soldiers could not have done
better.[9]

At the Chattahoochee Arsenal, some of the 6th Florida volunteers could not believe the tribulations that army life offered. Angus Gillis, a soldier in Company H,
wrote to a relative, "You ought to have seen us cooking . . . [I have helped] cook
several meals . . . but know no more about it than when I cooked the first." Another 6th Florida mess, the small group in which the soldiers prepared food and
ate, solved that problem early on: "Each one had his special instructions to give to
the other, but our combined culinary knowledge is not sufficient for the beaking
[*sic*] of bread. . . . A few days ago we came to the conclusion that we would not do
for cooks and we sent to Tallahassee and hired a boy."[10]

The soldiers at the arsenal woke at daylight and drilled for three hours each day.
Colonel Finley took the discipline of his regiment seriously, writing to his superior
in the Department of East and Middle Florida, "I can usefully employ as many as
six drill officers in the Regiment; being anxious to hasten its instruction, so as to
make it capable of being handled in the field at the earliest possible convenience."

To make better officers of the elected civilians, these gentlemen held their own drill session at 10:00 A.M. and Finley led a regimental dress parade every evening at 5:00. "So you see," wrote A. G. McLeod, "we have but little time to spare, especially the officers." Another soldier wrote of the intense training, "I reckon, we will get pretty well up on the traid be fore we leave camp."[11]

The soldiers of the 1st Florida were certainly well trained by early 1862, having endured months of drill in the manual of arms. Its ranks included soldiers who had heard the whistle of enemy minié bullets and others like Roddie Shaw who hoped to one day see battle. During the winter months the regiment underwent a transformation as a period of reenlistment began in Bragg's Pensacola army.

Most of Bragg's soldiers mustered in for a twelve-month enlistment. The general, fearful that his command would go home at the end of their terms, asked his veterans that November to reenlist for the war. The general appealed to the soldiers' sense of unit pride, claiming that if the soldier did not reenlist, he would join a new unit and be thrown in "with strangers and raw men, where he will have to go through all the drudgery of elementary instruction. . . . All his former acquaintances and *esprit de corps* will be lost, and he will be looked on as a raw recruit instead of a veteran." Bragg announced that he would grant furloughs to every man who reenlisted, and regiments that maintained companies of sixty-four or more officers and men were allowed to retain their old organization. The Pensacola soldiers began deciding whether to sign on for the war or take their chances in other units.[12]

The soldiers varied greatly as to whether they wanted to reenlist. William D. Randolph wrote home, "I think I wont [sic] join the infantry again for a million a minute and expenses paid." His brother, Thomas Eston Randolph, assured their father, "You need feel no uneasiness about my enlisting again, at least while I am here. I have seen enough of the 'Pomp and circumstance of war.'" However, Samuel H. Harris, who had earlier written that he would run away during the first fight, now had a change of heart, confessing, "I am willing for me to join for the war but not under our present officers . . . I expect to be a soulder the ballance of my life and if this war closes any time soon I will be very arguably disappointed." Still, he decided to soldier in a different regiment and did not reenlist in the 1st Florida.[13]

Many of the officers in the regiment, either disillusioned with the prospects of war or physically unable to continue, planned to retire at the end of their enlistment. As a result, a game of persuasion and politics ensued, as the officers who intended to remain coerced men from the lame-duck companies to enlist in their own units so as to boost their numbers over the minimum. Of this practice, William D. Randolph wrote that "the officers or at least the most of them are very busy trying to raise companies out of the Regt. for the war . . . many of the men have already joined and more are joining every day." By January some companies had met their quota, and the men were allowed to take their furloughs. Meanwhile, other officers still sought out volunteers for their companies so that they might keep their commissions.[14]

W. Capers Bird, the younger brother of Captain Daniel Bird, was one of the officers who had trouble obtaining enough soldiers for his company. Bird entreated "his fellow citizens of Jefferson County to come forward and enroll their names, and enable him to swell the ranks to one hundred." He enticed new recruits with the promise that "the position that the Regiment will occupy is delightful and it is the post of honor." Bird's company, whether through the flowery rhetoric or by other means, eventually reached its required number of men.[15]

By early March 1862, General P.G.T. Beauregard ordered Braxton Bragg to proceed with his Gulf Coast forces to Corinth. As regiments prepared to leave their positions on the coast, furloughed Floridians returned to their post on Deer Point. They rejoined comrades, such as Roddie Shaw, Samuel H. Harris, and the Randolph brothers, who refused to soldier in the 1st Florida any longer. In all, more than three hundred 1st Florida veterans reenlisted out of the six hundred soldiers that remained with the regiment at the end of 1861. Also by March, because of Anderson's elevation to brigade command, Lieutenant Colonel William Kelly Beard commanded the 1st Florida; Major Thaddeus McDonell served as the regiment's executive officer.[16]

As Bragg moved north to complete Beauregard's order, he left behind Brigadier General Samuel Jones to command at Pensacola and forward troops to the vital rail junction at Corinth. With the Pensacola army dispatched to the front to defend the Mississippi Valley, the Gulf city itself became expendable. On March 6 General Jones ordered Lieutenant Colonel Beard to hold a portion of his troops ready to evacuate their position on Deer Point, while the commander himself would proceed with two companies to locations up East Bay by steamer to destroy industries that might aid the enemy. On March 10, as the last major elements of Bragg's force departed Pensacola, Beard carried out Jones's order. That night his troops burned saw mills and steamships, and then marched overland to Pollard, Alabama. At the same time, the remaining 1st Florida companies on Deer Point were ordered to serve as a delaying force and defend that location against enemy attacks, and "reflect credit upon themselves and their state." Days later, these eight companies of the 1st Florida Regiment joined Beard at Pollard.[17]

On March 16, as the Floridians marked time at Pollard, an order arrived that required Beard to proceed with his soldiers to Corinth. General Jones wrote that Braxton Bragg was "anxious to have the Floridians with him." Bragg's anxiety would not yet be relieved, for damage to a rail line between Mobile and their final destination delayed the Floridians until late in the month. While the 1st Florida Infantry Regiment's soldiers who refused to reenlist mustered out at Montgomery, the remainder proceeded to Corinth as the 1st Florida Battalion.[18]

Upon their arrival at Corinth, Lieutenant Colonel William Kelly Beard's tenure with the 1st Florida Infantry ended, as Braxton Bragg appointed him acting inspector general of *his* newly formed 2nd Corps, Army of the Mississippi. By default, Major Thaddeus McDonell, the young lawyer from Alachua County, commanded the 1st Florida Battalion. The battalion numbered four companies totaling 328 soldiers and was assigned to Anderson's Brigade of Daniel Ruggles's Division in Braxton Bragg's 2nd Corps. The Floridians joined the 17th and 20th Louisiana Infantry Regiments, the Confederate Guards Response Battalion, and the 9th Texas Infantry in Anderson's unit. The brigade also included the 5th Company of the New Orleans–raised Washington Artillery.[19]

There was not much time for the Floridians to become acquainted with their new comrades in Albert Sidney Johnston's newly designated Army of the Mississippi, for the enemy was near and Confederate plans for an attack were afoot. To support a Union strategy in the west of clearing the Mississippi River of Confederate control after the fall of Fort Donelson, Major General Henry W. Halleck, commanding the Federal Department of Missouri, decided to use Grant's victorious army to seize Corinth from the Confederates. As the historian Larry Daniel has pointed out, control of Corinth, with its rail junction, meant that Memphis would fall and with it the river forts north of the important town. Though the original move up the Tennessee River was meant only to target the rail lines that passed through Corinth, the plan soon evolved into one where the army would encamp in southwest Tennessee at Pittsburg Landing, situated near small Shiloh Church and twenty miles from Corinth. Once Grant's force consolidated its numbers, a movement toward the city would begin.[20]

As the Federal Army gathered on the banks of the Tennessee River, General Albert Sidney Johnston adopted the plan of his second-in-command, P.G.T. Beauregard, for dealing with this incursion into Confederate territory. After moving into position near the Federal encampment, the forty thousand soldiers of the Army of the Mississippi would strike for Pittsburg Landing, cutting the Federal Army off from the river and its supplies. Once stranded in the wilderness of West Tennessee, Grant's army would have to surrender.[21]

Late on the afternoon of April 3, the Army of the Mississippi, comprising mainly raw soldiers, began a disorganized march toward the Federal encampment. Poor roads and confused marching orders hampered their progress, and when the army deployed to attack on the morning of April 5, rain caused another delay. Not until the morning of April 6 could the army launch its assault. As dawn broke, Federal patrols bumped into Rebel picket lines and firing began in earnest. In Bragg's 2nd Corps, which occupied the second line of the Confederate battle formation, the 1st Florida Battalion's 250 active soldiers waited for their opportunity to move forward.[22]

General William Hardee's 1st Corps moved forward just after 5:30 A.M., pushing through the Union patrols and into Federal encampments just south of Shiloh Church. Bragg's soldiers were close behind, with Lieutenant Colonel Beard delivering the order to Anderson to advance at 6:15. "As I rode down the lines," Beard later wrote, "I shook hands with many of them. . . . All seemed filled with bright hopes—anxious to win a name and place in their Country's gratitude." The Floridians, along with the other regiments of Anderson's Brigade, moved forward on the line of the Pittsburg-Corinth Road.[23]

The Floridians pushed through what Lieutenant Colonel Beard referred to as "a deep ravine where from the nature of the wood we could do nothing" and halted. The ravine Beard referred to was Shiloh Branch, a stream that lay within a gully surrounded by woods and overgrown with thickets. The 53rd Ohio's tents were pitched upon high ground that dominated this tributary, and though Brigadier General Patrick Cleburne's Brigade succeeded in breaking the Union line above the stream, their attack had stalled due to stout resistance. Unused to this turmoil, the Floridians faltered in their advance.[24]

The chaos resulted mainly from Federal artillery fire that was both heavy and accurate; one shell fragment ripped open Major McDonell's thigh as he led his soldiers forward. As litter bearers bore McDonell from the field, command of the battalion devolved upon Captain Bill Poole of Company A. A Marylander, Poole was twenty-seven years old and the co-owner of a successful import company in Tallahassee. His only prior leadership experience was as the foreman of Rescue No. 1, a volunteer Engine and Hose Company in the capital city.[25]

Taking command, Poole could not make his battalion move against the heavy Federal artillery fire; instead, the Florida soldiers remained in Shiloh Branch, hugging the muddy bank, trying desperately to avoid the shell and canister flying overhead. The Floridians, shocked at the ferocity of the battle, remained in the ravine as some of Anderson's other troops forced their way through the 53rd Ohio's camp and surged forward toward Shiloh Church. Lieutenant Colonel Beard wrote that "some Regiments seemed indisposed to advance as rapidly as necessary but were soon reassured by the dauntless bravery and personal courage of Gen. Bragg." It could be that Bragg, still anxious to have the Floridians with him, had to coax the 1st Florida from the safety of Shiloh Branch, for the battalion did not rejoin the brigade until it passed Shiloh Church.[26]

By 9:30 A.M. the Federal volunteers just north of Shiloh Church found themselves fighting a delaying action across a field near the intersection of the Pittsburg-Corinth and Purdy-Hamburg roads. Colonel Ralph Buckland's Ohio Brigade formed a portion of this line, and though much reduced by stragglers, the Buckeyes poured a destructive fire into the onrushing 1st Florida Battalion. Leading the battalion's Company A, twenty-year-old First Lieutenant Lawrence "Laurie" Anderson encouraged his soldiers to move forward. A student in Tallahassee before the conflict, Anderson was a favorite of the battalion. He died in that field after a bullet shattered his brow and passed "entirely" through his head. In addition to Anderson, the 1st Florida Battalion lost many effective leaders in the mid-morning assault, including a captain and four lieutenants, all wounded in the attack.[27]

Though the assault on the Federals waned due to heavy fire, Confederate forces pushing northward to the right of Anderson's line succeeded in collapsing the Federal position. However, because of the influx of troops behind William Hardee and Braxton Bragg's attacking forces, and the Federal soldiers' natural inclination to retreat toward the boats, the Union Army swung like a gate toward the landing rather than into the wilderness. Therefore, Anderson's Brigade moved in a northeasterly direction during the day and that afternoon came face-to-face with a strong defensive line cobbled together by Brigadier Generals Benjamin Prentiss, Stephen Hurlbut, and W.H.L. Wallace. The line, which took form along what came to be called the "Sunken Road," was dubbed the "Hornet's Nest" by Confederates because of the ferocity of the combat.[28]

Against the western flank of this position, the 1st Florida Battalion made its last attack of the day. The Floridians advanced across a bald cotton field in an attack against the strong Federal line. Here, Brigadier General Anderson wrote, "the enemy's canister was particularly well directed, and the range being that of musketry, was well calculated to test the pluck of the sternest." Directly opposite the Floridians, holding their portion of the defensive line, lay two Iowa regiments. At one time the Floridians and Iowans were kindred spirits, as their two territories joined the Union together in 1845. Now they attempted to kill each other.[29]

Lieutenant Colonel James C. Parrott, commanding the 7th Iowa Infantry, wrote that his regiment "advanced to the edge of a field, from which position we got a view of a portion of the rebel forces." The Iowans "remained in that position until 5 p.m., holding the rebels in check and retaining every inch of ground it had gained in the morning." Colonel James Tuttle, commanding the brigade of Iowans, recalled proudly that the Confederates were "each time baffled and completely routed." Near sundown the Federal troops holding the right of this strong line began to give way to fresh Confederate attacks, creating a salient that the Confederates slowly collapsed.[30]

As daylight faded, the Army of the Mississippi captured nearly 2,300 of Prentiss's defenders, but the victory was in vain, for throughout the afternoon the Union soldiers delayed the Confederates, giving Grant time to devise a defensive line on a ridge not far from Pittsburg Landing. The salient also claimed the life of Albert Sidney Johnston, who, while leading an attack on the right, was mortally wounded. Dying minutes later from the loss of blood, command passed to Beauregard, who called a halt to the day's fighting after a few scattered attempts against Grant's new line.[31]

Anderson's Brigade spent that night in an abandoned Federal camp. Rain fell, soaking the soldiers who could not find a tent. Around them lay a battlefield where "the scene was a most horrible one. The dead and dying and wounded lay scattered all over the field, and horses, wagons, tents torn to pieces, and all other evidence of terrible strife." At Pittsburg Landing that night bustling activity never ceased, as steamboats made trip after trip across the Tennessee River, bringing the soldiers of Don Carlos Buell's Department of the Ohio onto the battlefield.[32]

On the morning of April 7, Captain Bill Poole, who was unable to speak because he had spent the previous day yelling commands over the volume of fire, relinquished command to Captain Capers Bird. Shortly afterward, Grant's force, along with elements of Buell's army, surged forward in a savage counterattack. During the day, the 1st Florida Battalion, along with the remainder of the Army of the Mississippi, was pushed back across the battlefield of the previous day, occasionally launching their own counteroffensives. That afternoon, however, fearing the army might disintegrate, Beauregard ordered a retreat to Corinth.[33]

Over the next few days the Army of the Mississippi straggled into Corinth to count its losses and mend its wounds. When Captain Poole sat down on April 12 to write his version of the 1st Florida Battalion's part in the battle, brigade surgeon Cary Gamble's casualty report informed him that two officers and fourteen enlisted men were dead, and the wounded numbered fifty-seven. These losses amounted to 30 percent of the 250 soldiers that had marched forward on the morning of April 6.[34]

The Floridians' sixteen dead were only a small fraction of the 1,723 Confederates killed in the battle. On April 7 Capers Bird, the officer who had asked the men of his hometown to join his regiment, joined the 8,404 rebels who sustained wounds. Though total Union casualties numbered over 13,000 when the killing ended, the Federal Army remained at Pittsburg Landing, convalescing and waiting for the order to advance on Corinth and finish the campaign they had begun that winter.[35]

The Battle of Shiloh made veterans of the 1st Florida Battalion soldiers who had not fought on Santa Rosa Island. Some, such as Lawrence Matthews, found that active soldiering was much more taxing than sentinel duty at Pensacola. Matthews, a resident of Pensacola, wrote after Shiloh that "the duties were too severe and altogether beyond my powers of endurance." Despite the Confederates' seemingly lackluster performance during the two-day contest, Shiloh brought Florida positive attention as a state across the Confederacy for the first time during the war. Anderson wrote in his official report of the fight, "the desperation with which" the Floridians "fought brings new luster to the arms of the State they represented, and paints imperishable fame upon the colors they so proudly bore." Lieutenant Colonel Beard immodestly wrote of his former regiment, "It has won for itself an enviable reputation and done credit to the state. Thank heaven the old 1st has shown what it could and would do in time of need. Its flag will show where the fight was hottest."[36]

Nearly a month after the Battle of Shiloh, in the first wave of unit consolidations imposed upon the army, the 1st Florida Battalion, by Special Orders No. 51, merged with the two-company Confederate Guards Response Battalion. The Guards, a New Orleans–raised unit, had also suffered heavily at Shiloh, and Bragg, in an attempt to provide the two units with strength enough to render effective service on the battlefield, created the Florida and Confederate Guards Response Battalion. Under the command of Major Franklin Clack of the Guards Response Battalion, sickness prevented the new unit from ever maintaining more than 190 soldiers for duty during any time that spring.[37]

Following a decline in Confederate morale in the aftermath of the disasters at Forts Henry and Donelson, the casualties of Shiloh shocked the Confederacy. In Florida the loss was magnified, coming as it did on the heels of the invasion of the state's shores. However, the people of Florida could be proud of their little band that advanced through the thickets and ravines of Shiloh and earned a token of respect from their commanders and fellow soldiers. In the months ahead, more of their fellow Floridians would join them in the Western Theater, embellishing the name of Florida and enduring more of the savagery of war.

5 To Maintain Inviolate the Sacred Honor of Florida

January–May 1862, East Florida

In March, as the 1st Florida Infantry Regiment departed Pensacola for Corinth and the troubled situation in the west, a malaise descended upon Florida. The strike on the state's coast that John Milton had long feared came to fruition that month as a joint Federal army-navy operation moved on Fernandina. Coming soon after the attacks on Forts Henry and Donelson, the invasion lowered Floridians' morale and caused some to question the Confederate government's request to transfer troops from the state.

The attack on Fernandina came during a renewed series of coastal offensives by the Federals that were intended to close Southern ports to blockade runners and at the same time secure bases of operations for blockaders. The Federals had already seized the mouth of Hatteras Inlet and Port Royal, South Carolina, in 1861. The 1862 attacks built on these earlier successes and achieved an initial victory with the capture of Roanoke Island on February 8, 1862. The conquering of Roanoke allowed the Federal Army to occupy several North Carolina ports and netted 2,675 prisoners.[1]

Amelia Island, with its fine harbor, offered a Roanoke-like opportunity for the Federals as the Confederate force occupied an offshore position that the Union Navy might easily isolate. Brigadier General Horatio G. Wright looked to make a strike against Florida, suggesting on January 31 that they "land on Amelia Island to engage and cut off, if possible, the retreat of the rebel force." Wright planned to hold the enemy in place with an amphibious landing, even as a flotilla of warships "pushed as rapidly [as] possible up the Amelia River [Nassau Sound] past Fernandina, to intercept the retreat of the rebels, to prevent the destruction of the railroad bridge, and to save any rolling stock of the road."[2]

Even before the Yankee fleet appeared off Amelia Island, the Confederates were making arrangements for the post's evacuation. Although General Robert E. Lee, commanding the Department of South Carolina, Georgia, and Florida, discussed the possibility of strengthening its garrison on February 14, five days later he wrote Brigadier General James Trapier advising a different strategy. "The force that the enemy can bring against any position where he can concentrate his floating batteries," argued Lee, "renders it prudent and proper to withdraw from the islands to the main-land and to prepare to contest his advance into the interior." Looking to Roanoke Island as an example, Trapier concurred and advised Lee that his

force "was not well equipped nor armed" and had but "a short supply of ammunition and heavy ordnance." On February 24 Trapier obtained permission to evacuate the island, with General Lee insisting that Trapier save the cannon for use elsewhere.[3]

One of the reasons the force on Amelia Island was not well prepared to defend
against a Federal attack was the fact that in January the 3rd Florida, armed with
rifled-muskets, was dispatched to the Cedar Keys to meet a supposed threat there
and to New Smyrna to guard the offloading of shipments brought in through the
blockade. The 4th Florida and 24th Mississippi infantry regiments were assigned to
defend Amelia Island. Yet sickness complicated these regiments' ability to defend
the island. Communicable diseases, obtained from the close living in the camps
and standing shoulder-to-shoulder during drill, had spread through the ranks.
Other ailments caused by poor sanitation facilities and the elements plagued the
men as well.[4]

Mumps and measles, with its accompanying pneumonia, made their appearance on Amelia Island in early 1862, causing numerous deaths and filling the hospitals with the sick. Assistant Surgeon Mathers wrote home during the evacuation,
"Death is making a broad road through the 4th Regiment I think they have lost
thirty or forty men Since they landed here." At nearby Callahan, the 1st Florida
Cavalry suffered similarly; in early February "in one company of 70 men, 23 were
laid up as shown by the sick report." After the 3rd Florida's Jefferson County companies departed from Fernandina in January to guard Mosquito Inlet near New
Smyrna, Lemuel Moody conveyed, "I am sick know with measles . . . I am stay-
ing at the hotell[.] Naily all ower company is down know with measles. they was
only thirty-five sick this morning." In Lake City, Washington Ives scribbled in his
diary, "Nearly every day there is a death at one of the Hospitals."[5]

On March 2, as the rush to remove the guns and soldiers from Amelia Island
continued, and at a time when sickness hit several Confederate regiments hard,
twenty-seven Federal ships appeared off the island. Much of the evacuation had
proceeded well, as Mathers related, "they are dismounting and Sending the Guns
away now all the horses have bin Sent away and the work of tearing every-thing
up is now going on."[6]

Out of thirty-three cannon mounted on the island, the Rebels removed eighteen and spiked the remainder. Colonel Edward Hopkins, overseeing the retreat,
also saw to it that trains carried civilians to safety. At 2:00 P.M. on March 3, the last
4th Florida companies retreated from the island and set fire to the railroad bridge;
the Federals quickly took possession of Fernandina. After surveying the island's
fortifications, a *New York Times* correspondent paid tribute to Colonel William
Dilworth's and the 3rd Florida's hard, yet futile, work of the previous fall: "The
fortifications were very strong. . . . Had the enemy chosen to make any resistance
we must have suffered severe loss in an attack." To add insult to the Confederate's

injury, however, two weeks after Fernandina's fall several companies of the 4th New Hampshire occupied Jacksonville.[7]

Though General Lee had ordered the evacuation of the position, General Trapier and Colonel Hopkins became the scapegoats for the loss of Amelia Island. Though Colonel Hopkins saved his regiment and most of the equipment on the island, newspaper editors throughout the Confederacy wrote scathing columns blaming him for the loss of another coastal installation. The *Savannah Republican* raged, "the men were eager for a fight, but were held back by their commanders," and that "much was lost owing to the inefficiency of the Colonel in command." Hopkins, perhaps overcome by the stress of the operation and stung by harsh criticism, remained sick in Lake City for the remainder of the month. James Trapier asked for, and was granted, a transfer to the Army of the Mississippi.[8]

As the Federal forces consolidated their hold on Amelia Island, the 1st Florida Cavalry began earning its keep. General Trapier had stationed the majority of the unit in Nassau County the previous January because "the site was favorable as a Camp of instruction, that, they could be more cheaply supplied than at any other point" and be within "supporting distance of Fernandina." Also, three companies were encamped at Camp Mary Davis, just south of Tallahassee, where they could guard against coastal incursions against the capital. After a quiet winter its troops were suddenly busy with scouting the Atlantic shore and observing Federal activity on Amelia Island. Having been upgraded to a regiment with the addition of two companies in December, W.G.M. Davis became colonel and led the unit, G. Troup Maxwell gained promotion to lieutenant colonel, and William Tennent Stockton was appointed major.[9]

Major Stockton brought with him a caliber of discipline taught only on the Hudson. A native of Pennsylvania, Stockton graduated eighth in the United States Military Academy's Class of 1834 and was commissioned as a Brevet 2nd Lieutenant of Artillery. After service at the Augusta Arsenal and at Fort Wood, Louisiana, he was transferred to Pensacola, where he performed surveying duty. Stockton also served at Tampa, where he was engaged in the early Second Seminole Indian War battles of Camp Izard and Oloklikoha. He resigned his commission on May 31, 1836, though, and settled in Quincy where he eventually purchased a plantation and managed a post road service. Commissioned a captain in 1861, he spent that year in East Florida mustering state troops into the Confederate service.[10]

Given the task of drill instructor of the 1st Florida Cavalry, Stockton used the time not spent reconnoitering Amelia Island to put the troopers through their paces. "My work is very arduous," he assured his wife, "for the training of 500 raw men whose officers know very little, and the men less, is a very different thing from drilling my own Company. But they shall learn. I have a school of the officers every night to recite from their books. Some of them are dull enough." That same month he wrote, "Yesterday, 22nd, I had a review of the command. It was admirably done and I am well satisfied with the service I have rendered."[11]

The intense training was necessary, for in January a group of Florida politicians passed a resolution requesting that Trapier transfer the 1st Florida Cavalry to Sidney Johnston's Kentucky army. General Lee wrote to Trapier, concurring with the transfer, but to do so only "if you can without impairing the efficiency of your command." The request was formalized on February 18, 1862, when Judah P. Benjamin wrote to General Lee to "order the cavalry regiment of Colonel Davis from Florida to Chattanooga immediately to report to A. S. Johnston." The capture of Amelia Island put a stop to this movement, however, and the regiment's companies remained in Nassau County, monitoring the Yankees on the island, and near Tallahassee.[12]

With the threat that Amelia Island and Jacksonville's capture posed to East Florida, soldiers of the 1st Florida Cavalry who hailed from this region penned a protest to the governor, explaining why they would not go to Tennessee. Written by Captain Noble Hull, the document was dispatched to Governor Milton and read, in part, "A few weeks ago, we were perfectly willing to go anywhere ordered but, Sir with the enemy all around . . . our homes and families threatened we cannot think of leaving the State unless there is an Army left here sufficient to protect our families and interests." Governor Milton, once determined to see the 1st Cavalry disbanded, wrote back sternly: "If the First Florida Cavalry Regiment should refuse to obey or resist the order the regiment would be dishonored and disgraced and payment refused for past services . . . I repeat hasten to the Battlefield where victory will insure the Independence of the Confederate States of America and in the achievement of . . . a Victory let Florida be distinguished by the noble daring of her Sons." Milton's letter either inspired or coerced the 1st Florida Cavalry's soldiers to accept their orders for deployment to Albert Sidney Johnston's western force. However, further development on the Florida coast caused another delay.[13]

In January 1862 Brigadier General Trapier dispatched the 3rd Florida Infantry's Jefferson County companies to New Smyrna on Florida's Atlantic coast to guard vital shipments run through the Federal blockade. Under the command of Major John Barnwell, a South Carolina officer and friend of Trapier, the soldiers were dispatched up the St. John's River and then marched overland to their destination. The Floridians remained at New Smyrna several weeks, "eating," wrote Lemuel Moody, "oysters and oranges and fish," while the blockade runner *Kate* made several dashes in from the Bahamas and discharged many tons of arms and equipment, including "6,000 Rifles, 50,000 lbs. of powder, 600,000 Cartridges, gun caps, blankets . . . sufficient to equip an army of 6000 men complete." Because of Florida's poor transportation network, with no rails and few roads leading to the coast, the equipment was stored near the beach until the government could gather adequate wagons to move the precious cargo.[14]

Situating their camp on the mainland so as to guard both the mouth of the inlet and Mosquito Lagoon, the Confederates kept a constant vigil out to sea. However, Major Barnwell seemed unconcerned with the possibility of a Federal attack
on his position. The Jefferson County companies, armed with Enfield rifles, gave
the major confidence that he could hold out against all odds. "If the enemy does
find us out and make a boat attack," Barnwell wrote rather nonchalantly, "I shall
whip them, as the rifles can range beyond the river [Mosquito Lagoon], and I have
never seen such shots as these Floridians." Undoubtedly upset at being stationed
on the Florida coast, the major added as an afterthought in parentheses: "(about
all this country is worth for)."[15]

On March 23 sailors and marines from the Union gunboats *Penguin* and *Henry
Andrews* rowed through the inlet in an attempt to disrupt the Confederate operations. Piloted by a runaway, five launches rowed ashore on the mainland and the
Federals advanced inland. Dan Bird and William Girardeau's companies, secure
in concealed positions, took them under fire. The Rebels succeeded in driving the
sailors back into the lagoon, killing seven and taking three prisoners.[16]

The thwarting of this attack, which occurred just as the Confederates prepared
to move the arms northeast to the railroad at Gainesville, caused Colonel Dilworth
to believe that the Federals in Jacksonville would advance on the railroad terminus
at Baldwin to cut the lines there. This bold move might result in the capture of the
weapons and munitions, or at least cause the Confederates to continue transferring
the shipment north by horse and wagon. Because of this development, Colonel
Dilworth ordered the 1st Florida Cavalry to Baldwin, where they would remain
until the weapons safely left the state.[17]

As the Jefferson County companies of the 3rd Florida guarded New Smyrna,
the remainder of the regiment joined the 1st Cavalry at Baldwin to prevent any
attempt by the Federals to intercept the munitions convoy. The 4th Florida encamped at Sanderson, thus providing a mobile reserve on the Florida Atlantic and
Gulf Railroad. To keep the Federals off-balance, Colonel William Dilworth instituted a campaign of harassment near Jacksonville, mainly seeking to overwhelm
enemy pickets and discourage any thoughts of an inland advance. One raid, taking place on the night of March 25, saw thirty-nine Floridians dispatched to assault an outpost near Brick Church at LaVilla. In a violent exchange of gunfire,
five 4th New Hampshire soldiers were killed and three Yankees were seized. In
the skirmish, the 3rd Florida lost its first soldier to enemy fire when Lieutenant
Thomas Strange of the Columbia and Suwannee Guards was mortally wounded.
These skirmishes and active patrols continued throughout the last week of March
and into April until the Federal Army evacuated Jacksonville on April 9. Upon
leaving Jacksonville, the 4th New Hampshire was transferred to defenseless St. Augustine, where it began the continuous Union occupation of the Ancient City.[18]

With the munitions being transported north, and as the 1st Florida Cavalry

Regiment prepared to move to the front, the 7th Florida Infantry organized in Gainesville. The state united nine militia companies that had been organized in late 1861 and early 1862, and for good measure added a Florida Coast Guard company stationed near Tampa. The regiment drew two companies each from Alachua and Marion counties, while Bradford and Putnam contributed one apiece. The South Florida frontier districts of Manatee, Sumter, and Hillsborough each provided companies of tough pioneers as well. Likewise, a number of exiled Key West residents soldiered in the Coast Guard unit, Company K. Because its soldiers hailed from strong Democratic regions, it was no surprise that ex-governor Madison Starke Perry was elected colonel.[19]

Leaving the governor's office in October 1861 after an extended term as a result of Florida's secession, Madison Starke Perry returned to his Alachua County plantation for several months of peace. At forty-eight years old, the former executive remained an imposing figure, though his once lantern jaw had given way to a sag. Born in the Lancaster District of South Carolina, Perry migrated to Alachua County where he owned acreage near Micanopy. A strident Democrat, Perry had long been active in Florida politics, and he served as a state senator in 1850 and 1855 before winning the governorship in 1856. The ex-governor constantly worried about his health, and wrote in July 1862 after arriving in Tennessee, "I regret that I ever consented to take charge of the Regt."[20]

The man elected lieutenant colonel furnished the leadership that the oft-sick Perry could not. Robert W. Bullock, a pudgy, ruddy-faced North Carolinian who called Ocala home, was thirty-three years old in 1862. A resident of Florida since 1844, Bullock served as clerk of the court in Marion County and in 1860 practiced law with St. George Rogers, a future Confederate congressman. During the 1850s the young man had married, dabbled in entrepreneurship, and captained a mounted company during the Third Seminole Indian War. His biographer writes that Bullock was "popular and respected in Marion County," and this high regard carried over to other companies of the 7th when election time came.[21]

Tillman Ingram, a cousin and political crony of Madison Starke Perry, became the major. A native of South Carolina, the thirty-nine-year-old Democrat had served in the state house in the 1856 and 1858 sessions and in the state senate in 1860–61. The owner of a plantation he dubbed Oak Hall, Ingram won the bid for and constructed Alachua County's new courthouse in 1856.[22]

As the majority of the regiment converged on Camp Lee, located just outside Gainesville, the companies of former judge James Gettis and educator Robert Blair Smith remained on duty at Tampa. The soldiers in Gainesville had an easier time than did their comrades in the 6th Florida: instead of sleeping in tents, which had not been provided, the soldiers were quartered in houses and thus for a time enjoyed beds and fresh sheets. Captain Samuel D. McConnell, the Ocala lawyer, commanded Company G in the new regiment. At twenty-eight, the Georgia native had previously served as principal of the East Florida Seminary and just before secession had begun practicing law. McConnell had married the previous summer, and his wife was expecting their first child. McConnell spent an uneasy and stressful April waiting for news from his wife and putting his soldiers through the basics of drill.[23]

In Tampa at the encampment of Company K, the scene was livelier. Robert Watson, a twenty-seven-year-old naturalized citizen originally hailing from the Bahamas, had worked as a carpenter in Key West. Because of his known Southern sympathies and because Federal troops held onto the installations on the island, Watson left in late 1861 and the following spring found himself a member of the Coast Guard, and then Company K, whose members called themselves the Key West Avengers.[24]

Though drill remained the order of the day for the new soldiers, the former Key West men found time for hunting, boat races, and harassing their comrades. In one instance, Private John Pratt was found sleeping with a slave woman employed as a cook for the company. Watson and others rode the unfortunate Pratt, straddling a fence post, down to the shore and dumped him into the waters of Tampa Bay. Watson wrote, "We then gave him a lecture, told him what it was done for, and that if he was caught doing the like again that we would give him thirty nine lashes."[25]

Throughout the remainder of April and early May, the 7th Florida's companies remained at Camp Lee near Gainesville and at Tampa Bay. As those soldiers were introduced to the army, their fellow Floridians in the 1st Cavalry and the 3rd and 4th infantry regiments prepared to leave Florida for active service. Though some in the 7th Florida hoped to remain in the state to stay close to loved ones, it was not to be. The 6th and 7th were also, despite their limited training, ordered to Tennessee.

Even before Albert Sidney Johnston's force moved forth from Corinth on the march to Shiloh, Jefferson Davis dispatched a letter to the Confederate Congress implying that "in order to maintain which we are now engaged all persons of intermediate age not legally exempt for good cause, should pay their debt of military service to the ardent and patriotic." Afraid that more regiments would depart for home at the end of their enlistments, leaving a depleted Confederate Army, Davis continued in his letter, "I therefore recommend the passage of a law declaring that all persons residing within the Confederate States, between the ages of eighteen and thirty-five years, and rightfully subject to military duty."[26]

In response, the Confederate Congress passed a law on April 16 that acted on Davis's recommendations and more. Congress not only required the service of all eligible men between the ages of eighteen and thirty-five but extended the enlistment terms of all twelve-month men to three years "from their original date of enlistment." The law provided some incentives, as it allowed soldiers to reorganize for the war, which meant electing new regimental and company officers. Further-more, the law allowed a grace period for those who did not want the label of con-script, permitting them to voluntarily join an existing organization.[27]

The law came at a vital time, for in late April the weight of another disaster was felt by the fledgling nation. In gathering reinforcements for Albert Sidney John-ston's army, Pensacola was not the lone Gulf port to lose its garrison. The much more important city of New Orleans lost many of its defenders to Corinth, as well as its small fleet of gunboats, which were dispatched to defend Memphis. On the night of April 24, Flag Officer David Farragut's West Gulf Blockading squadron steamed past the forts near the mouth of the Mississippi and dropped anchor with the city under their guns.[28]

Like so many other regiments that were ready to go home when their enlist-ments ended, the 3rd and 4th Florida infantries were saved by the Conscript Law. Their men grumbled among themselves and to their relatives at home about their dissatisfaction. Colonel William S. Dilworth feared that his men would not re-enlist out of concern that they would be relegated to duty in Florida. He wrote to Adjutant General Samuel Cooper, "I apply for authority . . . to raise a regiment for the war and have it ready by the time my present term of service expires." At New Smyrna, Benjamin Waring Partridge, a private in the 3rd Florida's Jefferson Rifles, apparently put off by his commanding officer, said that "I don't expect many of the Jefferson Rifles will reenlist under Captain [William O.] Girardeau." At Jackson-ville, where the 4th Florida encamped following the Federal evacuation, Georgian Seaborn Harris avowed in May, "I am afraid the same man will be our Colonel again."[29]

As the 3rd and 4th Florida remained behind to reorganize, the 1st Florida Cavalry finally departed for Tennessee after yet another postponement. Colonel W.G.M. Davis related on April 24 that "I shall leave here as soon as my Regiment is paid off and all the absent men are collected which will be the first of May. I have had a good deal of sickness in my Regt. since I came to East Florida, and but for such causes I would have been in Georgia on my way." Also, during April, the decision was handed down to dismount a portion of the regiment.[30]

Alluding to this occurrence in his reply to Noble Hull, Governor John Milton wrote that the dismounting occurred at the behest of the Confederate authorities, as its military leaders wished "to receive you as an Infantry Regiment at Chatta-nooga. I entertain no doubt that as an Infantry Regiment, you would render more service to the country with less fatigue to yourselves and much less expense to the Government." Ironically, the governor's early prediction of the unsustainability of a cavalry unit came true and was a major factor in the decision. In April, W.G.M. Davis wrote that the mounts, owing to "an entire absence of long forage . . . with few exceptions, are so reduced as to be entirely unfit for any service . . . the regi-ment is entirely unfit to proceed to Tennessee as a cavalry corps." As a result, in the

fashion of the legions raised by Wade Hampton and William Phillips, three of the
1st Florida Cavalry's companies remained mounted, while seven companies converted to infantry. Both battalions moved north on or around May 1 and arrived
in Tennessee on the first of June.[31]

As the troopers of the 1st Florida Cavalry rode and marched from the state, the
3rd Florida Infantry Regiment gathered at Midway, a station on the Florida Atlantic and Gulf Railroad between Tallahassee and Quincy, and prepared to depart
for Corinth. Here, women from Monticello presented the unit with a regimental
flag, which an anonymous soldier declared would "come back victorious, or will
be stained with the rich blood of many a brave Floridian." At Midway the soldiers,
under the provision of the Conscription Act, also elected new officers. William S.
Dilworth remained the regiment's colonel, and after Lieutenant Colonel A.J.T.
Wright resigned, Lucius Church succeeded him as second-in-command. In Church's
place, Edward Mashburn of Madison County became major. Several company officers also quit or failed to gain reelection, including William O. Girardeau of the
Jefferson Rifles. The regiment then marched to Chattahoochee on July 11 and
loaded onto four steamers for the journey to Columbus, Georgia. The soldier who
wrote the anonymous letter to the *Floridian and Journal* declared the 3rd Florida
left "to represent Florida on a new and untried field of action. We go to illustrate
her upon the bloody fields of Tennessee and Kentucky, and when we meet the
enemy face to face, then we will think of our sunny 'Land of Flowers,' think of
loved ones left behind, and it will nerve our arms with strength, inspire our hearts
with courage, and enable us to maintain inviolate the sacred honor of Florida."[32]

Private Edward Clifford Brush, a seventeen-year-old former student in the St.
Augustine Blues, was one of two hundred soldiers crowded on the lower deck of
the *William H. Young.* Angered by the steamer's cramped quarters, the young man
blamed the problem on a policy that "none but Commissioned officers are allowed
on the upper deck." Disembarking at Columbus on May 12, the soldiers marched
through the city and made a favorable impression on the populace. "They are
armed mostly with Enfield rifles and sabre bayonets," wrote the editors of Columbus's *Daily Sun,* "and bear evidence of having been well drilled and disciplined for
service." Boarding cars for the supposed journey to Corinth, one of Company C's
Hernando County Wildcats "had a wild cat skin stuffed and placed at the head of
the engine which bore us to Montgomery." By May 26 the regiment, after traveling
by ship down the Alabama River, reached Mobile, where it remained for nearly
two months.[33]

While the 3rd Florida departed the state, the 4th Florida Infantry Regiment,
encamped near Jacksonville, also prepared to repair to Corinth. Recruits, called
into service by the Conscription Act, filed into its camp to join, one of whom was
eighteen-year-old Washington Ives Jr. A native Floridian, Ives was reared in Lake

City where his father practiced law with M. Whit Smith. In 1861, during the initial rush to join the colors, Ives remained in school in Jacksonville. Although he had the opportunity to join a company that attached itself to the 2nd Florida, he did not: "I do not think I shall join a military company for yet awhile for I have the honor to be the last boy who kept his name to the Lake City Guards which was got up in January." Back in Lake City in April 1862, he received news of the Conscript Act and a week later traveled to Jacksonville to join a company of the 4th Florida. He enlisted in Captain William H. Dial's Madison County company and began his service on April 28.[34]

Before the 4th Florida left the state, the regiment reorganized and experienced several changes in its command structure. In the first and foremost of these electoral decisions, the 4th Florida soldiers replaced Edward Hopkins with James Hunt, a young Bradford County lawyer. Hopkins probably knew his defeat was imminent, for he wrote to the secretary of war: "I am desirous of going into active service if defeated in the election. . . . Full returns have not as yet been received, but judging from the fate of company officers who performed their duty, it is by no means unlikely. And a reelection under the circumstances would not be agreeable." Hopkins lost the election, and his fellow conservative Matthew Whit Smith resigned. Major Wylde L. L. Bowen was elected lieutenant colonel and the regimental adjutant, Edward Badger, won election as major.[35]

Edward Nathaniel Badger would prove himself one of the most reliable and effective officers in the Florida Brigade. Born in South Carolina in January 1841, Badger resided in Ocala with his father, Dr. James Badger, and attended the East Florida Seminary located in that town. He left school in October 1856 during the Third Seminole Indian War and, lying about his age, enlisted in a volunteer cavalry company. In early 1861 Badger earned a degree from the Cumberland University Law School. After spending a year as the 4th Florida's adjutant, Badger, at age twenty-one, became its third-in-command.[36]

With their elections completed, the 4th Florida departed Jacksonville and arrived in Chattahoochee on June 7. Boarding the reliable *William H. Young* and another steamer, the *Munnerlyn,* on June 11, the 4th Florida reached Columbus on June 12. The ever observant editor of the *Daily Sun* recorded: "It is due to the regiment to state that during their stay in this city, the deportment of the men generally, has been characterized by gentility and good breading [*sic*]. . . . A regiment as jealous of its reputation for good behavior, may justly excite expectations of brave deeds upon the fields of battle." Arriving in Mobile on June 21, the 4th Florida pitched their tents near the 3rd Florida.[37]

By 1862, having performed garrison duty on the Atlantic Coast over the previous year, the 1st Florida Cavalry and 3rd and 4th Florida infantry regiments were more than ready for active service. Freed from the relative boredom of coastal duty, the 3rd and 4th infantries had also rid themselves of incompetent officers, replacing them with former lieutenants and non-commissioned officers who had demonstrated the ability to lead well. Yet, rather than engaging in battle immediately, the infantrymen would languish in Mobile throughout June and most of July, performing tiresome sentry duty. Yet whatever their obligation, like the men of the 1st Florida Infantry, the soldiers strove to prove the capability of Florida's troops.

6

Our Cause Is Just and We Need Not Fear Defeat

Floridians' Rationales for Fighting the Civil War

By late spring 1862, more than 10,000 Floridians had enlisted in the Confederate Army. Each newly minted soldier had his own reasons for participating in a rebellion against the federal government. The historian Chandra Manning has asserted that the war's combatants were willing to fight because they "recognized slavery as the main reason for the war." Emboldened by their interpretations of the most crucial issue of their day, Northern and Southern boys surged forth to battle. Though less than 2 percent of 78,699 white Floridians owned slaves, these citizens and their non-slaveholding neighbors maintained a "conviction that survival—of themselves, their families, and the social order—depended on slavery's continued existence."[1]

Southern society was based on the bedrock of human bondage; simply stated, these Americans' ultimate goal was to achieve and maintain slave-owner status. As a young lawyer in Mississippi, Jesse J. Finley embodied these ambitions when he spoke of removing to Texas. "West of the Sabine," the Tennessee native wrote, "they can make four thousand pounds of cotton to the acre." The whole country, he believed, promised "individual prosperity." Because of the black race's degradation, even poor whites in the South were assured that they "could never fall into the lowest social stratum no matter how frequently they move, geographically or economically." In the same vein, slavery ensured segregation, thus ensuring that blacks could never interact with the white race on the basis of equality. St. Augustine citizens railed against even this possibility in a manifesto published in December 1860. In part, East Floridians argued that "the Northern people under the influence of the evil spirit of Abolitionism, have resolved to emancipate our slaves, placing them upon equality with ourselves, our wives and our daughters."[2]

The Florida press had, particularly since John Brown's failed raid in October 1859, stressed the evils of the Republican Party and their supposed designs to end slavery. With a Republican triumph almost certain in the 1860 election, editors worked at a feverish pace to make Floridians aware of the danger the new party represented. Holmes Steele, the editor of the *Jacksonville Standard,* asserted that "a large majority of the people of the North are hostile to the institutions of the South, . . . in other words the South shall not expand in the territories, that [slavery] shall ultimately be destroyed in the States, that it is in their power to do it, that it must be done." The week before the November election, the *St. Augustine Examiner* warned its readers of the forthcoming watershed vote: "The danger is imminent to our Southern institution. It is not to be disguised that the election of a Black Republican Abolitionist President is a foregone conclusion."[3]

Samuel Pasco, the Massachusetts-raised schoolteacher, was obviously influenced by the periodicals and consequent debates. He held contempt for these "Yankee hirelings who put themselves side by side with the African negro to put down free men." Samuel Darwin McConnell, who in 1860 gained acceptance to the Florida bar, wrote to his fiancée of the crisis: "I think the South has submitted to the North long enough, and if there is ever to be disunion, the time has come. I know it is a serious matter, but I am of the opinion that we of the South will be better off by it."[4]

During November and December 1860, voters in communities across the peninsula convened meetings to endorse secession. The men, many of whom would soon shoulder arms against their former countrymen, placed their convictions in elaborately worded yet often fallacy-filled documents. These proclamations, which listed grievances against the Republican Party and the North, essentially conveyed the ideals for which the Confederate soldiers fought. In Wakulla County, the citizen committee claimed they were "willing to remain in the Union so long as we can have our constitutional rights and our interests are protected, and the fugitive slave law strictly enforced in all the free States and agitation of the slavery question in Congress to cease." The Southerners warned, "without this we are for immediate secession." Voters in Cedar Keys came to the consensus that Florida's departure from the Union was necessary because that course of action exhibited "the only feasible method of resisting successfully the aggression of the North, upon our domestic institutions and sacred Constitutional Rights."[5]

The majority of the Floridians who met to discuss the ills of the country—like those who gathered in St. Augustine—believed the wags who claimed Abraham Lincoln's "whole political life, has been devoted to this crusade against Slavery." Hamilton County's committee, like the Ancient City's residents, thought that the "election of Abraham Lincoln and Hannibal Hamlin to the Presidency and Vice Presidency of the United States ought not to be submitted to." The Florida Baptist Convention provided religious conviction to the state's citizens, denoting "the Christian as well as the political welfare of our whole population, and more especially of our slaves, deem it proper . . . to express a cordial sympathy with, and hearty approbation of those who are determined to maintain the integrity of the Southern states."[6]

Both slave owners and non-slaveholders joined the Confederate military during the course of the war. In examining the rosters of regiments that eventually became a part of the Florida Brigade in conjunction with corresponding census records, one finds that most of the enlistees did not own slaves. These men went to war to preserve the social order that assured poor whites they would never, as long as slavery remained in place, occupy the lowest caste in Southern culture. The slaves "performed essential, basic tasks so that others—in the South, all white people—did not have to tackle demeaning duties." These volunteers also joined the army to protect their families against the supposed attempt by the Republican government to let "loose four millions of slaves upon us unrestrained, who will at once, embark in the work of murder and rapine."[7]

The historian James McPherson has estimated that one-third of all Confederate soldiers hailed from slave-owning households, and Joseph Glaathar points out that this connection to slavery went deeper, for Southerners also "rented land from, sold crops to, or worked for slaveholders." In the ranks of the Florida Brigade, however, the number of men who actually owned human chattel was considerably lower, and those Florida Brigade soldiers who owned slaves usually held title to "nine slaves or less." Samuel Darwin McConnell, whom the 1860 Census (Slave Schedule) listed as the owner of two servants, was typical of the slaveholders who enlisted in the Florida regiments. Very few gentlemen who owned large numbers of slaves went to war. Instead, these plantation sires dispatched their heirs—teenagers and young men in their twenties—to fight the Yankees. It was unusual to find planters like Daniel Bird, who owned forty-four slaves, serving in the Florida Brigade.[8]

Besides the few who called themselves planters, the Florida Brigade's citizen-soldiers represented numerous peacetime occupations. Most had followed agricultural pursuits before the conflict, working subsistence farms in West Florida, growing cash crops in the countryside north of Monticello or along the Peace River, or raising citrus trees near the Atlantic. Landless individuals also participated in farming before the war by hiring their labor out to local landowners or renting land. Some soldiers had toiled for long hours before hot forges, and others turned scraps of wood into furniture and assisted in constructing houses. Also included in the Florida Brigade's ranks were masons, painters, printers, mechanics, and tailors. They were community leaders who served their counties as elected officials; they were ministers who navigated their flocks through the world's trials and tribulations. Attorneys, physicians, merchants, and schoolteachers represented the professional classes in the regiments. Academy students, as well as medical apprentices and legal scholars, also comprised a sizable minority of Florida's soldiers.[9]

Bell Wiley estimates in his *Life of Johnny Reb* that Rebels "within the 18–29 range [were] approximately four-fifths of the total" number of soldiers in his sample, and James McPherson has written that the average age of the Rebels at the time of enlistment was 26.5. Yet in some Florida companies, men between the ages of 18 and 29 represented less than 60 percent of the total number of soldiers. Though some had been born in the 1820s, many of the soldiers had just entered their formative years as their state seceded, giving the companies a youthful character.[10]

When Gadsden County soldiers marched toward Chattahoochee in April 1861 to become the 1st Florida Infantry's Company G, the soldiers' average age was but twenty-three. The average age of soldiers in Hillsborough County's own 4th Florida, Company K, raised in June 1861, was twenty-two. The 3rd Florida's Company B, comprised of the Ancient City's elite, was young as well, with "16 of the men . . . under the age of 17." The Blues' ages averaged to twenty-four.[11]

Florida's citizens who enlisted in 1862 following the passage of the Confederate Conscript Act were closer to McPherson's average than were their neighbors and kin who joined the service during the war's first days. The 6th Florida's companies surveyed maintained an average age of twenty-five, as did the 7th Florida's Company E. The average age of soldiers serving in Robert Bullock's and Samuel Darwin McConnell's 7th Florida Company G was twenty-seven.[12]

Though the regiments belonged to Florida in name, the troops were a motley assortment. Most had been born in the Deep South—namely South Carolina, Georgia, and Alabama—and had migrated to Florida in the 1830s and 1840s in search of cheap land and fortune. Joseph Glatthaar, in his study on the Army of Northern Virginia, estimated that "eighty percent of the men who would ultimately serve in the army in Virginia and who entered the service in 1861 were born and lived in the same state." The Florida Brigade certainly did not mirror Lee's vaunted force in this statistic. Instead, the Florida regiments' makeup was very similar to that of Texas's Confederate outfits, for like Florida, the Lone Star State was relatively young and had served as a haven for immigrants since the 1820s. The historian Richard Lowe, writing about Walker's Texas division that served in the Trans-Mississippi, discovered that "almost half of the men in the division (47.2 percent) had been born in Alabama, Georgia, Mississippi, or South Carolina."[13]

The 1850 census showed that 86 percent of Alachua County's residents had been born outside the state. These numbers correlated with the statistics for Alachua County's Company H, 1st Florida Infantry, in which 82 percent of the soldiers claimed locations outside Florida as their birthplaces, with Alabama, Georgia, and South Carolina natives alone accounting for 71 percent. In the 6th Florida's Union Rebels, raised in Walton and Santa Rosa counties, of the soldiers whose birthplaces are known, less than half claimed Florida. Alabamians composed 37 percent of the company, and North Carolina, South Carolina, Georgia, and Mississippi all had representatives.[14]

The Jefferson Rifles boasted one of the highest numbers of Florida natives, and yet locally born soldiers still numbered less than half of the company's men. The St. Augustine company, with its soldiery descended from Minorcan and English colonists, also contained a high percentage of Florida natives in its ranks. At least sixty-seven of eighty-five men who listed their birthplaces were born within the state. On the opposite end of the spectrum, of the sixty-nine men in the 7th Florida's Company G also found in the 1860 census, only ten were native Floridians.[15]

With Florida's secession on January 10, 1861, the state's men joined preexisting militia companies or formed new units. With the Confederate call for troops later that year and into the next, recently raised Florida regiments absorbed the militia companies. Samuel Darwin McConnell, who joined a local cavalry company in early 1861, informed his fiancée: "our State is but thinly settled, and would need the services of every man who is able to do military duty, so that I would expect to do service if there is any necessity for it." He added jubilantly: "We of the South have not sought it, and blame can not rest upon us. Our cause is just and we need not fear defeat." Michael Raysor, a Jefferson County Rifle, wrote to his wife, "you know the situation of our country and somebody will have to do the fighting and it is as much my duty to defend our state as any body else."[16]

One historian has written that as the Confederates came together for various reasons, "they started to see themselves not just as citizens of their own states, but also as residents of the Confederate States of America." Defending this Confederate nation that was constructed on a foundation of accusations and grumbles directed toward the old United States was on the minds of many Floridians. In 1864 Sergeant Archie Livingston expressed his reasons for fighting in a letter to his father: "My duty at present is in the field of practical service. . . . Our country is in imminent danger, requiring a faithful discharge of service from every young man." Roddie Shaw declared in 1862, "My country needs my services and till peace is declared I expect to remain with the Army." Archie Livingston's cousin John L. Inglis wrote to his extended family in Madison County, "the many kindnesses that I have received at your hands . . . constantly reminded me that in Madison I have something in reality to Battle for, besides Principle, Justice, and Self Government."[17]

Theodore Livingston, yet another member of the large Livingston clan, wrote with a touch of melancholy in 1864 that he thought the war was being waged to remove the Republican government from power: "Every one thinks we will be successful in the end, but a dear bought victory. . . . We that are left will have life to begin anew & God grant that we may select leaders, whose judgement will change this Republican Government & . . . political tricksters will not be allowed." Francis Nicks, a 3rd Florida private, also saw the Lincoln administration as the stumbling block to Southern security and penned, "every Person I hear Speake of it [the war] sais it will last as long as Lincoln's administration last I hope the old rascal will die." A 6th Florida soldier, Charles Herring, simply wrote that he would gladly die, ironically, "in the discharge of my deauty as a lover of freedom."[18]

Young and old, rich and poor, and having turned their backs on a variety of occupations, Florida's citizens joined the Confederate Army to maintain slavery's position within Southern society. Though these soldiers hailed from different backgrounds, in slavery all found a common ground for fighting: they enlisted to protect their property, to keep slaves from obtaining equality with whites, and to prevent poor whites from falling to the lowest rung of the social ladder. However, they could not have imagined how hard the fight would be or the ultimate toll it would take on their lives.

7

I Am Now As You Know in the Enemys Country
June–August 1862

Major General Henry Halleck's arrival at Pittsburg Landing signaled the completion of the Federal concentration there. On April 29 more than ninety thousand Union soldiers began the twenty-mile march toward the important rail junction of Corinth. Halleck, unwilling to suffer a surprise Confederate attack like Grant had experienced at Shiloh, entrenched his army each night, and as a result, the large force spent the first three weeks of May covering the ground between Pittsburg Landing and their destination. When the Federals finally reached Corinth and began settling in for a siege, General P.G.T. Beauregard decided to sacrifice the town in order to save his army. During the night of May 29, the Confederate force slipped away under the cover of darkness, marching fifty miles southward to the town of Tupelo.[1]

Though the retreat cost Beauregard his command, for the soldiers in the ranks the withdrawal was a blessing. During the month following Shiloh, Corinth had turned into a sanitation nightmare and sickness abounded. Private William D. Rogers, an Alabama-born, Milton resident serving in the Florida and Confederate Guards Response Battalion, described the new encampment at Tupelo as "a beautiful place and I think it is very healthy, also splendid water two things that we were sadly in want of at Corinth." However, the army's bout with sickness continued at Tupelo, where the consolidated battalion suffered seven deaths and listed no fewer than 164 as ill throughout June.[2]

Despite the sickness raging through the camps at both Corinth and Tupelo, James Patton Anderson and other brigade commanders continued to transform their veterans into even better soldiers. After the disorganized fighting at Shiloh, more drill was necessary, and Anderson at least gave his soldiers all they could stand. Beginning at 5:00 A.M. on weekdays the soldiers drilled for two hours then came back after breakfast for another hour and a half of company-level instruction. In the heat of the afternoon, the men drilled in regimental and brigade formations for two hours before concluding with a dress parade. Anderson ordered that "regimental commanders . . . establish schools for instruction for officers and non-commissioned officers." Any sergeants or corporals "found to be incapable of drilling squads [would] be reported to" their superiors and if necessary would "be reduced to the ranks, and their places filled with more efficient men."[3]

For the 3rd and 4th Florida at Mobile, the duty was no less strenuous. The 3rd

Florida arrived at the Mobile docks in a heavy downpour; Colonel Dilworth, despite his exceptional performance in Florida, failed to impress his soldiers once in Mobile. In the words of First Lieutenant Jacob E. Mickler of Company F, "he went to the hotel and left us all night and a day in the rain on [the] Mobile Wharfs." For reasons that remain unknown, Mickler penned of the colonel, "the Officers from the east look upon him with disgust and also some from the west."[4]

Despite its original orders to reinforce the Army of the Mississippi at Corinth, with the army's retreat the regiment was detained at Mobile and encamped on the west side of the city. Twenty-two-year-old private William C. Middleton of the Blues had injured his leg while in Montgomery and this ailment caused him to miss drill and guard duty. He jotted in his diary: "We sick are having a fine time, though some are too sick for any enjoyment." While waiting for his leg to heal, Middleton took in the city, where he dined on oysters and enjoyed a show at a theater.[5]

On June 8 orders arrived for the 3rd Florida to dispatch a guard detail to the city every night to serve as military police. Thereafter, each afternoon, a sergeant's guard consisting of three corporals and twenty-one men marched into Mobile for service that began each evening at 5:00 P.M. and lasted twenty-four hours. A few weeks later, the 3rd Florida had one hundred of its number acting as police in the city. This duty did not suit the Floridians at all, particularly the long hours without sleep.[6]

Lieutenant Jacob Mickler complained, "I do not like the duty Darling [of] guarding the City of Mobile and Yankee prisoners. It is very unpleasant unless you capture them yourself." Michael O. Raysor, a twenty-six-year-old farmer serving in the Jefferson County Rifles, noted of the time spent in Mobile, "we had to stand guard and do police duty in the city of Mobile and guard Yankee prisoners that we come on guard duty and could not stand up at all." Willie Bryant of the Jacksonville Light Infantry concurred, adding that "the duties are pretty tough, for this warm weather."[7]

The 4th Florida, arriving in Mobile after an uneventful journey, pitched their tents within a few miles of their neighbors and kin. Soon Colonel James Hunt's regiment was assisting the 3rd Florida in policing the city. New soldier Washington Ives vented to his sisters, "I am under such discipline that I can't leave the lines 2 hours in a day and am kept drilling or standing guard that I just can get along, and manage to sleep enough."[8]

Although the soldiers were exhausted from carrying out their new responsibilities, pride prevailed on the days before July 4, which the men spent brushing their uniforms, polishing their brass buttons, and cleaning their weapons. On Independence Day, the 3rd and 4th Florida along with the remainder of the renamed Army of Mobile paraded down the streets of the city to celebrate their former country's separation from England. Michael O. Raysor recalled, "[I]t was a grand sight thousands of spectators but just as we got in the town good they came up a heavy rain and give us a good ducking the streets was awful mud, they was one continual slough slough in mud and water all the time but we were every day soldiers and therefore we did not mind it."[9]

The soldiers' spirits were dampened, however, by the sickness that prevailed in Mobile. Some illnesses might have resulted from the 3rd Florida's remaining in the rain during the night they arrived; Michael O. Raysor believed that "the cause I think of my getting sick was that our Regt had to perform so much duty." Lemuel Moody lamented that "I have had the diarrhea nairly every since we have bin in Mobile it has all most beome cronik." Washington Ives informed his family that "at one time in Mobile as many as thirty of our company were on the sick list in a day and 7 men died in the reg't during its stay." During July's third week it appeared the regiment's health had improved, for a visitor to the 3rd Florida's camp wrote that only thirty of the regiment's members were on the sick list.[10]

Not a week had passed following the successful completion of the campaign to take Corinth when President Lincoln used telegraph wires to press his western generals for a drive on Chattanooga. Lincoln had long advocated an advance into Tennessee's mountainous region because he thought its people had little in common with the remainder of the Confederacy and that their allegiance remained with the Union. In fact, the majority of its citizens worked small farms and felt snubbed by the slave-owning aristocracy in Middle and West Tennessee. The East Tennesseans' indignation increased in May 1861 when Tennessee governor Isham Harris "had attempted to undermine the results of the February vote against separation, and they characterized his use of the legislature to pass the ordinance of secession rather than calling a state convention to decide the issue, as unconstitutional."[11]

In an even stronger statement of where the region's sympathies lay, when Tennesseans voted in favor of the legislature's ordinance of secession in June 1861, 70 percent of East Tennesseans opposed the measure. Lincoln wished to occupy the area as soon as possible "because he was eager to show all potentially loyal Southerners that they would have the effective support of the national government in opposing the 'slave-ocracy' that had stampeded their states into rebellion." Federal military planners considered the area important because of the Tennessee and Virginia Railroad. The seizure of these rails, which, after the fall of Corinth, represented the only continuous east-west rail line of the Confederacy, would severely injure the South's already deficient transportation capabilities. On June 18, as the Florida regiments made their way to the front, a Union division occupied Cumberland Gap and threatened to push into the East Tennessee Valley.[12]

In Middle Tennessee, following the fall of Nashville, one of Don Carlos Buell's divisions under Ormsby Mitchel advanced to the Tennessee River at Bridgeport and halted there to wait for the remainder of the army. In June, Halleck informed

Buell of the opportunity to not only satisfy Lincoln's wish to occupy Tennessee but also launch a fatal strike at the heart of the Confederacy. "Old Brains" Halleck lectured his subordinate: "After considering the whole matter I am satisfied that your line of operations should be on Chattanooga and Cleveland or Dalton. . . . By moving on Chattanooga you . . . are on the direct line to Atlanta." Halleck thus ordered Buell to march overland, rejoin his advanced division, and then occupy Chattanooga. In mid-June, Buell's Army of the Ohio began a ponderous advance into the hills of northern Alabama. The Federals faced only a few thousand Rebel soldiers, and they were stretched thin to watch both Cumberland Gap and Chattanooga. These soldiers were commanded by a soldier whom the Floridians called one of their own: Edmund Kirby Smith.[13]

During June, however, as the situation in East Tennessee became critical and the front at Tupelo quieted, Bragg dispatched reinforcements to the mountains to help fend off Buell's advance. The 1st Florida Cavalry, Dismounted, having arrived at Chattanooga in early June, also moved ten miles west of Chattanooga to the Narrows. Dubbed the "Canyon of the Tennessee," here the river tightened between Walden Ridge and Lookout Mountain, creating a hazard for boatmen and a scene of natural beauty for spectators. Stationed atop of the southern wall of the canyon at Raccoon Mountain, the regiment was charged, according to Major William Stockton, with "holding the mountain passes to prevent the enemy from crossing the Tennessee between Chattanooga and Bridgeport, i.e., to the same side on which Chat. is."[14]

The 1st Florida Cavalry's dismounted troopers gained national recognition for its service on the river, as it fought several small but violent actions with Federal soldiers. Richmond's *Daily Dispatch* noted two occasions where W.G.M. Davis's men both beat back Federal probes and conducted their own patrols across the river. Major Stockton wrote that the soldiers were "shooting at each other . . . every day." The old soldier pondered "this deliberate shooting at human beings, as coolly as [if] they were only a large species of game and quietly taking arms & equipment, as one would the hide and venison."[15]

To reinforce the 1st Florida Cavalry, Dismounted, the 6th and 7th Florida infantry regiments were ordered to report to the threatened front. "We leave for Tennessee today," wrote Charles Herring of the 6th Florida's Company G, "[a]ll in good of life and high spirits talking to th[eir] sweet[hearts] as like they would be back in two weeks. . . . Oh I hear the boat coming. I must close." Lieutenant Hugh Black, a Liberty County politician serving in Company A, penned a quick note to his wife: "We are now loading the boat to leave for Tennessee. . . . I cannot leave without causing a difficulty and therefore I will go but will not be gone very long before I return perhaps to remain . . . I hope that you will reconcile yourself to your fate."[16]

The 6th Florida arrived in Columbus on June 16, just days after the 4th Florida, and by June 18 was in Chattanooga. Lieutenant James Hays in Company D recalled with pleasure the rail journey: "After we left Columbus, nearly every house we passed they were out with their handkerchiefs waving and hollering, throwing bocaies [sic] and apples into the cars as we would pass by. From Atlanta to this place beat all. . . . They were perfect swarms of young ladies standing on the road with their flags flying." For Hugh Black the rail ride was more tedious, for northwest of Chattanooga "the car that myself and the remainder of our company was in ran off the track and very near crushing the whole concern to attoms."[17]

A letter to Columbus's *Daily Sun,* which maintained a circulation in West Florida, noted that during its journey north the 6th Florida had "been complimented for the quiet and gentlemanly deportment of both officers and men." At first dispatched to the Narrows, Edmund Kirby Smith quickly ordered the regiment to Knoxville, intending it to help defend that point against a Federal advance from the mountains. Arriving in the East Tennessee town, the Floridians found the greeting very cold, a stark contrast to the cheers they had received during their rail journey through Georgia. A. G. Morrison informed a friend, "The yankees are all over this portion of the country, and there are many citizens here who are no better than them. The ladies in town are howllowing out Confusion to Jeff Davis, history to Abe Lincoln."[18]

The 7th Florida came on quickly, departing from camps near Jacksonville, where the majority had spent the early days of June, and from Tampa. Captain Samuel McConnell told his wife: "My regiment is ordered to Tennessee, and will start tomorrow for Tallahassee, and remain near there until fully equipped." The 7th soon embarked on the overworked Chattahoochee River steamers and reached Columbus on June 14–15, where they waited several days while the men were uniformed. A wag in Company H, which was nicknamed the Marion Hornets, wrote lightly of his regiment's marches in verse, noting of the stop in the River City, "Here it were well I should not tell/ All the things in this place done./ How the soldiers act is a fixed fact—/ All should their actions shun. Some drinking hard, some standing guard/ Much money spent for naught/ With frolic, fun, the day begun/ With it the time was fraught." From Columbus, the majority of the regiment's companies were dispatched to reinforce the 1st Florida Cavalry, Dismounted. However, Company K, after having to move from Tampa to Chattahoochee, did not reach Columbus until July 11; the Key West Avengers took advantage of the town's pleasures. Robert Watson wrote that while in the city he "took several drinks, ate supper, and passed the evening among the 'Ladies.'"[19]

With six Florida regiments now stationed throughout the Western Theater, from Tupelo to Mobile and in Tennessee, the editor of Columbus's *Daily Sun* who witnessed the majority of these soldiers pass through his city paid tribute to the Land of Flowers. "The patriotic little State," he proclaimed, "with a voting population not exceeding 12,500 now has in the field over 10,000 men. . . . Not only has she furnished these troops, but she has given the hated Yankees evidence of [the] prowess and gallantry of our sons."[20]

On the banks of the Tennessee, the soldiers of the 7th Florida pitched their tents near those of the 1st Florida Cavalry, Dismounted, at a point appropriately named Camp Kirby. The trip north from Florida, much of it spent in open cars, caused a bout of noticeable sickness in the regiment. Captain McConnell wrote from the Tennessee River, "Mr. Watkins, the Orderly Sergeant of my company died at Columbus last week. He was left there sick as the Regt. passed through. Some of my men are still behind as also members of all the companies." Lieutenant Colonel Bullock ruefully informed his wife that "the health of the Regt is very bad—now about two hundred of six hundred on sick report." Colonel Madison Starke Perry, who did not join the regiment until it readied for departure at Chattahoochee, was appalled by the number of men who were sick: "I have witnessed more suffering since I took charge of the Regt. than in my . . . previous life. My feelings are hourly harrowed up by the suffering which in many instances I am unable to alleviate."[21]

While sickness raged through the regiment, there also remained the business of war. "We are on the banks of the Tenn River & the enemy on the opposite side," Lieutenant Colonel Bullock informed his wife. His friend from Ocala, Samuel D. McConnell, remarked of the new camp, "The enemy's forces are encamped on the opposite side of the river several miles off but near enough for their drums to be distinctly heard. Their camps can be seen from the top of a high hill near this place." Yet Knoxville seemed to be the more threatened area, and on July 4, as the 3rd and 4th regiments tramped through the muddy streets of Mobile, the 7th Regiment departed from the Narrows and also moved to Knoxville. The regiment's poet composed: "Oh, Muses, give me your aid;/ Again we'll travel on;/ We left Camp Kirby, where we stay'd/ One Fourth of July morn,/ And the 'Hornets' took the cars,/ Hunting, still hunting, for the wars." Nearly a month behind their comrades, Company K finally detrained at Knoxville on August 2.[22]

With the arrival at Chattanooga of John McCown's Division from Tupelo, the 1st Florida Cavalry, Dismounted, was withdrawn from its exposed position in the van of Smith's force and ordered to Knoxville as well. Once there, Colonel W.G.M. Davis took command of a newly organized brigade consisting of the three Florida regiments and the Marion Artillery, a Florida battery. The troopers could be proud of their work, as they had gained both a reputation and experience on the banks of the Tennessee. However, it had taken more than just the 1st Florida Cavalry, Dismounted, to scare Don Carlos Buell into halting his forces before reaching Chattanooga.[23]

The route of advance assigned to Buell ran parallel to the Memphis and Charleston Railroad, which navigated the hilly region of northern Alabama. This rail line was, for two major reasons, entirely inadequate and could in no way support the operations of a major offensive. First, when Buell prepared to move his force east in early June, "Only two locomotives and a dozen box cars operated between Corinth and Tuscumbia." Second, because the Memphis and Charleston was in such poor condition beyond Tuscumbia, Buell's "army would be forced to repair the railroad until it reached Mitchel in northern Alabama." On June 12, Buell communicated to Ormsby Mitchel that for the advance to continue, rail links to several depots, including Nashville, were needed. Work parties began repairing the Nashville and Chattanooga and Nashville and Decatur railroads.[24]

Besides spending invaluable time making the railroads suitable for carrying munitions and rations, General Buell also had to construct defenses to cope with roving Confederate cavalry who constantly threatened the newly operational rail lines. To contend with the menace, "[b]lockhouses were built along the Nashville and Chattanooga route while stockades were constructed on the Memphis and Charleston line. . . . All of this took time, energy, and manpower."[25]

Until the rail lines were completed, Buell refused to conduct an active offensive toward Chattanooga and instead inched his army along the repaired line. On July 12 Federal work gangs put the last touches on the Nashville and Chattanooga line, which joined the Memphis and Charleston at Stevenson, Alabama. The next day Confederate horseman Nathan Bedford Forrest wrecked this line near Murfreesboro, causing a week of delays. By the time Buell moved forward again, the van of the Army of the Mississippi detrained in Chattanooga, its soldiers eager to change the fortunes of war in the west.[26]

Because the relationship between Jefferson Davis and Beauregard had been strained since an exchange of words in the aftermath of First Manassas, Davis used Beauregard's abandonment of Corinth as an excuse to sack the Louisiana-born general. When Beauregard departed Tupelo for an Alabama spa, the Confederate president used the opportunity to promote Braxton Bragg to command the Army of the Mississippi. William D. Rogers, serving with the Florida and Confederate Guards Response Battalion, noted of the change, "I think Old Bragg will take us where the Yanks are at least he says so, he says he intends to take Cincinatti [sic] to pay for New Orleans."[27]

Bragg assumed command of the Army of the Mississippi on June 20 and began contemplating his options. A march to retake Corinth was immediately discounted because good water between the two towns was scarce and the Rebels lacked the number of wagons needed to move supplies. Furthermore, Grant's Army of the Tennessee still occupied northern Mississippi. During July, as Kirby Smith pleaded with Bragg for more reinforcements and as the idea of a Middle Tennessee offensive formed, Bragg considered relocating his base of operations to Chattanooga. With McCown's men now in Chattanooga, Bragg's plan was feasible. Orders to move were passed to nearly thirty thousand soldiers stationed at both Tupelo and Mobile.[28]

On July 22 the 1st Florida Battalion, separated five days earlier from their New

Orleans comrades, boarded a southbound train in Tupelo. The journey, which newly promoted lieutenant Augustus McDonell called "anything but a pleasant one," took the four small companies to Mobile and then north to Montgomery via Alabama River steamers. The Gainesville merchant remarked that when the veterans reached Montgomery and were back in civilization, they could not withstand the temptation of the city. "Notwithstanding the General order forbidding the officers and men from leaving their Commands," McDonell wrote, "mostly ⅔s of them . . . ran the Blockade and went up to the city and had a gay time generally. Some of them got Slighty [sic] inebriated and talked too much thereby letting the cat out of the bag."[29]

While the 1st Florida Battalion's deployment to Chattanooga was accomplished with relatively few hindrances, the 3rd and 4th Florida's soldiers were less fortunate. The 3rd Florida departed from Mobile on July 20, embarking on the steamer *R. B. Taney.* Throughout July 21, the vessel steamed against the current, slowly making headway toward Montgomery. For the majority of the 3rd Florida's soldiers, crowded onto the *Taney's* deck, the voyage was uncomfortable. William Middleton recalled that at one point during the first night all were awakened to "shrieks . . . and the cry of a man overboard, the boat stopped but the man was not found." While this event unnerved the soldiers, the next morning they stirred to find the ship hard aground on a mud flat. To lighten the *Taney* so that it might float free, the men "had to go ashore and walk through the swamp a mile." Rejoining the ship, the men finally reached Montgomery seventy-eight hours after leaving Mobile. Once the regiment boarded the cars at Montgomery, only two days were needed to travel from the former Confederate capital to Chattanooga.[30]

The 4th Florida fared even worse after it entrained on July 22. Seventy-five miles south of Montgomery, Washington Ives remembered, disaster struck as "the car on which Capt. Miot's co. was, broke down and if it had held on to the engine would have killed us all, but thanks to Providence I escaped unhurt, and the Engine tore loose and ran down the road leaving ½ the regt. in a deep Clay Cut at 2 A.M." He continued, "I tell you it was quite a scene . . . lights dancing here and there men calling others to find out who had been killed etc." Two of Ives's comrades died in the wreck and a number were wounded. Once the regiment's injured were tended to, the soldiers continued to Montgomery, where Colonel James Hunt allowed the regiment time to prepare rations since they had not eaten for more than a day. For this act of compassion, and for delaying their movement to Chattanooga, Hunt found himself under arrest once the regiment reached its destination.[31]

Departing Montgomery, the journey became more bearable for the Floridians. Ives remembered that while their train halted in Marietta, Georgia, "some young Ladies in a piazza fronting . . . the Depot sang several war songs such as Maryland, Bonnie Blue Flag, and Cheer Boys Cheer. The Singing was excellent. As we came along some apples and peaches also min[i]ature Con. flags were thrown to us, and at every sight of a female Cheer after Cheer echoed from the cars." The 4th reached Chattanooga on July 25 and camped near the 3rd Florida. Washington Ives announced his arrival in Chattanooga to the family by writing, "I am now as you know in the enemys country."[32]

Once bivouacked at Chattanooga, the Floridians found time to enjoy themselves by exploring Lookout Mountain and the surrounding countryside. Lieutenant Jacob Mickler, who would soon obtain his discharge from the 3rd Florida's Jacksonville Light Infantry, described the region to his wife: "You can Darling from Mount Lookout see 4 different states—namely North Carolina—Georgia—Alabama and Tennessee. It is Darling the highest mountain in the South." Washington Ives spent the better part of one day visiting "the Saltpetre Cave in Lookout Mountain . . . the Cave is miles deep (on a level) and the entrance is just on the R. R. which runs on the foot of the Mount . . . I would not go far into the Cave because some of the avenues are not yet explored." Willie Bryant of Company A hiked "Look Out Mountain . . . and tho a very fatiguing trip on foot, enjoyed it, and got a good dinner too." Lieutenant McDonell also made the trip up the mountain, noting as he sat on a ledge, "beneath are little farms and beautiful plots . . . with little farm houses which gives the whole a picturesk view."[33]

While the Army of the Mississippi assembled at Chattanooga, the 1st Florida Battalion gained reinforcements. During the summer months, Shiloh casualties, including Major Thaddeus McDonell and Captain Capers Bird, returned to the ranks. McDonell and Bird both had endured a rather harrowing convalescence. The two men had begun their recovery in a makeshift hospital in Huntsville but were made prisoners of war by Ormsby Mitchel's Division. Exchanged in May, they rejoined their old command in time for the movement to Chattanooga.[34]

Joining the battalion in Chattanooga as well were six West Florida and Alabama companies commanded by Lieutenant Colonel William Miller and known collectively as the 3rd Florida Battalion. Formed in 1861 and early 1862, the companies were in the state's service for a year, during which they garrisoned different points in West Florida. In February 1862 Colonel Miller petitioned and received permission from the Confederate War Department to raise a regiment. By June the enterprising Miller had gathered together the six state companies and formed a battalion.

The 3rd Florida Battalion was, for a time, stationed just north of Pensacola, which the Yankees had occupied following the Confederate evacuation of the city. That same month, Governor John Milton applied to the newly appointed secretary of war, George Randolph, to consolidate Miller's troops with the 1st Florida Battalion. Randolph granted Milton's request on July 5, and soon the battalion began its own trip to Chattanooga.[35]

A New Yorker by birth, William Miller was reared in Louisiana and attended Louisiana College. The colonel was regarded by many as a man of "fine education" and gained praise for his high "attainment in Mathematics." A Mexican-American War volunteer, he soldiered under Zachary Taylor, during which time he "had acquired some knowledge of Military Service." Migrating to Florida in 1850, he settled in Milton, where he read law and managed a saw mill. In politics, Miller was a staunch Democrat and had represented Santa Rosa and Escambia counties at the 1860 Florida Democratic Convention.[36]

Miller's companies were comprised of West Floridians and Alabamians, with companies hailing from Santa Rosa and Walton counties and from Alabama's Conecuh and Escambia counties. This was the second year of soldiering for the men from Walton County, though the first had been spent within fifty miles of their homes. The soldiers, some of whom were Scots-Irish Presbyterian kinfolk and Knox Hill Academy classmates, were stationed at Camp Walton near East Pass on the Gulf. There, they protected Choctawhatchee Sound against Yankee incursions. Daniel G. McLean wrote regularly from Camp Walton, noting in August 1861, "We are all well & well satisfied; with the exception of 3 or 4 back woods fellows." Later, he sadly informed friends at home: "When we first came down here we were mighty good. . . . We would read our Bibles twice a day & would not play cards or do anything of the sort. After a while we got to reading only once a day & then we got so we only read at Sundays . . . I have positively not played cards but four times since I came & that was when I just came but some of the rest are playing all the time."[37]

Assigned to the 3rd Florida Battalion under William Miller in April 1862, the soldiers saw little action other than obstructing the Escambia River and destroying the recently completed Florida and Alabama Railroad from Pensacola to the Florida-Alabama line. If the soldiers had not suffered previously from disease, they certainly did at Camp Pringle near Bluff Springs, Alabama. Daniel McLean, appointed as a hospital steward, bemoaned, "Everyone here is sick nearly & dying. No pleasure only when we are sleep. . . . Hardly notices a man dying, at all; never think about going to see him buried & it is only about 150 yds to the grave yard." They escaped the unhealthiness of Camp Pringle in early July and made their way to Chattanooga.[38]

There, on August 15, 1862, the 1st Florida Battalion's four companies and the 3rd Florida Battalion's six consolidated. In an instant, the grizzled veterans of Shiloh, whom Washington Ives described as looking "completely wild," and the raw West Floridians became comrades. The fused command was renamed the 1st Florida Infantry Regiment, and like its predecessor, it contained reduced numbers. Lieutenant Colonel Miller became colonel in the new organization, and Major Thaddeus McDonell gained promotion to the lieutenant colonelcy of the regiment. Glover Ailing Ball, who possibly served as the 3rd Florida Battalion's executive officer, was appointed major. Ball, a twenty-eight-year-old Connecticut Yankee, made a striking appearance in his uniform, standing 5'10½" with a head of black hair. Reared in Tallahassee after his father migrated south, Ball was a painter by trade; he had no previous military experience.[39]

Together in Chattanooga, the Floridians found time to visit friends and family in the regimental camps. They were there, however, for soldiering, not socializing, and on August 17 elements of Bragg's army began crossing the Tennessee and rumors abounded of a pending offensive. Already on August 12, W.G.M. Davis's Brigade, with the whole of Kirby Smith's Army of East Tennessee, had begun its march north into the Cumberland Mountains. The soldiers assumed that the day would soon come when they would test their mettle on the battlefield. Inwardly, they probably maintained fears of how they might act in combat. Outwardly, like Washington Ives, many proclaimed that when the time came "Florida will not be ashamed of her sons."[40]

8 Another Luminous Page to the History of Florida

September–October 8, 1862

The Kentucky Campaign, waged during the late summer and early fall of 1862, was designed to liberate Middle Tennessee, but a poor command structure and unbounded ambition carried the Confederates into the Bluegrass. While their fellow Floridians earned laurels fighting in Virginia, the soldiers of the Western Theater regiments viewed this as their chance to prove themselves on the battlefield. Many would be disappointed. Although the majority of the soldiers did not participate in any battles, the campaign's adversity served to harden the Florida troops and in the end produced better soldiers.

Braxton Bragg and Kirby Smith sowed the seeds for a Kentucky invasion at a meeting held in Chattanooga on July 31. The commanders agreed that after Kirby Smith flanked Cumberland Gap, thereby forcing the Yankees to abandon the strategic pass, the Army of the Mississippi and Kirby Smith's Army of East Tennessee would destroy Buell's force somewhere in Middle Tennessee. After Buell's destruction the two armies would advance into the Bluegrass and liberate the state from Federal domination. Bragg's plan contained a fatal flaw, however, because he and Kirby Smith commanded separate departments. And only when their armies united would Bragg, the senior officer of the two, have any mandate over Kirby Smith's Army of East Tennessee.[1]

While Bragg hoped to deal with Buell's army in Middle Tennessee, he endured much pressure for a march into Kentucky. Bluegrass politicians, living in exile within the Confederacy, attempted to convince the general that Kentuckians wished to secede but first needed the Union Army removed from their state. Kentucky cavalier John Hunt Morgan, leading one of Bragg's cavalry brigades, informed his superior after returning from a raid in his home state that its citizens would rise to support the Confederacy in the event of an invasion. Morgan estimated that thousands of Kentuckians would willingly join Bragg's force.[2]

While Bragg waited for his wagon train and artillery, which moved overland through Alabama to reach Chattanooga, Kirby Smith's force began its march toward the Cumberland Mountains. The 1st Florida Cavalry's three mounted companies, attached to the van of the offensive, prepared for hard riding and possible fighting. On August 13 Kirby Smith's cavalry slipped undetected into the mountains southwest of Cumberland Gap. Behind the cavalry column, the gray infantry plodded along on dusty roads, wondering what their destination might be.[3]

Colonel W.G.M. Davis's Brigade, attached to Brigadier General Henry Heth's small division, departed Knoxville on August 13. Robert Watson, having arrived in East Tennessee with the 7th Florida's Company K only a week earlier, wrote, "We took up our line of march at 5 P.M. for Kentucky via Big Creek Gap. We have no tents in future and have to carry our knapsacks, rifle, forty rounds of ammunition, haversacks and three days provisions, and canteens." The Florida soldiers, unfamiliar with long, trying marches, particularly over the uneven topography of East Tennessee, found the first few days demanding, to say the least. "We marched until midnight," Watson penned before dozing off, "when we halted and turned in, every man in the Regt. completely used up." The aspiring Byron in Company H rhymed, "For day and night we traveled on/ O'er mountains high and steep,/ 'Neath the hot rays of August sun,/ O'er rivers dark and deep."[4]

The column tramped north over a series of ridges and reached Big Creek Gap on August 17. Lieutenant Hugh Black of the 6th Florida wrote from the pass, "the road from Knoxville to this place was the dustiest road that I ever saw, it was just like marching through a solid bed of ashes and the heat was very great." Though the Big Creek Gap offered passage through the Cumberland Mountains, the soldiers would find it difficult to traverse. A Confederate Army engineer described the gap as a "second-class wagon road" that was "rough, rocky and steep."[5]

The Floridians suffered particularly on the passage, as Kirby Smith assigned Heth's Division the responsibility of guarding the army's wagon train. Lieutenant Colonel Robert Bullock portrayed the crossing as "the hardest trip I ever made in my life." He reported that the Florida soldiers "had to delay, waiting for the wagons, and pulling them up the mountains." Lieutenant James Hays noted, "[T]here have been three companies of our Regiment working all day rolling wagons over the mountain, we put over two hundred. . . . We are the blackest lot you ever saw for we havent [sic] shifted our clothes since we left Knoxville."[6]

Long before Kirby Smith's infantry reached the gaps, his flying cavalry column under John Scott entered London, Kentucky. This small hamlet, located thirty miles from the Kentucky-Tennessee border, sat astride Daniel Boone's Wilderness Road. Kentucky's early settlers had entered the state via that trail, and in 1862 it was the artery on which Cumberland Gap's supplies flowed. Thus, Scott's fast strike cut Cumberland Gap's lifeline, and his troopers also seized 160 supply-laden wagons. A day later Kirby Smith's infantry reached Barbourville, ten miles south of London, where they, too, captured an unsuspecting Yankee supply train.[7]

During the weeklong mountain passage, the soldiers survived on both the rations in their haversacks and produce from nearby fields and orchards. Lieutenant Hays explained, "[T]he men drew only beef and bread enough for one meal per day, and that was all they got, and some days they could not get bread and had to live on ground corn without salt—it is a wonder they all didn't die." Lieutenant Black survived on "roasting ears," though at Barbourville the captured Federal supplies provided some soldiers with "coffee and sugar which," the lieutenant explained, "added a great deal to our comfort." Forage from nearby farms and orchards also provided the soldiers' rations once they exited the mountains. Alex McKenzie Jr., also a 6th Florida soldier, wrote, "Since we arrived in Ky. we have faird exceedingly well. This is undoubtedly the finest county in the World. Small grain & fruit in abundance & the finest stock I recon in the southern states."[8]

The roads that Kirby Smith's army used to enter the Bluegrass became littered with the infirm and tired. The hard marching over the rough terrain and dusty byways caused blistered feet, sore muscles, and breathing problems. The climate in the mountains also brought on various sicknesses among the soldiers. James Hays observed of the weather, "the days are as warm as it is in Florida; at nite it is nearly cold enough for frost." The 7th Florida established a hospital in Boston, Kentucky, where the regiment deposited its sick.[9]

Robert Watson, who developed a severe fever at Big Creek Gap, was among the sick soldiers left along the route. The ailing soldiers survived on forage for nearly two weeks before a Federal patrol discovered the stricken Rebels. The Federals, unable to care for their new prisoners, promptly paroled the Floridians. During the first week of September, Watson and several others, feeling well enough to walk and understanding they could not fight again until they were exchanged, began the trek south to Knoxville. For these men, avenging Key West would have to wait.[10]

While Kirby Smith allowed his soldiers a week's rest at Barbourville, he implemented a change in strategy. Though the Confederates sat astride Cumberland Gap's supply line, the Union division there had food enough to last a month. George Morgan, the Federal commander, was determined to hold out as long as possible. Kirby Smith, unwilling to besiege the strategic pass, informed Bragg he needed to move farther north to obtain supplies. In reality, Kirby Smith moved his army toward Lexington to please Jefferson Davis, who still believed that "Kentucky's heart was with the South." Kirby Smith, hoping to lead the liberation of President Davis's native state, had designs for an invasion even before he promised to cooperate with Bragg in Middle Tennessee.[11]

On August 25, following the week of rest, Kirby Smith put his aptly renamed Army of Kentucky in motion on the Wilderness Road, moving toward the heart of the Bluegrass, with Colonel Davis's Brigade occupying a position near the rear of the column. Excitement arose the next day when the 6th and 7th Florida regiments, along with the Florida-raised Marion Artillery, were dispatched to Williamsburg, a village fifteen miles southeast, to deal with a supposed threat to the Confederate flank. Hugh Black wrote after the campaign that the diversion was caused by "a few stragglers," but the regiments remained at Williamsburg until August 28 before finally marching to rejoin the army.[12]

In an attempt to catch up with the main force, Colonel Davis pushed his Floridians hard up the Wilderness Road. The movement was in vain, however; while marching on the morning of August 30, the men heard the distant rumble of cannon ahead on the pike. The firing originated from Richmond, a town south of Lexington. There, Kirby Smith was winning a stunning victory against a cobbled-together force of raw Union regiments. By sunset Kirby Smith's army had routed the enemy, killing and wounding more than 1,000 Federals, and capturing 4,000. The Army of Kentucky's casualties numbered just over 450 killed and wounded. Despite a forced march that lasted a day and a half with but one hour of rest, the Floridians failed to reach Richmond in time.[13]

When the tired Floridians marched past the battleground the following day, the untested soldiers encountered terrible sights and sounds. The 7th Florida's poet put the dismal scene in verse: "Ah, saddening sight!—stretched o'er the ground/ Lay victims of the fight,/ In death's embrace—the ghastly wound/ Too hideous for the sight;/ And horses scattered here and there/ Did thus the fate of battle share." United with the army once again at Richmond, Davis's Brigade entered Lexington on September 5 where they were greeted with, in the words of Major William Stockton, "cheers, with smiles, with tears of joy."[14]

Davis's Floridians did not remain long in Lexington, for Kirby Smith, having acted on impulse in rushing to seize the Bluegrass, found himself in enemy territory and unsure of what to do next. Kenneth Noe, the foremost historian of the Kentucky Campaign, has noted that "a strange and sudden reversal occurred as Kirby Smith abandoned the offensive and mentally dug in. . . . Clearly he had never considered what to do once Lexington was in his hands." Rather than fall back toward Cumberland Gap and besiege the Union division, which had abandoned the pass and escaped into northeastern Kentucky, or march toward Middle Tennessee to support Bragg, he decided to occupy the region and wait for recruits to flock to the Confederate cause. Colonel Davis's troops occupied Kentucky's capital, Frankfort, and remained there for the next month. Of the occupation duty in the capital, the 7th's artist wrote, "Oh, Frankfort! governmental seat,/ thou burial place of Boone,/ Thou echoed'st to the soldier's feet/ At midnight, morn, and noon,/ And muskets, on thy pavements hard,/ Rang as the Hornets kept their guard."[15]

Back in Tennessee, John Calvin Brown, wearing the wreathed stars of a Confederate general on his collar, was glad to be a free man once more. Captured at Fort Donelson the previous February, the black-bearded Tennessean was exchanged in early August and on the last day of that month became a brigadier general. Thirty-five years old that year, Brown had read law before the war and had voted for the Constitutional Union ticket in 1860. Returning to the army after his internment, Bragg assigned the lawyer-turned-warrior to the 1st Brigade in James Patton Anderson's Division. Brown, who would one day be the governor of Tennessee, displayed courage and demonstrated a knack for leadership on the battlefield. He led his troops from the front and was wounded several times before the conflict ended. The Tennessean's new brigade contained only three regiments: the 1st and 3rd Florida infantries and 41st Mississippi Infantry.[16]

Brown's infantry was a mix of experienced campaigners and green but eager volunteers. The 1st Florida Infantry provided his veterans, as many of the regiment's soldiers had fought at Shiloh. Yet the 1st Florida also contained the untested West Florida companies that had recently arrived in Tennessee. The 3rd Florida Infantry, though well disciplined, remained unbloodied and its soldiers were anxious to prove their mettle. The Madison County planter Lucius Church commanded the regiment during the campaign, as Colonel William S. Dilworth had been "put under arrest on some trivial grounds and this act of injustice" caused him to miss the campaign. The 41st Mississippi, organized earlier that summer, remained an unknown quantity mainly due to a lack of training. Battery A, 14th Georgia Artillery Battalion, an outfit formed and armed in April and May 1862, was also assigned to the brigade.[17]

On August 19 Brown's Brigade, serving in General Anderson's Division of Major General William J. Hardee's right wing, received orders to strike camp and prepare rations for an imminent movement. The next afternoon the regiments formed into columns and marched through Chattanooga. Washington Ives, watching from the 4th Florida's encampment, painted the scene for his father: "It would have made you feel proud to have seen the gallant 3d Fla. leave its encampment on Wednesday evening to cross the River, its rank and file was 600 strong and it looked nearly as large as a brigade, as they left their Band struck up a martial air." Brown's three regiments crossed the Tennessee on ferries and started into the foothills of the Cumberland Plateau.[18]

On the Tennessee River's north bank, the soldiers faced ground similar to that which their comrades had encountered weeks earlier outside Knoxville. Like their fellow Floridians in Davis's Brigade, these soldiers had not faced such steep grades, as their state's highest point reached only two hundred feet above sea level.

In part, Willie Bryant blamed the tough marching on the fact that the soldiers were "overloaded in our anxiety to carry luxuries." Like so many other volunteers had already discovered, the 3rd Florida men learned that the added weight of extra clothing and unnecessary knickknacks hampered their progress. Parting with such items became quite easy on the road north of Chattanooga. W. C. Middleton, a twenty-five-year-old serving in the St. Augustine Blues, recalled in his diary, "the road all the way was strewn with old clothes, and blankets, and sick old men." Twenty-year-old Benton Ellis, a former student in Company C, wrote years later, "my brother Jimmie and I . . . had not gone three miles before we discarded the blankets and knapsacks and made the campaign with the clothing we had on us, in fact we left everything except our shirts and pants, shoes and hats." Brown's Brigade remained encamped several miles north of the river for a week, waiting for the army to gather for the coming campaign.[19]

The 4th Florida remained in camp near Lookout Mountain as the various commands departed for the campaign. By orders of General Bragg, the 4th Florida remained in Chattanooga where they and several other regiments formed a base of operations under the command of General Sam Jones, who had directed the evacuation of Pensacola months earlier. It is likely General Bragg detained the 4th Florida because both its colonel and lieutenant colonel were dangerously ill. Lieutenant Colonel Wylde L. L. Bowen survived to fight another day, but the young colonel James Hunt succumbed to an unknown sickness. The regiment at this time numbered only 483 privates, and rather than preparing for a battle with Buell's army, it spent the last weeks of summer in routine and boring work guarding commissary stores near Chattanooga.[20]

Braxton Bragg's Army of the Mississippi assumed the offensive on August 29 when his columns advanced northeastward over a precipitous height known locally as Walden Ridge, an extension of Lookout Mountain. The ridge loomed over Chattanooga from a distance and through the late summer haze its heights seemed an attractive bluish-green. A closer inspection, however, revealed less-inviting ground that would trouble the inexperienced campaigners. The ridge towered at least a thousand feet above the surrounding countryside, with many points rising above two thousand feet. The roads were in poor condition, often ascending steeply to the summit. At its base, just miles north of Chattanooga, Willie Bryant described the obstacle as "a perpendicular cliff."[21]

Upon hearing that Kirby Smith had occupied Lexington, Braxton Bragg decided he would not fight the decisive battle in Middle Tennessee. Understanding that to defeat Buell's force he needed Kirby Smith's assistance, Bragg determined that his divisions would march into the Bluegrass. Once the two armies united and combined with the thousands of Kentuckians who would undoubtedly flock to the Confederate banner, he would crush the Yankee army. However, as James Lee McDonough has noted, once Bragg made the decision to move to Kentucky and because he had no direct control over Kirby Smith, the two generals would make "no unified movement" and have "no clearly defined objective."[22]

Second Lieutenant John Livingston Inglis of the 3rd Florida's Company D was twenty-five years old in 1862. Though born in England, Inglis was of Scottish heritage and immigrated to Florida, where he had Madison County relatives, in the 1850s. By 1861 Inglis called Wakulla County home, and he managed a small iron works there. Enlisting as a private in 1861, he was elected sergeant during the first company election and then during the reorganization became second lieutenant.[23]

Marching with his regiment, Inglis described his physical condition after a few days of marching as "feet blistered, shoulders sore and worn out." William Raulston Talley, a cannoneer in Battery A, 14th Georgia Artillery Battalion, explained in his memoirs, "the road we were traveling was rough and soon we got to places real steep and as the horses would stall the infantry were detailed all along the road at the steep places to help push our guns up." Benton Ellis recalled that one man "had to carry a large rock and when the mules, after a desperate struggle would move a short distance and stop, we had to scotch the wheels with the rock." Willie Bryant wrote simply, "What we have suffered on this march those only can know who have experienced it, it is impossible to describe it, or for the mind to realise it by description . . . thousands have ben left sick at houses and hospitals established along the road."[24]

The Florida regiments descended from Walden Ridge into the Sequatchie River Valley where the soldiers earned a brief rest at the village of Dunlap. One problem that plagued the Confederate and Union soldiers alike during the late summer campaign was the lack of water on the Cumberland Plateau. Drought served to dry the region's creeks, and what little water remained was stagnant, covered with green film, and filled with bacteria. John Inglis simply denoted the lack of fluids by writing: "water scarce." The hot, dry dust of the mountain roads filled the soldiers' mouths, making the situation worse. "East Tenn," declared Willie Bryant, "is booked in my memory as the most abominable section of the country I have known."[25]

After marching through Sparta, which Samuel Pasco described as "quite a little place," the outlook brightened. The infantry still marched between ten and twenty miles each day during the second week in September, but the marching culminated with the crossing of the Cumberland River on September 10. There, the men had an opportunity to wash the grime and dirt from their clothing and bodies. After fording the river, the army passed through fertile country that provided ample forage and water. Charlie Hemming, a teenager soldiering in the 3rd Florida, described the landscape as one in which "the corn was in tassel and the red apples, in the orchards and fields on the roadside, made a picture not to be forgotten. Everywhere the people turned out, en masse, to give us food, or to cheer the passing army." Samuel Pasco described the landscape as the regiments descended the Cumberland Plateau as "most beautiful and picturesque."[26]

On September 12, as his division crossed the Kentucky state line, Anderson returned to the land he cherished. The Floridians expressed astonishment at the state's political division. From town to town, the Army of the Mississippi did not know which type of response their "liberating" columns would evoke. Samuel Pasco noted that Barron County, just north of the state line, "is strongly for 'Union' and the family who lived where we camped have all their sympathies enlisted on that side." Yet the next day citizens of Glasgow "enthusiastically cheered," and "flags and snow white handkerchiefs waved. Shout after shout went up from the stalwart soldier as he witnessed this demonstration of fidelity to our cause."[27]

Having reached Glasgow after a forced march, the soldiers bedded down for well-earned rest. However, during the night of September 15–16 the regiments were roused to their feet and many stomachs may have tightened as they marched toward the rail town of Munfordville. Lieutenant Inglis confessed that as the column trudged toward the sound of firing artillery, he was "afraid to be about in first fight." The attraction of capturing an isolated Union garrison brought James Chalmers's Brigade to Munfordville, which was strategically situated on the Green River. The Louisville and Nashville Railroad's tracks passed through the town, though this railroad did not figure into Bragg's invasion plan. The town's defenders, numbering nearly 5,000, were entrenched in poorly placed fortifications on the river's south bank. Expecting an easy victory, Chalmers marched on Munfordville, where he suffered a repulse with the loss of 280 casualties. Bragg, incensed at this defeat, decided to take the entire Army of the Mississippi to the town to avenge Chalmers's defeat.[28]

In his diary Lieutenant Augustus McDonell described the army's arrival at Munfordville on Monday afternoon: "[O]ur . . . men were soon placed in position so as to command every point of the enemies fortifications. Gen. Bragg then . . . demanded a surrender of the place, which was refused." The Federal commander, Colonel John Wilder, who would later gain fame as the leader of an elite brigade of mounted infantry, asked for proof that Bragg maintained superior forces surrounding the fortifications. As daylight faded and twilight engulfed the opposing forces, Samuel Pasco laid down on a blanket, "anticipating a fight in the morning."[29]

The next morning, as Joe Hooker's troops slammed into Stonewall Jackson's Corps near a small church on the west bank of Antietam Creek, Wilder's paroled men marched from their fortifications. The previous evening, to convince the Yankee colonel of Bragg's dominant numbers, Wilder had been given a tour of the Rebel lines. The sight of the Army of the Mississippi arrayed for battle caused the colonel to concede defeat. As sunlight struggled to break through an overcast sky, Bragg's soldiers, the Floridians included, lined the road to watch their former countrymen pass.[30]

John Inglis, who described his own soldiers as "ragged, barefooted . . . hungry" with "skins dark and burnt," could not help but note that the surrendered Yankees "looked fat, clean and had new uniforms." Pasco concurred, as he admiringly wrote in his own diary, "[T]hey looked fine in their blue uniforms." Young W. C. Middleton wrote that the Union soldiers were "well dressed" and "well feed [sic] . . . what a contrast to our ragged, foot-sore, and weary soldiers who marched for weeks over mountains and valleys on very short rations." As the Federals passed, the atmosphere turned festive; Inglis wrote, "[O]ur men [were] joking [with] each other, our bands played 'Ain't I Glad I Got Out of the Wilderness.'" The surrender also became an opportunity for the Floridians to replace items they had discarded while crossing the mountains. Pasco observed that "quite a trade in canteens sprung up as they passed." The English-born principal "bought a Yankee overcoat and india rubber cloth."[31]

The Confederates gained a hollow victory at Munfordville, as the detour caused a delay in their joining up with Kirby Smith's Army of Kentucky. For a time shortly after the Munfordville "victory" Bragg believed that his army would fight the campaign's decisive battle on the Green River's banks. For as the Army of the Mississippi accepted the surrender of Wilder's garrison, Don Carlos Buell's Army of the Ohio was encamped at Dripping Springs, only thirty miles southwest. Buell did not know his counterpart's intentions, "believing that the secessionists would . . . swing back and attack Nashville from the north." Thinking that Buell's army would move against him, "Bragg . . . ordered his army . . . to concentrate at Munfordsville. They would use Wilder's works to anchor an imposing defensive line, one that would shred Buell's army."[32]

Bragg remained in position at Munfordville for two days, his infantry waiting tensely for what was certain to be a fight. Samuel Pasco, who served during the campaign as General Brown's brigade clerk, decided that he would not miss the battle. On the morning of September 18, he left headquarters to "take part in the anticipated fight." He found the 3rd Florida "in line of battle on a high hill," but rather than engaging the Yankees he and his comrades "sat and talked till dusk." Meanwhile, Lieutenant Inglis continually walked behind his company's line as he "got anxious for their approach" and reminded his untested Floridians "to not waste a shot, be sure of hindsight and only fire when distance and aim was sure as for . . . a deer."[33]

The battle for Kentucky was not to be waged on the banks of the Green River; Bragg changed his mind. Rather than attempt to fight Buell with inferior numbers, the Confederate general would eventually move east and finally unite with Kirby Smith before giving battle. Kenneth Noe has summarized the decision as a correct one, adding, "Buell easily could have flanked Munfordsville without giving battle at all. Had he gotten in Bragg's rear at Elizabethtown, there would have been no junction with Kirby Smith, and probably no further Confederate advance as well." However, Bragg's decision allowed Buell's army, which had suffered from the same harsh marching conditions as their Rebel foes, an open road to Louisville. At any rate, Bragg's men left their entrenchments on September 20 and moved toward Bardstown, where supplies from Kirby Smith awaited.[34]

From the outset, the Floridians and all of Bragg's men enjoyed themselves at Bardstown, a small village where numerous roads converged. Though the town maintained a spur to the Louisville and Nashville Railroad, after a new railroad connecting Louisville to Cumberland Gap was constructed, bypassing the town, its importance waned. Despite this misfortune, Bardstown remained significant to Braxton Bragg because it was only thirty miles from Louisville. From the hamlet, Bragg could both watch Buell's army and maintain excellent communications with

Kirby Smith. During the brief two weeks that the Army of the Mississippi en-camped in Bardstown's fields and meadows, "a brief summer love affair between the town and the army" developed "that lasted at least until overwhelmed mer-chants closed their doors rather than accept Confederate money." The only draw-back to the town was its lack of water, a problem the soldiers faced the entire cam-paign: "little water remained for the soldiers to drink but the warm, muddy pond water they had grown accustomed to."[35]

The Floridians reached Bardstown on the afternoon of September 24. They en-countered the "streets lined with citizens," and the bands struck up "'Dixie' and 'Bonnie Blue Flag.'" Despite their bedraggled state, the 3rd Florida's soldiers snapped to attention at the edge of town and displayed the discipline that the *Daily Sun*'s editor had praised. John Inglis wrote that "men came up took places. Colors un-furled, Bayonets fixed, 'Right Shoulder shift,' dressed files, Bands to front, and fine order and . . . at a quick swinging step we went through B. Town." The sol-diers soon discovered that even the town's Unionists were cordial, as one evening a family named Grigsby invited several Florida officers for dinner. Colonel William Miller, Lieutenant Colonels Thaddeus McDonell and Lucius Church, and the Bird brothers and Augustus McDonell arrived to find "a very nice dinner prepared for us." Brown's Brigade encamped several miles from town on the Louisville road to serve as pickets and warn of any Federal advance.[36]

The combination of poor water and foraged food caused many Floridians to spend the Bardstown respite in one of the town's hospitals. Charles Hemming spoke for hundreds of his comrades when he recalled subsisting on "roast corn and ripe pumpkin, of which the fields by the road were full." He continued, "this diet made me sick, as well as many others." Lieutenant Henry Reddick, serving in the 1st Florida, became ill and was confined to an infirmary housed in a school. He was joined by numerous other 1st and 3rd Florida soldiers, including Michael Raysor, a member of the Jefferson County Rifles. The strenuous marching and poor con-ditions caused one 3rd Florida soldier to remark, "[M]ore than half our Regiment is left behind and they will be a long time catching up."[37]

On October 1 a distraught and nervous Bragg finally caught up with Kirby Smith in Lexington. Bragg made this trek across the heart of Kentucky for sev-eral reasons, the least of which was that he was unable to rally Kentuckians to the Confederate cause. Despite Bragg's efforts to encourage men to enlist, none had, and the general turned to the Confederate Conscription Act to induce Kentucki-ans to enter the service. To enable this legislation to take effect in Kentucky, a pro-Confederate government had to be installed, and by coincidence the Richmond-recognized Kentucky governor, Richard Hawes, had traveled north with the Army of the Mississippi.[38]

From Lexington, Bragg and Kirby Smith traveled to Frankfort to inaugurate Hawes. They made this journey knowing that Buell's army, rested and reinforced, though suffering from discord among its generals, had already departed Louisville searching for a fight. Assuming Buell's main target was Frankfort, Bragg decided to give battle north of Bardstown; hence he ordered his chief subordinate, Major General Leonidas Polk, to move the Army of the Mississippi in preparation for a strike on the Army of the Ohio's flank as it moved east. Polk, believing that the enemy columns were marching on Bardstown, disobeyed Bragg and retreated east to Danville. This move left Kirby Smith's troops at Frankfort exposed and necessitated a withdrawal, but before this retreat occurred Bragg doggedly went to the capital on October 3 with the intention of placing Hawes in the gubernatorial seat.[39]

Colonel Davis's Brigade still garrisoned the capital when Bragg and his entourage reached the city. On October 4, Bragg saw Hawes's inauguration through to completion, but even as citizens gathered for the event, they could hear the distant sounds of artillery. A soldier in the 6th Florida, writing on the day of the festivities, recorded, "I hear them now, cannonading at Shelbyville. I expect a hot time this evening or tomorrow. Jenerals Braggs and Buckner is in town. A Goverer of Kentucky was appointed and today innaugaurated." Davis's Brigade would have to wait for a fight, for Kirby Smith's troops departed the town that evening. The jester in the Marion Hornets made light of the evacuation, writing, "They made a Governor,—at least/ They partly made him,—and a feast,/ That is, when he was half installed/ They stopped to take their dinner, And e're the crowd was called/ Old Bragg shook like a sinner;/ And quickly sprang into the saddle—/ And then began the great "Skeddadle!"[40]

While Davis's Brigade withdrew southeastward to Versailles, General John Brown's Floridians and Mississippians departed from Bardstown early on the morning of October 5, leaving many of their sick comrades. The troops made a series of night marches, always forming their eastward-facing columns after midnight and moving until the next afternoon. Meanwhile Bragg, lacking good intelligence, could not determine which Federal column—that advancing on Frankfort or the one pursuing Polk—comprised Buell's main body. This problem was multiplied by the fact that when Bragg ordered the two armies to converge at Harrodsburg, Kirby Smith refused and "kept his army so that it could protect the approaches to Lexington." Searching for an opportunity to attack, Bragg believed he discovered one on October 7. Major General William J. Hardee, a veteran soldier and known to the men in the ranks as the author of their manual-of-arms, reported from Perryville that only an isolated portion of Buell's army trailed Polk's force. Bragg ordered the Army of the Mississippi to concentrate in that small town to crush the minor arm of Buell's army moving upon them. Not only was this an opportunity, but it became necessary to halt this unknown force from threatening Bragg's left flank and moving to cut him off from Tennessee. Bragg ordered an early morning attack on October 8, and after that quick victory, the Army of the Mississippi would move to join with Kirby Smith to confront the remainder of Buell's army.[41]

The Floridians in Brown's Brigade reached Harrodsburg on the afternoon of October 6, and the soldiers dispersed into their messes for dinner. Edward Clifford Brush wrote in his diary that he and his comrades feasted on turkey before dozing off around midnight. Less than two hours later, the soldiers were rousted from their blankets and, dazed and sleepy, formed a column facing west toward Perryville. Brush, attached to the ordnance wagons, penned, "The troops made all haste towards Perryville where the enemy is supposed to be." John Inglis described the men, though very tired, as marching "in fine spirits . . . men joked, and hoped to be first in."[42]

Brown's Brigade arrived in Perryville on the morning of October 7, having passed through the town just thirty-six hours earlier. John Inglis wrote of his affection for the town: "people all kind to us. Lots of Whiskey offered but officers emptied it all out." He described the village of five hundred souls as being in "fat country." Not only would the soldiers have "plenty to eat," but several creeks near the town contained pools of precious water. Upon its arrival Anderson's Division was divided, with Brown's soldiers and one brigade positioned north of the town and two others guarding the extreme left of the army. Before going to sleep, Edward Brush wrote, "A general engagement is expected tomorrow."[43]

On the morning of October 8, Bragg arrived at Perryville, incensed that Polk and Hardee had not launched the ordered attack. But already before dawn, firing began as the Army of the Ohio's I Corps moved on the small town and its water. After pushing back Confederate skirmishers, the Union soldiers deployed into lines of battle on a series of ridges northwest of the town. Their ranks overlooked Doctor's Creek, which contained small pools of the precious liquid. With this new development, Bragg himself planned an assault in which he hoped to envelop the Federal position with a flanking attack by Major General Benjamin F. Cheatham's Tennessee division. Cheatham's soldiers would "attack in echelon, brigade by brigade." Once this division broke the Federal line, "Hardee then would advance his divisions into the fleeing blue mass to finish the job."[44]

After awakening that Wednesday morning, the Floridians rolled up their blankets and stacked them along with their knapsacks before forming ranks. Thomas Benton Ellis, assigned to the brigade's wagons, left his post so that he might fight alongside his brother. He wrote in his memoirs, "I deserted my position . . . and set out to find my company and did find it in line of battle." At 11:00 A.M. Brown's Brigade marched to a ridge west of Perryville where the "corn had been cut down," and the men lay down on the eastern face awaiting the order to advance into the fray. The ridge descended steeply into an irregular, grassy valley before sloping upward again. Beyond this knoll, the ground gave way to form a V-shaped depression, a portion of which had further given way to form a small sinkhole. Across this second valley, and plainly visible from the Rebel lines, the Union forces held a formidable position on yet another ridge. On Brown's flanks, Joseph B. Palmer's Battery of the 14th Georgia Artillery and Charles Lumsden's Alabama Battery unlimbered and fired on the Federal position.[45]

The artillery duel began just after noon and the Floridians and their Mississippi comrades endured the most terrible effects of this ensuing slugfest. Yankee solid shot, intended for the Rebel artillerymen, rolled over the hill's crest and onto the Floridians, while shells burst over their heads, showering them with metal. The men instinctively pressed themselves flat against the ground, but the regiments still took casualties. Samuel Pasco, writing to the *Family Friend* ten days after the battle, described the bombardment as "perhaps the most severe fire of artillery . . . of the war." Willie Bryant explained the terror to his mother: "For an hour we fired we lay on the ground under a hill exposed to shot and shell which killed and wounded several." Colonel William Miller wrote years after the fight, "[S]ome fragments of bursting shells fell among us wounding several of our men."[46]

By 1:00 P.M. the firing to the north raged heavily. Rather than hit the Federal flank, Cheatham's force instead struck the blue line head-on, and the battle dissolved into chaos with the Confederates suffering heavy casualties. With the Tennesseans engaged in combat that one veteran described as "the very pit of hell," Bragg ordered Brown's Brigade into the fight. The command "'Attention,' rang along our line," John Inglis wrote. "[U]p jumped the 1st Brigade, Genl. B lined us up as if on drill, drew his sword, and with the command, 'forward, guide right, march,' we started from a march to a trot." Captain Holmes Steele, a former mayor of Jacksonville and the Jacksonville Light Infantry's first captain, served as the 3rd Florida's adjutant at Perryville. In an account given after the war, Steele proudly noted, "It would have done your soul good to have seen with what martial tread the brave 3rd Florida marched by the side of the gallant and tried 1st and the no less gallant 41st Mississippi. Under a terrific fire of shot and shell the 1st Brigade marched to the position assigned them."[47]

As the sounds of battle raged around them, the soldiers surged forward, hats pulled low, sweaty palms gripping the stocks of their weapons. Some of the regiments' men remained behind, for in the valley "there were many black locust thickets" and their footwear had long since disintegrated due to the hard marching. One who ignored the briars was fifteen-year-old Francis Rutledge Gould of the St. Augustine Blues, who went into the fight despite his lack of shoes. The soldiers of the 1st Florida who had experienced Shiloh were probably more reserved marching toward the Federal line, for as James McPherson has written, these veterans were "no longer . . . anxious for the fray." However, 3rd Florida soldiers like young Francis Gould were eager to prove their worth in a fight. When it came to battles, raw volunteers such as those that filled the 3rd Florida's ranks were "not at all pre-pared for the nightmare experiences in store for them."[48]

As the 3rd Florida surged forward, the troops began yelling, mimicking the ac-tions of a brigade the soldiers had watched advance earlier in the day. With the "Rebel Yell" emanating from their throats and taken with excitement, the volun-teers let their emotions get the better of them and their trot turned into a run. Soon the 3rd Florida's soldiers were, in the words of John Inglis, "into brambles, high as our heads, and in horrible bad order." General Brown, riding forward, "cussed us for being too quick, dress up or you will be cut to pieces in such order." As the 3rd Florida re-formed ranks and marked time under fire, the 1st Florida and 41st Mississippi finally caught up to their position and the brigade continued its ad-vance. The soldiers trudged up the knoll; upon reaching the top, they viewed the ridge, one hundred yards away, which marked the Union position.[49]

An early death unnerved and sobered the troops of the 3rd Florida. Thomas Mosely, a twenty-two-year-old teacher serving in Madison County's Company G, had been promoted to acting sergeant major of the regiment only that morning. As the troops crested the hill that put the Floridians and Mississippians in full view of the Federal line, a bullet shattered Mosely's forehead. Archie Livingston, a cousin of John Inglis and Company G soldier, wrote that none died that day "more loved than Thos Mosely." Soon the firing began in earnest.[50]

The veteran boys in blue holding the ridge belonged to the brigades of Colonels Leonard Harris and William H. Lytle, both part of General Lovell Rousseau's Di-vision. Supported by three experienced batteries, the line was indeed formidable. Already, the Federals had dispersed an attack by the Mississippians of Colonel Thomas Jones, who left his dead and wounded strewn on the western slope of the ridge and in the valley. Rousseau's midwesterners faced a disadvantage, however, as the engagement with Jones's troops had somewhat depleted their ammunition. Despite this hindrance, the Yankees were determined to hold their position. A sav-age contest ensued.[51]

The fight, which began around 1:30 P.M., lasted until 4:30 P.M. and consisted of a series of sharp firefights, each followed by an advance by Brown's Brigade. At least three of these charges were repulsed, and a period of reorganization fol-lowed before the Confederates tried again. This cycle repeated itself throughout the afternoon.[52]

Young Charles Hemming was wounded in the right arm by shell fragments not long after the firing started and sank onto the ground. As he lay stunned and un-able to move, "Dan Byrd [sic] of Monticello, ran and picked me up and gave me some brandy from his flask; then having my shoulder tied up, he sent me to the rear." Hemming recalled that the walk back to the field hospital was terrifying: "I got with many others directly in the line of falling bullets. . . . They seemed to go by like a swarm of singing bees, and I expected any minute to be struck again, but I got through without any accident." Benton Ellis suffered an injury to his left elbow not long after entering the fight. He continued loading and firing his weapon until he departed to help a wounded comrade leave the field.[53]

John Love McKinnon, serving in the 1st Florida, also fell wounded. Having sustained an injury to his left arm, McKinnon lay on the field through much of the engagement, wondering, "'Is this the glory of the bloody battlefield we read of in books?'" While lying in the grass, he watched as a shell exploded above General Brown's mount, killing the unfortunate animal and severely wounding the general. Command of the brigade passed first to Colonel William F. Tucker of the 41st Mississippi and then, after he was wounded, to Colonel Miller. One of his soldiers recalled, "[W]here the balls fell thickest his commanding form was to be seen, cheering on his men by voice and example."[54]

The fight grew so intense that the 1st Florida's entire color guard became casualties; its banner was lifted by a staff officer who bore it through the remainder of the engagement. Willie Bryant, a 3rd Florida soldier, wrote that during the tremendous firing, he "had many narrow escapes, men shot down on every side of me, balls striking near me and once as I lay on the ground taking aim a ball so filled my eyes with dirt as to blind me for some time."[55]

As late afternoon arrived, the brigade's ammunition ran low and the regiments partially withdrew to meet the ordnance wagons that rushed onto the field to resupply the fighting men. Before doing so, however, officers rummaged through the cartridge boxes of the dead and the wounded and passed the rounds to men on the firing line. While exposing himself to hand out cartridges, Captain Capers Bird received his second wound of the war, this time a severe injury to his thigh. Captain William Poole suffered the same fate. Major Glover Ball also fell wounded while performing this task, a bullet having passed through his neck.[56]

Edward Clifford Brush arrived on the battlefield with the ordnance train. "On our way thither," Brush later recorded, "the shell fell around us like rain. . . . I assisted in getting one or two of the members of our company who were wounded a comfortable place in a barn near by—It is truly an awful sight to witness." Similar to the experience of the 1st Florida, the 3rd Florida's officers were killed and wounded in great numbers during the sharp exchange of fire. By the time the 3rd Florida withdrew back down the hill to replenish its cartridges, Major Edward Mashburn and Captain Daniel Bird commanded the regiment, for Lieutenant Colonel Church went down early in the fight with a chest wound. By late afternoon Lieutenant Inglis fought through the pain of a broken collar bone to command his men. Every commissioned officer in the St. Augustine Blues was wounded on the battlefield; the most severely injured was Lieutenant Irvine Drysdale, who lost an eye.[57]

With their cartridge boxes refilled by 4:30 P.M., Colonel Miller's troops returned to the arduous task of displacing Lytle's men from their position. The Rebels now had a numerical advantage, for the brigades of Generals Patrick Cleburne and Dan Adams were moving up on the left, and S.A.M. Wood's regiments surged past on the Floridians' and Mississippians' right flank. With ragged firing coming from the Union lines, Miller ordered an advance and the brigade started down the western face of the hill. Holmes Steele remembered, "The 1st and 3rd Florida moved down upon them directly in their front while the 41st Miss. and a Tennessee Regt. approached them on their flank." After Miller's men fired a concentrated volley at the 10th Ohio, the lone regiment of Lytle's Brigade to resist the assault, the Confederates surged up the trying slope. "Here it was close to each other," John Inglis recalled, "in among the guns, we jumped on them downed the gunners and chased the 10th Ohio as they fell back, but few of them left." Willie Bryant wrote jubilantly, "we . . . made the Yanks 'skedaddle' in good style; they can't stand our charges and yell unless they have a much superior force." Here, the raw Floridians demonstrated their inexperience with battlefield conditions, for in firing at the fleeing Buckeyes they hit some of their comrades in the 41st Mississippi who had moved across the Floridians' front during its successful flanking attack.[58]

Following the last assault, which Theodore Livingston labeled "a most desperate charge," the regiments paused to reorganize. As the men halted to catch their breath, they mourned the death of one of the regiment's most popular officers. Sometime during the final attack, Captain Daniel Bird fell with a shot through his heart. Bird's shaken soldiers carried his body to a nearby farmhouse but, as Livingston wrote, "whether the Yankees buried our dead or not we dont [sic] know."[59]

Despite their losses, Miller's regiments followed Patrick Cleburne's Brigade as it moved past to continue the pursuit, which after a mile was ended by the settling darkness. Theodore Livingston came to better understand the harshness of war during the chase: "As we drove the Yankees off the field, of course we had all their dead and nearly all their wounded. Poor fellows as I passed them, some were dying and others begging for water and asking for their wounds to be bandaged."[60]

As night came the Floridians, drained of emotion, bivouacked where the pursuit had ended. By moonlight they roamed the battlefield and helped remove the wounded; many rifled the Federal dead for rations and trinkets. "Some of the Boys could find sardines, Butter, and crackers," described Theodore Livingston, "and every good thing showing what a difference in our living and theirs." "I was too busy attending the wounded on the battlefield that night to get many trophies," explained Willie Bryant weeks after the initial shock of the fight had worn off, "but I have . . . a good pocket knife, and a canteen and tin cup. . . . I also have a haversack with some parchd. coffee and hard bread."[61]

Many Floridians remained too shocked by the sight of the battlefield to think about picking the pockets of the deceased. Edward Clifford Brush wrote in his diary: "[The] dead and wounded are lying on the field in every direction. The wounded groaning and begging for help." A horrified Theodore Livingston could pen only that "[m]en were laying every three or four steps, shot every way imajin-able [*sic*]. . . . You could see blood, blood everywhere." John Inglis tried to forget "the groans of the dying and the cries for water of the wounded."[62]

That evening Bragg received intelligence that the remainder of Buell's force was arriving on the battlefield. Though he had mauled a Federal corps on the eighth, he believed his force was too exhausted to continue the fight the next day, particu-larly against unfavorable odds. Therefore, Bragg ordered a retreat to begin after midnight, the objective of which was to reach Harrodsburg, where he could easily rendezvous with Kirby Smith's divisions. Ironically, Buell's entire army had been within marching distance of Perryville during the battle, but due to a phenomenon known as acoustic shadow, the sounds of the battle bent back to earth and Buell, only three miles away, heard nothing. This freak occurrence saved Braxton Bragg at a time when his cavalry failed him.[63]

At their advanced positions, the Floridians did not receive word of the retreat until 2:00 A.M., and shortly thereafter "the men were quietly aroused, formed in line and without noise moved over the battlefield." The brigade began marching at 3:00 A.M., with the wounded John Inglis riding on a captured mule. The hasty retreat angered many of the Floridians as they had dumped their knapsacks, hav-ersacks, and blankets at the site of the previous night's camp and now there was no time to return to gather their items. Clothing, food, and personal belongings were all lost, according to Willie Bryant, due to the "bad management of the Of-ficers in command." With a full moon casting its glow upon the battleground and with Federal pickets only a quarter mile distant, William Miller's Brigade slipped away to the northeast.[64]

The Battle of Perryville cost the Florida regiments dearly. The 3rd Florida began the fight with 275 soldiers, while the 1st mustered only 167 the morning of the battle. The latter regiment endured casualty numbers similar to those of the 1st Florida Battalion at Shiloh: 12 died on the battlefield and 53 suffered wounds of varying severity. The regiment listed 6 as missing. The 3rd Florida lost 14 killed in action and 86 incurred injuries. Four more did not answer roll call that evening and were presumed captured. Twenty-six of the two regiments' wounded died of their injuries. The Floridians' officers' corps suffered particularly during the con-test, as many promising commanders were killed or wounded.[65]

However, non-combat fatalities cost the units more than the Perryville engage-ment. In the 1st and 3rd Florida, 30 soldiers died of various diseases. Moreover, 133 soldiers were captured after Union soldiers came upon the numerous make-shift hospitals Bragg left along his line of march. W.G.M. Davis's Floridians suf-fered even greater losses. The 6th and 7th Florida infantries and 1st Florida Cav-alry Regiment lost 40 men to illness during the invasion. A further 170 became Union prisoners.[66]

The Floridians and their fellow soldiers in both armies accomplished an incredible feat simply by enduring the terrible conditions of the Kentucky Campaign. The 1st and 3rd Florida infantry regiments covered, by the measure of various company clerks, at least seven hundred miles, while Davis's troops marched just over six hundred. All suffered under a hot sun, withstood rough terrain, and bore it all in spite of a lack of water.[67]

At Perryville, John Brown's troops learned of the terrors of the battlefield and performed relatively well. Willie Bryant proudly noted that during the fight he "felt considerably excited and a *little* dread, at first, but no fear . . . impartially, I am satisfied with myself." Many others also felt pleased as they had finally, after a year of inaction, experienced the combat for which they had volunteered. Many more battles would follow, but Kentucky served to transform the surviving Floridians from inexperienced volunteers to seasoned campaigners. In the words of Holmes Steele, the soldiers at Perryville, indeed both Florida brigades, had "covered themselves with glory and have given another luminous page to the history of Florida." The men would have proudly agreed with this remark and stood ready to perform the next task asked of them.[68]

9 Our Company and Regiments Mourns the Loss of Their Very Best

October 9, 1862–January 10, 1863

The fall months of 1862 witnessed the Confederate tide recede from Kentucky, culminating with the Battle of Murfreesboro. This time might have been one of recovery and wisely used to recoup the losses suffered in the Kentucky Campaign; indeed, Colonel W.G.M. Davis's Floridians in East Tennessee did earn a respite during December. The suspension of campaigning for Colonel William Miller's troops, however, was short lived; before 1862 ended the troops were again engaged in heated combat. The troops spent the holidays away from family and friends, casualties mounted, and yet another retreat was ordered. Small wonder, then, that morale plummeted during winter's first weeks.

At Harrodsburg, while Braxton Bragg and Edmund Kirby Smith pondered their next move, surgeons, their assistants, and townspeople cared for the several thousand wounded. The injured John Inglis, riding upon a saddle of blankets on a mule's back, passed through the town on the morning of October 9 and stared with horror at the "piles of amputated limbs at Houses used for Hospitals . . . waggon loads of them both Yank and Confed." John Love McKinnon of the 1st Florida, wounded in the arm at Perryville, found himself in one of the hospitals. Late in life he maintained gratitude for Harrodsburg, whose "good ladies came to the hospital day after day, taking to their homes such wounded soldiers as could be moved . . . and they never forgot to care for those who had to remain."[1]

When Bragg ordered a withdrawal southward to Bryantsville on October 10 to protect his lines of communication and retreat, the majority of the wounded remained in Harrodsburg. The next day Bragg decided to abandon Kentucky entirely, and the Rebel columns retired to the southeast. This region of southeastern Kentucky through which the army passed was barren of food, causing a paucity of rations. To make matters worse, the weather steadily deteriorated during the last half of the month; when combined with the poor state of the soldiers' clothing, the conditions caused even those with the strongest resolve to question their motives.[2]

Lieutenant Inglis wrote that the men's daily ration during the retreat consisted of one piece of hardtack that the soldiers supplemented with corn and acorns. Others risked punishment by stealing livestock to obtain sustenance. The temperatures

plummeted and the first snows fell as the columns cleared the Cumberland Mountains and marched toward Knoxville. The Floridians, the majority of whom had
never seen snow, were particularly affected. Samuel Pasco, who had the benefit of
a headquarters wagon and a cabin in which to sleep, wrote during the cold snap,
"[W]e have to build large fires to keep warm. The men are very destitute of clothing & shoes & there is much suffering in consequence."[3]

During the last week in October an intense storm hit the East Tennessee Valley,
dumping several inches of snow onto the Floridians and their comrades. Archie
Livingston explained that the snowfall "found many, many soldiers entirely unprepared for the occasion. Numbers were without shoes & blankets and only clothed
by a shirt and [pair of] pants of thin material and even unprotected by a tent or
tent Fly." Willie Bryant complained that because the soldiers were without tents,
the cold "gave us fits." The soldiers stripped nearby fields of wooden fence rails to
use as firewood despite an order to the contrary.[4]

While Colonel William Miller's Brigade encamped near Knoxville, the 6th
and 7th Florida infantry regiments bivouacked just to the northeast at Blaine's
Crossroads under the command of the newly promoted brigadier general W.G.M.
Davis. The 1st Florida Cavalry, Dismounted, remained at Cumberland Gap, collecting stragglers as they arrived and dispatching them to their units. Before the
month was out, Davis's infantry joined the 1st Florida Cavalry, Dismounted, in
the mountains. Casmero O. Bailey, an Alachua County resident serving in the 7th
Florida, wrote on October 31 that "Maj [Tillman] Ingram came back from Knoxville and he brought the order for us to go to Cumberland Gap. . . . I expect we
will see a hard time of it at the gap but I am in hopes we will not have to stay there
all winter." Major William T. Stockton wrote of his soldiers' attitudes after hearing the news: they "hate awfully the idea of going back to the mountains." Captain Samuel McConnell wrote after spending a week in the higher altitudes: "In
the Gap is the coldest place imaginable."[5]

In Knoxville during November's first days, Colonel Miller's soldiers had a brief
hiatus before their next move. Their spirits rose with the temperature and tents
were distributed. Willie Bryant contemplated the Kentucky Campaign with its
many hardships and commented, "I think I may now say I have gone thro' everything which I will ever have to endure in the service, and . . . I feel no uneasiness
for the future." Samuel Pasco was encouraged by the sound of "church bells ring-
ing in town" and described spending the nights listening to regimental bands playing "as we smoke our pipes."[6]

For some in the 3rd Florida, the return to Knoxville meant an end to their soldiering days. The April Conscription Act allowed non-conscripted men under
eighteen and over thirty-five years of age who had originally enlisted for one year
to obtain their discharge. The soldiers above thirty-five who had enlisted for three
years had to remain in the service. Though the 1862 Conscription Act set July 16

as the date for discharge, W. C. Middleton wrote that Colonel William Dilworth informed the eligible soldiers that "they had to remain until the 5th of August." During the rush to prepare for the Kentucky Campaign and because the campaign progressed so rapidly, the regimental clerks had little time to deal with the military bureaucracy regarding who was eligible for discharge. Thus the last days of October and the first half of November saw a flurry of discharges signed, and a number of Floridians headed home.[7]

Samuel Pasco wrote on October 29, "they are beginning to discharge the non-conscripts," many of whom had studied under the former principal at the Waukeenah Academy. Pasco related that a Board of Examination sat and acted upon all of the discharge applications. In the 3rd Florida, all who applied were discharged, amounting to a loss of fifty-six men. Edward Clifford Brush, the sixteen-year-old veteran of Perryville, was released from the St. Augustine Blues on November 1 and departed for home the next day.[8]

By the time the last of the qualified applicants obtained their discharge on November 18, the Floridians serving in the renamed Army of Tennessee were encamped near Tullahoma. General Braxton Bragg had decided to "invade Middle Tennessee" even before he departed from Kentucky, and during the first weeks of November he shuttled his troops toward the Volunteer State's most vital region. Bragg ordered this move so as to claim the Kentucky Campaign had liberated at least a portion of Middle Tennessee and to secure the foodstuffs of the area.[9]

Colonel Dilworth joined the brigade briefly during its journey, even assuming command of the unit for a few days. News arrived, however, informing the colonel of the death of one of his children, and he was given the opportunity to return to Florida to gather his regiment's absentee soldiers. Dilworth and a small staff that included Samuel Pasco departed for Florida on November 28. They would not return to their regiment until February.[10]

Once in Middle Tennessee the Kentucky Campaign veterans reunited with the 4th Florida Infantry. The 4th Florida, commanded since the death of James Hunt by Colonel Wylde L. L. Bowen, along with the remainder of the Chattanooga garrison, advanced into Middle Tennessee that October under the command of Brigadier General Nathan Bedford Forrest. Forrest's joint cavalry and infantry force was dispatched to Middle Tennessee to keep the area free of Union forays from Nashville. To complete this objective they occupied Murfreesboro, a small town of four thousand that sat astride the Nashville and Chattanooga Railroad, only thirty miles from the Tennessee capital. Washington Ives described the village as being "as pretty a town as I been in yet it is built around the court house Square . . . the same form as Lake City but the buildings are brick, the Town Clock on the CH can be heard to our camps, the spires of two churches can also be seen one spire is covered with a bright metal and glitters beautifully in the sunlight." Ives and his fellow soldiers would come to know the town and surrounding countryside well, as they would fight in the immediate area twice before the war ended.[11]

In late October reinforcements arrived at Murfreesboro in the form of a veteran division commanded by a former U.S. vice president. The Floridians would come to respect and admire General John C. Breckinridge, under whom they would serve for the next year and a man many had voted for in the 1860 presidential election. A Kentuckian by birth, Breckinridge was forty-one that year. A lawyer by profession and a loyal Democrat, Breckinridge served in both the Kentucky legislature and the U.S. House before being elected to the vice presidency in 1856. Dark-haired with a piercing stare and in the process of growing a handlebar moustache, the former politician had served at Shiloh and then led an unsuccessful attempt to liberate Baton Rouge. Arriving in Knoxville too late to participate in the Kentucky Campaign, the Kentuckian and his troops were dispatched to Murfreesboro by Bragg.[12]

Breckinridge absorbed the Chattanooga garrison into his division and in December his troops, part of Lieutenant General Leonidas Polk's Corps, were encamped just north of the town. The 1st and 3rd Florida, still serving with James Patton Anderson's Division in General William Hardee's Corps, were advanced west of Murfreesboro to Triune. At that location they would defend against any possible Federal attempt to flank Bragg's position. This alignment changed on December 12 when Anderson's Division was disbanded to "achieve greater numerical balance" in the Army of Tennessee's two corps. The 1st and 3rd Florida gained transfer to Breckinridge's Division and were brigaded with the 4th Florida, 20th Tennessee, and 60th North Carolina infantry regiments. The two regiments did not move to join Breckinridge at Murfreesboro, however, and remained at Hardee's position through the end of the month.[13]

Braxton Bragg assigned Brigadier General William Preston, another Kentuckian, to command this new brigade. Thin, with graying hair, the forty-seven-year-old Preston held a Harvard law degree, and after fighting in Mexico he spent the 1850s in politics. His service culminated with an appointment as President James Buchanan's ambassador to the Spanish court. A brother-in-law of Albert Sidney Johnston, Preston served on the former's staff until Johnston's death at Shiloh. The brigade was Preston's first command assignment since the evacuation of Corinth; he, like Breckinridge, would soon become a thorn in Braxton Bragg's side.[14]

The 1st and 3rd Florida and the venerable 20th Tennessee represented Preston's veteran troops. Organized during the spring of 1861, the 20th Tennessee had been bloodied at both Fishing Creek and Shiloh and had served with Breckinridge at Baton Rouge. The 60th North Carolina was a new regiment and, like the 4th Florida, had never experienced a battle. Henry T. Wright's Tennessee Battery was attached to the brigade as well.[15]

Before this reorganization, tensions between Colonel William Miller and Lieutenant Colonel Thaddeus McDonell reached a breaking point. McDonell apparently harbored resentment toward Miller for obtaining the colonelcy of the 1st
Florida. The Alachua County lawyer requested a reassignment to a military court
on December 5, saying in part, "the Regiment to which I belong is reduced in effective strength to the size of a company, and that the Colonel commanding the
Regiment although possessing good sound qualities is totally ignorant of military
tactics."[16]

The conflict was solved that month when Braxton Bragg found a place for Mc-
Donell on his staff. While the 1st Florida's numbers did not correspond with Mc-
Donell's low estimate, in November the regiment counted only 247 soldiers present; it can only be assumed that the 3rd Florida's strength was very similar as a
result of the Kentucky Campaign casualties. Other regiments in the Army of Tennessee had likewise shrunken in size, diminishing their effectiveness on the battlefield. Bragg, faced with the predicament of having many regiments severely un-
dermanned, decided to consolidate.[17]

Sometime in December the 1st and 3rd Florida were united under the overall
command of William Miller. The order, if similar to that of an edict combining
two Tennessee regiments, called for the organization of the Florida regiments "into
one organization of ten Companies," and though "the Regts and the Companies
of each Regt will be mustered for pay seperately—for all other purposes the united
Regts shall be considered one organization." The ten companies of each regiment
were likewise consolidated so that each regiment formed a battalion of five companies. Ranking commissioned and non-commissioned officers remained in place,
and excess officers became supernumeraries and were usually sent home until casualties necessitated their return to duty.[18]

The consolidation helped fasten the bond between the 1st and 3rd Florida regiments that had first developed during the Kentucky Campaign's hardships. This
union also symbolically joined the state's regions, as soldiers from all four areas
would now fight side by side under the same officers and beneath one banner.
There was little time to familiarize themselves with each other, however, for the
holiday season came on quickly and with them came the Yankees.

As Christmas approached, packages began arriving in the Floridians' camps from
family and friends. Many soldiers had written to their loved ones in October to
apprise them of the bitter conditions in Tennessee and request certain items of
clothing. Writing from Knoxville, Archie Livingston asked his mother to "please
get our woolens ready so as soon as we learn of our destination you can send on."
B. L. Rice of the 4th Florida asked for new pants, for his current pair were "badly
worn." Willie Bryant, having been transferred to the Jefferson Rifles, was certain
"a good supply [of warm clothing] will soon be sent from Monticello for the two

companies in this regmt. and I being in one come in for a share if I need any thing." Washington Ives added, "If the Ladies of Florida make up clothing for any troops I think the 4th ought to be remembered, for we nearly freeze, and do as much as any regiment now out."[19]

Reid Mitchell, in his influential work *Civil War Soldiers,* has written that volunteers "felt a particularly acute grievance when it seemed that members of their own local communities did not respect their efforts." Florida's soldiers had no reason to feel similarly during the winter of 1862–63 or at any time during the conflict for that matter. Florida's women, whether working in sewing societies or alone, put their needles and thread to work early in the war and by 1862 had produced all types of clothing. In the year after Florida's sons were dispatched to the Western Theater, her daughters "produced 3,735 pairs of cotton drawers, 2,765 cotton shirts, 169 woolen jackets and coats, 809 woolen pantaloons, and 1,000 pairs of cotton socks." The soldiers' mothers, wives, sisters, and daughters also labored in the kitchen, preparing food to send to the front; their fathers and brothers often sent pocketknives and toiletry items. This home-front patriotism served to aid all the state's soldiers and strengthened the attachment between the state's citizens and her fighting men.[20]

The packages, arriving either by express or in the hands of returning comrades, found their way to the Murfreesboro encampments in time for Christmas. The couriers and soldiers found the army preparing winter quarters and discovered that the men seemed relaxed and unconcerned about possible Union attacks. One historian has noted that "Bragg's camp hardly resembled that of an army scarcely thirty miles from a superior enemy." The army's officers held numerous parties and Major General Leonidas Polk, the former Episcopal Bishop of Louisiana, officiated at General John Hunt Morgan's wedding. Captain Jacob A. Lash, a 4th Florida company commander, wrote to his wife about a party thrown by Breckinridge's Division on Christmas Eve. He noted, "We are all invited to attend it is expected that all the Elite of the citty will be out."[21]

Most managed to find some joy that Christmas season, which for some was their first away from home. Alcohol remained popular for celebrating the holiday and as a remedy for homesickness. Near Murfreesboro, Washington Ives gained a swallow of Colonel Wylde Bowen's ginger punch. Henry T. Wright, a 1st Florida lieutenant, remembered gathering with numerous comrades on Christmas Eve and "drank 3 ½ buckets full (or empty) of nog."[22]

At Triune William D. Rogers, a sawyer in civilian life, celebrated Christmas a day early. On December 24 his new clothing arrived from home and that evening he "took a good wash all over, and next morning shaved and dressed up." He related that "everything fit the nicest you ever saw, couldn't have been made to fit any better if they had been cut by a tailor . . . I have no other clothing now except one jacket but what was made at Home." He wrote that his mess celebrated on Christmas Day by having "a first rate dinner which consisted of Bake Goose, Beef Steak, fresh Pork, sweet and Irish potatoes corn bread" and "biscuit."[23]

Packages for Benton Ellis and his brother James arrived on Christmas Day and contained clothing, shoes, and socks. The boys also received good food and promptly "invited the whole company to dine with us which they readily accepted." On Christmas night, after the soldiers had bedded down for the evening, a few ungrateful scoundrels on whom the reason for the season had been lost stole what food remained. Years later Benton would only say, "I was hurt and disgusted."[24]

Benton Ellis was fortunate to be spending the holidays among his thieving comrades. One of several thousand prisoners of war captured during the Kentucky Campaign, Ellis spent November and December returning to his regiment. The Army of the Ohio, as well as the Federal division occupying Cumberland Gap, netted stragglers along the roadside and became the keeper of Confederate sick and wounded in several Kentucky towns. Over three hundred Floridians were taken prisoner during the offensive, and most were transported to Louisville soon after their capture.[25]

In July 1862 Union and Confederate negotiators came to an agreement by which prisoners might be exchanged. Under these accords, "captured soldiers were to be paroled and sent back within ten days and were to remain out of service pursuant to the terms of their paroles until exchanged." The negotiators designated Vicksburg as the intermediary point for trading prisoners. While paroled, soldiers were not allowed to participate in any form of military activity. Confined outside Knoxville after receiving his parole, Robert Watson became disgusted with the inactivity and wrote to fellow Key West resident and Confederate secretary of the navy Stephen R. Mallory for relief. Watson related that Mallory replied, "the authorities have a right to keep us here until exchanged." Receiving a pass to visit Atlanta, Watson and a comrade went to Florida instead, determined to spend the winter in warmer climes.[26]

The Floridians captured at the height of the campaign who were well enough to travel soon reported to Louisville to be exchanged. Both Henry Reddick and Benton Ellis recalled rough treatment at the hands of the Federal guards there; Reddick said he was searched and lost everything but his clothes. Ellis remembered becoming angry after his pocketknife and tobacco were confiscated.[27]

The paroled prisoners found even worse conditions at Cairo, Illinois, where they were confined for a short time before being shipped on to Vicksburg. John Love McKinnon, captured at Harrodsburg, described the prison at the southern Illinois port as being a "low, wet place with but little shelter, cold drizzly rain, or hominy snow falling all the time, no place to make a fire to warm by . . . no blankets of any kind to sleep on." Ellis called Cairo the "dirtiest and filthiest place I ever saw." McKinnon wrote that a local Freemason took pity on Confederate members of the order and provided "a good load of blankets for us all. This was quite a treat and we blessed him."[28]

The first batch of paroled prisoners from Kentucky arrived in Vicksburg by steamer in November, and more arrived throughout the last days of fall. Samuel Harris, the 1st Florida veteran who had declared that he expected "to be a soulder the ballance of my life," had reenlisted in the 6th Florida in 1862. Captured in Lexington, Harris was suffering from a number of ailments and died a paroled prisoner on a ship bound for Vicksburg.[29]

Able-bodied prisoners such as Benton Ellis reported for duty at Murfreesboro immediately, while the wounded received furloughs home. Michael Raysor, taken at a Bardstown hospital, had not recovered sufficiently to return to duty. The Jefferson County planter spent Christmas in a Chattanooga hospital and only on December 29 was he able to return to his regiment.[30]

On the day after Christmas a cold front passed through Middle Tennessee, bringing rain and plummeting temperatures. That same day Major General William Starke Rosecrans, who replaced the bungling Don Carlos Buell as commander of the Army of the Ohio, pushed southeast from Nashville. The Lincoln administration wanted Rosecrans to attempt an early winter campaign. The president needed a boost after his fortunes had declined somewhat during the fall due to both Democratic gains in the midterm elections and the Emancipation Proclamation. By Christmas the ever-cautious Rosecrans decided the flow of supplies through Nashville was sufficient to permit a strike at Bragg's forces.[31]

Rosecrans marched the three corps of his retitled Army of the Cumberland toward Murfreesboro over separate roads, hoping to confuse Bragg as to his true intentions. Due to poor cavalry reconnaissance, Bragg was unable to determine his foe's destination for a full day. Finally, on December 27, he ordered his army to concentrate at Murfreesboro. The 1st and 3rd Florida, with Hardee's Corps at Eaglesville, broke camp and began their twenty-five-mile march early that day. The trek was undertaken, in the words of Henry T. Wright, "through mud knee deep, to say nothing of the creeks and sloughs which . . . ran across our path." William Rogers complained, "[I]t took us two days to get there the roads were so bad."[32]

Tramping into Murfreesboro on December 28, Colonel Miller's regiment found the Army of Tennessee arrayed for battle northwest of the city. Bragg's force deployed on both banks of Stones River, a narrow stream that meandered from the southwest before entering an oxbow curve that sent its flow northwest. The land on either side of the river consisted of cultivated fields and cedar groves. Breckinridge's Division was encamped just east of the river, his four brigades forming the right flank of the army. General Patrick Cleburne's men formed to Breckinridge's rear. Over the next few days Rosecrans's force slowly moved into position directly opposite Bragg's lines, the blue infantry stretching for more than two miles west from Stones River. On December 30 Bragg held a council of war at which he expressed his intention to attack the following morning. The general planned to strike at the Federal right with overwhelming force and roll it back onto Stones River. Cut off from his supply lines, and with his back against the river, Rosecrans would have to surrender. While Cleburne's Division moved to the west bank of Stones River to participate in the early morning assault, Breckinridge's troops remained in place.[33]

Before daylight the next morning, Hardee's and Polk's divisions slammed into the Federal right. Washington Ives wrote later of the morning's fight, "the fighting is . . . generall . . . and You can hear the cheering on both sides and [see] the smoke, the fighting is a mile W. of us The Cannons seem as if they never will stop." By early afternoon Bragg's army had, in the words of the novelist-historian Shelby Foote, pushed the Federal Army back "three miles . . . until now the Union line of battle resembled a half-closed jackknife, most of it being at right angles to its original position." However, the Confederates failed to seize the Nashville Pike, Rosecrans's supply route that bisected the battlefield from northwest to southeast. With his main force exhausted from the morning fighting, Bragg decided to commit his reserves in an assault directly up the Nashville Pike. A successful attack would throw the Federals into confusion and give Bragg a decisive victory. The Rebel attacks would aim at a knoll of cedars known to locals as the Round Forest.[34]

Bragg's first assaults against the Round Forest came with units of Polk's Corps, but the bishop launched the assaults in brigade strength, making them easy pickings for the Union defenders. By midday of December 31, these veteran soldiers, assisted by several artillery batteries, had repulsed two brigades of Mississippians and Tennesseans. The Rebels fell back in confusion, leaving the surrounding cotton field to their front covered with their dead and wounded.[35]

Determined to throw more troops at the salient in the afternoon, Bragg turned to his last uncommitted troops: Breckinridge's Division. Bragg had attempted to utilize these soldiers earlier in the fight, but Breckinridge had argued that he needed to address a Federal buildup on his own front and refused to release his brigades to the west bank of the river. By early afternoon Breckinridge realized no threat existed and complied with Bragg's latest order to advance two brigades to attack the Round Forest.[36]

General Breckinridge first dispatched the troops of Daniel Adams and John K. Jackson to assist in attacking the position. These units attacked around 2:00 P.M. and were slaughtered: Adams's command lost 544 men and Jackson's 303. Washington Ives explained that he had listened to the previous attacks on William B. Hazen's line and that the sounds of battle seemed "as regular and quick as touching the two lowest keys on a Piano, and the cannon are firing as fast as you can think." Just as Adams's and Jackson's men were beginning their assault, an "aid rode up to Gen Preston and I suppose ordered us into action . . . we were ordered to load. . . . Col Bowen gave us all directions about how to aim etc." The regiments "waded the River about half leg deep and Double quicked to where they were fighting." Along with General Joseph B. Palmer's troops, Preston's Brigade was about to enter the fray.[37]

While the veteran 1st and 3rd Florida and 20th Tennessee had experienced the destructiveness and confusion of battle before, the scenes of the smoky battlefield were new to the soldiers of the 4th Florida and 60th North Carolina. Washington Ives expressed horror at viewing "ambulances . . . crossing" Stones River "with the wounded, . . . a little Soldier . . . was in one of the ambulances and appeared to be hit in four or five places his back I think was broken, but he bore it like a man, except as the wagon would jolt he'd groan." As the 4th formed its line of battle Ives, looking forward to the cotton field, saw "the first dead man I had seen, lying on his back with a cannon ball hole through his breast which I could stick my head in."[38]

General Preston's Brigade was ordered to advance parallel to the Nashville Pike and directly at Hazen's Federals. The general deployed his brigade with Colonel Miller's 1st and 3rd Florida, 531 strong, on the far left; the 60th North Carolina extended the line to the east. The 4th Florida, fielding 458 soldiers and led by twenty-two-year-old Colonel Bowen and twenty-one-year-old Lieutenant Colonel Edward Badger, came next. The 20th Tennessee stood on the brigade's right flank. Ives remembered, "as soon as we were formed we marched straight forward, and then the Yankees began to play their Battery upon us."[39]

As the brigade moved to the attack Colonel Miller's 1st and 3rd Florida were taken out of the assault almost immediately. Having to realign its formation to move past a regiment that blocked its path, the 1st and 3rd Florida peeled off to the west. This meant it quickly gained the cover of a large cedar forest, but this maneuver also exposed its right flank to a severe punishment from the Union guns. The 1st and 3rd Florida reached the safety of the cedars and tried to advance beyond the forest to rejoin the attack. When severe fire forced them back, Colonel Miller contented himself with holding his position in the woods. The Perryville veterans loss included two killed, thirteen wounded, and two missing on December 31. William Rogers related that although the 1st and 3rd Florida suffered little, "every other Regt in our Brigade got into it pretty deep and suffered severely."[40]

The 4th Florida and 60th North Carolina advanced through the cotton fields just south of the Round Forest, the men stepping over the dead and wounded of the previous assaults. To their right rear sat the elevated bed of the Nashville and Chattanooga Railroad, which both had crossed. Up ahead, through the smoky haze, the Florida soldiers glimpsed the dark ruins of the Cowan House, and they could make out the picket fences that surrounded the property. The soldiers reached the Cowan House's wreckage in good order but had to break ranks to pass through the fence and did so "amid a most galling fire of grape, bomb-shell, and canister." Indeed, Captain Jerome Cox, commanding the 10th Indiana Battery, explained that by the time Preston's Brigade made its assault, his "ammunition was exhausted,

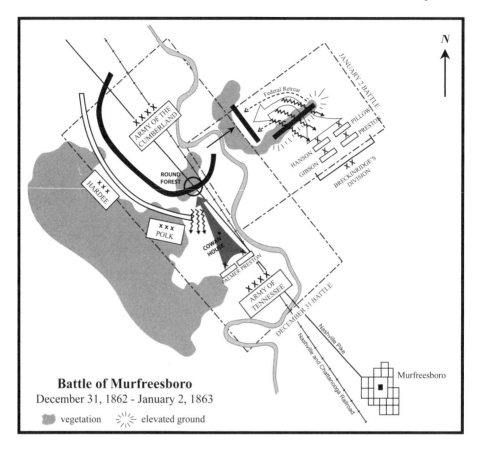

Battle of Murfreesboro
December 31, 1862 - January 2, 1863

   vegetation   elevated ground

with the exception of canister. . . . We held our fire until they were within 400 yards, when we could completely see the devices on their colors. We completely broke up their lines and scattered them in great disorder over the field in front." The 4th Florida's flag, described by an officer of the 60th North Carolina as "the largest flag I have ever seen" and with "crimson . . . so bright that it could be seen for five miles," probably drew the attention of the Yankee cannoneers.[41]

As the men passed over and around the fence in droves, companies became intermingled and officers pushed through the chaos, trying their utmost to keep order. Washington Ives complained that the 60th North Carolina "crowded us so that we were all . . . out of place an then 9 Co's of the 60th Turned an ran like sheep," contributing further to the confusion. At the same time these two regiments were falling apart while maneuvering through the Cowan House property, the 20th Tennessee faded toward the river where its men found "protection" in a "neck of wood along the river bank."[42]

Once beyond the Cowan obstacle, Colonel Bowen worked to re-form the 4th

Florida's line and then someone gave the order to fire. As the regiment threw a few scattered volleys at the Yankees, Ives watched fellow Company C soldier John McKinney fall with a piece of metal through his throat. McKinney "fell on [Ives's] feet and the blood spirted in a stream about as large as my forefingers, poor fellow, he could not speak though, but grabbed at the wound and tried to raise up." A shell fragment partially dismembered the left foot of color guard member Seth Osborne. W. M. Jones, a 4th Florida soldier, wrote that Osborne "sat up, took out his pocket knife and cutting off his foot which was held by a muscle, he crawled back of the line."[43]

Observing the 4th Florida's punishment at the hands of this unleashed violence and realizing the madness of remaining as targets for the Union artillery, a mounted General Preston braved the intense fire and rode toward the regiment's color-bearer. Seizing the banner, the old politician yelled over the din, "Forward Fourth Florida!" and made his way toward the woods where the 1st and 3rd Florida had found protection. The 4th Florida and the remaining 60th North Carolina soldiers followed. As Preston rode beneath one of the cedars, a branch knocked the flag from his grip. Color Sergeant William Jackson was following Preston closely; he picked up the dropped banner and exclaimed, "General, command me. I will carry the flag wherever you wish." Their adrenaline pumping, their faces darkened by powder, the Floridians and North Carolinians could breathe more easily after reaching the forest. Save for some sporadic firing, this last advance ended the first day's fighting at Murfreesboro.[44]

In their first fight, the untried 4th Florida had been asked to assault a heavily defended position that veteran troops had failed to reach in three previous attempts. The Cowan House property had sowed confusion in the ranks as the troops tried to pass through the yard and around outbuildings and then re-form. The Union batteries played havoc on the regiment from the moment the attack began, particularly as it tried to rally after the period of disorganization. The failed assault saw six killed, fifty wounded, and a single soldier missing. Preston's Brigade lost a total of 163 during the December 31 attack on the Round Forest. The survivors, their trousers wet from crossing Stones River, bedded down for an uncomfortable New Year's Eve among the dead of both armies.[45]

With the coming darkness, the temperatures sank; as the lines remained close together the commanders allowed no fires. On top of this discomfort, the soldiers had dropped their knapsacks and blankets before going into action. Washington Ives wrote that the 4th "broke Ranks to sleep on arms, but it was very little sleeping that any of us did for I like to have died of Cold, my teeth chattered all night we did not have our blankets and the ground was . . . frozen." W. M. Jones remembered that "I was nearly frozen as I lay on the ground that night among the dead." William Rogers complained that "we had a cold time for we were too close to the enemy's lines to have a fire and it was freezing weather."[46]

As the soldiers shivered beneath the cedars at midnight, 1862 passed quietly into 1863. The previous year had begun with high hopes, with the Floridians guarding their state's coast. Over the previous twelve months they had witnessed the Federal occupation of portions of their state, become combat veterans, and hardened themselves to the rigors of soldiering. On the night of December 31, most soldiers were more concerned with their present predicament than worried about the future. Little did they realize that 1863 would bring hardship and death; neither would help bring the conflict to a close.

Braxton Bragg believed that 1863 would dawn with a Confederate victory. On New Year's Eve, the Army of Tennessee pushed the Federal line back to within sight of the Nashville Pike but could not seize the vital roadway. Cavalry intelligence led the commanding general to believe Rosecrans was preparing to retreat. However, when it appeared the Army of the Cumberland would remain on the battlefield, Bragg faltered; Thomas Connelly surmised that "Bragg's entire strategy for Murfreesboro had been to force Rosecrans to retreat in a single day's action. . . . Evidently he had prepared no plans in case there should be a second day's battle." At a meeting of his corps commanders early on January 1, Rosecrans had decided to remain in position. Throughout the day "sharpshooters harassed the enemy's pickets, and there were sporadic exchanges of artillery, a few of them rather fiercely contested."[47]

On the morning of January 1, the Floridians awoke to the welcome news that they could build fires; later, a detachment brought their blankets over from the opposite bank of the river. Yet Federal artillery batteries threw rounds into the forest throughout the day, making life uncomfortable for the Floridians. The exploding shells brought severed cedar branches down on the soldiers and wounded two 4th Florida men. Lieutenant Seaborn Harris, who had declared the previous May he would serve no longer under Colonel Edward Hopkins, could finally stand no more. Walking to the edge of the wood, Harris stood defiantly in the open while he lit "a straw in a stump hole on fire with which to light his pipe." As he did so, a shell fragment passed through his coat, missing the dauntless officer by inches. Harris pulled up his coat and, peering through the hole at the Yankee lines, exclaimed, "'I will make you pay for that.'"[48]

The Floridians remained on the west bank of Stones River until 2:00 P.M. on January 2. The previous day a portion of Lieutenant General Polk's Corps advanced into the Round Forest, which Rosecrans had abandoned to shorten his line. Now, Bragg feared that Federal troops on the Stones River's east bank would rain artillery fire down on Polk's exposed position. The general believed that he needed to eliminate this threat and called upon Breckinridge, whose division had suffered less than any other on December 31, to make the assault.[49]

Breckinridge immediately launched a protest, claiming "he was certain Rosecrans was heavily placed on the bluff on the side of the river opposite the proposed line of attack. The ground was higher than his, and his artillery could hit him in front and flank, turning the attack into disaster." The commanding general could not be swayed from his decision and ordered the Kentuckian to attack at 4:00 P.M. General Polk would initiate the attack fifteen minutes earlier by placing artillery fire on the Federal position. Bragg, the old artilleryman that he was, ordered Breckinridge's artillery to assume an offensive role as well, following the infantry into battle to support the attack.[50]

At 2:00 P.M. Preston's Brigade left the cedar forest that had sheltered the men for the previous two days and countermarched to the Stones River's east bank. There, Breckinridge formed his division into two lines. Like their division commander, none of Breckinridge's brigade commanders possessed professional military training; each had practiced law before the war. Brigadier General Roger Hanson's Kentucky Brigade, which would gain fame during the conflict as one of the Confederacy's best, took position in the front line. Gideon Pillow, a political general and Mexican-American War veteran with a poor service record, aligned his Tennesseans next to Hanson's troops. The brigade of Colonel Randal Gibson, who was serving in place of the wounded Daniel Adams, and Preston's men formed ranks two hundred yards to their comrades' rear.[51]

At the appointed time, Breckinridge's 4,500-man division began their attack; Benton Ellis recollected that the divisional commander rode down Preston's line "and made a speech to us and told us to keep good order and charge like men." Their advance would take them through open fields toward the ridge on which Colonel Sam Beatty's 2,000 Federal troops waited. Beatty's line, its right flank resting on the Stones River, stretched northeast along the ridge. The Kentuckians and Pillow's Tennesseans quickly overran the Federal line, forcing the Yankees back in confusion. As the Confederates streamed over the ridge, hell exploded in their faces. The historian Larry Daniel writes that John Mendenhall, the Army of the Cumberland's artillery chief, gathered fifty-seven guns on the western bank of the river; soon the gunners were firing with a rapid pace at Breckinridge's soldiers.[52]

William Rogers confessed that the battle was so terrible that he never wanted "to go into another such a fight as long as I live." The Confederates pursued the retreating Federals through the heavy artillery fire; their objective was now McFadden's Ford where the enemy was crossing the river. Overhead, shells flew from Breckinridge's artillery, which had taken position on the ridge to the soldiers' rear and began an unequal contest with the massed Federal guns. In addition, to Breckinridge's right a brigade of Federals remained on the east bank, firing into the Rebels' flank. As the units approached the river, Miller's 1st and 3rd Florida became intermingled with Pillow's men, while the 4th Florida lay prone and waited as the first line engaged the enemy.[53]

Under the cover of the artillery fire, numerous Union brigades counterattacked across the river. The Kentuckians, with their commander Roger Hanson mortally wounded, fell back in the face of this onslaught and Pillow's troops gave way as well. W. M. Jones reported "the Fourth Florida was lying down when the other regiments passed back over it." Colonel Bowen wrote that only after the regiments ahead of the 4th Florida retreated did the men fire "with that deliberate accuracy that characterizes the Florida woodsman." The Tennessee native explained that he "determined to hold as long as practicable, that if possible, we might form a nucleus upon which to rally the broken line."[54]

The 1st and 3rd Florida remained in line as well, firing at the advancing Federals. Lieutenant Albert Livingston, another of the Madison County brothers, attested that the fighting on the banks of the Stones River was "much nearer . . . than at Perryville [and] at one time [the lines] were only about 40 or 50 yards apart." Benton Ellis wrote that as the 1st and 3rd Florida troops tried to stem the tide, he "heard a ball strike some of the boys. . . . It was dear boy Jimmie that received that bullet in his right groin; but he said nothing but kept shooting." Eighteen-year-old James Light Ellis collapsed soon after; he was captured and died in a Federal field hospital on January 19.[55]

On line with the 4th Florida, the regiment's color-bearer, William T. Jackson, suffered a wound in the left shoulder that thereafter limited the use of his left arm. The regiment's banner was raised by three other men, all of whom successively fell either killed or wounded. Finally, John A. Mathis seized the flag and carried it to safety. Washington Ives related, "[T]he nearest the Yankees came to getting me was shooting a hole in my pants and cutting hair off my right temple." Although men were falling all around him, the young Columbia County man wrote that he "did not feel any different while under fire than I do at any kind of work. I took 20 deliberate shots picking my man every time, and one time I saw the man fall, but the others I could not see on account of the smoke."[56]

Some soldiers in the 4th Florida expended their forty rounds that afternoon on the river; Ives fired twenty times using a .69 smoothbore that "got so dirty that I had to tear Cartridge and wet every load of Buck and Ball." W. M. Jones got off eighteen rounds before the regiment began to fall back. The firing was so heavy from both sides that Albert Livingston exclaimed, "[I]t did not look as if one would Escape."[57]

As the Yankee counterattack became too much for the Floridians and their comrades, a retreat to the rear began. Benton Ellis explained that the 1st and 3rd Florida "made several stands" as they retreated up the ridge and down the opposite slope. Fleeing as fast as his feet would carry him, William Rogers confessed that when the withdrawal began "I was badly scared my back itched the whole time, But thank God I escaped untouched."[58]

Passing over the ridge, Colonel Bowen came upon Wright's Tennessee Battery then commanded by Lieutenant John W. Mebane. The battery had remained to cover the retreat of the division and soon the enemy had closed within deadly range. As twilight came on, young Bowen rallied his soldiers around the guns and sought to buy time for the artillerymen to limber their pieces. The colonel wrote that while protecting the battery, his "command sustained its heaviest loss." Ives estimated that the 4th Florida held its ground for fifteen minutes, allowing the Tennesseans to move their guns to safety. When the regiment was ordered to fall back, the Yankees "were in 40 yds of its left and 85 [yards] of its center." Left near the battery's former position was the mortally wounded Seaborn Harris, who had vowed to pay the Yankees back for his ruined coat. He, like James Ellis, died at a Federal hospital.[59]

Major John Lesley of the 4th Florida asserted in his report that when his regiment finally retreated it was "the last to leave the field." Washington Ives substantiated this claim, writing home that "the 4th was the last on the field and few as it was it kept back about 40 times its number of Yankees until the other confed regts had got out of the most danger." The Federals continued to fire on the Rebels as they broke for the safety of their own line. Running for his life, Washington Ives halted suddenly "as a man right ahead of me got his brains shot out and I was so close behind him that if I had not stopped I'd have fallen on his body." General Preston managed to rally his brigade near the unit's original position to resist the Yankee advance, but darkness was falling fast and the pursuit soon ended.[60]

That evening the regiments mustered for roll call to determine the casualties suffered during the disastrous attack. The 1st and 3rd Florida numbered 456 officers and men for the January 2 fight; 5 were killed outright and 73 were wounded. Colonel William Miller was numbered among the latter, as he had suffered a severe hand wound. William Rogers wrote that the colonel suffered the loss of a thumb and was furloughed home to Florida to recuperate. The injury ended Miller's tenure with the 1st and 3rd Florida. Forty-one soldiers were listed as missing, but most of these, like James Ellis, had been too badly wounded to retreat and were left on the field. The total losses for both days' combat were 138 of the 531 soldiers present for duty on December 31.

Murfreesboro served to effectively decimate the 4th Florida Infantry. The second day's action cost the lives of 28 soldiers; 79 sustained wounds during the seventy-minute fight. Thirty were missing that evening, bringing the number of casualties suffered that day to 137. B. L. Rice would never need the pants he requested from his mother, for he was one of those mortally wounded on January 2. Of the 458 who formed for battle on December 31, 194 were either killed or wounded. Among Breckinridge's 19 regiments engaged that day, the 4th Florida suffered the most killed and the second-highest number of casualties. The regiment never fielded more than 300 soldiers in a fight again.[61]

On the morning of January 3, Braxton Bragg decided to retreat from Murfreesboro, and that evening his troops marched south. Lieutenant Augustus McDonell penned in his diary, "It was rainy yesterday when we started back and it continued

raining the wind blowing very hard all night—marched twenty miles through it."
William Rogers, who retreated from Shiloh and Perryville, informed his parents
with disgust that Murfreesboro was "called a drawn battle, but I think we were
whipped." Washington Ives, who passed through his first trial by fire at Murfreesboro, disagreed, arguing "Our Army is not whipped, we killed more Yank's than
they did Conf[ederate]s but we were worn out." At any rate, Albert Livingston was
correct when he soberly told his mother, "Many of our brave men were killed at
the fight near Murfreesboro our company and regiments mourns the loss of their
very best." Preston's Brigade reached Tullahoma on January 7, and in that vicinity
the Army of Tennessee halted.[62]

By January the Floridians in both Bragg's and Kirby Smith's armies were in
winter quarters. The 1st and 3rd Florida and 4th Florida regiments had suffered irreplaceable casualties at Murfreesboro, but the latter regiment's green soldiers were
now veterans and Colonel Wylde Bowen and Lieutenant Colonel Ed Badger had
gained valuable combat leadership experience. The 1st and 3rd Florida lost its experienced colonel in the fight and would soon be commanded again by Colonel
William Dilworth, who had yet to endure the horrors of battle. There was no joy
as the soldiers pitched their tents; Washington Ives described the soldiers as "worn
out and down hearted." Daniel G. McLean in the 1st Florida explained, "I never
think of peace now." At its outset, 1863 looked glum for the Floridians in the
Western Theater. Soon, however, nature's cycle would cause winter to give way to
spring: the snow would melt, the roads would harden, and a new campaigning
season would begin.[63]

10 I Expect We Will Stay Here All Winter

Winter–Spring 1863, Tennessee

In the week following the Murfreesboro battle, Braxton Bragg shepherded his battered Army of Tennessee southeastward, away from the scene of carnage. William Rosecrans's Army of the Cumberland, occupied with burying the dead and tending to the wounded of both armies, was in no condition to pursue. General Bragg halted the retreat within the Highland Rim, "an oval belt of steep ridges" that surrounds Middle Tennessee. The northern edge of this geographical feature "contains a broad series of ridges which reach elevations of thirteen hundred feet"; Bragg chose this location not only because it appeared easily defensible but also because of the rich Duck and Elk river valleys that lay within the sheltered region. The general planned to allow his troops to live off the area's foodstuffs that winter. Bragg made the railroad town of Tullahoma his headquarters and General William Hardee's Corps encamped nearby. Soon after the army established their quarters, Daniel McLean informed a relative: "I expect we will stay here all winter, if we are not run off by the yankees."[1]

The beginning of 1863 found the Department of East Tennessee's soldiers deployed along the vital railroad that snaked through the valley in a generally southwest to northeast direction. With terrible weather making a crossing of the Cumberland Mountains by a large number of troops impossible, the Federals in Kentucky posed little threat to the Confederates. Yet that winter the Rebels would find trouble in the form of East Tennessee Unionists and deserters.

The winter of 1862–63 was the first that the Florida regiments spent away from their home state. Whether performing manual labor at Tullahoma or scouring Appalachian hollows for Tories, these troops remained active that winter. Also, respite from Union threats allowed the regiments to hone their discipline, and all spent countless hours on the drill field. For General W.G.M. Davis's Brigade, the months saw two critical command changes, and the majority of the 6th and 7th Florida's soldiers underwent their baptism by fire on the outskirts of Knoxville. Although the winter lull halted most major military operations, the Florida soldiers found the hiatus provided no break from the rigors of soldiering.

General William J. Hardee's eleven thousand soldiers limped into Tullahoma during the second week of January following a strenuous march through harsh weather. In other winter quarters during the war, troops constructed crude cabins to escape the elements; at Tullahoma the Floridians lived in their tents. The soldiers fashioned makeshift chimneys to help warm their scant dwellings; seasonable storms that swept through the area brought rain, falling temperatures, and snow. Lieutenant Henry Wright marveled at the climate's "changeableness, last week it was so cold that creeks were all frozen and snow covered the ground. Today it is so warm that even a light coat is . . . apprehensive." Francis Nicks of the 3rd Florida complained, "[T]his is the worst country I ever saw in my life it rains all the time and when it ain't raining it is snowing." Daniel McLean declared that the worst part about the wetness was that "the ground gets so muddy."[2]

By the time the Army of Tennessee entered its winter encampment at Tulla-homa, the troops had long since devoured the provisions that had arrived at Mur-freesboro in time for Christmas. Therefore, the Floridians' primary fare that winter consisted of army rations, meaning "Fresh pork, meal occasionally a little molas-ses and salt." McLean lamented the quality of the meals, remembering that "[w]hen we were on the march we could occasionally get a chicken or Irish potatoes, Turkey, or something of the sort and make a little change." Florida's citizens, how-ever, continued to support their soldiers in the field; McLean, who was from West Florida, pointed out that "some of the fellows from East Fla, get any quantity of . . . eadibles from home." Washington Ives wrote home that "I long for fish birds and oysters I could almost shed tears I wanted some so bad, and Eggs." Ives asked his parents "to raise as many chickens and Gardens in Fla as is possible" to supply the state's soldiers, for he avowed that it was "camp fare that is killing off . . . many good soldiers."[3]

During the Middle Tennessee encampment the number of men who became ill steadily rose; the Army of Tennessee's hospitals recorded 137,000 patients dur-ing the first five months of 1863. McLean, who served as an orderly in the 1st and 3rd Florida's hospital, noted that "we average 4 to 5 a day sent to the Hospit. gen-erally have Pneumonia." This was not uncommon, as this disease "prevailed to the greatest extent in the more elevated and northern regions of the Southern Con-federacy, and in the armies which were subjected to the severest labors, privations, exposures." The Army of Tennessee's soldiers were certainly subjected to exposure at Tullahoma, not to mention the fact that they had just endured the Murfrees-boro Campaign. When the 1st and 3rd Florida shifted their camp to a muddy, bare field in early February, Lieutenant Augustus McDonell bemoaned, "We had sickness enough before the change, but I'm confident it will . . . double."[4]

In the weeks following the Murfreesboro retreat, Washington Ives told his par-ents, "I am poor, being reduced by sickness." Ives's ailments included a severe cold and jaundice, but he found that his sickness strengthened his bonds with his com-rades. The young man related that his messmate, Sam Sessions, "has acted a broth-ers part by me in my sickness." Though his condition improved briefly at the end of January, in February Ives was confined to a Georgia hospital. Obtaining a fur-lough, he would not return to his regiment until July. Another soldier, Benton Ellis, mourning his brother's death and suffering from an attack of acute rheumatism, also spent several weeks in a hospital.[5]

Another casualty of the sickness that swept through the Tullahoma camps that winter was Lieutenant Colonel Lucius Church. The Madison County officer resigned his commission in early February, claiming to "have been afflicted with a Rheumatic affliction which . . . has totally disqualified me from exercising the duties of my Office." Upon Church's departure, Edward Mashburn became lieutenant colonel of the 1st and 3rd Florida.[6]

Near Cumberland Gap in November, General Davis's 1,800 soldiers with no tents and poor clothing, endured the elements at their worst. Although the Confederates knew they needed to guard the strategic pass, the Floridians wished they could depart the mountains before winter arrived. Early in the month, 6th Florida private A. G. McLeod wrote, "[O]ne thing I know, if we are stationed anywhere up here many will not survive the winter. The Snow was six inches deep here last Saturday and Sunday." Colonel J. J. Finley, dissatisfied with his regiment's station, pleaded with Adjutant General Samuel Cooper for help: "[W]e are now here without tents and without axes and tools for building huts—and I really wish an easier and less exposed service for my poor men." Major William T. Stockton reported "all heart & interest in the Regt. is departed. We seem to be dumped down here, without tents, food almost, cooking utensils . . . feed for our horses." Lieutenant Colonel Robert Bullock found Cumberland Gap disagreeable because he felt it "out of the world as far as Civilization and society are concerned."[7]

During the first week of December the Floridians received the welcome order that moved the regiments southwest to Knoxville, the "metropolis of East Tennessee." The forty-five-mile march to Knoxville was one of the roughest endured by Davis's soldiers during the entire war. As told by the Marion Hornets poet: "at morn the road was icy hard,/ 'Twas slippery mud at noon,/ Each must his steps with care regard,/ Or muddied he was soon." Lieutenant James Hays confessed to his wife, "[I]t was the worst traveling I ever saw . . . you don't know anything about cold weather." Lieutenant Colonel Bullock wrote: "I have read about soldiers of the Revolution being tracked in the snow by the blood that came from their bare feet, but I always thought it was an exaggeration; but I am now convinced that it was true, for I saw on the march from the Gap here, any quantity of blood that came from the feet of the men who had no shoes . . . their feet so badly cut up by the rocks and frozen ground."[8]

A principal threat to Confederate forces in the East Tennessee Valley in 1863 came from loyal Tennesseans' active resistance. However, the region's Unionists had not always advocated violence toward the Rebels. In fact, following the 1860 presidential election and the Lower South's secession, these citizens had followed a moderate approach in opposing a government in which they believed only a few would hold power. Pressed on by dynamic and earnest leaders such as William

G. "Parson" Brownlow, the population's conservative element believed that East Tennessee's elitists, along with "demagogues from lordly cotton plantations had brought on the conflict and, in the Confederacy, were creating the aristocracy they had long desired." Brownlow preached to his followers that in the Confederacy "only slaveholders would be allowed to vote."[9]

By no means were East Tennesseans abolitionists. Many were, like Brownlow, in favor of the institution. The difference between the East Tennesseans and pro-slavery Southerners in the cotton states was that the region's ex-Whigs "still believed it possible to protect slavery within the Union." Before Fort Sumter's fall, four-fifths of the region's voters cast their ballot against a proposed secession convention. East Tennessee's votes, combined with moderates from across the state, doomed that measure to failure.[10]

However, after the Confederates fired on Fort Sumter and President Lincoln ordered the loyal states to provide seventy-five thousand volunteers to put down the rebellion, the Tennessee legislature "approved a declaration of independence from the United States." When Tennessee's voters approved this step on June 9, East Tennessee conservatives met in Greeneville on June 17, where instead of advocating the use of violence to throw off Confederate rule they dispatched a committee to "present a memorial to the Tennessee legislature requesting that East Tennessee and the Unionist counties of Middle Tennessee be allowed to form a separate state." The legislature turned down this offer because of the vital railroad that passed through the region.[11]

During the early summer of 1861, Confederate authorities adopted a lenient attitude toward the Unionists and refused to station many troops in the region. In August, however, reinforcements moved into the area and East Tennessee's Confederate district attorney charged more than one hundred local citizens under the newly passed Alien Enemies Act. The final breaking point came in November when, in anticipation of a Union invasion, East Tennessee Tories burned five railroad bridges between Chattanooga and Bristol. After Confederate soldiers carried out a harsh retaliation against those suspected of participating in the burnings, the violence increased as "Unionists would operate in smaller-bands, seek limited objectives, and rely on the weapons of ambush, harassment, and intimidation to achieve their purposes." Into this whirlwind were thrust Davis's Floridians.[12]

The historian Noel Fisher has written that "a favorite tactic was to snipe at marching Confederate troops from the sides of narrow, wooded roads." Davis's Brigade first encountered these guerillas as the regiments marched through the Cumberland Mountains during the Kentucky Campaign. Lieutenant James Hays explained that the 7th Florida marched into an ambush five miles from Barboursville, Kentucky. Lieutenant Colonel Bullock wrote that when his regiment recovered from the initial shock of the attack they killed five bushwhackers and captured twenty-two. The 1st Florida Cavalry, Dismounted, also suffered at the hands of the insurgents, as William Stockton reported his regiment's early losses in the march as "one killed & 4 wounded." "We, the Southern Army," Stockton explained, "was presented as cruel & brutal. Robbers was the best name we received."[13]

Though the winter weather precluded an invasion by a sizable Union force, this did not stop small-scale Federal raids from exacting a toll on the region. In late December a thousand blue-clad cavalrymen emerged from the Cumberland Mountains and wreaked havoc upon several trestles and munitions depots in the extreme northeastern tip of the state. Davis's Florida Brigade, due to this incursion and the continued Unionist menace, spent the winter dispersed along the railroad, charged with guarding its essential bridges.[14]

General Davis and newly promoted colonel G. Troup Maxwell's 1st Florida Cavalry, Dismounted, encamped at Strawberry Plains, a depot fifteen miles northeast of Knoxville that gained importance because of the nearby 1,600-foot Holston River bridge. The majority of Colonel Finley's 6th Florida was stationed at Strawberry Plains as well. However, the 6th Florida's Company H engaged in "building a stockade and guarding the Hiawassee Bridge" near Charleston on the East Tennessee and Georgia Railroad. Private A. G. McLeod enjoyed the time his company spent at this pleasant community, writing, "[W]e have been invite[d] to a party one or two nights every week since we came here."[15]

Seven 7th Florida companies were bivouacked ten miles from the Virginia border, where the soldiers stood a watchful sentinel over the Watauga River bridge, one of the spans burned during the December raid and had since been rebuilt. Casmero Bailey delighted in being stationed in a region where "we have butter eggs chickens and etc." Meanwhile, Captain Samuel Darwin McConnell commanded a three-company battalion that guarded Loudon, a town thirty miles southwest of Knoxville. McConnell's three companies were dispatched to this new posting a week before Christmas. Though McConnell was proud to have been chosen to command at such a vital location, the captain confided that he would "prefer the pleasure of seeing my wife and child to all such compliments."[16]

By January 1863 the conflict between the Confederates and the Tories reached a viciousness previously not witnessed in the Appalachians. Though General Davis and his Floridians spent much time building stockades and blockhouses to safeguard the railroad, they also became embroiled in this rancorous conflict that winter. Evidence regarding the full degree to which the Floridians were involved remains sketchy. However, it is safe to say that these troops did create some hardships for the region's Unionists.

Perhaps the most infamous incident to emerge from the Appalachian conflict remains the Shelton Laurel Massacre. Confederate deserters and Unionists set in motion a series of events on January 8 when a party raided Marshall, North Carolina, searching for salt. This preservative was needed during the winter months when residents cured meat for the next year. A severe shortage of salt in the winter of 1863 caused it to be "hoarded by the loyal Rebels and kept from the hands of the poor rural mountaineers suspected of Union sympathies." Lieutenant James Hays wrote that "some of the citizens came down to Knoxville and reported how they were doing and asked for help," and on January 17, General Henry Heth, then commanding the Department of East Tennessee, dispatched General Davis into North Carolina to investigate.[17]

General Davis's force included two hundred Floridians, as well as the 64th North Carolina and Colonel William Thomas's Legion; the latter two units contained soldiers native to the Great Smoky Mountains. Departing from Strawberry Plains, the expedition had but a short march before reaching the French Broad Turnpike, which passed directly through the troubled area. Lieutenant Hays recorded that upon leaving, General Davis had remarked "that he never would take a prisoner, so I guess they will fair rough if they come up with them." Davis would soon come to rue these words, if he indeed spoke them. The former lawyer used a softer language in his official orders to his subordinate commanders, requesting them to "pursue and arrest every man in the mountains, of known bad character." The general gave explicit instructions for "all the citizen prisoners to be turned over to the civil authorities of Madison [County]."[18]

General Davis established his headquarters at the antebellum resort town of Warm Springs and began examining the evidence. He quickly concluded that "there is no organization in the mountains of armed men banded together for the purpose of making efforts to destroy bridges or to burn towns" and that "the attack on Marshall was gotten up to obtain salt, for want of which there is great suffering in the mountains. Plunder of other property followed as a matter of course." However, the situation grew steadily worse because the raiders directed some of this plundering at the homes of soldiers serving in the 64th North Carolina, including that of its colonel, Lawrence Allen. The historian Phillip Shaw Paludan asserts that General Heth provided explicit instructions to the 64th, saying, "'I want no reports from you about your course at Laurel. I do not want to be troubled with any prisoners and the last one of them should be killed.'" Using harsh methods of interrogation, Allen's Tarheels rounded up fifteen suspects and several days later executed them.[19]

General Davis and his Floridians remained near Greeneville, Tennessee, and Warm Springs, North Carolina, for the majority of the operation, and it is unclear as to whether the commander knew of the 64th North Carolina's transgressions. Davis wrote at the time that "Col. Allen's Sixty-fourth North Carolina Regiment and the men of his command are said to have been hostile to the Laurel men," but this probably refers to the bad blood that existed among the regions' citizens regarding the battle over secession. In February, after North Carolina governor Zebulon Vance learned of the massacre and demanded an inquiry, Davis explained that he knew "nothing of the facts, the transaction having taken place before I was placed in command of the troops operating in North Carolina." He was in command of the expedition at the time but probably still at Greeneville sifting through evidence when the massacre occurred. Because Davis's wartime papers have not survived, the Florida general's role in the Shelton Laurel Massacre may never be known. It is likely that Allen followed Heth's orders and that Davis knew nothing of these instructions.[20]

The January expedition marked one of two times that winter that the Floridians penetrated the Great Smoky Mountains in search of Unionists. In late February, General Alfred E. Jackson, commanding in place of an absent General Davis, led a brigade-sized unit into western North Carolina to forcibly remove Tories and their families. General Davis had suggested this policy in January, writing to Governor Vance: "I have proposed to allow all who are not implicated in any crime to leave the State and to aid them in crossing into Kentucky. . . . They will be driven to do so from necessity, as I learn our troops have consumed all the corn and meat in the settlement. If the people alluded to agree to emigrate I will cause them to be paid for their property used by our troops."[21]

General Jackson's troops, which included elements of the 6th Florida and 1st Florida Cavalry, Dismounted, set out from Limestone Depot on the Virginia and Tennessee Railroad and entered the mountains in three columns, each converging on the country north of Asheville. The expedition traversed treacherous terrain, and the march coincided with some of the worst weather to hit the region that winter. Dr. Henry McCall Holmes, an assistant surgeon in the 1st Florida Cavalry, Dismounted, accompanied his regiment and wrote on March 1, "it commenced snowing and sleeting . . . the sleet cut & struck our faces, was very cold." These poor conditions occurred while the soldiers had "some steep and difficult ascents to make, a horse could not have gone where we went indeed a cat would have thought it a hard trip." Lieutenant Hugh Black remarked that "the last day of February and the first day of March I did the hardest traveling and traveled the shortest distance that I ever did in my life."[22]

Holmes wrote that the Confederates swept through the region "hunting bushwackers [sic] as the Tories there are called" and implemented Davis's policy of removal. Lieutenant Charles Herring wrote that the 6th Florida "caught several & burned and destroied every thing in the mountains as we went, collected the families & sent them out. The girles would curs and blagardeuss ahead of any thing I ever heard befor." A 6th Florida company clerk recorded that his unit "made a march of twenty-one miles over the mountains" and on March 8 arrived at Strawberry Plains. Despite these efforts, the Confederates would never quell Unionist sentiment in the North Carolina mountains. As the expedition neared its conclusion, General Daniel Donelson, then commanding the Department of East Tennessee, noted that General Davis's command "is necessarily in a scattered and bad condition."[23]

While Davis's troops chased bushwhackers and stood sentinel over the East Tennessee railroad, the Floridians in Bragg's Army of Tennessee remained equally active. They spent their days erecting breastworks and fortifications and tramping across muddy drill fields. These soldiers had not cared for either activity during the first year of the war and their attitude had not changed.[24]

Francis R. Nicks, who served in the 3rd Florida, wrote home that his regiment was continuously "building batteries and shoving breastworks up and cutting hammock preparing to have a fight." Lieutenant Augustus McDonell complained that this labor came before everything, including worship. McDonell recorded that on one Sunday morning, as the 1st and 3rd Florida slogged through water that was sometimes waist deep, the troops came across General Hardee. The corps commander took pity on his soldiers and allowed them to take the day off. McDonell wrote that the soldiers "could not resist the temptation to hollow" and their yells "echoed over hill and valley as they marched back to camp on double quick time." Private William Rogers assured his father that "if old Rosy runs afoul of us here behind our breastworks which extends about ten miles he is certainly gone under."[25]

Larry Daniel has noted that at Tullahoma, the Army of Tennessee "underwent a period of intensive refresher training and refinement of skills." Rogers wrote that his consolidated company was detailed as sharpshooters and "drill every day in Skirmish Drill. I like the drill very well but I don't know whether I will like the mode of fighting." Samuel Pasco, who returned from Florida in February with his regiment's absentees, wrote that the 1st and 3rd Florida held target practice during the winter hiatus. In addition to drilling their soldiers, the officers used some of their spare time to review various manuals in order to remain sharp regarding maneuvers. Roddie Shaw, who enlisted in the 4th Florida in the fall of 1862, held the rank of sergeant major in his regiment. He hoped one day to become a commissioned officer, writing, "day after day I sit under my fly . . . studying tactics, . . . I have to study very hard to go through on Battalion drill, and should I ever be promoted I will have use for it in passing the proper examination."[26]

The soldiers' sweat and hard work on the drill field paid off on March 23 when General John Breckinridge held a review of his division for Generals Hardee and Polk. Part of the ceremony included a contest to determine Breckinridge's finest regiment. The 1st and 3rd Florida, ably led by Lieutenant Colonel Edward Mashburn, represented Preston's Brigade and was defeated by the 18th Tennessee. The Volunteer State's soldiers flawlessly executed a bayonet charge and then all, including the colonel's horse, fell to the ground as if evading an enemy volley.[27]

When General William Preston's soldiers had any leisure time, they found various activities to amuse themselves. Samuel Pasco, who, as the 1st and 3rd Florida's regimental clerk, remained occupied with paperwork during the days, relaxed in the evenings by playing euchre with the officers. Many soldiers spent their days in the forests near camp hunting squirrel, rabbit, and other small game. Lieutenant

Henry Wright enjoyed the yields of these excursions, remembering that his rations were supplemented by "'Squirrel Gumbo.'" At the Tullahoma encampment, the soldiers gained much enjoyment from games of town ball. William Rogers closed a letter to his parents by confessing he was stopping to "join the Boys in a game of Ball which has become a great amusement here." Roddie Shaw wrote that baseball fever had swept through his regiment: "while I write the Regt. is engaged in a game of town-ball one of our greatest sources of amusement."[28]

Floridians in both Middle and East Tennessee also began attending religious services with more frequency. Revivals occurred in all of the Confederacy's armies that winter and spring. While this spiritual awakening had positive effects on the troops, there were those among the Florida regiments who failed to see the need for divine guidance and redemption.[29]

Civil War historians seem to agree that the revivals of 1863 occurred as a result of the increased bloodletting of 1862 and the availability of religious literature. Bell Wiley has claimed that renewed interest in religion developed among the Confederates because "the wearers in gray came from communities where the church was fervid, aggressive, and influential, and where revivals were common." The missionaries who visited the armies during these months also helped spark the soldiers' interest in religion.[30]

Missionaries were necessary because, as Larry Daniel estimates, at the Middle Tennessee encampment "there were four or five brigades without a single chaplain, and the army barely averaged one per brigade." This statistic does not include the Florida regiments at Tullahoma, for very active chaplains served both the 1st and 3rd Florida and 4th Florida soldiers. Both Samuel Pasco and Washington Ives mentioned that their respective regimental chaplains, William J. Duval and Robert L. Wiggins, regularly held Sunday services. In East Tennessee, however, the soldiers relied on traveling preachers because both the 6th and 7th Florida's regimental chaplains resigned in April 1863.[31]

By May the Florida regiments' revivalism was in full swing; Michael Raysor wrote home, "[W]e have preaching every Sunday morning & evening and night & every night during the week, they are three or four preachers & among them is Mr. Wiggins that was at the camp meeting in Jefferson County. . . . The spirit of the Lord has come to our Regt at last & hope the work may continue." First and 3rd Florida lieutenant Augustus Tippins applauded "a fine Sermon Preached by the Chaplin of the 4th Fla. the text was (O that there was one heart that would keep all my commandments allways) I thought it was a beautiful foundation."[32]

The revival in the Department of East Tennessee began in the spring as well, the inevitability of which might be gleaned from Lieutenant Hugh Black. He explained that at Strawberry Plains "we have a good opportunity for embracing religion, but there is few who avail themselves of this opportunity, there is three nice churches at this place and there is preaching in each of them . . . there is also an excellent singing society at this place and the soldiers are invited to attend." Once missionaries began arriving in the East Tennessee Valley encampments in May, revival began and continued until the Confederacy abandoned the region in August. Colonel Bullock said that at Knoxville he "heard two of the best sermons I ever heard in my life. The celebrated Dr. Stiles preached last night and it was truly grand. His eloquence exceeded anything I ever heard." At Loudon in June, Lieutenant James Hays found comfort in the words of a "Missionary Baptist; the first one that I have heard since I left Florida, and it was given up by all hands that he was the best we have heard since we have been in service. He was from Virginia, and was traveling from one army to another."[33]

While conversions during the revivals promised redemption on a personal level, Drew Gilpin Faust asserts that Confederate commanders believed religion would also provide "significant assistance in the thorny problem of governing the frequently intractable Confederate troops." As many 7th Florida soldiers joined the church during the summer, Colonel Bullock used the opportunity to expel vice from the regiment. Robert Watson, recently returned from Florida, related that an issued order stated: "Any commissioned officer, non. com. officer, or private found drinking, gambling, or swearing, should be court martialed and punished severely, also that tomorrow was fast day, and that there would be preaching in the regiment." Watson, who did not participate in the church-going, nevertheless looked upon the revivals as a blessing. He explained, "[O]ur boys will stand a better chance to get more [forage] for the psalm singing hypocrites will be afraid of being found out and being expelled from church. Our company has always been looked upon as hard cases, but I suppose we will be called the ungodly company now."[34]

The 1863 revival was beneficial for the Confederates serving in the Western Theater in several ways. In the Army of Tennessee, coming as they did after the failures in the Kentucky Campaign and at Murfreesboro, church services helped rebuild the soldiers' morale. Newfound faith likely helped the Floridians in the Department of East Tennessee endure their sojourn in the mountains. Religion also reinforced the troops' comradeship: "for many soldiers the companionship provided by these meetings afforded the soldiers a way to escape . . . frightening times." A year later at Dalton, the troops would once again participate in revivals to help them deal with the losses incurred later in 1863.[35]

Before summer arrived, Davis's Florida Brigade endured two pivotal command changes and squared off against Federal troops. In May two key officers tendered their resignations, thus reshaping the command structure of Davis's Brigade. One departure saw the loss of an officer who was hardly missed at all, as he had rarely been present with his troops. The other was a thoughtful and resourceful leader.

Colonel Madison Starke Perry had commanded his regiment only a few weeks following the retreat from Kentucky. Claiming ill health, the politician-turned-soldier departed Tennessee in November, and soldiers like Captain McConnell wished "he may resign and stay there, as he is regarded by the whole Regt. as a nuisance." Obviously the colonel had not endeared himself to his soldiers in Kentucky, perhaps concerned more about his own health than that of his troops. On learning of Perry's imminent return in April, Bullock griped, "[B]efore I go into another campaign with Col Perry, I will resign & come to Florida . . . I would make almost any sacrifice before I would serve under him." Perry's May resignation letter to General Samuel Cooper acknowledged a "physical inability to discharge the duties of the office."[36]

Colonel Perry admitted in his letter that "the great struggle in which we are engaged for the right of a free people to govern themselves will receive no determent by my resignation being pretty well conceived that Ex Governor and Ex Congressmen make better politicians than soldiers." Despite his poor record, Perry maintained supporters among the regiment, mainly Alachua County Democrats of whom he was chief. Casmero O. Bailey informed his father of the colonel's decision, adding that "I am very sorry for it . . . I do not like Col Bullock."[37]

Despite the ill feelings some soldiers maintained toward Bullock, who was now promoted to colonel, most agreed that the regiment would greatly benefit if newly promoted Lieutenant Colonel Tillman Ingram resigned as well. By 1863 Ingram had not developed into an effective military leader, and he never would. After ascending to command the 7th Florida, Bullock refused to take a furlough "for Col. Ingram is not fit to command at any time." Casmero Bailey, the staunch Madison Starke Perry defender, agreed that Ingram could not stand before an officer examination board and earn his commission. Robert Watson would comment in December 1863 that Ingram "knew no more about tactics than my old grandmother."[38]

With Perry's resignation, the 7th Florida lost an often absent and thus ineffective officer. Bullock had gained invaluable experience while commanding the unit during Perry's frequent absences. Though the new colonel had to deal with an impotent executive officer, Bullock instituted his own brand of bravery and discipline, measures that Perry failed to provide. From all accounts it appears that Bullock served ably under fire.

General Davis, who for a short time commanded the Department of East Tennessee that spring, also claimed impaired health and quit the service the same week as Perry. Davis explained to General Samuel Cooper that he resigned because the war had caused the "entire neglect of my private affairs." The general's departure marked a significant loss to the Florida troops, as he had led his brigade capably for the previous ten months. Not only did he demonstrate a knack for leadership at the brigade level, but his thoughts on the defense of East Tennessee during his tenure as commander showed that the former attorney put forth a truly concerted effort to study military tactics and strategy.[39]

With Davis's departure, Colonel Robert C. Trigg assumed command of the brigade. A Virginian, Trigg was a graduate of VMI and the onset of war found him practicing law in Christianburg. Originally a captain in the 4th Virginia Infantry, Trigg had helped his brigade earn the moniker "Stonewall" at First Manassas. In the fall of 1861, after overseeing the 54th Virginia's organization, he became the regiment's colonel. Following service in western Virginia, the 54th Virginia was ordered to East Tennessee and was eventually placed in Davis's Brigade. Trigg's admirers and superiors called the officer a "strict disciplinarian" and an "energetic soldier."[40]

Colonel Trigg commanded his scattered brigade for a month before it faced the enemy for the first time on the field of battle. On June 14 William P. Sanders, the Union commander from Kentucky, set out from Mount Vernon, Kentucky, with 1,500 troopers. The cavalry pointed their mounts southward toward the East Tennessee Valley. Sanders, hoping to emulate the December foray, had orders "to move up, destroying the road as much as possible, burning bridges, breaking up culverts, and destroying rolling stock." While the early winter raid had been undertaken to merely harass the Confederates, Sanders's movement would precede a Federal invasion of the area.[41]

After destroying the depot at Lenoir's Station, only twenty miles from Knoxville, Sanders's troopers wrecked the railroad and telegraph lines between that point and the "metropolis of East Tennessee." As the Federals advanced to Knoxville along the north bank of the Tennessee River on the afternoon of June 19, two Confederate cavalry companies, dispatched by Trigg, met them several miles west of town and a hot skirmish ensued. Colonel Trigg used the time bought by this desperate delaying action wisely, allowing his force, consisting of the 7th Florida and 54th Virginia and various citizens and convalescing soldiers, to fortify the town's streets "with cotton bales." Trigg also "positioned his artillery on hills behind the Dumb and Deaf Asylum on the north side of town and near Temperance Hall in East Knoxville." As Trigg's troops worked frantically, Colonel Finley's 6th Florida arrived to reinforce the garrison.[42]

Once the sun set, Sanders pushed several Kentucky companies toward the city to occupy the Confederates' attention. The Union commander's troops performed their diversion well, and as firing occurred Sanders shifted the remainder of his brigade to the north side of Knoxville. As his decoy force traded shots with Captain William E. June's 7th Florida company, one raw Floridian became convinced that June's soldiers had "prevented a night attack, which they doubtless had in contemplation." More trickery occurred that night as the Confederate artillery commander, disguised as a farmer, wandered into the Yankee lines and provided false information regarding the forces guarding the city.[43]

Daylight found the 7th Florida deployed on Temperance Hill, an imminence east of town, with their lines stretched north across the railroad. The 6th Florida was in the line of battle on a hill also north of the city, ready for the threat that soon materialized. Sanders's troops "came up in solid columns on the north side of town and commenced firing at our Batteries . . . with cannon and Minnie rifles." Benjamin R. Glover, a 6th Florida solider, noted, "We returned the fire with 6 cannons, the fight lasted about 3 or 4 hours."[44]

According to Hugh Black, as the artillery duel intensified, 6th Florida soldiers "would yell as if playing a game of town ball instead of fighting a battle. When a ball would go to high they would holler at the Yankees to shoot lower and when it struck the hill below us the[y] would say to the Yankees they were shooting too low, and when a ball not come near they would cry out 'lost ball.'" The Federals finally found their aim and a solid shot killed Lieutenant Bert Snellgrove of the 6th Florida. James Hays also saw a Federal round kill three Confederate cannoneers: "I was but a short distance when three fell, all killed by the same ball, it cut two of them nearly in two. It took off both the other mans legs—it was a bad looking sight."[45]

Realizing the "farmer" had deceived him as to Knoxville's strength, Sanders called off his attempt to seize the town after several hours of artillery fire. The Florida soldiers could feel proud of their accomplishment, for under Colonel Trigg's direction and with the aid of well-placed artillery, they successfully defended Knoxville. This did not, however, mean that Sanders was finished; before he returned to Kentucky, his soldiers burned both the Strawberry Plains and Mossy Creek bridges.[46]

Two weeks after Sanders's East Tennessee raid the campaign season in Tennessee began in earnest, as Rosecrans's Army of the Cumberland began a series of maneuvers meant to flank Bragg from his position at Tullahoma. By then, Breckinridge's troops were no longer with the Army of Tennessee, having been dispatched to Mississippi to bolster declining Confederate fortunes there. The winter quarters at both Tullahoma and in East Tennessee bore fruit for both Florida brigades. The troops' morale surged after hearing good news from other fronts and as a result of the revivals, their drill and discipline improved, and the 6th and 7th Florida gained confidence from participating in a fight, even though it was only a skirmish. The six-month hiatus (five for Breckinridge's troops) had given the wounded and sick a chance to return to the ranks and in general allowed the soldiers time to rest and prepare for whatever the last half of the year might bring.

11 This Seems to Be Our Darkest Times

May 26–July 15, 1863, Mississippi

In 1863, as the eastern armies clashed at Chancellorsville and Gettysburg, western forces of both nations dueled in Mississippi. The Confederates could not underestimate the importance of Vicksburg, Mississippi, for as long as the Rebels held the river town, foodstuffs and other war material passed from Louisiana, Texas, and Arkansas to the east bank of the Mississippi. Not only did the Federal forces wish to close this avenue of supply, but with the capture of Vicksburg and the downriver stronghold of Port Hudson, the entire length of the Mississippi would again be safely in Union hands. When Grant's forces began their offensive several miles south of the river town in mid-May, the Confederates rushed reinforcements from Tennessee to counter the thrust.

The soldiers of Colonel William Scott Dilworth's Florida Brigade spent May 23, 1863, striking their tents and preparing their equipment for a move. Rumors spread like wildfire throughout their Fairfield, Tennessee, encampment regarding the destination of their division. A visit by Major General Breckinridge to the brigade's headquarters that evening ignited further speculation. Though the ultimate destination remained a mystery, the men in the ranks learned that orders called for them to be at the Wartrace Depot the next morning by 7:00 A.M.[1]

General Braxton Bragg chose General Breckinridge's Division to reinforce the threatened Mississippi front not for their prowess in battle but because of a rift that had occurred between the two generals the previous winter. The Army of Tennessee historian Thomas L. Connelly writes that Bragg "had been critical in October of Breckinridge's failure to reach Kentucky in time to be of service." Bragg's campaign into the Bluegrass rested on the theory that pro-secessionist Kentuckians would take up arms and fill the ranks of his army. To do this, he relied on the native Kentuckians within his army, namely Brigadier General Simon Bolivar Buckner, to appeal to the pro-secessionist elements. Bragg had also hoped that Breckinridge and his division, then serving in Louisiana, would be able to reinforce his army for the offensive. Breckinridge's force reached Knoxville by early October and was ready to advance into the Bluegrass in support of Bragg when word arrived that Bragg was in retreat.[2]

Kentuckians failed to rally to the Confederate colors despite the pleas of Buckner and provisional Confederate governor Richard Hawes, who had been installed into office by Bragg in an elaborate ceremony in Frankfort. However, without popular

support and after the defeat at the Battle of Perryville, Bragg was forced to withdraw from the Bluegrass State. By late October, Bragg's demoralized, tired, and
hungry army was trudging through the rugged East Tennessee mountains, moving toward Knoxville. Unwilling to admit that he was the reason for defeat, Bragg
began blaming the Kentuckians in his force, particularly Breckinridge.

The feud worsened following the Battle of Murfreesboro when Bragg bore the
brunt of sharp criticism following his decision to retreat farther into Middle Tennessee after the second day of battle. In another round of finger-pointing, Bragg
accused Breckinridge of misconduct during the assault on January 2. Throughout
the spring while the Army of Tennessee recuperated in camps around Tullahoma
and Wartrace, the battle of words continued in the official reports. Samuel Pasco
recorded in his diary the thoughts of many soldiers on the matter; on May 1 he
noted, "Gen'l Bragg's official Report of the Murfreesboro battle came out to-day;
it is a tissue of misrepresentations against the good name of the noble Breckinridge and will create great indignation among the troops of this army who idolize
Breckinridge." The conflict between the two continued until Bragg was asked to
send reinforcements to Mississippi. Because there was no one he wished to be rid
of more than Breckinridge, his May 23 orders banished the Kentuckian and his
division from the Army of Tennessee.[3]

The former commander of the Florida Brigade, Brigadier General William
Preston, was also reassigned from the Army of Tennessee during the spring. Like
Breckinridge, Preston was a Kentucky politician. Following Murfreesboro, where
he led his brigade admirably, he earned the ire of Bragg by siding with Breckinridge during the spring feud. In late May, in another of Bragg's calculated moves
to rid the army of his "enemies," Preston was transferred to service in western Virginia. Following the removal of Preston, Colonel William Dilworth assumed temporary command of the reduced brigade—reduced because the 20th Tennessee
stayed behind to defend their native state.[4]

Though the brigade's four regiments were at the station before the appointed
time, it was close to 3:00 P.M. before the train began steaming south. After a stop
in Chattanooga to switch trains, the engines ran through Tunnel Hill on the
northernmost spur of Missionary Ridge and then made the sharp turn southeast
onto the Western and Atlantic Railroad, which would carry Breckinridge's soldiers
toward Atlanta. As the train steamed through the hills of north Georgia, many
men began speculating correctly as to their ultimate destination. Samuel Pasco,
who rode in the same car as Colonel Dilworth, wrote in his diary on May 25, "We
then started towards Atlanta and now we all believe Mississippi to be the destination of our Division."[5]

The 1863 journey through Georgia reminded many veterans of their rail movement of the previous summer when they had traveled to Chattanooga from either
Mobile or Tupelo. As their trains moved through north Georgia in 1863, the sol-

diers of the Florida regiments were greeted by familiar scenes. Pasco wrote, "We had a very lively time at Ringgold & Dalton. Our band played finely and attracted a large crowd."[6]

A day later, when the brigade reached Marietta, Pasco recalled: "Plenty of pretty ladies turned out; they were very desirous to see Breckinridge who is on our train and he appeared." The trains arrived at Atlanta on May 26 and the soldiers had to move their equipment from the Western and Atlantic to cars on the Atlanta and West Point. As the locomotive picked up speed for its southbound run and with black smoke spewing from its funnel, the hospital steward Theodore Livingston stood on the platform and watched his brother Archie and other comrades from the 1st and 3rd Florida "standing on the Cars, with their Hats off and shouting all sorts of fashions." The soldiers reached West Point on the Chattahoochee River that night, and the next day the train crossed the Alabama line. Pasco noted, "It rained this morning when we left and the men are terribly crowded inside the cars and on top for there is a scarcity of cars. The rain gradually cleared away and we had a charming day." What the soldiers saw in eastern Alabama was a land untouched by the war—a stark contrast to the region they left behind in Middle Tennessee. "The country is beautiful," wrote Pasco, "the crops of corn and grain abundant and at every little station crowds of ladies came out to welcome us."[7]

At Montgomery the force was split: part of the division was sent by river steamer to Selma, and the rest remained on the train until they reached Mobile Bay. The train that took the southern route passed near the homes of some of the men of the 1st and 3rd Florida. As the train rumbled through southern Alabama towns, many homesick soldiers jumped from the moving cars in an attempt to desert.[8]

By May 29 as the Floridians traveled toward the threatened front, the situation in Mississippi was rapidly falling apart. Only ten days earlier, Major General Ulysses S. Grant's Army of the Tennessee completed a two-hundred-mile march ending before Vicksburg. After landing his forces twenty miles below Vicksburg, Grant marched his troops to the state capital of Jackson, fifty miles inland from the river city, before turning west against their objective. On May 19 Grant's army had covered the last fifty miles and had, in the process, fought and defeated the Vicksburg garrison under the command of Lieutenant General John C. Pemberton at Champion's Hill, forcing it to retreat into the city. Having brought more than 30,000 men against the Vicksburg defenses with nearly 30,000 reinforcements on the way, Grant immediately attempted two frontal assaults. The Union commander threw his forces against the entrenched Confederates on the day his army reached the city and again three days later. Both were repulsed, with Grant's veterans suffering over 1,500 casualties. "After the failure of the 22d," wrote Grant in his official report, "I determined upon a regular siege."[9]

As Grant's army began digging into the Mississippi soil to construct entrenchments and gun emplacements to encircle Vicksburg, fifty miles to the east at

Jackson, General Joseph E. Johnston was organizing a relief force for the besieged city. However, by early June Johnston wrote of his army, "this force (about 24,000 infantry and artillery, not one-third that of the enemy), it was deficient in artillery, in ammunition for all arms, and field transportation, and could not be moved upon that enemy (already intrenching his large force) with any hope of success." In addition, "Grant had positioned seven divisions behind the Federal siege lines at Vicksburg, specifically to prevent relief of the city." Therefore, even after 5,000 reinforcements arrived in the form of Breckinridge's Division on the last day of May, Johnston remained idle at Jackson.[10]

On May 28 the van of Breckinridge's Division, including Colonel Dilworth and at least part of his brigade, reached Mobile Bay. Here the soldiers were crowded onto a steamer for transport down the Alabama River and across the bay. On the western shore of the bay, the soldiers re-embarked on trains that traveled along the Mobile and Ohio Railroad as it wound northwestward to Meridian, Mississippi. From Meridian less than a day was required for the trip to a location on the Southern Mississippi Railroad five miles east of Jackson.

The trains could not approach the city itself because the bridges over the Pearl River had been destroyed in early May when Grant's army occupied the city. As equipment was unloaded from the cars and tents were pitched, rain began to fall. The climate prompted Private Michael O. Raysor to write home of the Floridians' situation: "This country is not as good as Tennessee I am sorry we left their [sic] but I can't help it soldiers has to do what they are told to do."[11]

On June 5 Brigadier General Marcellus A. Stovall, a newly promoted brigadier from Georgia whom General Bragg assigned to the brigade on May 25, arrived in Jackson and assumed command from Colonel Dilworth. Formerly colonel of the 3rd Georgia Infantry Battalion and a merchant in civilian life, the forty-five-year-old Stovall was a veteran of Murfreesboro. The following day the brigade received reinforcements in the form of the 47th Georgia Infantry Regiment.[12]

Throughout June, Breckinridge's Division remained encamped on the outskirts of Jackson with orders from General Johnston to "establish lines of pickets on the various roads converging to Jackson." The Floridians were assigned to the area southwest of the town where, by the order of General Breckinridge, each regiment spent one day out of four on the picket line.[13]

As spring ebbed, cannons from Grant's army and Federal gunboats shelled the Vicksburg defenses daily. From their encampments around Jackson, more than forty miles from the river city, the Floridians reported hearing the rumble of cannon fire from the siege lines. "We heard heavy firing in the direction of Vicksburg all last night and day until 10 o clock," wrote William Rogers of the 1st Florida. Samuel Pasco wrote in his diary, "We are glad to hear the guns again this morning for it silences the groundless rumors of the fall of our stronghold."[14]

As the supplies of the Vicksburg garrison dwindled, Jefferson Davis renewed

a feud with Joseph Johnston that had begun in the months following First Bull
Run. Davis became exasperated as both he and the Confederate War Department
constantly urged Johnston to move in support of the besieged city. Yet the general
balked at each request from Richmond, pleading numerical inferiority to Grant's
army. As a Vicksburg historian has recently written, during the campaign Confederate "authorities sent what they could, but it was never enough—Johnston needed
more, more, more."[15]

However, during the last half of June, Johnston attempted to vindicate himself
with some form of action after receiving word from General Pemberton that "his
provisions would enable him to hold out no later than July 10." Maintaining be-
lief in his commanding general, Private Michael Raysor told his wife that "Gen
Johnson [sic] is not idle he will have Grant out of here before long." Yet despite
this eleventh-hour attempt to relieve Vicksburg, the feud between the president
and general turned particularly bitter and would remain a nuisance for the Confederates during the remainder of the war.[16]

Though official orders had not been issued, rumors circulated through the
camps on the outskirts of Jackson that the army would soon move to relieve the
Vicksburg garrison. Returning from furlough on June 21, William Rogers found
the men of his company ready to move out. "I had to turn in my knapsack as soon
as I got here," he wrote. Rogers went on to note that the soldiers were traveling
light, with only "an extra shirt a [pair] drawers a [pair] socks which we have to
carry folded up in our Blankets. From that it looks like they intend us to do some
heavy marching."[17]

The same day Samuel Pasco noted in his diary that "[d]rivers are called for
the supply train which I suppose betokens an early departure." But another week
passed before orders arrived at brigade headquarters from Breckinridge, ordering
a march to Clinton. "The reveille disturbed our slumbers at 3 and we at once rose
and loaded the waggons. We marched out into the road at day break but it was
sunrise before Gen'l Stovall appeared to lead the brigade," wrote Pasco on July 1.[18]

Over the next few days, as the eastern armies clashed at Gettysburg, Johnston's
columns marched westward under a scorching Mississippi sun. Charles Hemming
wrote, "The heat was intense, and the water was most execrable as well as scarce. I
have never forgotten that experience. We had to drink the stuff that was absolutely
alive with animal life, and sometimes we had to drink it when animals without any
life were upon its surface."[19]

Michael Raysor wrote to his wife from Bolton Station, "Only two days coming
here and the hottest days I ever felt a great many men fainted it was so hot and I
heard that some died. But thank God I stood it first rate and am well and hearty."
Pasco also wrote of the heat on the first day's march: "We had a terrible march;
many dropped fainting by the roadside; three it is said died. I never felt such in-

tense heat; water was scarce; the air was filled with thick clouds of dust and the General stopped but once on the march to rest and then only for a few minutes."[20]

By July 5, unaware that Vicksburg had capitulated the previous day, the Florida Brigade camped on the Champion's Hill battlefield. Johnston spent the first few days of July "probing for a soft spot in the Union line, trying to find an opening, a way to break through to Pemberton with his four infantry divisions," and found that the thirty thousand Union soldiers under the command of Major General William T. Sherman "had fortified and barricaded every road in the area between Big Black Bridge and Snyder's Bluff, and were prepared to hold these strongholds against double their numbers." No attempt at a breakthrough would take place, as on the morning of July 6, orders came from Johnston for his divisions to countermarch east toward their starting position at Jackson.[21]

"There is no confirmation yet of the news of the fall of Vicksburg," wrote Samuel Pasco on July 7, "but our movements evidently show that it is believed at Head Quarters." He further noted, "Waggons and vehicles of every description have filled the road since daybreak. Citizens are taking their families and servants to a place of security and all our army is falling back towards Jackson." The army was indeed in retreat toward the capital on July 7, as "Johnston realized that General Grant, having eliminated Pemberton's army, would turn upon his force."[22]

Johnston speculated correctly as to Grant's plans, for as the Confederates began their retreat on July 7, General Sherman had already launched his expedition toward the Mississippi capital. In fact, the city of Vicksburg had not been in Union possession twenty-four hours when Sherman's force, numbering around forty-six thousand, began to advance eastward from their lines around Vicksburg. Sherman's veteran soldiers, like their Confederate counterparts, carried only the necessities of a campaign, which included their blankets, ammunition, and five days' rations. Their swift marching would allow the Federals to reach the outskirts of Jackson on July 10, only three days behind Johnston's men.[23]

The Florida Brigade arrived in Jackson during a rainstorm on the night of July 7. The 1st and 3rd Florida had an especially tiring day, as the soldiers had been delayed after being deployed to "picket duty on two roads while our trains were passing." To make matters worse, the soldiers were without their tents, which meant a night spent under a steady rain. Pasco wrote of the night, "I was soon thoroughly chilled but exhausted by the fatigue of the march I fell into a sound sleep."[24]

During the ensuing days, the men of Johnston's army strengthened the line of fortifications that had been constructed around Jackson before Grant's advance through the town in May. Soldiers built embrasures of cotton bales and constructed rifle pits and breastworks to form a semicircular-shaped line that enclosed the city. The Floridians worked equally hard on their portion of the fortifications; Samuel Pasco wrote, "[T]he line of breastworks has been greatly extended by our Brigade during the day and our Regiment will have to work half the night on them."[25]

By July 10, when Sherman's soldiers reached Jackson, they confronted a formidable Confederate line. North of Jackson, Major General W. W. Loring's Division anchored the right flank on the Pearl River. To the left the line extended southwest, secured by William H. T. Walker's Division, whose left flank joined the division of Major General Samuel French. The entrenchments of French's Division ran almost due south, and Breckinridge's troops covered the southern line of fortifications. The former vice president's left flank rested on the Pearl River. The Florida Brigade held the center of Breckinridge's line, flanked on the right by Robert Cobb's Kentucky Battery and the left by the Tennessee Battery.[26]

On July 10, as the Union force approached Jackson, Companies C and H of the 3rd Florida were detached to picket duty in front of the Confederate lines. The day turned out to be memorable—not because of the arrival of the Union Army but because of the find made by members of the picket line. Pasco wrote in his diary that evening: "a lot of tobacco was found deserted about a half mile to the front and rather the Federals should enjoy it our men overhauled it all and carried away a good deal. Some private property left there to be sent off on the train which did not come in from Brookhaven yesterday. Nearly everything was taken off or destroyed to prevent the Federals from getting it." Herrmann Hirsch, a member of Pasco's Company H, wrote in a letter to an acquaintance in Mobile that at the depot there was also an abundance of "flour, Sugar, Bacon, Rice, Peas, & Salt & everybody made full use of it." The good fortune of the soldiers from Florida did not end with the raid on the depot. Later that evening, as Pasco wrote in his journal: "Cavalry were driving some beeves by our line and a refractory bull refusing to go with the common herd was shot down and turned over to the skirmishers. [Brigadier General Daniel] Adams' men and ours stripped off the flesh quicker than a lot of hungry buzzards could have done and beef in all forms was soon very abundant; steak, heart, liver, kidney, broiled, toasted, fried, and barbecued."[27]

Charles Hemming, by then recovered from his Perryville wound, had quite a different experience on picket duty in front of the Confederate entrenchments. Years later, when writing his memoirs, he recalled: "One day, before the pickets' lines had been drawn so close together, the boys told about a spring that they had found between the lines, and several of us went out to fill our canteens. The path we pursued was narrow and winding. Lo and behold, as we emerged from the brush to the opening where the spring lay, we ran across several Federal soldiers who were there for the same purpose. None of us had any arms, nor was the greeting between us unkind. We chatted a little, filled our canteens, and went back to our respective commands." In another instance, the veteran recollected that "I was out on the picket line with some of the boys one night, and the pickets of the Union army were so close that we could hear them . . . pulling corn in a small field that intervened between us."[28]

By July 11 General Sherman had succeeded in positioning his forces around Jackson's fortifications. Major General John Parke's IX Corps lay north of the city while Major General Frederick Steele, commanding Sherman's old XV Corps, moved against the line held by Walker's Confederates. Major General Edward O. C. Ord's XIII Corps, which had been reinforced by several divisions of the XVI Corps, was positioned on the southern flank of Sherman's advance. The previous day Sherman had ordered his army to "gain ground to the front whenever they can do so without too great a sacrifice of life." After intensive skirmishing on July 11, as the Federal commanders attempted to carry out Sherman's orders, the commanding general called for an extensive bombardment of Jackson beginning at 7:00 A.M. the following morning. "Each gun," Sherman dictated, "will fire not to exceed thirty rounds, shot and shell in proper proportions. The shots will be directed against any groups of the enemy's troops, or in direction of the town of Jackson."[29]

Daybreak on July 12 once again found Companies C and H of the 3rd Florida deploying on the picket line, relieving Companies A and F. "I got a position on the extreme left of the Company," wrote Pasco, "and took my post in a fence corner with the rails thrown down at either end." A Union battery, acting on Sherman's orders to fire into the Confederate lines, "took its position in a field beyond us and soon opened a destructive fire. . . . Adams' pickets fell back and soon after we had to follow. The shot and shell fell in all directions ploughing up dirt in front of us and on either side as we retreated."[30]

Hermann Hirsch, who was on picket duty with Pasco, remembered in a letter written two weeks later that as the skirmishers fell back, "one of my Companie was struck by a cannon ball in the hip & his side got badly shattered." The man in question was eighteen-year-old Thomas Linton Pettus. In the excitement and rush to reach their own lines, none of his comrades had time to provide aid to the mortally wounded soldier.[31]

Charles Hemming recalled of the bombardment, "Their batteries were posted in such a way as to rake the lines where our pickets were established, and, like all soldiers, we took the best shelter we could get. I was behind a little standing oak tree that did not measure more than three inches in diameter." Soon the barrage slackened, and Pasco recalled that the skirmishers were dispatched two hundred yards from the main lines; it was here they received the attack of a Federal brigade.[32]

The previous day, Federal divisional commander Brigadier General Jacob Lauman had been ordered by General Ord to move toward the New Orleans, Jackson, and Great Northern Railroad tracks just south of Jackson and brush away Confederate pickets in the vicinity. General Ord instructed Lauman to "make a reconnaissance, and, if it is necessary to form a line and attack to drive the force in front, do so." The order contained no mention of an attack on the Confederate main line. Lauman was an able commander who had served with Grant's army since Belmont, but for some reason on the morning of Sunday, July 12, he superseded his written orders and commanded Colonel Isaac Pugh's Brigade to make an advance against the Confederate entrenchments.[33]

Pugh was a veteran of the western campaign with more than two years' service by July 1863. Pugh's Brigade, which was a part of Lauman's Division, XVI Corps, consisted of four veteran midwestern regiments: the 41st and 53rd Illinois, 3rd Iowa, and 33rd Wisconsin. The brigade was reinforced that day with the addition of the 28th Illinois.[34]

Following an advance through the cornfield in which Charles Hemming had heard Union soldiers picking ears and then past the downed fence that had been the position of Pasco's skirmish line, Pugh ordered a halt to his brigade's movement. In his own words, "I did not like the appearance of the field, and I did not intend to advance farther without orders." The colonel called for his superior to come and view the situation firsthand. Lauman surveyed the field and promptly ordered Pugh to continue toward the enemy's fortifications.[35]

As Pugh's regiments advanced, the eighteen cannons of Breckinridge's Division and rifles of Dan Adams's Brigade began firing at the Federals. Benton Ellis recalled the awful scene that followed: "They advanced by platoons, and when well into the old field, our artillery opened up on them—I think it was Cobb's battery . . . I never saw such slaughter as our guns made,—they were nearly all killed, captured or wounded. I never saw so many dead men in all my life." The description Charles Hemming gave of the devastation matched that of Ellis: "When the line opened and the battery turned loose, hundreds were mowed down like grass before a scythe." Rinaldo Pugh, the Federal brigade commander's son, wrote home days later, "[I]t was the most terrible fire that man was ever sent into. It is a miracle that any of us got off of that bloody field alive."[36]

While the artillery was responsible for most of the Union casualties that day, the skirmishers of the 1st and 3rd Florida in advance of the fortifications played a role in the victory. According to Samuel Pasco, the skirmishers "threw out our left to flank them." Perpendicular to the Union advance, the Rebels "began firing . . . and kept it up until we had them opposite to us, but they paid no attention to the Pickets' firing, but continued the charge towards our main line and artillery." The Union troops advanced that afternoon to a point within 120 yards of the Confederate line. There the men in blue were finally halted by the blasts of double canister from Breckinridge's cannon. Unable to take anymore, the survivors of the useless attack began a pell-mell retreat to the rear.[37]

While the pickets moved to sever the retreating Yankees' escape route, a part of the Florida Brigade led by Major Rice Graves, Breckinridge's chief of artillery, advanced with soldiers from the trenches to provide the hammer to the skirmishers' anvil. These maneuvers enabled the Florida Brigade to capture a great number of prisoners. "We cut them off and captured a good many," wrote Samuel Pasco of the maneuver undertaken by the 1st and 3rd Florida's skirmishers. "Our company was much complimented for its conduct." Charles Hemming gave this description of the scene that transpired: "Then the order was given to charge, and we leaped across the breastworks in the face of the advancing column, just in front of our regiment. Capt. Saxon, the commander of our sharpshooters, was the first to cross the trenches. All the boys were moving quickly to the front, and in a few minutes, when we got to where the Federals were, they threw down their guns, and we took in three battle flags and a hundred and fifty prisoners within the space of fifteen minutes. As they would fall and throw down their guns they would cry out, 'Do not hurt me!' But we did not hurt prisoners; that was not the kind of war we waged." Benton Ellis noted that many Rebels seized trophies other than battle flags from Union prisoners, as "soldiers at once began to appropriate their guns knapsacks and Haversacks and also their pocketbooks, and as much as they wanted." Ellis continued, "I exchanged my old Enfield for a new one, took a rubber blanket and a fine new hat—that was all I wanted. The Haversacks were filled with good rations, and when we got to Camp, we made good sure enough cough [coffee], and with the hard tack and ham, we had a fine dinner."[38]

As the sun set that evening, Union commanders tallied their official casualties at 510 out of the 880 soldiers who had made the attack. These losses included 67 killed, 294 wounded, and 149 captured. In addition, the Florida Brigade captured the colors of the "28th, 41st, and 53rd Illinois' Regiments." These prizes, described by the *Richmond Daily Dispatch* as bearing the "spread eagle bird on a blue field, with the regimental inscription in gold," were sent directly to General Johnston's headquarters. The commander penned the following reply to General Breckinridge: "Do me the kindness, also, to express to the First and Third Florida, Forty-seventh Georgia, and Fourth Florida Regiments the pride and pleasure with which I have accepted the splendid trophies they have presented me. Assure them that I equally appreciate the soldierly courage and kindly feelings to myself which have gained me these noble compliments."[39]

For his part in the fiasco, Jacob Lauman was immediately removed from command by General Sherman. Casualties in Breckinridge's force that day were small, numbering just fifty during the seven-day siege. Yet one of these, Tom Pettus, lay somewhere between the lines, unable, in his wounded condition, to move. That night, Pettus's condition remained at the forefront of Sam Pasco's thoughts.[40]

Writing of the episode in 1909, Pasco remembered that throughout the night, "the wounded men between the lines begged piteously for water and a number of the Union soldiers were, at great risk, relieved and brought into our lines." The next morning the 1st and 3rd Florida prepared to send out a small party to give water to the wounded. Pasco wrote that he "felt convinced that Tom Pettus was still in the woods and asked . . . permission to go with the party."[41]

Permission was granted and Pasco joined the relief detail, which also included some of Pettus's old classmates. The picket line advanced to provide cover for the group and, as Pasco noted in his diary, "the Yankees fired at us but we kept cautiously along. Several of their wounded were there and we supplied them with water as we advanced." Pasco's 1909 account recalled that an Illinois soldier whom the 3rd Florida men provided with water "called to his comrades not to fire at these men for they were helping the wounded."[42]

The firing soon ceased, and the detail continued their mission of mercy. As they approached the fence that had marked the previous day's skirmish line, Pettus was found. Clarence William Smith, a member of Company H, also penned an account of the rescue. Smith wrote that the wounded man "recognized his comrades and begged for help and water." Pettus was carried by Pasco and two members of Company C "towards our line, the bearers not stopping until a skirt of woods, near by, was reached." There the wounded man was placed onto a blanket and borne into the Confederate trenches. Despite his comrades' valiant efforts, Pettus eventually died: "[His] condition was hopeless, and, though he received the best care and attention that was possible under the circumstances, he lingered till the next day and died."[43]

On July 14 the stench from the Federal corpses before the Florida Brigade's lines had become unbearable. General Breckinridge wrote to General Johnston, pleading, "The enemy's dead in front of my position are becoming quite offensive, and I cannot have them buried because of their skirmishers firing on my burial parties. They have even fired on my litter-bearers while their own wounded were being brought in." That afternoon a truce was put into place to allow for the burial of the bodies. During the short respite, Pasco noted that at 4:00 P.M. "the bugle was sounded and the brief period of peace was ended, and after a sufficient time had elapsed for all to get within the lines, blank discharges from artillery announced that we might go on with the work of destruction once more and the snapping of musketry along the lines recommenced very soon. Sixty three were buried by our Brigade."[44]

Two days later, on the night of July 16, 1863, General Johnston evacuated the Mississippi capital. Pasco wrote, "The Bridge was ready to be burned as soon as all the troops could cross and ours was the last Brigade. . . . Shells were laid by the road side & guards placed to keep us off them, large piles of cotton were burning and we were leaving ruins behind us." The Florida Brigade and Breckinridge's Division reached Morton, Mississippi, four days later, where it encamped until August 26.[45]

For the soldiers of the Florida Brigade and Breckinridge's Division, the mission to Mississippi had been a failure. The Confederacy no longer controlled the Mississippi River and Grant's army had captured more than thirty thousand soldiers and vast numbers of weapons on July 4. Less than two weeks later, Sherman forced Johnston's army from Jackson and captured the Mississippi capital for a second and final time. Coupled with the repulse of Robert E. Lee's army at Gettysburg, Vicksburg's fall marked the beginning of the end for the Confederacy.

Writing from Morton on July 22, Michael Raysor despaired: "Times look gloomy but I hope they will brighten before long this seems to be our darkest times." Indeed, the brief triumph the Floridians experienced at Jackson was but a fleeting instant in a long period of defeat. Nonetheless, the battle of July 12 was the Florida Brigade's finest hour. On that afternoon they fought like the hardened veterans they had become and assisted in blunting a Union assault on their lines. In the process, they took 149 prisoners and 3 battle flags.[46]

Their victory was set against a backdrop of defeat, but there had been a few bright spots in Mississippi. Samuel Pasco's rescue of Tom Pettus at Jackson was one such occasion. This scene was repeated time and again on numerous Civil War battlefields. For Lieutenant Colonel Edward Badger of the 4th Florida, the siege proved a personal success as well. While visiting the city in June, a fellow officer introduced the young lawyer to *his* sister; a whirlwind courtship followed and Matilda Leavel became Badger's fiancée soon after. The two married in March 1864.[47]

The Floridians were at their zenith in the summer of 1863. Their regiments were, for the most part, still large in number and could perform effectively on the battlefield. However, the summer and the disease that accompanied it would take its toll, and at Chickamauga, fought in mid-September, the three regiments would field a total of only five hundred men. Their regimental banners, however, would soon bear the word "Jackson"—a simple reminder of a small triumph during a period of defeat on a hot Mississippi afternoon.[48]

12 Napoleon's "Old Guard" Never Fought Harder

July 16–September 21, 1863

During the first full week of the summer of 1863, a season that proved invaluable to the Federal war effort, the Army of the Cumberland swept Braxton Bragg's force from its Tullahoma encampment in Middle Tennessee in a series of brilliant maneuvers. General William Rosecrans followed this campaign several weeks later with another movement designed to flank the Confederates out of Chattanooga. This effort ended along the banks of Chickamauga Creek in northern Georgia, after which both Florida brigades became attached to Bragg's Army of Tennessee. General Marcellus Stovall's unit steamed back to Tennessee via rail and Colonel Robert C. Trigg's Brigade, along with the Army of East Tennessee, abandoned its namesake region to join forces with Bragg.

During the last days of a disastrous summer, these men would engage in one of the most ferocious and confusing battles of the war. For the Floridians, some became heroes, some became veterans, and many fell as casualties. None who fought there would forget the carnage that was Chickamauga.

Nearly two weeks after Rosecrans's Tullahoma Campaign ended successfully and Grant's force captured Vicksburg, Joseph E. Johnston's position at Jackson was growing precarious. In giving his reasons for evacuating the town to Jefferson Davis, Johnston informed the president that "Sherman . . . would concentrate upon us the fire of nearly two hundred guns. It was also reported that the enemy had crossed Pearl River in rear of their right flank." Because of these developments, on July 16 Johnston had informed his subordinates that "in the opinion of the commanding general, the safety of this army renders necessary retrograde movement."[1]

That night, Johnston's tired army evacuated Jackson; the soldiers shuffled eastward, their faces illuminated by pyres of cotton bales and munitions that had been set afire to prevent them from falling into Yankee hands. The soldiers also passed engineers deploying torpedoes meant to delay any Yankee pursuit. The Department of the West's troops' initial destination was Brandon, only ten miles from their former position; from there, Johnston informed Jefferson Davis that he intended "to hold as much of the country as I can, and to retire farther only when compelled to do so."[2]

Remaining at Brandon only a few days, General Johnston finally halted his withdrawal near Morton, a Southern Mississippi Railroad town in the central part of the state that consisted of "half dilapidated and deserted stores" and "pretty little houses." General Sherman, "due to the intense heat, dust, and fatigue of the men," resolved not to follow the Rebels in force and dispatched only a single division to continue the pursuit to Brandon. Sherman decided instead to use the bulk of his troops to ensure "Jackson is destroyed as a military point." During the last two weeks of July, while the Yankees devastated the railroads near the capital and demolished anything of value to the Confederates, the Department of the West's troops pitched their tents near Hurricane Creek.[3]

The Floridians spent one month of their three-month Mississippi exile encamped at Camp Hurricane. Washington Ives favorably compared their central Mississippi campsite to Florida, describing the landscape as "covered with growth of pine and black jack, very little grass growing in the intervals between the trees" and "with the surface generally rolling." The pleasant scenery was only one of the benefits that the soldiers found in their new bivouac. Samuel Pasco wrote in his diary that Stovall's Brigade "now have very fine water and the hill we are on gives us a fine breeze though there is very little shade."[4]

Thanks to their successful performance at Jackson, the Floridians' morale remained high even though they wore ragged clothes and subsisted on the same poor fare as at Tullahoma. Washington Ives criticized the pound of beef and cornbread the soldiers received as their daily ration as "barely enough to sustain life." He pointed out that "if the sugar and Molasses which was burnt at Murfreesboro and Jackson had been issued to the men, we would have some now." Like the area around Tullahoma, the farms near Morton offered little relief. An officer serving in the 60th North Carolina described the region as "poor and thinly settled but few of the people have provisions enough for their families, and so of course, it is a bad chance for a soldier to do any foraging." The hard campaigning had also taken a toll on the soldiers' clothing, turning their garments into rags. Washington Ives wrote that in his regiment, the men "with few ecceptions [sic] had not changed their clothes in (7) seven weeks," and "large numbers . . . are barefoot."[5]

What might have further raised the troops' spirits instead garnered mixed reactions from the soldiers. On July 23 General Johnston announced a number of furloughs for his army's soldiers: a two-week leave for one of every twenty-five men in each regiment, and one for every two company grade officers. Samuel Pasco reported days after the proclamation that "everybody is pleased and desirous of having the first chance." Washington Ives, on the other hand, vented that "about as many officers got furloughed as privates, notwithstanding the hardships and privations the Privates have to endure." He added that "great dissatisfaction prevail among them, not so much . . . from our late reverses as . . . the treatment theyve recd from their officers and the Confederate Governemnt." Michael Raysor conceded to his wife that he had hoped to gain leave, "but trying is all in vain." Raysor mentioned that too few men gained furloughs to have a positive effect.[6]

The combination of a limited number of furloughs and the Mississippi heat and frequent cloudbursts threatened to sap the Floridians' esprit de corps, but Washington Ives explained that his comrades would "turn misfortunes into merriment and can laugh as heartily and pass as good a joke as any set of mortals on earth, and indeed some live for no other purpose than to keep the rest lively and in good spirits." Ives wrote in one of his letters home that as Colonel Wylde L. L. Bowen attempted to conduct a dress parade, a Kentucky soldier yelled his own set of commands, confusing members of the 4th Florida and infuriating the young colonel. Samuel Pasco described that while the 1st and 3rd Florida soldiers were not busy performing their duties, the men worked "building a long shelter for each Company which will keep off the sun and slight showers of rain and add very greatly to the comforts of the men and appearance of the camp."[7]

For the 1st and 3rd Florida, a morale boost might have come from an unlikely source: politics. Colonel William S. Dilworth, after being approached to campaign for a seat in the Confederate Congress, declined the offer. Dilworth probably understood the anger in the ranks toward the partial furlough system, which gave more officers than enlisted men an opportunity to travel home. His publicly printed letter declining the offer to run for Congress was no doubt intended to smooth things over with his men: "no position of honor, profit, or ease, shall call me away from the post of duty."[8]

As the soldiers completed their shelters, their diets gained diversity as the farmers of central Mississippi began harvesting their crops. Samuel Pasco wrote, "[T]he country people are beginning to bring in wagon loads of produce to sell the soldiers." These peddlers, seeking to benefit from the soldiers encamped near their farms, asked extremely high prices for their foodstuffs. To counter this profiteering, General Johnston recommended General John Breckinridge "send out details from each regiment, with one or two wagons, into the country around where you may be enabled to purchase vegetables and luxuries at reasonable prices." These expeditions returned, Pasco observed, with "a pretty good supply." Washington Ives commented, "We now draw a lb. of flour per man per week . . . if salt was not so scarce, we would live well."[9]

On August 16, 1863, the Army of the Cumberland, which had lain idle for six weeks following its successful Tullahoma Campaign, moved yet again. Characteristically deploying his corps so as to confuse and mislead his enemy, Rosecrans had his force move on a wide front. While XXI Corps occupied Bragg's attention by threatening a juncture with a Federal force descending into East Tennessee, XIV and XX Corps marched to Bridgeport from whence they would sweep into northwestern Georgia. The objective was to maneuver Bragg out of Chattanooga; this was accomplished by September 8, and Confederate "deserters . . . told of utter demoralization within the ranks of the Army of Tennessee." Rosecrans, prepared to take advantage of Bragg's misfortune, launched his army into the mountainous terrain of North Georgia intending to cut the Army of Tennessee's line of retreat.[10]

Within days of the Federal movement, Bragg telegraphed Johnston requesting reinforcements. Johnston agreed to send nine thousand troops with an understanding that they were "a loan to be promptly returned." On August 26 Breckinridge's Division received orders to report to Bragg as part of this relief force; after
a miserable, though semi-successful sojourn in the Magnolia State, the Floridians
were going home to the Army of Tennessee. While in Mississippi they had learned
of Sherman's tenacity and Johnston's cautious tendencies; they would encounter
both men and their habits again.[11]

For the fourth time during the war, the 1st and 3rd Florida and the 4th Florida
regiments embarked upon railroad cars, this time at Morton on August 27, to
travel to a threatened front. Numerous engines and cars were assembled for the
transport; Samuel Pasco wrote, "[T]he men were crowded on different trains just as
room could be found." Washington Ives's railroad woes continued on the journey,
for not long after leaving Morton "something became the matter with the Engine
and she cut loosed and left us in the road until 2 Oclock P.M. on the 27th when another Engine came and pulled us to Meridian." Ives also soberly commented that
on the trek from Meridian "the 1st 3d and 4th came on one train with all their baggage and 49 horses and the brigade commissary to Mobile, and yet when we left
Florida one engine could scarcely pull the 4th alone." Perhaps this not only represented the attrition that had whittled away at each regiment but also symbolized
the war's fusing together men from Florida's different regions. The regiments followed their old route though Mobile, Montgomery, and Atlanta, and finally arrived at Chickamauga Station on September 1.[12]

Bragg also garnered reinforcements for his army from East Tennessee. More
than a month before the Battle of Chickamauga, the department entrusted to defend that region, commanded by Major General Simon B. Buckner, became the
Army of Tennessee's III Corps. The East Tennessee soldiers had augmented Bragg's
troops in late June when they were rushed to Tullahoma to participate in the fight
against Rosecrans, a fight that never occurred.[13]

After spending a monotonous July in the northeastern corner of East Tennessee,
Colonel Trigg's Brigade bivouacked on August 25 at Loudon with the remainder of
Buckner's III Corps. With General Ambrose Burnside marching on East Tennessee
in conjunction with Rosecrans's advance against Chattanooga, the Confederates
could not hope to successfully defend against both thrusts. Bragg chose to concentrate his soldiers against Rosecrans, thus forsaking East Tennessee in the process.
In early September Bragg ordered Buckner's troops to Charleston, Tennessee, to
watch the Tennessee River's upper reaches for any sign of Union activity. Lieutenant Hugh Black, who knew nothing regarding events in northwestern Georgia,
confessed, "[W]hat caused our authorities to evacuate East Tenn is more than I am
able to say but think that it was done for prudential reasons." Lieutenant Colonel
William Stockton, detached from his regiment since December, voiced his pride
in the 1st Florida Cavalry, Dismounted, to his wife: "[O]ur little regiment is in

the finest possible order and march like 'soldiers.' I think they will fight well, for I believe they have every confidence in their officers."[14]

In the last days of August, Bragg was still uncertain as to Rosecrans's intentions. Poor cavalry intelligence and the Federal troops northeast of Chattanooga caused Bragg to seriously consider the possibility of a union between the two Federal armies operating on the Tennessee front. However, as Larry Daniel points out in his study of the Army of the Cumberland, Bragg knew "that the force in the Sequatchie Valley [just north of Chattanooga] was not Rosecrans's entire army, having been aware since late August that at least one Union corps arrived at Bridgeport." However, it was only when Bragg received information confirming that two Federal corps were in the mountains of northwest Georgia and moving eastward that the general developed a plan to withdraw southward and meet the Federals as they emerged from the mountains.[15]

After evacuating Chattanooga on September 8, the Army of Tennessee's three corps, commanded by Leonidas Polk, Daniel Harvey Hill, and Simon Bolivar Buckner, marched southward to intercept Rosecrans. Colonel Trigg's Brigade tramped along under the divisional command of Brigadier General William Preston, who had led the 1st and 3rd Florida and the 4th Florida into battle at Murfreesboro. During the second week of September, this division was to participate in an attack on an isolated Federal division in a valley near the headwaters of Chickamauga Creek. Timidity among the Confederate commanders charged with leading this advance prevented any battle. As Dr. Henry McCall Holmes wrote of September 11, "[we] got into line of battle on mt. ridge, sides in front almost perpendicular, very strong position. We advanced for awhile but found no Yanks except one dead one, they had left, got away from us."[16]

During the week before the Chickamauga battle, Bragg had one other opportunity to strike an isolated portion of Rosecrans's force, and once again his subordinates failed to implement his orders. On September 17 Bragg had received intelligence that the bulk of Rosecrans's army lay within McLemore's Cove and that his own force overlapped the Federal left. Bragg then formulated a plan in which his army would roll the Army of the Cumberland into McLemore's Cove, where, cut off from Chattanooga, it would be destroyed.[17]

On September 18 Bragg's troops seized several of Chickamauga Creek's bridges and fords and the general planned an overwhelming attack to take place the next morning. What resulted was a confusing series of isolated attacks in which the gray-clad soldiers, rather than finding Rosecrans's flank, ran into the front lines of several Federal divisions. Robert Watson wrote that on September 19, Trigg's Floridians "fell in and marched off at 5 A.M.," crossed Chickamauga Creek at Thedford's Ford as daylight broke, then formed the left flank of Bragg's forces west of the creek. General Preston positioned Colonel Trigg's regiments in line behind his other brigades, commanded by Archibald Gracie and John Kelly. Trigg's four regi-

ments formed their lines of battle in a cornfield tucked within a bend of Chickamauga Creek. For a time there was peace, and the men built fires to provide warmth;
Watson recalled they "ate . . . breakfast of sour cornbread and water."[18]

These fires, built for the soldiers' comfort, soon added unneeded misery to their
lives; the numerous blazes drew the attention of Union general John Palmer's divisional artillery, located southwest of the Chickamauga Creek bend. Soon the Confederates lay flat to avoid the rounds that were, in the words of Colonel Jesse Finley, "passing over, and near, diagonally in many places from right to left, frequently
striking in front and ricochetting [sic] over my men." Not long after the barrage
began, a shell exploded over the 6th Florida's Company D, showering the troops
with fragments. A single splinter passed through Lieutenant James Hays and First
Sergeant Samuel Staunton, killing them both. Only a month before Hays, anticipating a furlough, had informed his wife in jest, "[I]f I do come home don't have
too many orders for me to obey, for if I find there are too many orders, I shall
back out and not come home." Now he would never go home again. Hays and
Staunton, along with Sergeant William R. F. Potter, became the first 6th Florida
soldiers killed that day; they were joined by many of their comrades before the sun
set. After taking these casualties, Trigg's Brigade moved forward slightly to the east
slope of a ridge where they found cover from the deadly missiles.[19]

At noon, General Preston ordered Trigg's Brigade to the front of his divisional
line. Positioned on Gracie's right flank, Trigg aligned his regiments and shook the
entire 1st Florida Cavalry, Dismounted, into a skirmish line that covered his brigade's front. While Colonel G. Troup Maxwell's regiment had yet to become engaged in a fierce battle, they had experienced the dangerous thrust-and-parry work
of skirmishing both in Florida and along the Tennessee River. The line cautiously
moved forward several hundred yards through thick woods until it emerged in a
cornfield.[20]

This land, the Viniard farm, would see some of the battle's most ferocious fighting. Beyond the green corn lay other cultivated plots that were bisected by LaFayette Road, which ran north-south. This trace proceeded along the length of the
battlefield and provided both an avenue for reinforcement and a retreat for Rosecrans's army. At 12:00 P.M. only Colonel John T. Wilder's mounted infantry brigade protected this vital location against any Confederate threat.[21]

In a battle of oxymorons, the 1st Florida Cavalry's horseless troopers found
themselves trading shots with Wilder's mounted foot soldiers. While Stockton explained to his wife that his soldiers "had things pretty much our way," Maxwell described a different situation in his official report: "[A]fter the deployment was effected we became hotly engaged with the enemy's sharpshooters (under very great
disadvantage, as my regiment was armed chiefly with short-range guns of inferior
quality)."[22]

Indeed, Wilder's mounted infantry were armed with the potent seven-shot Spencer Rifle, allowing them to make things uncomfortable for the 1st Florida Cavalry's skirmishers. According to Colonel Maxwell, this uneven contest continued for nearly two hours and even after one of Union general Jefferson C. Davis's artillery batteries unlimbered and began firing at the Floridians. Stockton wrote, "[A] battery opened on us at about 300 yards in a corn field & hurt us badly." The 1st Florida Cavalry's troopers avoided taking heavy casualties during this sharp engagement, and only when General William Carlin's Brigade of Jefferson C. Davis's Division formed and moved across the field toward the Floridians did they break for the safety of their own brigade.[23]

During the afternoon, north of the popping skirmish that occurred across the cornfield, Confederate and Union divisions fought a fierce engagement that seesawed through thick forests and crop-laden fields. These Confederate attacks failed in part because of Bragg's assumption that he outflanked his opponent. In reality, his force assaulted the center of a Union corps. Another factor that hampered these assaults is that they were conducted in a piecemeal fashion, with divisions advancing one at a time into the fray. Throughout the day, Rosecrans shifted his blue-clad troops toward the sounds of the guns, reinforcing the Union line as needed.[24]

By early afternoon Generals W.H.T. Walker and Frank Cheatham had unsuccessfully launched their western troops at the Union line; the gray-clad soldiers incurred heavy losses in the process. The next assault was spearheaded by the first of the Army of Northern Virginia's soldiers to have reached Bragg's army. Dispatched by President Jefferson Davis and a reluctant Robert E. Lee on September 9, two divisions of Lieutenant General James Longstreet's I Corps traveled by rail to reinforce the Confederacy's beleaguered western force. On September 19, only three brigades of John Bell Hood's Division were present on the field of battle. Hood combined his hardened veterans with General Bushrod Johnson's Division and proceeded to slam into General Jefferson C. Davis's blue-coated soldiers in the southern section of the battlefield. This attack drove Davis's Federals toward the Viniard farm.[25]

General Jerome Robertson's Texas Brigade formed the extreme left of Hood's line, and "as soon as Robertson came under fire," Hood "asked Bragg for reinforcements to protect his left." Bragg relayed the order to Buckner, who in turn commanded Preston to enter the fray. Preston dispatched Trigg's soldiers to support the Texas Brigade. Casmero Bailey wrote, "[W]e were ordered forward which we did in quick time." Colonel Trigg's regiments, following the sounds of the battle, soon reached the eastern boundary of the Viniard farm and came under the same artillery fire that earlier pestered the troopers of the 1st Florida Cavalry, Dismounted. The Floridians arrived at the right time, as their advance placed them on the flank of a fresh Union brigade that was crossing the cornfield in an attempt to strike the Texas Brigade's own flank.[26]

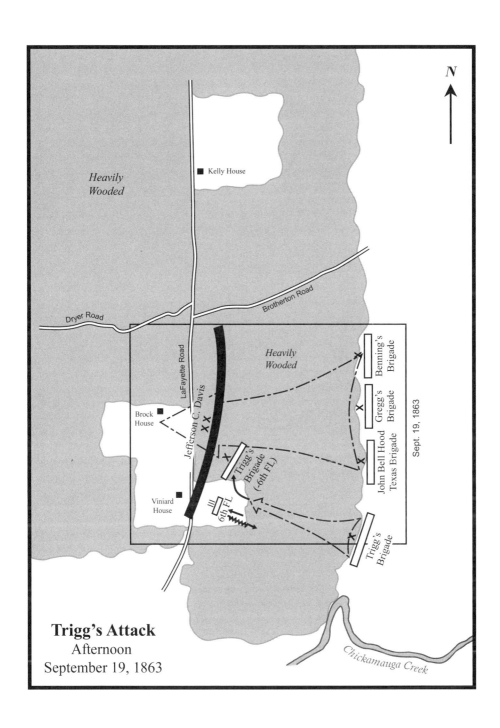

N

Kelly House

*Heavily
Wooded*

Dryer Road

Brotherton Road

LaFayette Road

Jefferson C. Davis

*Heavily
Wooded*

Benning's
Brigade

Gregg's
Brigade

John Bell Hood
Texas Brigade

Sept. 19, 1863

Brock
House

Trigg's
Brigade
(-6th FL)

6th FL

Viniard
House

Trigg's
Brigade

Trigg's Attack
Afternoon
September 19, 1863

Chickamauga Creek

The East Tennessee soldiers, in position along a split-rail fence on Robertson's left, soon unleashed a volley into the flank of the newly arrived Federals and, in Trigg's words, they "broke in confusion to the left and rear." Casmero Bailey confessed that because of the smoke, "I stood some time without fireing [*sic*] looking for something to shoot at, but I could not see anything and the boys kept shooting so that I thought I would shoot too, so I shot right ahead of me." With the Federal brigade in retreat, Colonel Trigg ordered his regiments to pursue and aimed for the artillery batteries on the far edge of the field. The order was, according to a 6th Florida soldier, "executed with enthusiastic gallantry and success." Proud of his soldiers, Colonel Finley wrote, "[T]he regiment moved forward through the open field at a double-quick to the crest of the ridge, the distance of about 300 yards." Colonel Trigg, who accompanied the 6th Florida, discovered at this juncture that the remainder of the brigade had not heard his order to advance.[27]

Soon realizing their error, the brigade's other regiments quickly crossed the eastern fence and moved double-quick to reinforce the 6th Florida. Robert Watson described his regiment's confusing movement as a charge into a cornfield and then "within about 400 yards of their battery we were ordered to right flank and marched at the double quick to the right." The reason for this sudden turn of events was that the Texas Brigade had encountered new resistance and Robertson dispatched a staff officer to commandeer Trigg's regiments. In describing the regiments' move to reinforce Robertson's troops, Casmero Bailey informed his father, "[T]he grape and shell came thick and fast we kept on until we came to the woods where we were ordered to lie down which we did in a hurry." With the 1st Florida Cavalry, Dismounted, 7th Florida Infantry, and 54th Virginia assisting the Texas Brigade, the 6th Florida remained alone and exposed in the cornfield.[28]

Several Federal artillery batteries placed by Major John Mendenhall, the bane of Breckinridge's Division at Murfreesboro, concentrated their fire on the 6th Florida. Federal infantry also added their small-arms fire to the inferno. Hugh Black, who suffered a broken arm during the disastrous assault, wrote from an Atlanta hospital, "I never was in just such a place before it is strange to me how any one escaped for I assure you that the bullets seemed to search every nook and corner of the field that we were in." John R. Ely, the 6th Florida's adjutant, proudly informed the *Florida Sentinel*'s readers that the West Floridians, "outnumbered by overwhelming odds, at least five to one—fought with a coolness and determination, which has covered with glory and shed a new lustre upon the arms of gallant little Fla." Unable to withstand this punishment, Colonel Trigg ordered Colonel Finley, whom Benjamin Glover described as being "as brave as a lion" during the fight, to retreat toward the woods.[29]

By sunset the Confederate attacks in the southern portion of the field had ended; to the north, General Patrick Cleburne carried out a dusk assault that also ended in a stalemate. Trigg's Brigade settled in for a cold night in the woods just east of the Viniard cornfield. Robert Watson wrote, "I scarcely slept a wink all night but lay shivering with cold all night. The groans and shrieks of the wounded and volleys of musketry and falling of trees made it impossible to sleep." That night, Casmero Bailey stood picket along the rail fence on the eastern edge of the corn-field and grew sick looking at "men shot in every place and form."[30]

Many of the dead seen by Bailey and the wailing wounded heard by Watson be-longed to the 6th Florida. That regiment was decimated on the afternoon of Sep-tember 19, suffering 35 killed and 130 wounded in only a short time. Benjamin Glover was counted among the latter, as during the attack he was struck in the head by a spent ball. Nevertheless, John R. Ely proclaimed, "Napoleon's 'Old Guard' never fought harder than did the representatives of our gallant little State on that memorable field." Colonel Finley could not share in his adjutant's jubilation and bitterly reported that his soldiers "purchased whatever reputation they may have won upon the sanguinary field at a fearful cost of life and blood." The 1st Florida Cavalry, Dismounted, and 7th Florida Infantry suffered three killed and thirty wounded during the day's fight.[31]

While Trigg's soldiers engaged in mortal combat on September 19, their friends, neighbors, and relatives in Stovall's Brigade spent the day south of the battlefield near Glass's Mill. Bragg had assigned Breckinridge the task of providing the ar-my's rear guard; as the major fighting occurred to the north, only Benjamin Helm's Kentucky Brigade and two artillery batteries saw action in an intense skirmish on the west bank of Chickamauga Creek. While the bulk of Breckinridge's Division moved north at Bragg's order, the 1st and 3rd Florida remained at Glass's Mill to picket against any Union attempt to turn Bragg's left flank. At 10:00 P.M., a cou-rier arrived ordering the regiment to rejoin their division. After their guide became confused in the darkness, the 1st and 3rd Florida wandered about on the east bank of Chickamauga Creek all night and did not locate their brigade until 8:00 A.M. the following morning. If Breckinridge had attacked that morning as Bragg had ordered, the 1st and 3rd Florida's tardiness would have kept them from partici-pating in the assault.[32]

The previous evening Bragg had announced to his commanders that the army would continue attempting to push Rosecrans's force into McLemore's Cove. Also, late on September 19 Bragg reorganized his army into two grand wings, with Leonidas Polk commanding one and James Longstreet the other. D. H. Hill's Corps and Breckinridge's Division were placed under Polk's direction. Though Bragg had or-dered the attack to take place at dawn, Polk never mentioned this to Hill or Breck-inridge, only that the attack was to occur the next morning. Hill, instead of launch-ing his troops at the Federals at daybreak, allowed them to eat breakfast.[33]

One positive development that arose from the delay was that Hill used the early morning to scout the Federal line. Discovering that the Yankees had constructed breastworks from hastily cut timber along its length, Hill adjusted his line to outflank the Union defenses. At 9:30 A.M. Breckinridge formed his division on the army's right flank, placing Daniel Adams's Louisiana Brigade and Stovall's Florida Brigade north of the Union entrenchments, while Benjamin Hardin Helm's "Orphan" Brigade on the left would strike the Army of the Cumberland's northern line at an oblique angle. Samuel Pasco remembered that Breckinridge's "Div. was forming into line as we came up and dusty tired and hungry as we were we filled up our place but a good many were missing who had dropped out from exhaustion."[34]

On the morning of September 20, the Federal front extended from north to south for several miles along LaFayette Road. George Crittenden and Alexander McCook's Corps were in the southern end of the line; General George Thomas's divisions in the north took the shape of a semicircle that bulged east of LaFayette Road. Breckinridge's Division was to strike the northern edge of this bulge.

On that Sunday morning, Stovall's Brigade contained only 818 soldiers. The 1st and 3rd Florida, led into a major engagement for the first time by Colonel Dilworth, mustered 273 soldiers and took up position on the brigade's right flank. Bowen, the youthful but effective combat leader, and Lieutenant Colonel Edward Badger commanded the 4th Florida. That regiment fielded only 213 soldiers for the battle and formed the left flank of the brigade's line. The 60th North Carolina and 47th Georgia occupied the center.[35]

Moving forward at 9:40 A.M., Adams's and Stovall's brigades pushed westward through thick woods toward LaFayette Road. According to Samuel Pasco, the Rebels "swept through the woods with a line of skirmishers ahead driving the Yankees like sheep." Peter Cozzens has described the Federal resistance north of Thomas's main line as "feeble." In a short time, Stovall's and Adams's brigades had crossed LaFayette Road and then turned south to assault the Federal flank.[36]

As Stovall re-formed his unit for the next phase of the attack, he repositioned the 1st and 3rd Florida on the left to watch for any movement toward his brigade's own flank. With Adams's men engaged west of the road, Stovall's troops emerged into Kelly Field, which was at the immediate rear of Thomas's line, just after 10:30 A.M. The Federals responded to this threat sporadically, with blue-clad units rushing to the hotspot. This hastily formed Yankee line would attempt to check Adams and Stovall along the northern edge of the field.[37]

Stovall's regiments rushed forward toward their foes and traded volleys with the surprised Yankees across the cleared land. Colonel Dilworth, whose regiment fell upon the northern portion of Thomas's line, captured an advanced line of Federal rifle pits. At the main line of breastworks, however, the enemy offered stern resistance and blue- and butternut-clad soldiers exchanged shots at only twelve paces. Dilworth described how "Samuel Neeley, the color bearer, fell near the breastworks, and Robert McKay, of the color guard close to his side, both severely wounded, and 4 of the color company were left dead on the field." Charlie Ulmer, a young corporal and one of Samuel Pasco's former students, seized the colors and "bore them bravely through the rest of the contest."[38]

The regiments could not withstand the heavy volume of fire the Federals placed on them for long. In addition, to the west, Daniel Adams went down with a severe wound and his brigade fell apart under well-placed small-arms fire. Artillery fire soon stripped the 47th Georgia of any fight it had, and the 60th North Carolina, at odds with the Floridians since Murfreesboro, gave way under intense pressure. With only the Floridians remaining in the woods north of Kelly Field, the Federals applied pressure on their front and both flanks. Samuel Pasco confessed, "[W]e had to fall back to save the Regiment from being captured." A soldier from Ohio wrote of the battle, "As they faltered we charged on them and hurled them back as fast as they had come on this charge."[39]

By 11:30 A.M. Breckinridge's Division had fallen back to its starting position. General Cleburne's troops, whose attack fell on Thomas's east-facing breastworks, were also unsuccessful. Breckinridge's attack lasted roughly ninety minutes, and the 1st and 3rd Florida suffered 92 casualties. Samuel Pasco wrote that most of these occurred during a ten-minute period. The 4th Florida endured similar losses, counting 9 killed, 67 wounded, and 11 missing. Stovall's other regiments, the 47th Georgia and 60th North Carolina, suffered fewer losses. The butcher's bill in Breckinridge's other brigades was steeper: 396 of Adams's soldiers became casualties, and the "Orphan" Brigade lost 471 soldiers, including Benjamin Hardin Helm, the unit's commander and Abraham Lincoln's brother-in-law.[40]

Although Breckinridge was unable to turn the Federal flank, his attack, combined with that of Cleburne, still managed to contribute to the Confederate victory. Thomas, commanding at Kelly Field, clamored for reinforcements during the late-morning hours. What resulted was "not only an organizational mess and the confused movement of many units, but also the further weakening of the center and right." When Rosecrans dispatched a unit to fill a gap created by a division supposedly on its way to assist Thomas, a real breach opened in the southern portion of the Federal line led by Crittenden and McCook. At that moment, 11:15 A.M., General James Longstreet's wing rushed forward to the attack and the Army of the Cumberland's right disintegrated.[41]

While numerous Federals, including Rosecrans, fled the field, a patchwork line formed a new right flank on a series of hills, collectively known as Horseshoe Ridge, just to the west of Kelly Field and LaFayette Road. Throughout the afternoon, Longstreet's wing made numerous, disjointed attacks against the new Federal position.[42]

By 4:00 P.M. on September 20, General Preston's Division had yet to engage the enemy that day. Robert Watson and the 7th Florida, after getting little sleep during the cold, loud night, awoke that morning as veterans, built fires for warmth, and ate breakfast. Though General Longstreet had ordered Preston's Division to lend its numbers to the Horseshoe Ridge fight, the Kentucky general only committed his two unbloodied brigades. Trigg's unit was dispatched to the southern flank to guard against a possible cavalry attack. After Gracie's and Kelly's brigades launched vicious but unsuccessful assaults against the Union position, Preston called once again on Trigg's tenacious unit. While Colonel Finley led the 6th Florida and 54th Virginia toward the fighting on Horseshoe Ridge, Trigg kept the 1st Florida Cavalry, Dismounted, and 7th Florida Infantry on guard for the supposed threat.[43]

While these regiments remained idle, Colonel Finley's two regiments formed on the Confederate left flank and joined in the assaults to take Horseshoe Ridge. These units' attacks came late in the fight as the Union forces were attempting to disengage. Nevertheless, the fighting was still ferocious and deadly. In later years, two veterans remembered that the 6th Florida was repulsed twice in its attempts to reach the top; on the third try amid "shot and shell" that "fell like rain," the 6th Florida lost Lieutenant John Wilson, one of its most promising and respected officers. One of the soldiers recalled, "[S]carcely had we started up the hill when a cannon ball struck the Lieutenant . . . on the leg, shattering the bone." Wilson died while being transported to a hospital in southern Georgia.[44]

When the 1st Florida Cavalry, Dismounted, and 7th Florida were finally summoned to the scene of action, the late summer sun was beginning to set. The 7th Florida soldiers looked forward to trying out their new weapons; as Casmero Bailey recalled, "[W]e went in on Saturday with muskets and when we went in on Sunday we had either springfields or enfields we captured them all on the field guns and cartridge boxes were strewn an the boys threw away their old muskets and got a gun to suit themselves."[45]

On the way the 1st Florida Cavalry, Dismounted, became lost and wandered near the Union line; this carelessness caused several casualties. Lieutenant Colonel Stockton was counted among the wounded; as the officer was peering over the crest of a rise, "one ball struck in front of my face, as I was watching the Yankee manoevers [sic], and dashed the gravel into my eyes so sharply that I was blinded for a while." Shaken by this sudden encounter, the 1st Florida Cavalry, Dismounted, withdrew from the enemy's fire and no longer participated in the battle.[46]

Colonel Robert Bullock's 7th Florida Infantry fared better in reaching Snodgrass Hill with Colonel Trigg as twilight settled over the bloody ground. After a quick conference, Trigg and Kelly decided they could bag the few Yankees remaining on the west slope of Horseshoe Ridge, and Trigg proceeded to guide the 6th Florida toward the Federal flank and rear. Meanwhile, the 7th Florida edged up the hill on the enemy's front. Robert Watson described the advance: "We went in at double quick and got to the foot of the hill at dark. The enemy seeing us sent a man towards us to see whether we were their own men or not with directions to fire if we were enemies, but we took him before he could fire his gun, therefor [sic] the Yankees took it for granted that we were their own men. We then proceeded to the top of the hill within 50 yards of them and halted and took 30 prisoners. . . . They tried to escape by running but they ran into the 6th Florida and were all captured."[47]

Casmero Bailey wrote home that his regiment "took . . . one stand of colors the Flag was a beautiful thing it belonged to the 21st Ohio." The 21st Ohio, armed with Colt Revolving Rifles, held the right flank of the Horseshoe Ridge position all afternoon, and as darkness descended fought a rearguard action to allow the remainder of the army to retreat. The regiment, in historian Steven Woodworth's estimation, "fought one of the most heroic defensive battles of the war that day." In addition to the hard-fighting 21st Ohio, Trigg's Brigade captured portions of two other Union regiments that evening, though the exact number of prisoners varies from source to source. The Floridians and Virginians also seized five stands of colors, and among the spoils of war were numerous rifles and accoutrements.[48]

Prior to the final drama playing out on Horseshoe Ridge, the Federals still holding the north salient near Kelly Field received orders to withdraw. At the same time, Bragg ordered General Polk to launch an overwhelming assault on this sector of the Federal line. John Love McKinnon recalled that late in the day "several lines of battles were formed in the oak scrub thicket as close as to the enemy's lines as we dared to go. All were commanded to lie down on the ground as flat as flounders and as quiet as beetles and await orders." Pasco wrote, "Three lines were formed & we swept the field completely routing the foe. We pursued only to the Chattanooga road and the air resounded for many minutes with the prolonged cheers of our delighted boys." The Federal soldiers who had held this line throughout the day retreated toward Chattanooga. At any rate, this attack and Trigg's flanking maneuver were the last Confederate movements on September 20.[49]

That night the Floridians of both brigades slept among the dead and wounded upon the battlefield. Washington Ives remained in the rear during the fight, managing the detail cooking rations for the 4th Florida, and arrived after the fighting ended with food, which brightened the soldiers' already jubilant spirits. Ives observed that among Stovall's Florida regiments "the Florida Boys Stand up like heroes." In Trigg's Brigade the soldiers were also exultant, but Jacob Yearty of the 7th Florida seemed to speak for all when he penned, "I hade heared talk of batles and have bin in too small ingagements before this one but I cold not draw eny ideas untill now I have a ful understanding of what it means." The losses suffered by the 6th Florida served to sober the entire command.[50]

Though Bragg stymied Rosecrans's advance at Chickamauga and in the process won the Army of Tennessee's first victory, the casualty figures were astounding: more than eighteen thousand men were killed, wounded, or captured during the two-day fight, including Hays, Stockton, Black, and Raysor. Though Raysor suffered only a minor injury to his left hand, his health suffered. He died in Jefferson

County on January 27, 1864, exclaiming: "I am going home; I am going home to Heaven." He was twenty-seven years old.[51]

For Raysor's surviving comrades in the 1st and 3rd Florida and 4th Florida regiments, the Battle of Chickamauga provided yet another laurel that testified to their bravery and discipline. Well led, this time by Colonels Dilworth and Bowen, these small units had turned the Federal flank and remained until superior numbers forced them to retreat. Coming on the heels of the Jackson victory, Chickamauga marked the zenith of these young Floridians' careers as soldiers.

The 6th and 7th Florida infantries and 1st Florida Cavalry's performance in the fight might be considered mixed. On September 19, these green soldiers swept a veteran Federal brigade from the Viniard cornfield, and only the order from Jerome Robertson kept Trigg's Brigade from seizing several Federal artillery batteries. The 6th Florida suffered needlessly because of this confusion. During this trying time, however, Colonel Finley developed into an effective combat leader; Bragg hailed him as "'the old Hero.'"[52]

Late in the day on September 20, the 6th and 7th Florida made a name for themselves when they participated in the capture of the few remaining Federal units on Horseshoe Ridge. Although Bullock should be credited with magnificently maneuvering his unit up the hill, this event was more a case of being in the right place at the right time. Had the Floridians been committed an hour or two earlier, they, like the Confederate regiments that had participated in the afternoon attacks, would have suffered similarly dreadful losses. G. Troup Maxwell's direction of the 1st Florida Cavalry, Dismounted, during that afternoon was dismaying and possibly cost him a generalship later that year.

Retreating from the battlefield in the darkness, the Federal Army passed through the gaps of Missionary Ridge, an irregular spur of Lookout Mountain that formed the western border of the Chickamauga battlefield. From its heights, the Floridians gazed down upon Chattanooga, the town that Rosecrans's defeated army now occupied. Few could have known then—and few could have thought after Chickamauga—that their fortunes would be tied to the western slopes of Missionary Ridge. Yet after the last week of November 1863, the Florida Brigade would forever be linked with the disaster that occurred there.[53]

1. Brigadier General Jesse Johnson Finley, photographed after the war. (Photo courtesy of the Florida State Archives.)

2. Captain John Livingston Inglis, an immigrant who fought for the Confederacy. (Photo courtesy of the Florida State Archives.)

3. Roderick G. Shaw. (Photo courtesy of the Florida State Archives.)

4. Washington M. Ives. (Photo courtesy of the Florida State Archives.)

5. (*above*) Samuel Pasco, as he appeared when he served as a U.S. senator (1888–1900). (Photo courtesy of the Florida State Archives.)

6. Colonel William Miller, 1st and 3rd Florida Infantry (Consolidated). (Photo courtesy of the Florida State Archives.)

7. Brigadier General Robert Bullock, 7th Florida Infantry. (Photo courtesy of the Florida State Archives.)

8. Lieutenant Colonel Edward N. Badger, 4th Florida Infantry. (Photo courtesy of the Florida State Archives.)

9. William D. Rogers, following his transfer to the 15th Confederate Cavalry Regiment. (Photo courtesy of the Florida State Archives.)

10. Major Jacob A. Lash, 4th Florida Infantry. (Original in author's collection.)

13 I Have Never Known Them to Fail in the Hour of Trial

September 21–December 2, 1863

In the two months that followed the Chickamauga victory, the Army of Tennessee tried unsuccessfully to starve the Army of the Cumberland, which held on precariously at Chattanooga, into submission. During this time, General Braxton Bragg, as a part of a series of moves meant to rid his army of dissent and to reward his supporters, created the Florida Brigade, effectively uniting his six Florida regiments into a single unit. The Floridians first fought together in this new formation on November 25, 1863, on Missionary Ridge, which overlooked Chattanooga. Though this battle saw the Confederates defeated, the Floridians added to their hard-fighting reputation and brought additional honors to their small state.

On the morning after the firing ended along Chickamauga Creek's west bank, the smoke still lay thick in the hollows of the battlefield. General Marcellus Stovall's Florida Brigade's soldiers awoke long before the sun shed its light on the terrible scene, having been aroused from their blankets in the early hours of the morning when word arrived that cooked rations had reached their bivouac. In the darkness the soldiers devoured their first meal in two days. Stovall's elated troops spent the next few days visiting their wounded comrades and even seized the opportunity to bathe in Chickamauga Creek to wash the grime and powder stains from their bodies.[1]

The soldiers in Colonel Robert Craig Trigg's Brigade of William Preston's Division found the aftermath of their first major battle appalling. Jacob Yearty, a 7th Florida soldier, wrote that his regiment "bured the dead too days and did not get half of them bered and they are getting to smell so bad that it is impossible to bury the rest of them we could not get neare all of our men bured." Robert Watson, serving in the same regiment, described spending September 21 "carrying off the wounded and burying the dead all day. It was a terrible sight, friend and foe lying side by side." Preparing a peaceful rest for the dead remained low on the Confederates' list of priorities, though, and on September 22 Trigg's troops marched to the western base of Missionary Ridge, where they engaged in constructing breastworks. Stovall's regiments reached Confederate lines near Chattanooga on the same day. Samuel Pasco wrote, "[W]e had a beautiful view of the town below [from atop Missionary Ridge]. They [the Union Army] appear to be crossing the river on pontoons but are in line of battle to resist us if we crowd them."[2]

Following the retreat from Chickamauga, a portion of the defeated Army of the Cumberland maintained a defensive position at Rossville, southeast of Chattanooga, ready to contest the jubilant Rebels. However, due to "the bold maneuvering of Forrest's cavalry . . . and the unfounded rumor of the impending arrival of additional large Confederate reinforcements, Rosecrans had given up a key defensive perimeter and withdrawn his army into the immediate environs of Chattanooga." By retreating into Chattanooga the Federal general placed his army in a stranglehold, for with the Army of Tennessee commanding Lookout Mountain, the Union force could rely only on a few rough wagon roads, including a trace over Walden Ridge, the bluff that proved so hazardous to the Confederates the previous year, for resupply. With his opponent in a difficult position, Braxton Bragg determined to starve the Union Army into submission while waiting for an opportunity to strike at one of the Federal flanks.[3]

Bragg positioned John Breckinridge's Division in the part of the siege line that ran along the western base of Missionary Ridge. The bivouac of Stovall's Brigade was near where Moore Road crossed the ridge; the regiments spent their days either improving their breastworks or on picket duty between the two armies. Prior to the Atlanta Campaign, when enemy sharpshooters posed a constant and deadly threat, the time some Floridians spent on the sentinel lines near Chattanooga represented the closest contact they had with their enemy away from the battlefield. Only three miles separated the Rebels' encampment from their foes in Chattanooga, and their picket lines stood only two hundred yards apart.

In the crisp, late September weather, the Confederates engaged in heavy firing with enemy sentinels; these fights resulted in occasional casualties. Major Jacob Lash informed his wife that because the armies were in such close proximity, throughout the days "ours and Theirs Bands Play in opposition." Dr. Henry McCall Holmes of the 1st Florida Cavalry, Dismounted, recalled being awakened "by Hail Columbia, Star Spangled Banner & Yankee Doodle from the Yankee Band."[4]

On a cold October 10, Federal soldiers in and around Chattanooga heard prolonged, roaring cheers erupting from the Confederate lines at the foot of Missionary Ridge. President Jefferson Davis's arrival and subsequent tour of the main line of breastworks brought forth cries of jubilation from the soldiers. After the review the Floridians wrote to family and friends of the experience, providing candid opinions of the Confederacy's executive. Sergeant Major Roddie Shaw looked upon the ailing man with sympathy, observing that Davis "looks quite thin." Colonel Robert Bullock concurred with Shaw, explaining, "I do not think he is by any means very imposing in his appearance. I was introduced to him & had a short conversation with him. He is a very frail looking man." While the troops yelled and screamed as the commander in chief halted before each unit, Davis, according to Washington Ives, "rose up to the front of our flag and took off his hat . . . not a man opened his mouth . . . Davis rode away gratified at their soldierly demeanor, and evidently thought that their silence showed more respect than the screams of men who seem to be so frantic."[5]

Bitter infighting and political intrigue among the Army of Tennessee's high command had prompted Jefferson Davis to travel to southeastern Tennessee early that fall. This visit and its aftermath impacted the army's command structure and directly influenced the Floridians' future as well. Strangely enough, the scheming and intrigue that infected the army's generals in the aftermath of Chickamauga also occurred in two Florida regiments, as their soldiers attempted to create changes of their own and ease certain officers from command.

Braxton Bragg's conflict with his subordinates, which had begun the previous year following Perryville, flared up once again in the aftermath of Chickamauga. Bragg's removal of General Leonidas Polk from command on September 29 due to his lackluster performance at Chickamauga became one factor in this unhappy turn of events. Polk's sacking was initiated at the same time the army's corps commanders began a writing campaign to remove Bragg. After President Davis had dispatched his aide, Colonel James Chesnut, to the army to determine the depth of the dissent, Chesnut "wired the president that the Army of Tennessee urgently demanded his personal attention and that he should make the trip if at all possible."[6]

Even after hearing corps and divisional commanders berate the commanding general, Davis decided to keep Bragg in his position. The commanding general, then, according to the historian Wiley Sword, believed Davis's confidence in him "was carte blanche to remove his most vocal and dangerous detractors." Lieutenant General Daniel Harvey Hill was the first subordinate Bragg dismissed following Davis's visit. Hill's removal (allegedly for not attacking as ordered on September 20 and for actively campaigning for Bragg's sacking) would have significant and permanent ramifications for the Floridians.[7]

Bragg elevated Major General John C. Breckinridge to corps command on November 8. Although Breckinridge had had disagreements with Bragg, he had not joined the latest conspiracy and the commanding general rewarded this competent fighter with a promotion. In losing their beloved division commander, the Floridians gained a new leader under whom they served, for better or worse, until the war's end.[8]

With Breckinridge elevated to corps command, Bragg chose William Brimage Bate, a thirty-seven-year-old Tennessean, to lead the Kentuckian's old division. Although Bate's formal education had ended when he was sixteen, the future general later earned a law degree from Cumberland University. Prior to the war, Bate found success as a Democratic newspaper editor and also served as a state senator. A supporter of Governor Isham G. Harris's secessionist policies, Bate became colonel of the 2nd Tennessee Infantry at the beginning of the war and served in Vir-

ginia before returning west. Colonel Bate was severely wounded at Shiloh and returned to active duty in time to command a brigade during the Tullahoma and
Chickamauga campaigns. Bate would turn in his best performance at Missionary
Ridge, as in his previous battles he had demonstrated a lack of creativity in tactical
maneuvers and an inclination to send his troops against the Federals in disastrous
frontal assaults.[9]

While Bragg pursued his enemies within the army with a vengeance, the Floridians themselves attempted to create a change of their own. After the Battle of
Chickamauga, Colonel Wylde Bowen became ill with what doctors diagnosed as
erysipelas. By the end of September, the colonel had been removed to a Georgia
hospital to recover. Disgruntled with both the infirmity of their colonel and their
dwindling regimental numbers, the 4th Florida's officers applied to have their regiment consolidated with the 7th Florida.[10]

The 4th Florida's Marion County company and the regiment's interim leader,
Lieutenant Colonel Edward Badger, likely initiated this move. The 7th Florida's
Robert Bullock was junior to Colonel Wylde Bowen, and *he* understood that the
latter would receive command of the regiments should they unite. Bullock, recognizing that he would become a supernumerary, wrote to his wife: "I was, at first,
very anxious for it, because I hoped to be able to be sent off on some duty where
I could have you with me." Bullock admitted that he felt good about the idea of
Badger serving as the consolidated unit's executive, for he thought "Badger . . . is a
first rate officer; much better than [Tillman] Ingram, who is really an old fudge."[11]

Indeed, for the twenty-two-year-old Badger, the conflict had proven beneficial. The Marion County resident had, since May 1862, been promoted from lieutenant to lieutenant colonel, become engaged, and suffered no injuries. He commanded his troops ably at Murfreesboro and Chickamauga, and Bullock's wife,
Amanda, informed her husband that soldiers on furlough in Ocala "seem to think
the world of Col Badger . . . that his men all love him." Colonel Robert Trigg put
a quick halt to any talk of a consolidation, explaining that he did not want to lose
Bullock in the shuffle.[12]

In November, however, Colonel Trigg lost command of his brigade. In that
month, in an attempt to realign his army so as to "dissolve the anti-Bragg cliques"
and reward his supporters, Bragg began a wholesale shifting of various regiments
and brigades throughout his force. Bragg's Special Orders No. 294, issued on November 12, 1863, produced these transfers. The order that created Finley's Florida
Brigade grouped the Florida regiments together and noted that "the Senior Colonel will take command until Brigadier is appointed." However, the senior colonel,
William Scott Dilworth, was on a forty-day furlough after falling ill following the
Battle of Chickamauga. The leadership of the Florida Brigade thus fell to Colonel
Jesse J. Finley.[13]

In reality, only Finley had been considered for command of the brigade. His performance at Chickamauga assured his promotion. Likewise, Colonel Troup Maxwell's bungling on September 20 probably removed him from any consideration. This turn of events came more than a month after General Simon Bolivar Buckner provided Adjutant General Samuel Cooper with his opinion of Maxwell's and Finley's potential for higher command. The East Tennessee commander rated both colonels as "excellent officers, perhaps not fully the equals of Col. Trigg, but either would make a good brigade commander." Buckner added that in "character necessary to command . . . I think Col. Maxwell is the superior of Col. Finley."[14]

Colonel Dilworth had his supporters in the army as well. Just prior to Chickamauga, General Breckinridge nominated the 1st and 3rd Florida's commander for the rank of brigadier general. Breckinridge described Dilworth as having "shown the qualities of a competent and faithfull officer." Though General William Hardee endorsed Breckinridge's request, Jefferson Davis did not sanction Dilworth's promotion. The Confederate president instead was swayed by Governor John Milton's request that Finley receive the promotion. The governor's petition is impressive: Milton a Democrat, endorsed a former Whig, thereby demonstrating a dissipation of Florida's political divisiveness.[15]

Only four days after Bragg created the Florida Brigade, the Confederate Congress approved Finley's wreathed stars. Standing nearly six feet tall, General Finley exhibited a formidable presence on the battlefield. The war had given the fifty-one-year-old general his first gray hairs and robbed him of his youthful appearance. By 1863 Finley also wore a thick beard that caused him to look his age. The Florida Brigade would, in title at least, be his for the remainder of the war.[16]

The formation of the Florida Brigade truly bonded the state's citizen soldiers, as it fastened large numbers of troops from each region under and tied the state's reputation in the Army of Tennessee to one command. The Florida Brigade's hierarchy mirrored the political power structure in the state, with a West Floridian at the top and East and Middle Floridians as subordinates. Ten years earlier it would have been unthinkable for the latter regions to approve of a West Floridian as a commander.

Despite jubilation over the Florida Brigade's formation, which garnered attention in their letters and diaries, the Floridians in the trenches at the base of Missionary Ridge still endured bad weather, a poor diet, and inaction following the Chickamauga victory. Although these conditions were a constant source of irritation for the soldiers, they endured them just as they had at other points during the war when the going became exceedingly difficult. However, they were not lacking in clothing and seemed better prepared to face the oncoming winter than they had been the previous year. This fact seemed to ease the rigors of daily existence. Meanwhile, from the picket lines they watched the Yankee army grow stronger and awaited the inevitable clash of arms.[17]

The autumn weather plagued both sides equally. Freezing rain fell upon the Floridians huddled behind their entrenchments at the foot of Missionary Ridge and upon the sentinels on the picket line; tents were a bygone luxury and overcoats were few. Sergeant Archie Livingston complained to his brother-in-law and state representative Enoch Vann that the Floridian men were "without sufficient Tents & flies, and rain continues to fall." Willie Bryant, having returned to the regiment after extended duty at Braxton Bragg's headquarters, complained, "[I]t goes devilishly tough with me at first, particularly as the weather has been horrible since my return, rainy, cold, and windy, . . . and our Brigade is without tents." Lieutenant Henry Wright wrote disgustedly that he and his messmates might have been comfortable, but "all our clothes, cooking utensils, tents, mess chest, and Bed clothes were lost on the trip from Miss."[18]

Throughout October the Floridians' primary enemy remained the annoying weather, for no harm would come from Yankee small-arms fire. Following a truce declared on September 27 so that both sides could exchange their Chickamauga wounded, the pickets of both armies refused to kill while in the line of rifle pits that snaked between them. Wiley Sword has aptly described the ensuing cease-fire as consisting of "friendly exchanges of goods, impromptu discussions and innocuous fraternization." An anonymous soldier wrote that Confederate "pickets and the Yankey pickets are within 200 yds. of each other. The boys when out on picket swap papers, exchange coffee for tobacco etc. . . . Both parties lay down their guns & meat each other half way. & have a regular chat." Though the foot soldiers honored the truce, the artillerists continued to fire rounds at their enemies. One of the victims of artillery fire was Lieutenant Francis Marion Mitchell of the 4th Florida, who was mortally wounded by solid shot on November 2.[19]

While besieging Chattanooga, Bragg's army subsisted on the rations that a single rail line could deliver. The general's attempts to feed his soldiers were hampered by the fact it took time to distribute cooked food to the troops at the front, as well as by the fact that Lee's Army of Northern Virginia received favored status from the Confederate Commissary Bureau. T. J. Robertson of the 6th Florida informed his friend Benjamin Glover, "[W]e don't git one third enough of Beef, and no Bacon atall 3 days rashings of Beef makes 2 meals and the bread stuff only lasts one day and a half." Willie Bryant described his fare as "corn meal, poor beef, and 2 in 7 [days] flour and bacon." Lieutenant Reason W. Jerkins of the 7th Florida, one of the fortunate soldiers who had ready cash, visited a "Settlers [sic] Shop" to supplement his meager fare "& bought 4 lbs pottoes @ 50 cts $2.00 . . . I thought I wanted to taste one . . . as I have not ett one or two messeses sence I left home." Newly promoted quartermaster sergeant Washington Ives complained of the diet on November 10: "[W]e have not drawn a pound of meat in five days, nor see any prospect for more. In lieu of meat we get two and three quarters (2 3/4 oz.) ounces of sugar in place of a pound of beef or a third of bacon."[20]

Regardless of the lack of meat, the conditions at Chattanooga were no worse than at Tullahoma earlier that year. In fact, Washington Ives wrote that in November the soldiers in his regiment were "getting along remarkably well and are by far more healthy than anyone could expect." By late October, the 1st and 3rd Florida numbered 375, a higher total than the regiments had carried into battle at Chickamauga. The soldiers had reason to rejoice in October when the army received new winter uniforms, which Ives described as "jackets of kersey, Blue Cuffs, Pants, . . . Shoes, Caps, Shirts, etc." The young quartermaster sergeant further informed his father that the men received "new English Blankets. . . . A single one is large enough to cover a double bed and the texture is far superior to the blankets usually brought south with goods."[21]

The soldiers further improved their chances against the weather by constructing crude cabins at the foot of Missionary Ridge. This was no easy task; Henry McCall Holmes observed, "[W]e have cut down all the timber on the mountain." Robert Watson and his messmates, using alternative materials, created a "hut which is built of poles, corn stalks, straw, and dirt. It makes a warm and comfortable hut, but I don't think it is healthy." Lieutenant Jerkins and several officers of the 7th Florida were fortunate enough to have a tent and pitched it near the ridge's base. On November 17 Jerkins noted, "Mie boys is buisey building a chimnly." With their new clothing, blankets, and shelters, the Floridians settled down in mid-November for a tolerable existence, even if the food shortage continued. In Chattanooga, General Ulysses S. Grant was preparing to put an end to the Florida Brigade's tenure on Missionary Ridge and drive the Confederates into the mountains of north Georgia.[22]

Fresh from his capture of Vicksburg, Grant arrived at Chattanooga on October 22 after assuming command of a new military department that comprised all Union forces between the Appalachian Mountains and the Mississippi River. The War Department also transferred the Union Army of the Potomac's XI and XII Corps to Tennessee, as well as William T. Sherman's XV Corps from the Army of the Tennessee. In the last week of October, at Grant's directive, the Army of the Cumberland and the newly arrived easterners participated in a joint strike to clear Longstreet's troops from Lookout Valley and thus secure a supply line to Chattanooga.[23]

Soon after the Yankee reinforcements arrived, Bragg's own army was weakened by President Davis's detachment of Longstreet's two divisions to liberate East Tennessee. Bragg, infuriated by Longstreet's failure to halt the Union thrust in Lookout Valley and still holding a grudge against Lee's "Old Warhorse" for his part in the early October command fiasco, happily complied with Davis's order. However, while a defeat in East Tennessee might cause Grant to dispatch a portion of his Chattanooga force to deal with the threat, "his communication line would remain intact via the river and railroad into Middle Tennessee."[24]

With Longstreet's forces moving into East Tennessee, General Grant began planning the defeat of Bragg's reduced force. He decided to use General Sherman's Vicksburg conquerors to seize the northern end of Missionary Ridge and cut Bragg's line of retreat at Chickamauga Station. General George Thomas, then commanding the Army of the Cumberland, prepared for the flanking maneuver that would threaten the Confederate center after Sherman had seized the ridge's crest. On November 23 General Thomas's soldiers opened the fighting when they seized the Confederate picket line that lay between Missionary Ridge and Chattanooga.[25]

Samuel Pasco wrote that the Florida Brigade, which had occupied entrenchments between Missionary Ridge and Lookout Mountain since the Federal advance against Longstreet's flank, relocated to its old position at the foot of Missionary Ridge on November 22. Robert Watson, always angry when he was forced to miss a meal, detested the Federals even more for the timing of their assault, which came "at 2 P.M. . . . just as I was about to eat my dinner we were to fall in and march to the breastworks at double quick so I had to go without my dinner." On November 24 General Joseph Hooker led a mixed force of easterners and westerners against Lookout Mountain and captured that prominence; as night fell Pasco watched from the Florida Brigade's breastworks as "after dark the contest was renewed on this side of Lookout . . . the flashing of guns appeared like myriads of fire-flies or glow worms shining on the distant mountain sides."[26]

On the night of November 24, Braxton Bragg, after conferring with his corps commanders, ordered his troops to occupy newly constructed fortifications atop Missionary Ridge. The historian James McDonough has noted that the problem with this line of entrenchments was that they lay "along the physical crest rather than what is termed the 'military crest'—that is, along the top-most geographic line rather than along the highest line from which the enemy could be seen and fired upon . . . these works severely handicapped the defenders." Confederate general Arthur M. Mannigault wrote that these works were not only laid out poorly but of "very inferior quality . . . low, and only afforded protection to the lower part of the body, and against the fire of artillery were rather a disadvantage than otherwise." Breckinridge's Corps defended the southern end of the ridge, with A. P. Stewart's and Bate's divisions aligned from south to north on the crest. The Floridians' own James Patton Anderson commanded the division that extended the Rebel line farther north.[27]

On the night of the twenty-fourth, General Finley led three regiments of his brigade into the entrenchments on the crest of Missionary Ridge. Some did not reach the trenches atop the seemingly formidable position until after midnight, but at dawn on November 25, 1863, Lieutenant Colonel Edward Mashburn's 1st and 3rd Florida and the 6th Florida, with youthful Colonel Angus McLean commanding, stood ready to meet the enemy. Finley's right flank rested on the Moore Road, with his left connecting with Colonel Randall Gibson's Brigade. Colonel

G. Troup Maxwell commanded the three regiments, including his own 1st Florida Cavalry, Dismounted, which remained in rifle pits at the foot of Missionary Ridge. His detachment also included Bullock's 7th Florida and Badger's 4th Florida. This force of nearly seven hundred soldiers joined several thousand men in defending this advanced line.

On November 25, General Sherman's troops began their anticipated assault against the northern end of Missionary Ridge, while Grant ordered General Hooker's soldiers to outflank the Confederates in the south. General Thomas's Army of the Cumberland was to "charge and carry the rifle pits at the foot of Missionary Ridge. Nothing more was intended." Grant's plan began to falter, though, when Hooker's advance started late and General Patrick Cleburne's troops thwarted Sherman's assaults to seize the northern end of the ridge.[28]

As the day wore on, the Floridians would have heard the heavy volume of fire coming from the northern end of the ridge; at 1:00 P.M., Bragg ordered the Orphan Brigade, also serving in Bate's Division, to assist against Sherman. To fill the gap left by the Orphans, Bate shifted his line to the right, meaning the Floridians' left flank would sit on Moore Road, very close to the house that served as Bragg's headquarters. Samuel Pasco maintained that Colonel Robert Tyler's men successfully completed this move, but Thomas's attack began before the Floridians could complete the maneuver. As a result, Finley had to stretch his line uncomfortably thin to connect with both Tyler's right and Gibson's left. To confuse matters more, during the early afternoon hours General Breckinridge sent word to his troops holding the advance line of entrenchments to retire up the ridge after firing one volley. Unfortunately, William Bate had previously ordered his troops defending this line to "fight to the last resort," and some of his soldiers, including the Floridians, never received Breckinridge's revised orders.[29]

At 3:00 P.M. the soldiers on the crest and at the foot of Missionary Ridge watched twenty-three thousand soldiers of the Army of the Cumberland deploy nearly two miles from the Confederates' position. At 3:40 P.M. this force began its advance toward the ridge; though he considered the Yankees his mortal enemies, Lieutenant Jerkins wrote, "[O]h, what a purity sight it was to see them charge in 3 solide colums across the old field as blue as indigo mud and their arms glittered like new." While the artillery atop Missionary Ridge opened almost immediately, the soldiers in the rifle pits at the base of the ridge waited until the enemy closed to within three hundred yards before firing. Immediately after delivering one volley, the soldiers to the left and right of Maxwell's advance force beat a hasty retreat up the ridge. Upon seeing the Rebels fleeing, the Federals of the assaulting columns broke into a run toward the advanced line.[30]

In the trenches, Colonel Maxwell determined to follow Bate's orders, and his soldiers loaded and fired until the blue-clad enemy had "reached the rifle pits on my right and were close in my front." Robert Watson wrote that he and his com-

rades "mowed them down until they were within 30 yards of us and then we retreated up the hill." Washington Ives added that the withdrawal of General Alexander
Reynolds's Brigade from the rifle pits on the right of Maxwell's men allowed the
Federals to "follow them partly up and getting higher up the hill . . . than the Floridians. The latter were compelled after firing several rounds at the advancing foe,
to climb the ridge under terrible fire."[31]

Robert Watson claimed that ascending the ridge's western slopes was the "worst
part of the fight for the hill was dreadful steep and the enemy kept up a continual
fire and threw a continual shower of bullets among us, and I only wonder that they
did not kill all of us." The historian Peter Cozzens has noted that when General
Philip Sheridan's Federals reached the rifle pits they discovered many Floridians
for whom "surrender seemed preferable to trying to scale the sheer ridge with their
backs to the oncoming Federals." Others wanted badly to escape but found themselves too weary to attempt to climb the seven-hundred-foot precipice. Lieutenant
Colonel William Stockton was one of the latter; he wrote his wife from a Union
prison camp, "I was unable from exhaustion, to leave the field, when all was lost
in our part of it. . . . Two of my men, were killed at my side, while successively attempting to assist me." The Yankees seized Stockton in the rifle pits, and farther
up the heights the bluecoats came across Colonel Bullock, who was, in the words
of his biographer, "a beefy man" and quickly "became winded" in his attempt to
reach the top. Jerkins was one of those fortunate enough to reach the crest, and
he recorded he "came through saff through a shower of shot and shell . . . I recon
that I could hear a 1000 whistle at a time and bums bursting all . . . round and
over us."[32]

At the line of rifle pits, the Army of the Cumberland's soldiers came under heavy
fire from Missionary Ridge, and it became obvious to these veterans that they
could not remain in the captured entrenchments. "So, in every mind there arose
one thought: get out of the rifle pits immediately . . . a continued advance to the
base of the ridge . . . seemed the only alternative to slaughter." Slowly, the soldiers
began inching their way up the ridge.[33]

The first Federal breakthrough on the ridge's crest came at an intentional gap
left in the Confederate line that General Alexander Reynolds's North Carolinians
and Virginians were to fill when they reached the top. These regiments, instead
of taking their proper place in line between Anderson's Division and Brigadier
Colonel Robert Tyler's Brigade of Bate's Division, fell back from the base through
Finley's troops atop the ridge. General Thomas Wood's Yankees quickly exploited
the breach and forced back Colonel William F. Tucker's Mississippi Brigade. A correspondent for the *Memphis (Atlanta) Daily Appeal* informed his readers that "the
enemy was not slow in availing himself of the great advantages of his new position. In a few minutes he turned upon our flanks and poured into them a terrible
enfilading fire, which soon threw the Confederates on his right and left into con-

fusion." General Finley, writing a month after the battle, agreed: "[T]he left centre (Hindman's Division) composed of veteran troops of tried courage, gave way in the most inexplicable manner . . . almost without resistance." Turning south, the Federals, joined now by more of their comrades who had successfully scaled the ridge, proceeded to capture a Washington Artillery section of two cannon and began firing into Tyler's flank.[34]

Colonel Tyler's Brigade collapsed under an intense barrage of small-arms and close-range artillery fire originating from the cannons seized by the Federals. Next in line to the south were Jesse Finley and his Floridians, holding on perilously in their thin line. An artilleryman of Havis's Battery, which the Floridians supported, claimed that the Floridians stood "only one man every eight feet apart" atop the ridge. Washington Ives agreed, claiming that Finley's "line amounted to nothing more than a skirmish line at some points." Owing to the poor layout of the fortifications atop the crest, soldiers there could not effectively defend their position once the Federals reached the foot of the ridge. To counter this defect, Bate advanced his firing line "to the verge of the ridge" in order to pour volleys down on the Yankees. Young Charlie Hemming wrote that "when the order came to fire, it seemed to us that hundreds fell, and at first their line wavered, but brave officers held them to their work and, cheering wildly they came at us again." Bate certainly performed well on November 25. He recognized early in the fight that because of Missionary Ridge's contours and the volume of smoke, the Federals might approach the crest undetected. To counter this threat, Bate dispatched skirmishers down the slope to provide advanced warning.[35]

Bate's Division atop the ridge held firm during the first hour of the assault. Only after 5:00 P.M., with the Federals exploiting the breakthrough on their right flank, did the line waver. As Tyler's men crumbled, Bate despaired that because of a renewed attack on his front, he could not spare any of his troops to protect his right flank. He soon discovered that the only soldiers available to stem the advancing Yankee tide were the 60th North Carolina, the regiment that had earned the ire of the 4th Florida at Murfreesboro. An overwhelming number of Yankees soon forced the 60th North Carolina to retreat; Samuel Pasco pointed out in his diary that the withdrawal of his own brigade was caused by the retreat "of the Brigade to our right."[36]

As the Federals threatened the Floridians' right flank, General Bragg and his staff rode up to the faltering line and "sprang to the front of the Florida Brigade, reckless of the terrible fire the enemy was pouring upon us, and cap in hand, endeavored to rally the men beseeching them to hold their ground, if not for his sake, for God and their country." The commanding general shook hands with the color-bearer, Charlie Ulmer, before riding to another threatened point in the line. Not long after his encounter with Bragg, Ulmer was killed; Archie Livingston raised the 1st and 3rd Florida's battle flag and bore it from the field. Bragg's words rejuvenated their spirits and the Floridians redoubled their efforts to hold their position; the line was soon restored.[37]

The Rebel left finally collapsed when the Federals forced a foothold among A. P. Stewart's troops and reached the ridge's crest. According to William Raulston Talley, the Federals on the ridge's slopes, along with those who "turned down our line" and those who turned north from "Bragg's HQ[,] . . . had the Fla brigade and our battery between three fires and we were ordered to retreat and we got." Charlie Hemming corroborates this; he claimed that as he turned away from the trenches, "from seventy-five to a hundred men of the Union army, just climbing the crest of the hill, were to my right, not over twenty or thirty feet away."[38]

Robert Watson, whose blanket received twenty-three bullet holes while he was scaling the ridge, recalled that the Floridians contested their position "until the enemy were on the top and had their flags on our breastworks." Watson wrote, "[W]e retreated down the hill under a shower of lead leaving many a noble son of the South dead and wounded on the ground and many more shared the same fate on the retreat. We retreated in great confusion, men from different companies all mixed together." Samuel Pasco decided the time had come to flee "when I saw half a dozen flags across the breastworks." Pasco had not gotten far when a ball passed through his left calf. While trying to mount a stray mule, Pasco's left leg buckled and he collapsed to the ground. The Englishman watched Charlie Hemming pass by "running faster than a young deer before the hounds." Pasco "cried out 'Charlie, don't leave me!'" Hemming never broke his stride and instead yelled as he passed: "'It's no time to stop now!'" Nevertheless, Hemming soon joined Pasco as a prisoner of war. John Inglis was more fortunate; he wrote later, "I am somewhat indebted to a good pair of legs which enabled me to show a clean pair of heels to [the] Yanks."[39]

Many of the men who escaped from the southern end of the ridge soon rallied just to the east, where Bate quickly forged together a line to prevent further pursuit of Bragg's defeated force. Bate placed General Finley in command of this delaying force and then pulled the 6th Florida farther east to form a reserve and second rallying point. Finley's line held until late that evening when General Breckinridge arrived and ordered the troops to withdraw. This final retreat ended at Dalton, Georgia, more than thirty miles southeast. There, Braxton Bragg's tenure with the Army of Tennessee ended at his own request; as he departed on December 2, one of the brass bands that serenaded the disgraced commander belonged to the 4th Florida.[40]

At Dalton, Bate discovered that his division had suffered 857 casualties at Chattanooga; he noted that most of those listed as missing "were Floridians who were in the trenches" at the ridge's base. Of Colonel Maxwell's 200 soldiers who began the day in the rifle pits, Washington Ives recorded that only 33 remained in the ranks that evening. The missing included Maxwell himself, Stockton, and Major Henry

Bradford, all of whom became prisoners of war. Ives's own 4th Florida had 172 soldiers in the works at the foot of Missionary Ridge and 23, including Lieutenant Colonel Badger and Major Jacob Lash, were present at the next roll call. Lieutenant Jerkins estimated that the 7th Florida lost 105 soldiers, killed, wounded, or missing. For the other regiments, only an incomplete tally can place the 6th Florida's losses at a minimum of 50. This means at Missionary Ridge, without including the unknown 1st and 3rd Florida's losses, the Florida Brigade suffered at least 471 casualties.[41]

Safe at Dalton, Daniel Hall of the 6th Florida inquired of his family back home, "I suppose you have heard of our Whiping before this time?" General Finley and others felt differently about the Missionary Ridge defeat and were quick to point out the bravery the Floridians had demonstrated during the fight. The brigade commander told Governor Milton, "My command fought with a courage and steadiness which elicited, as I am informed, the commendation of the Commander in Chief, and it is an admitted fact, that it did not retire from the field, until after the troops on our right and left had given way." Washington Ives reported, "Gen'l Bragg Breckinridge & Bates give Floridians great praise for the way in which they acted." John Inglis confided to relatives, "[T]he Florida Brigade behaved very well and of cours the old 3rd was as long in the line and longer than the Balance." A correspondent for the *Richmond Daily Dispatch* caused many a Floridian's chest to swell with pride when he wrote of their performance at Missionary Ridge, "I may say of the Florida troops generally that I have never known them to fail in the hour of trial."[42]

Thanks to the Floridians' hard fighting at Missionary Ridge, the brigade drew much praise from their superiors and admirers—but at the cost of hundreds of irreplaceable soldiers the brigade would dearly miss the following spring. In this same vein, the last-ditch defense of the Missionary Ridge rifle pits saw the 1st Florida Cavalry, Dismounted, and 4th Infantry all but annihilated. The regiments' field officers faced the possibility of Yankee prison camps for the remainder of the war. The battle saw Colonel Bullock's fears come true, as following his capture the poorly regarded Lieutenant Colonel Tillman Ingram assumed command of the 7th Florida.

In the days after the battle, the brigade's survivors reached Dalton and worked on their cabins in preparation for the winter; this would be their second such encampment of the war. At Dalton the soldiers recuperated, were refitted, thanks in large part to the supplies sent by Florida's citizens, and once more looked to religion for solace. Eighty miles southeast of Dalton, the Western and Atlantic's tracks reached Atlanta. The Floridians had glimpsed the city briefly as their trains had traveled through, both in the previous year and earlier in 1863; with spring would come the fight to defend the important rail hub and logistics center.

14 The Old Soldiers Are Much Better Satisfied

December 1863–May 5, 1864

Only days after the Missionary Ridge debacle, the Army of Tennessee halted its retreat at Dalton, a small railroad town situated on the Western and Atlantic Railroad in the mountains of northern Georgia. While the army remained encamped about the town for the next six months, the troops certainly did not remain idle. Though the soldiers spent the cold winter days at drill and standing for inspection, their morale gained a boost in the appointment of General Joseph E. Johnston and his implementation of a new furlough system. For the Florida Brigade, gaining adequate clothing and shoes became a significant outcome of the Dalton hiatus. By May, when new leaves covered the trees and the flowers bloomed, they stood well prepared and willing to contest the Federal Army for control of Georgia.

On the northern edge of Dalton, the Florida Brigade's campground was abuzz with activity during the first days of December. The soldiers worked in various capacities, cutting timber and constructing cabins for shelter against the oncoming winter. These huts, which Sergeant Archie Livingston described as having "chimneys and comfortable bunks, and upon the whole . . . dry and comfortable," were a necessity, as many of the brigade's soldiers suffered from a dearth of footwear and blankets. Many troops, particularly those who had fled from Missionary Ridge's base, fared worse, as any extra clothing they possessed was left in the rifle pits during the hasty withdrawal. Lieutenant Colonel Edward Mashburn wrote state legislator Enoch Vann, "[W]e are as Comfortable as the scarcity of blankets and Under Clothing will permit."[1]

Brigadier General Jesse Finley worked diligently to alleviate these deficits. In mid-December the general alerted Governor Milton to the fact that he had requested permission from General William J. Hardee to dispatch "one man from each company to proceed to Florida, to collect and bring to the command all the clothing, which the friends and families of our gallant soldier may have to send them, or which may be appropriated by the State." Washington Ives explained in a letter to his father that during the Christmas season the brigade had to rely on Florida's citizens for relief, for although "there has been a limited issue of Shirts, Pants, Jackets, Shoes etc. showing that the government is willing to supply us if it were able . . . the supply . . . are not equal to the demand." The citizens of Florida responded to General Finley's request with zeal, but precious weeks passed before the needed goods arrived.[2]

Pleasant news did arrive quickly, though, in the form of Lieutenants Daniel Knight and William Roberts, two officers who surrendered on Missionary Ridge. Days after their capture the two men escaped from their Yankee captors and made their way to Dalton. The lieutenants brought word of comrades who had been captured and killed in the battle, and that in turn allowed the casualties' loved ones to be notified. A family friend wrote to Amanda Bullock to inform her that her husband, Colonel Robert Bullock, though a prisoner, "was treated very well, and that he was quite cheerful." The brigade missed the Missionary Ridge prisoners considerably; by December the unit counted just over nine hundred effectives.[3]

During the months spent at Dalton, the regiments' command structures underwent alterations as well. Winter saw Angus McLean, the young lawyer, ascend to the colonelcy of the 6th Florida in the wake of General Finley's promotion. In lieu of Colonel William S. Dilworth's continuing absence due to illness, Lieutenant Colonel Mashburn commanded the 1st and 3rd Florida, and Lieutenant Colonel Tillman Ingram succeeded Colonel Robert Bullock in leading the 7th Florida. The most significant change in the Florida Brigade's composition was the consolidation of the 1st Florida Cavalry, Dismounted, and 4th Florida Infantry. The two regiments, thrown together under temporary commander Lieutenant Colonel Edward Badger, consisted of only five companies and numbered but 190 soldiers in early December. The 1st Florida Cavalry's three mounted companies were dismounted in early 1864 and joined the consolidated regiment as infantry. Of the brigade's plight, Benjamin Glover bluntly observed, "[O]ur Brigade is a fare [sic] sample of our army as it now stands."[4]

Very few of the soldiers captured at Missionary Ridge would ever fight again, for the federal government in late 1863 disregarded the 1862 agreement regarding prisoner exchange. This decision came after Vicksburg parolees were allowed to fight again before they were exchanged and then the Confederacy threatened to place captured black soldiers into servitude. Floridians who surrendered at Chattanooga found themselves incarcerated in "depots" throughout the Midwest: Camp Morton, Rock Island, Johnson's Island, and Camp Douglas.[5]

The holiday season did resemble 1862 in the fact that Christmas provided a glimmer of happiness during an otherwise bleak period. Dallas Wood of the 6th Florida's Company K still found grounds for complaints that day, however, arguing, "Christmas comes but once a year and then even poor soldiers can't get egg nog. However, we have some old spirits hear [sic] and they will make drunks come as quick as any thing." Evidently, as alcohol flowed freely through the Dalton encampment, many Floridians backslid from the religious lifestyle they had begun the previous year at Tullahoma and in East Tennessee. Officers and enlisted men imbibed alike. On Christmas Eve, a crowd gathered around General Finley's headquarters as the Florida Brigade's band serenaded their commander. Washington Ives recorded, "[T]he Brigade played 'My Old Kentucky Home,' & called for Gen'l

Finley who responded with a short and appropriate speech. It then, at Gen'l F's request, played Dixie, Marseille, and a beautiful waltz known by the band as the 'Lovely Waltz.'"[6]

Hearing the brigade band's music, Lieutenant Colonel Badger brought up the 4th Florida's band, which had been playing in the camps all evening, to also serenade the general. Ives explained with chagrin that the 4th Florida's band members embarrassed themselves because they had accepted drinks at each stop "until some of them had become 'How Come You So,' . . . Lt. Col. Badger was then called upon, but . . . he had been too long with the band to have a clear idea." Others, such as Archie Livingston and John Inglis, drank socially and did not join others in becoming inebriated. Teetotaler Dallas Wood confessed that he had no "desire to get drunk and would much prefer having a big dinner of old collards or turnips, and in fact think that they would be of more advantage to me than a barrel of whiskey."[7]

Despite the losses at Missionary Ridge, the subsequent retreat, and their winter encampment at Dalton, the Floridians remained full of fight. However, they were very concerned about the issuing of furloughs. Captain Inglis wrote, "[O]ur Army is in good Spirits, and willing to go in again at the expiration of the present service provided they are allowed a few days furlough. . . . The men . . . are willing to Fight, March, starve, or freeze, but ask for a short respite from it for a few days to rest, and see the loved ones they have defended." Washington Ives informed his father, "[F]rom what I see and hear, every day that unless the men are allowed furloughs . . . that at the end of the present term of enlistment, desertions will be very numerous." Benjamin R. Glover stated the men of his regiment would not "fight without they are treated better."[8]

A solution to the soldiers' complaints came in the person of General Joseph E. Johnston. A fifty-six-year-old Virginian who led both the Army of Northern Virginia and the Department of the West, the Confederacy's failed attempt at a unified command structure, Johnston came to lead the Army of Tennessee by default. General Johnston and President Jefferson Davis, to put it mildly, did not have the best working relationship; their quarrels began before the war, and the animosity between the two grew during the conflict, particularly following the Vicksburg fiasco. When Johnston assumed command of the Army of Tennessee on December 27, 1863, it was only because Davis had to choose between Johnston and Pierre G. T. Beauregard, and the president disliked Beauregard more than the Virginian. Washington Ives described his new leader as "5'9, grey hair, blueish eyes, and fullish face . . . and broad nose." The slightly built general soon instituted measures meant to soothe the disgruntled army.[9]

Even before General Johnston assumed command, interim commander General William J. Hardee issued General Orders No. 227, allowing one in every thirty enlisted men, and one officer per company, leave "for any period not exceeding thirty days." After General Johnston arrived at the army, he modified the order so as to allow one furlough for every twenty-five enlisted soldiers. Interestingly, the same men who voiced opposition to Johnston's summer furloughs seemed to appreciate the general's winter proclamations. Washington Ives saw a change in attitude as "the old soldiers are much better satisfied than they were a month or two ago and I believe the spirit of the men is greatly increased by the late system of furloughs instituted by General Johnson [*sic*]." John Inglis wrote, "General Johnston is still giving furloughs . . . I never saw men so attached to a Genl as our Army is to him. The men are greatly encouraged by the furlough system."[10]

Keeping the Army of Tennessee pleased that winter was of the utmost importance because of the dearth of Confederate Army recruits at that point in the war. In his annual message to the Confederate Congress in December 1863, Jefferson Davis highlighted the vital problem of the Confederacy's declining manpower. The president asked congress to extend the Conscription Act of 1862 to include men older than forty-five so as to free up able-bodied soldiers from rear-echelon duties; he also wanted slaves used to perform certain jobs, such as driving wagons and cooking. Davis also informed the legislative body that according to the current draft law, the enlistments extended in 1862 would end in 1864. Davis wanted new draft laws because "the difficulty of obtaining recruits from certain localities and the large number of exemptions have prevented sufficient accessions in many of the companies to preserve their organizations after the discharge of the original members." In short, unless the congress passed new draft legislation, the Confederacy would lose a portion of its army in the forthcoming year.[11]

Congress relieved President Davis's fears in February when it passed an amended Conscription Act. This draft law required all those in the service to remain until the war's end and all able-bodied men between the ages of seventeen and fifty to enlist. Therefore, when a wave of reenlistments passed through the Confederacy's armies in January and February, these proclamations were demonstrations of patriotism and protest rather than binding agreements between the soldiers and their government. Roddie Shaw pled that reenlistments were needed so that the soldiers were not "kept in service under conscript acts." By reenlisting, symbolically at least, the soldiers exercised their liberty in deciding to fight until the war's end.[12]

Confederate soldiers bemoaned the new conscription act's lack of a clause that permitted regimental reorganization, so cherished in the Conscription Act of 1862. Influential politicians and the soldiers' own generals stood resolutely opposed to any form of electioneering. Secretary of War James Seddon argued that officer elections that winter could remove experienced veterans and place ill-prepared soldiers in command of regiments and companies. With 1864 looming as perhaps the most important year in the Confederacy's short life, the War Department had no desire to stand in the way of success. In the end, Washington Ives reported that the Confederate Congress decided not to allow reorganization and "all the officers seem well satisfied, knowing that we will not be allowed to organize."[13]

Florida soldiers, at least, protested the government's refusal to sanction regimental elections, a right the American volunteer claimed. Roddie Shaw wrote that in late January, when numerous other regiments had reenlisted for the war, "none of the Florida troops have made a start in that direction. They all want . . . reorganization." When the 7th Florida's committee eventually sat to write a reenlistment proclamation, they claimed that though the soldiers maintained "the utmost and unequivocal confidence in the fidelity and wisdom of our legislatures," they were disappointed in the Confederate Congress's decision and "most respectfully ask that we, as a Regt. of volunteers, may be permitted to reelect our own regimental and company officers, claiming it as a right belonging to all volunteers." Despite all of this, General Finley reported to Governor Milton on February 7, "[M]y command is rapidly re-enlisting for the war, which when done, will give it a still greater claim upon the respect and confidence of our beloved and noble little State."[14]

In February 1864 the Florida Brigade's supply deficiency reached a critical point. General Finley informed Governor Milton, "[I]f we had shoes and blankets, would be in very fine condition. Our destitution in the former article of clothing is deplorable—there being between seven and eight hundred men either barefoot or nearly so." Some relief arrived before Finley's letter reached Governor Milton's desk. In reply to Finley's December request, Tallahassee's ladies and children held several benefit concerts and a festival to raise money for clothing for the soldiers. Their contribution amounted to flannel shirts enough to outfit two companies and a single blanket. In March, donations of shoes and socks arrived, allowing Finley to report to the governor, "We received the shoes which were sent . . . last month. They came at a time when they were very much needed—and were, I assure you, in the highest degree acceptable to our brave men, many of whom at that time, were barefooted." Washington Ives wrote that "there was a lot of clothing issued to the troops consisting of shirts, pants, etc."[15]

For the 1st Florida Cavalry and 4th Florida, Consolidated, a new battle flag presented by McNaught, Ormond, & Company of Atlanta provided a morale boost and symbolized the fastening of the two regiments into a single entity. The committee that drafted a resolution of thanks to the company confessed that the new banner "has cheered our spirits in no small degree." It emboldened the soldiers to think that the citizens' "faith in Confederate valor and patriotism . . . is still as unbroken and fresh as when for the first time the star of the Confederacy rose bright and beautiful amid the blood and carnage of the victorious field of Manassas."[16]

On February 12, 1864, the Florida soldiers, along with other troops that had long served under General John C. Breckinridge, gathered in Dalton to say goodbye to their beloved leader. After General Bragg accused Breckinridge of drunkenness at Missionary Ridge, General Johnston replaced Breckinridge first with General Thomas Hindman and then with General William Hardee. Ives wrote that at their last meeting, Breckinridge told the Floridians "he was proud of his association with us." Robert Watson remembered the general "made a splendid speech in which he said he regretted very much that he had to part with his old friends the Florida troops. He complemented them highly for their bravery and etc."[17]

By the beginning of the next month, Robert Watson's tenure with the Army of Tennessee had ended as well, as the former carpenter and sixteen other Key West Avengers received their transfers to the Confederate Navy. Watson happily recorded that he and his fellow sailors were "as such a joyful lot of fellows as we were since the war began." Not everyone, particularly Captain Robert Blair Smith, was satisfied with the reassignment. Watson wrote that Smith "was greatly put out at it for it leaves him with but a remnant of a company." Before they repaired aboard the CSS *Savannah,* the newly minted seamen mollified Smith's wounded feelings by presenting him with a new sword.[18]

The entire 7th Florida had reason to celebrate in March when Colonel Robert Bullock was exchanged and free to report for duty. Though the exchange and parole system faltered in 1863, in February 1864 U.S. secretary of war Edwin Stanton ordered "an experimental boat under flag of truce to City Point, Va., with 200 rebel officers, with an officer to exchange them for a like number of U.S. officers held by the rebel authorities as prisoners of war." Bullock somehow became one of the two hundred exchanged and returned to duty with his regiment.[19]

Arriving at the 7th Florida's camp during the spring, Bullock witnessed gray-clad soldiers tramping about in the muddy fields around Dalton, performing close-order drill. General Johnston wanted his army to remain keen on maneuvers and sharp regarding their shooting. For Bullock's 7th Florida, as with other regiments in the army, the immediate aftermath of Missionary Ridge brought no respite from constant training. The soldiers had been taking part in brigade inspection and practicing battalion drill since December. By March, General Bate could inform Braxton Bragg, "[D]rills are the order of the day in this Army. I have Brigade or Division drills every suitable day . . . it (the Div) . . . is in good condition."[20]

Sergeant Archie Livingston wrote home in March as well, explaining that in the Army of Tennessee, "Army Reviews Corps Division & Brigade drills on hand. Hardee and Bate put us through it on Monday and oh it was shockingly cold." Washington Ives described to his sister, who had seen only local Florida troops on dress parade, a corps review in detail:

> At 8 AM each Regiment formed on its own ground, and then marched off each taking its proper place in line as they marched, after passing through Dalton we formed in line in an old field where all Breckinridge's Division got

together, here we were kept an hour & a half before everything and everybody was made to pass in review . . . each passed in column by companies yet it took about half an hour to pass at quicktime, the line being about a mile long . . . I never marched over any more slippery ground in my life . . . it would have puzzled a duck to walk the road without falling down . . . Gen Johnston, Cheatam, Anderson, Bates [sic] and Stovall were present at the colors, besides the different brigade commanders.

Lieutenant Roddie Shaw wrote that the muddy conditions of the ground during the review caused men to fall "by the dozens on all sides."[21]

In April, General William Hardee's Corps, to which Bate's Division had been transferred in March, held a mock battle to practice tactics under combat conditions. Archie Livingston recalled:

[O]ur division was arranged in line of battle to meet Walker's. Every man was supplied with blank cartridges and when the command "forward" was given, thus sounded a shout almost deafening from both sides. Artillery and musketry of Bate's, Walker's Cheatham's and Cleburn's [sic] divisions, made a display of smoke and noise representing perfectly the exact features of a deadly conflict with the enemy. However there was nothing of the death suffering and mental distress that more or less comes in every engagement with forces determined for success or death.

Ironically, the sham battle produced casualties: "after the infantry finished their part of the program they were formed into squares to resists the attacks of Cavalry. . . . Several Cavalry men were wounded . . . with paper wads, and . . . one horse . . . had been struck with a bayonet."[22]

On March 25 General Bate's men marched onto the parade ground to view the all-too-real effect of rifled-musket fire. The division formed a "U"; at the open end of the formation stood a single wooden post and nearby a freshly dug grave. Washington Ives wrote, "[A]fter standing in the cold and wet about 3/4 of an hour the prisoner appeared accompanied by the guard of 12 men and the Band of the 4th [Florida] Regt and his coffin borne by 4 men." William Keen, a 3rd Florida private, was the condemned in this instance and his charge: desertion.[23]

According to one of Keen's staunchest defenders, Major George Fairbanks, a Floridian serving with the Confederate Army in Atlanta, Keen deserted in November 1862 after receiving word that his wife and two children were ill with pneumonia. The *Gainesville Cotton States* asserted that after Keen reached Florida, he discovered "that the case was not as bad as had been reported." Keen, however, decided to remain in Florida, and Robert Watson recorded the camp rumor that

Keen had "made his brags that he could not be taken for he carried a double bar-
reled gun whereever he went." A conscript officer seized Keen and soon dispatched
him back to the 3rd Florida. During his transport to Dalton, Keen, fearing his
awaited fate, leaped from the moving train and broke several ribs.[24]

According to the historian Ella Lonn, during the Civil War more than 2,200
Florida soldiers deserted from their units. At least 333 of them served in the Army
of Tennessee's Florida Brigade. These soldiers left their posts for many reasons,
though one of the prime motivators for returning home was the Yankee threat to
Florida's citizens. With Amelia Island and St. Augustine both captured in 1862
and the constant menace of raiding parties launched by blockaders, many never
even left the state with their regiments. Given the available evidence, it would seem
that most were simply disillusioned by the defeats at Murfreesboro and Missionary Ridge and slipped away while the army retreated from those battles or sat in its
winter encampments at Tullahoma and Dalton. Others managed to become lost
in the hurried shift between Tennessee and Mississippi in the summer of 1863.[25]

Around 250 Floridians returned to the ranks, either forced by Confederate authorities to do so or on their own recognizance. An amnesty extended to deserter-
ers by President Jefferson Davis saved some of these men from suffering the penalty for their crime. However, sources show at least twenty-three were tried and
punished. All received sentences of hard labor and confinement, and some were
marked with a "D" on their hips. William Keen received death by musketry.[26]

Though the 3rd Florida's soldiers circulated a petition asking for the sentence's
commutation, some of Keen's comrades refused to sign the document. Major
Glover A. Ball wrote bluntly: "William Keen has not discharged his duties as faith-
fully as a soldier should have done . . . I regret that such a stain should rest upon
any member of this command." General Finley wrote to the anxious Major Fairbanks that the chaplains were meeting with Keen so that "he be prepared through
repentance toward God, and faith in our Lord Jesus Christ to meet the solemn
doom that awaits him!" Private A. G. McLeod declared, "[M]en who . . . desert
their country in the hour of trial richly deserve the penalty."[27]

A commutation never arrived. Before the firing squad performed their grisly
task, Keen "exhorted all to meet death a thousand times on the Gory Field, before
acting as he had." After the prisoner knelt, his arms were bound to the stake and a
handkerchief was placed over his eyes. Six soldiers discharged their weapons at the
condemned man; Washington Ives recalled, "I was looking at Keene at the time
and at the volley his head jerked back." John Inglis felt that the execution "had a
good effect on the troops."[28]

Though the men spent much of their time working to become even more proficient soldiers, the Dalton encampment also witnessed its share of revelry and religion. Many Confederate Civil War veterans' most treasured memory of army life

remained the snowball fights held during the winter encampments. Of the surviving Florida Brigade soldiers' collections, many contain at least one letter describing the amusement offered by the large, division-sized battles. On the morning March 22, after a night of snowfall, Finley's soldiers peered out of their cabins to behold a world blanketed in white. Duncan McLeod, a Walton County citizen serving in the 6th Florida, wrote home, "[T]he woods and distant mountains surrounding our encampment present a beautiful appearance." Before long, Finley's troops heard a commotion and soon saw Bate's Brigade formed in a "line of battle," with the view to give the Florida Brigade a test of their "prowess in snowballing." While at first an even fight, Washington Ives claimed that because the Orphan Brigade soon reinforced Bate's men, the Floridians capitulated. Before long, Bate's Floridians, Kentuckians, and Tennesseans had become friends once more and, with battle flags flying and General Finley commanding their motley band, moved "against [A. P.] Stewart's Division."[29]

John Inglis remembered watching General Finley at the head of his troops, leading "with the enthusiasm of a School Boy." Bate's "whole line impelled by . . . determination, threw themselves impetuously, broke their [A. P. Stewart's] lines, and scattered them in confusion." Soon, Stewart's soldiers were on the run and Bate's men followed, capturing "Colonels Captains often and privates." Stewart's veterans rallied, however, and with reinforcements "drove us back and completely routed us." A soldier serving in Bate's Brigade called the defeat "another Missionary Ridge affair, only on a smaller scale." In this debacle, Stewart's soldiers captured both General Finley and the 1st and 4th Florida's new battle flag. While the "enemy" soon paroled General Finley, they kept the banner and never returned it to the Floridians.[30]

In April, as spring bloomed in earnest, the soldiers turned once more to town ball for amusement. Washington Ives explained that "the boys are killing time in camp by playing ball, which is such good exercise that it will fit them for the fatiguing marches to be taken this summer. The Soldiers here are undoubtedly, at this time more lighthearted and like schoolboys than I ever saw them. Maj. Lash and Col. Badger often play ball with the men." The fiercest rivalry in the brigade was between the 1st Florida Cavalry and 4th Florida and the 6th Florida. The former regiment remained undefeated in their series with the West Floridians, though they tied the 7th Florida in the only meeting between the two regiments. The 1st and 3rd Florida missed out on most of the excitement, for General Bate dispatched the regiment to Resaca on April 15 to guard against any threats against the Western and Atlantic's trestle that spanned the Oostanula River. Washington Ives regretted the transfer, for "the 1st and 3rd & 4th are more like brothers than any other regt in our brig, so that the latter regt is sorry that the 1st and 3rd has gone."[31]

As in the previous year in East Tennessee and at Tullahoma, the soldiers turned to religion as a balm against their hardships and fears. After they had built their winter quarters the Florida soldiers constructed a brigade chapel. Washington Ives reported that in March the church "is thronged every time service is held."[32]

"If there was ever a genuine work of the Spirit," 4th Florida chaplain R. L. Wiggins marveled, "certainly it is now going on in the Florida Brigade of the Army of Tennessee." Chaplain J. H. Tompkies of the 7th Florida seconded this assessment when he proudly wrote of the brigade's chaplains' successes since the revivals had begun in mid-February: "[W]e have had the pleasure of welcoming one hundred and six of the officers and men into the different branches of the Christian church." Lieutenant Reason W. Jerkins explained to his daughter that on two sequential nights in March "we had a fine meating today & after Church thare baptizzin thare was 22 Diped," and "there was 10 more Men that Joined the baptis church Last Knight." John Inglis wrote, "[T]here is quite a revival going on here, and many of our hardy boys are being converted. I wish our whole Army were Christians."[33]

Sergeant Archie Livingston wrote that the church-going continued even after the 1st and 3rd Florida removed to Resaca: "A Religious meeting is going on every night with Our Regt and some Texas cavalry of Dibbrell's command. Many are joining the church and being baptized." In order to prevent the backsliding that had occurred at Christmas and to "exercise a Christian watch care over each other and to exert a salutary and religious influence over the whole command," the Christians organized a Brigade Christian Association. General Finley, likely a Christian since the 1840s, led this group as well.[34]

One factor that threatened to hamper the troops' religious nurturing, according to Chaplain Tompkies, was a "great scarcity of testaments and Bibles in the Brigade." Tompkies suggested that Floridians, who by providing clothing and food to the troops adhered to the Christian teachings of providing for the needy, "might do much towards supplying our soldiers with copies of the scriptures and religious readings in general." This shortage might have existed only in the 7th Florida, for Angus Gillis, a 6th Florida private, wrote on May 5, "[W]hen we do not attend preaching we lie up in our huts and read the Bible and religious tracts and newspapers distributed among us by our Chaplain (Mr. Tally)."[35]

As Gillis explained the religious habits of the Rebel soldiers at Dalton to his aunt, General William T. Sherman's Federal force began moving south from the Chattanooga area. With the Yankee columns observed marching toward their position, most Confederate soldiers expected a fight soon. The soldiers' confidence ran high; Washington Ives informed his father: "[W]e are all in good spirits and the opinion is general, that if the enemy advances against us we will use him roughly, if not annihilate him." Benjamin Glover wrote, "[I]f we have a fight it will be close around here, and the yankeys will get the worst whipping they every got."[36]

Roddie Shaw was particularly anxious for the fight, for his lieutenant's commission had arrived in January and he'd not had the opportunity to serve in his new rank: "I do not feel proud of it yet, as I think I have no right to if for skill and valor. But by summer I will either deserve it or the brand of a coward." The new officer understood how vital the upcoming campaign was. He warned in January, "This Spring will be the most important period of the war. . . . The mighty hosts of the invader will be driven back or Rebellion will tremble. . . . Johnston will do all in his power to gain some ground or hold his present line, but if it is necessary for him to fall back, let not the vile tongue of censure be uncaged."[37]

15 The Company and Entire Brigade Suffered Immensely and Accomplished Nothing

May 7–September 3, 1864

During the first week of May 1864, Federal generals Ulysses S. Grant and William T. Sherman put their armies in northern Virginia and Georgia, respectively, in motion against their Confederate opponents. While both generals endeavored to destroy the Rebel field armies, they also looked toward Richmond and Atlanta and sought to wage a "war of exhaustion"; the Northern commanders hoped to wreck Confederate resources and the enemy's will to resist. The eyes of both Southerners and Northerners focused on these campaigns, for already that year the Rebels had blunted Federal thrusts into Florida and Louisiana, and in the Shenandoah Valley. President Abraham Lincoln's reelection hopes hinged on the 1864 spring campaigns, as early that year even some of the president's own party doubted his policies could bring a successful end to the war.

General Jesse Finley's Florida Brigade stood in the midst of this maelstrom, awaiting the next Union movement at their Dalton encampment. As news of intense skirmishing reached the troops, Lieutenant Francis P. Fleming of the 1st Florida Cavalry and 4th Florida wrote of the already failed Yankee offensives and of the coming battles: "In no case have they gained a success. I trust that they will soon see the madness of their undertaking to subjugate us."[1]

Rising above Dalton on its western edge is Rocky Face Ridge. True to its name, this eight-hundred-foot-high mountain stretches in a general north-south direction for more than twenty miles and posed a steep and harsh obstacle that any Federal army attempting to invade Georgia had to overcome. The Confederates had fortified the ridge's gaps, barring passage through the mountain. On May 7, 1864, Rebel pickets stationed on the ridge's western edge encountered Sherman's bluecoated columns as they marched southward to offer battle. News of the skirmishing reached the Confederates at Dalton, and soon the various divisions rushed to occupy their entrenchments. From their perches atop the ridge, the Army of Tennessee's soldiers glimpsed their old foes of the Army of the Cumberland as they entered the valley before the Rebels' strong position.[2]

For nearly a week, General William B. Bate's Division manned the trenches that overlooked Mill Creek Gap; the general observed in his official report that during this time, "skirmishing with artillery and small arms occurred constantly."

Captain John Inglis, commanding a consolidated company in the 1st and 3rd Florida, wrote that while the Florida Brigade remained on Rocky Face, "we repulsed the Yanks in every attempt they made on our lines . . . with loss." Captain David Ewell Maxwell, a twenty-one-year-old who saw action at Gettysburg with the 2nd Florida Infantry and had been transferred to the 1st Florida Cavalry, Dismounted, upon receiving his commission the previous August, remarked that while he thought the Yankees lost numerous men, "our loss was comparatively small, from the fact that we were protected by breast-works." Maxwell allowed, however, "we were obliged to keep half of the companies up, so that by the time the retreat began we were pretty well worn-out."[3]

As the Atlanta Campaign began, the Florida Brigade, bolstered by convalesced wounded and soldiers who had returned from furloughs and extended periods of unauthorized leave, numbered over 1,200 soldiers. General Finley's troops began the campaign uniformly armed with the cumbersome and relatively ineffective .69 Springfield musket, which had been provided to the units sometime during the Dalton winter encampment. Veterans of the 1st Florida Infantry would have recognized the weapons as the same model issued at Pensacola in 1861. At a time when Federal units were armed with rifled-muskets and lever-action repeaters, the Floridians would find themselves at a distinct disadvantage in a firefight. Despite their poor weapons, the Floridians were, for the most part, led by experienced and well-respected officers at all levels. At the onset of the fight for Georgia, the soldiers' confidence in General Johnston and victory remained high.[4]

On the evening of May 13, the Army of Tennessee's soldiers may have wondered why the order came to fall back from their entrenchments and form marching ranks; even more puzzling was why they faced south toward Atlanta. The reason was that while Johnston's force busied themselves with blunting the various attempts by the Army of the Cumberland to seize the gaps, one of Sherman's other armies, the Army of the Tennessee, emerged from unguarded Snake Creek Gap within a few miles of the railroad town of Resaca and the Confederates' supply line. Though only a few thousand Rebels guarded Resaca, the Army of the Tennessee failed to launch an attack against the town, sparing Johnston's army an early defeat in the campaign. Only on May 12 did Johnston learn for certain that Sherman was moving on Resaca in force and the next day ordered his two corps to march for that place with all haste.[5]

At Resaca, the Army of Tennessee affected a juncture with Leonidas Polk's Army of Mississippi, just arrived from its namesake state. Johnston's reinforced army formed an inverted L-shaped line with its flanks anchored in the south on the Oostanaula River and northeast at the banks of the Connasauga River. General William Hardee's Corps occupied the center of the line, with Bate's Division forming the southern half of the apex; Finley's Brigade was stationed on the left of Bate's line. John H. Hill, assigned to General Finley's staff as a courier, recalled that upon their arrival at Resaca, the brigade's soldiers, though tired from a night march, immediately engaged in "building field works by taking down a worm fence and hastily covering up the rails with earth."[6]

Though the Union attacks on the afternoon of May 14 aimed at a point north of Finley's soldiers, the Florida Brigade's pickets remained active throughout the day, maintaining a brisk fire at their Federal counterparts. During the exchange, the Yankee sharpshooters caused an alarming number of casualties among the various regiments. After the Federal assaults against the angle faltered under a withering fire, General Sherman, as he had done at Jackson nearly a year earlier, made use of his numerical advantage in artillery and ordered a bombardment of the Rebel works. In the main line of entrenchments, the 1st Florida Cavalry and 4th Florida and 7th Florida found some protection behind their hastily built earthworks. The 1st and 3rd Florida and 6th Florida, lying in reserve to the rear of the entrenchments, received the worst of the cannonading. Of the firing, Captain Inglis wrote, "[W]e got the worst shelling here that we ever had, and yet held our position." His cousin Archie Livingston remembered: "[T]he Artillery firing at the two days fight at Resaca was the most terrific I ever witnessed. . . . We were exposed to an enfilading fire both from Artillery and sharp shooters." Surgeon Henry McCall Holmes estimated that the Floridians' casualties for the day totaled one hundred.[7]

During the fierce bombardment, as Federal gunners focused on Slocumb's Washington Artillery, a shell impacted against a tree growing near the Floridians' line, sending splinters flying in every direction. John Hill reported one of these fragments "struck General Finley in the face. He passed his hand over his face and saw the blood, and remarked: 'This is the first blood I have lost in this war.'" The following day, while enduring yet another enemy shelling, a Yankee round severed a heavy limb from a tree standing near Finley's headquarters; in falling, the limb crashed upon the general's shoulder. The general soldiered through the discomfort of this wound for two days, "believing his hurt . . . a mere contusion." However, with "the pain and inconvenience becoming intolerable, a surgical examination discovered the fracture, and he was ordered to the rear, extremely loath to leave his gallant brigade in such a crisis."[8]

Thus, within the first week of this important campaign, the Florida Brigade lost its popular and experienced leader to a broken collarbone. In late May Finley traveled to his Florida home to recuperate and would not rejoin his brigade until August. Colonel Robert Bullock, as the brigade's senior colonel, assumed command. One of his men described the new leader as "a man of farsighted and sure-footed judgement."[9]

The Army of Tennessee evacuated Resaca on the night of May 15 after General Johnston received word that Federal divisions had crossed the Oostanaula River downstream and once more threatened the railroad that supplied the Army of Tennessee. Johnston's force retreated south along the railroad to Adairsville, with Bate's and Cleburne's divisions acting as a rearguard. Though Johnston discovered no terrain suitable for sustaining a defensive battle at Adairsville, he did plan to launch a limited offensive to destroy a portion of Sherman's force. By dispatching Hardee's Corps to Kingston with the army's wagons, he hoped Sherman would divide his army so that it could march to outflank the new Confederate position. The corps of Generals John Bell Hood and Leonidas Polk would stand by near Cassville to surprise the Union force dispatched toward that town. The trap failed when General Hood, as he prepared to launch an assault at General John Schofield's Army of the Ohio, discovered Federal troops on his unprotected right flank.[10]

Following the aborted assault on May 19 and 20, the Army of Tennessee remained in defensive works below Cassville awaiting a Federal assault. However, Generals Hood and Polk voiced concern over the vulnerability of their works to Federal artillery fire and proposed a withdrawal. The fact that the Federal Army forced crossings over the Etowah River on the Confederate left flank enhanced the need for a retreat. Johnston's army fell back to Allatoona, where the road and railroad funneled through a narrow gap, hoping to establish a new position there.[11]

Despite the constant retreating since the campaign's inception and being exposed to enemy fire almost daily, the soldiers' morale remained high. Captain Maxwell explained to the folks at home, "[W]e . . . all are in fine spirit, although it has been somewhat dampened since we left Dalton, but still the confidence in our chief is unshaken." Lieutenant Francis P. Fleming, who like Maxwell had transferred to the 1st Florida Cavalry, Dismounted, in August after becoming an officer, also wrote, "[W]e have been falling back ever since giving up our position in front of Dalton, but the troops are in fine spirits and have every confidence in Gen Johnston, and that when he sees fit to make a stand will inflict a terrible blow upon the enemy." John Inglis confided, "[T]he late movements and hard life have been very trying to us, but confidence prevails everyone in this Army."[12]

As alluded to by Inglis, though high morale abounded, the fatigue of night marches and the stress of constant skirmishing began to take its toll on the men's physical condition. Sergeant Archie Livingston wrote to his sisters from a Georgia hospital after becoming ill: "the present campaign of the A. of T. has been one of the severest I ever went through in my life. Night marching, maneuvering and occasionally fighting has almost used me up. . . . Every time Johnston confronts him Sherman marches his army to the right."[13]

The Army of Tennessee rested near Allatoona on May 21 and 22, where some found time to bathe to remove the red dirt and powder stains from their bodies, although their uniforms remained filthy. General Sherman spent these days pondering his next move, eventually deciding on a course that would take his army south of Allatoona in an attempt to turn the left flank of Johnston's strong position. If the movement succeeded, Sherman could then strike for the Western and Atlantic Railroad at Marietta, southeast of Johnston's present position. Johnston's cavalry reported the Federal move nearly as soon as it began and, as a result, the general put the Army of Tennessee in motion for the crossroads town of Dallas. The Confederates won the race and began entrenching as soon as they arrived. Hardee's Corps occupied the Army of Tennessee's left flank at Dallas, and the army's line ran northeast for several miles.[14]

On May 25 and 27, General Sherman launched two ill-advised assaults on what he believed was Johnston's right flank; the fights at New Hope Church and Pickett's Mill resulted in heavy Federal casualties. While both engagements were north of the Floridians' position, heavy skirmishing occurred on their front during these days. Though the flanking movement had not succeeded in opening a route to Marietta, Sherman had achieved his objective of turning Johnston out of his Allatoona entrenchments, and on May 28 he decided to remove his army back to the line of the Western and Atlantic, from which he had departed to embark on his Dallas trek. On that same day, Johnston instructed General Bate's Division to probe the Army of the Tennessee's works and "ascertain his strength and position." Essentially, Johnston wanted Bate to push in the enemy's skirmishers and determine if McPherson's Federals were still in position.[15]

On the evening of May 27 under the cover of darkness, a detail from the 1st Florida Cavalry and 4th Florida slipped out of the main line of entrenchments to occupy the rifle pits in the brigade's front. Sometime prior to the movement Roddie Shaw began a letter to his uncle, intending to provide him with a detailed description of the campaign. The call to perform picket duty cut Shaw's writing time short, and the lieutenant ended the abbreviated letter by penning: "I leave now for a skirmish myself for 24 hours. Goodbye until tomorrow evening." Around 9:00 A.M. the next morning, Shaw, determined to prove during the campaign that he was a competent and brave officer, rose from the cover of his rifle pit, perhaps to yell an order. Somewhere across the field, a XV Corps soldier took aim at the dark-haired Rebel and pulled the trigger of his weapon. A split second later, a projectile tore through Roddie Shaw's neck, severing his spinal cord. Shaw died instantly. Several 1st Florida Cavalry and 4th Florida soldiers carried the twenty-three-year-old's body from the skirmish line and that afternoon buried him on Marietta Road. A Gadsden County resident's eulogy would have pleased the fallen soldier, as it noted that Shaw "was a gallant young man and his death is lamented by all who knew him." The wooden headboard carved by his comrades, its lettering inked with care, has long since disappeared; Shaw's burial location now is known only to God.[16]

The upcoming probe on the Army of the Tennessee's line gave Shaw's comrades little time to grieve and by nightfall the slain lieutenant's name was but one on a long, pitiful casualty list that grew exponentially that afternoon. Bate, in order to follow Johnston's instructions to probe the Army of the Tennessee's line, directed General Frank Armstrong's Brigade of "Red" Jackson's Cavalry Division to ini-

tiate the attack at 4:00 P.M. by pushing back the enemy's pickets and scouting the
Army of the Tennessee's main line of entrenchments; General Bate directed that if
Armstrong's cavalrymen discovered "little or no resistance, four cannon shots will
be fired in rapid succession" as a signal for the infantry to advance and invest the
entrenchments. Bate later claimed that he stressed upon his brigade commanders
that if they met "stubborn resistance behind defences, withdraw without assault
unless satisfied it can be carried." As Armstrong's dismounted troopers rushed forward, they encountered very heavy firing, indicating that McPherson's soldiers,
namely John A. Logan's XV Corps, still manned their fortifications.[17]

    While heavy firing raged to the south, the Florida Brigade lay behind their breast-
works, awaiting the order to move forward. On the 6th Florida's line, Colonel
Angus McLean finished explaining General Bate's orders to his subordinates and
stood atop the earthworks to observe the Federal line. With the hot sun beating
down upon his brow, the young colonel turned to a soldier below and asked for a
swallow from his canteen. The words had just exited McLean's lips when a Yankee
skirmisher's minié bullet passed through his head, and McLean collapsed back-
ward into the entrenchments. One of his many relatives in the regiment passed the
sad news to the folks in Walton County: "Mr. King caught him, I sprang to him
& assisted in laying him down & for a minute or two supported his head with my
hand. He never spoke or groaned. Closed his own eyes & died in a few minutes."
Lieutenant Colonel Lafayette Kenan assumed command of the 6th Florida following his superior's death.[18]

    McLean's and Shaw's deaths demonstrated to the soldiers they were fighting a
new brand of warfare. Save for the brief "sieges" of Jackson and Chattanooga, the
Floridians had never been in such close contact with the enemy for extended periods of time. During the Atlanta Campaign, the men were under constant fire
for days on end, where even the briefest exposure to a sharp-eyed Federal picket
might bring death.

    Within a short time after this tragic episode, Colonel Bullock gave the order for
the Florida Brigade to form lines of battle beyond the entrenchments and prepare
for the assault. Though Armstrong's men had encountered heavy resistance in their
attack and General Bate had dispatched couriers to his brigade commanders informing them to abort the attack, both General Joseph Lewis of the Orphan Brigade and Colonel Bullock somehow missed Bate's message. The couriers failed to
alert the two officers in time, and soon the Orphans and Floridians were advancing toward the enemy line. This would have tragic consequences.[19]

    With skirmishers sweeping before them and battle flags unfurled in the hot
afternoon haze, the Floridians and Orphans swept across a field cleared of forests,
much as they had done at Murfreesboro more than a year earlier and at Chickamauga the previous fall. Over the "pop-pop" of the skirmishers' guns, a veteran remembered hearing Lieutenant Colonel Edward Badger's voice "bidding the men

remember the State from whence they came." As the soldiers tramped forward across the thick underbrush, the fortifications of the Army of the Tennessee's XV and XVI Corps frowned down upon them from atop a ridge. Not long after the advance began, Federal skirmishers unleashed a volley that mortally wounded 1st Florida Cavalry and 4th Florida Lieutenant Frank Kilpatrick, who had recently lost his wife. Despite being stunned and staggered by the initial firing, the two Confederate brigades overran the Federal rifle pits, which lay a hundred yards from the enemy's main line of works, and engaged in hand-to-hand combat with the Yankees.[20]

One soldier remembered that at the Federal skirmish line the Floridians poured "a deadly volley into them, gave a real rebel yell, and charged with . . . force into their ranks, killing, wounding and capturing about one hundred of them, the balance fled in the wildest dismay to their breastworks." The Floridians and Orphans should have stopped their assault at the picket line, as the Federals' main works were in view and it was clear that they were occupied. But the two brigades continued their advance. J. C. McLean of the 6th Florida described in a letter that the Floridians passed over the rifle pits, remaining close on the heels of their foe, and "charged to the enemies breastworks & stopped . . . in a few yards of them."[21]

John Duke of the 53rd Ohio remembered thirty-six years later, "The charge of the Florida Brigade which the 53rd and 37th Ohio resisted and repulsed, was an extremely gallant one. . . . they came with their hands bowed down and their hats pulled over their eyes as if to hide from view their inevitable death." Once the Rebels were standing face-to-face with the Federals, their plight became clear. Lieutenant Henry W. Reddick remembered, "[T]here rose the Yankees in three or four ranks, I know it seemed to me that the air was blue with their uniforms. As they rose they fired volley after volley into our single line of battle." Duke also wrote of the fight, "Our murderous fire, while we had them in this death trap, was that of precision. Our aim was deadly." John L. McKinnon wrote that the 1st and 3rd Florida's color-bearer went down and a struggle ensued over the banner: "A commissioned officer jumped out of the pit with sword drawn, pointing to the flag, saying to his men in the pit, 'Take it! Take it!' I directed John Love McLean to direct his firing line at this officer." Eventually, Lieutenant Charlie Stebbins of the Jefferson County Rifles, though wounded, bore the flag to safety. Somewhere in the confusion, the 6th Florida's officer corps suffered a further blow when Major Robert H. M. Davidson went down with a portion of one foot mangled by an enemy bullet.[22]

An anonymous 1st Florida Cavalry and 4th Florida soldier wrote to the *Memphis Daily Appeal* that the Florida Brigade exchanged fire with their foes for twenty minutes, all the while sheltered in part by the poor placement of the Federal works atop the ridge and the irregular slope: "the hight [*sic*] of the hill, upon which the enemy were posted, and the [1st Florida Cavalry and 4th Florida] regiment being so close in under the same, is one reason why they suffered no more than they did." Finally, though, the Florida Brigade could take no more and they began a withdrawal under the cover of the hanging smoke. Left dead on the field was George W. Adams, who only four years earlier had been a student at Samuel Pasco's Waukeenah Academy.[23]

Sergeant Archie Livingston wrote simply of the short, horrendous fight, "the company and entire brigade suffered immensely & accomplished nothing." According to an account mailed to the *Gainesville Cotton States* two days after the charge, the Florida Brigade suffered 223 casualties in the brief fight. The historian Zack Waters, who wrote the first in-depth account of this lesser-known fight on the Dallas line, has asserted that the losses were nearer to 300. General John A. Logan's Federals losses totaled 379.[24]

At Jackson the previous July, the Floridians helped annihilate a Federal brigade; at Dallas, they were on the receiving end of the power and accuracy of rifled-muskets in the hands of entrenched, veteran soldiers. The Floridians, who had never before failed to carry out their role in an assault, suddenly became averse to participating in attacks on fortified positions. The soldiers felt the Dallas attack had been useless and that their casualties were taken in vain, and they wondered why two brigades had attacked a prepared Federal position.

Even though General Bate never ordered the signal cannon to fire, the Floridians and Orphans held their divisional leader in contempt for both the advance and losses suffered that afternoon for two reasons. First, unlike General Breckinridge following Murfreesboro, Bate had no army commander who was viewed with much scorn from the ranks. Furthermore, the Floridians and Orphans would not lay the blame for the botched assault at the feet of their own leaders. Thus, the troops directed their ire solely at Bate. The Dallas fight helps explain the half-hearted forays against entrenched enemy forces later in the Atlanta Campaign. Though in letters home the soldiers maintained a brave front to family and friends, their actions would speak louder than words.[25]

Though June brought miserable rains to accompany the usual Federal artillery and small-arms fire, the Floridians could be thankful that during that month they engaged in no heavy fighting with the enemy. Sherman, having gathered his armies near Acworth on the Western and Atlantic, used the first ten days of the new month to resupply his troops and repair the rail lines before moving against the Confederates' new positions. By the second week of June the Army of Tennessee occupied a strong position based around the heights of Kennesaw Mountain. General Bate's Division, however, occupied Pine Mountain, a knoll described by Bate as "an isolated hill rising some two or three hundred feet from the level of the plain with graceful slopes on either flank studded with timber. . . . This point . . . in advance of & separated from the line occupied by the main army & hence was found a serious obstruction to his [Sherman's] movement, a thorn in his pathway, which he could not well pass without being pierced in the flank and dared not assault." Washington Ives wrote in his diary that the Florida Brigade reached this new position on June 2 and by June 7 completed extensive earthworks. On June 10, the enemy advanced within rifle range of the pickets and the firing began anew.[26]

June 14 began, in the words of Washington Ives, "fair." Yet as the morning wore on, Yankee artillery on the plain below began firing rounds at any movement observed along the Confederate lines, making life uncomfortable for the Rebels. At 11:00 A.M. Generals Johnston, Hardee, and Polk arrived at the Florida Brigade's headquarters atop Pine Mountain to determine whether Bate's Division should be withdrawn; they were greeted by Colonel William S. Dilworth, who had recently arrived from Florida and taken command of the brigade from Bullock.[27]

While the generals examined the countryside from the crown of the knoll, Federal artillery, on Sherman's orders, fired several rounds at the gathering of officers. Following the passage of a solid shot over head, Colonel Dilworth asked the generals to remove to safer ground; as they did so "something had attracted [Polk's] attention and he stopped behind. A moment later . . . someone exclaimed: 'General Polk is killed!'" While awaiting an ambulance to remove the body, Generals Johnston and Hardee grieved the loss of their comrade and friend within Colonel Dilworth's headquarters tent. Lieutenant Albert Livingston of the 1st and 3rd Florida wrote home, "He was immediately behind our regiment at the time he was killed . . . Genl Polk's death is greatly lamented by all." That evening after sunset, Bate's Division retreated from Pine Mountain.[28]

The letters of three officers provide a glimpse into the mid-June condition of the Florida Brigade. Captain Hugh Black, recovering from an illness in an Atlanta hospital, wrote of the soldiers: "They are suffering terribly from sickness—*wether* [sic] is enough to kill them. Heavy rains have been falling for . . . two weeks and the Army has it all to take. The men are in an awful fix not being able to have any washing done for sixty days." Black continued, "[T]he army seems to keep their spirts [sic] and feel confident of success." Major Jacob Lash seconded Black's assessment, telling his wife, "I am quite dirty, havent [sic] changed clothes in four weeks." Albert Livingston, Archie's brother, explained to his family: "The troops are much fatigued but not the least depressed in spirits . . . I feel confident our armies will be victorious. All the boys feel that it cannot be any other way. All have unbounded confidence in our chief. . . . The 1st & 3rd Florida only number for duty at this time 120 men. The enemy & [disease] have made sad [inroads] in our regt. Though what few are left are as resolute & defiant as ever."[29]

By June 20 the Army of Tennessee soldiers had completed their new line encompassing the Kennesaw Mountain range. While Polk's Corps, commanded temporarily by the Floridian William Wing Loring, occupied heights on Johnston's right, Hardee's Corps entrenched on significantly lower ground in the center of the line. The commanding general positioned General Hood's troops on the left.

In spite of the relative quiet that descended on their portion of the battlefield, the Floridians lost several soldiers to death and wounds on the picket line. On June 26, however, the soldiers received a boost when the entire brigade exchanged their smoothbores for potent Enfield rifled-muskets.[30]

They may have hoped the Federals would give them a chance to exact revenge for Dallas. The next morning General Sherman seemed to give the Floridians their chance, as various segments of the line erupted in intense firing as blue-clad units moved to the attack. To clear the Rebels from their strong position, the Federal commander decided to throw his armies forward in an attempt to force a way through the Confederate entrenchments. The Union general felt the assault was his best option, as he was afraid to flank Johnston, fearing a Confederate attack on his vital railroad, and he was unwilling to allow an impasse to settle upon the north Georgia front. While the XV Corps, which had devastated the Floridians at Dallas, met with a similar fate on the northern end of the line, General George Thomas's Army of the Cumberland assaulted Patrick Cleburne and Benjamin Cheatham's divisions of Hardee's Corps. The portion of ground defended by Cheatham's Tennesseans became known as the "Dead Angle" because of the high number of Union casualties taken while attempting to seize the V-shaped entrenchments there.[31]

The Floridians began the day as Bate's divisional reserve, and soon after the firing began an order arrived to send a regiment to reinforce Cheatham's threatened line. The 1st Florida Cavalry and 4th Florida hustled southward at the double quick and arrived at the Dead Angle just as the attack faltered; the remainder of the Florida Brigade hurried up soon after. Washington Ives recalled that as the Floridians neared the Dead Angle, "the Federals in our front had reached the breastworks—some were on the top. . . . As we reached the works, the federals fell back, and we were ordered 'Hold your fire!' The dead and wounded lay thick."[32]

By midday all of Sherman's attacks had faltered and more than three thousand Federal soldiers had been killed. The Confederates lost fewer than a thousand during the day's combat. Even after the wanton bloodletting of the morning, and despite the fact that wounded men lay suffering between the lines, both sides continued to fire unceasingly. As dusk gathered, Lieutenant Colonel Edward Badger dispatched "litter bearers to bring in the nearest wounded, but their groans drew the fire from their comrades on skirmish line not one hundred yards distant. Two of the litter bearers were struck, but not seriously wounded, and they all rushed back over the works."[33]

Two days later, on June 29, in the words of 6th Florida soldier John Campbell, "their dead lay on the field until they began to stink," and the two sides finally agreed upon a cease-fire to remove the wounded and bury the deceased. Campbell wrote, "[T]he Yankies came up & talked with our men and appeared to be very social. It looked very strange sure to see them appearantly so friendly to each other." Campbell noted that at 4:00 P.M. "hostilities again commenced & the same men who were so friendly now commenced shooting each other. Oh, this war is a most horrible thing."[34]

In the days following the attack on the Kennesaw Mountain positions, General Sherman worked his army around the Confederate left flank, forcing Johnston to abandon his strong position on July 2. Only a week later on July 9, portions of Sherman's force effected a crossing of the Chattahoochee River, less than ten miles from Atlanta. The next day Johnston, rather than contest the Federals' hold on the southern bank, withdrew his army yet again toward the city. Following the retreat to within five miles of Atlanta, the Floridians enjoyed nearly a week of inactivity, during which time Enoch J. Vann and a comrade arrived in the town. The Florida politician came to the threatened city on a mission of mercy, namely to establish a Florida Relief Committee to distribute food, clothing, and medicine to the wounded Floridians recovering in Atlanta's various hospitals. Vann's diary of the journey and his letters dispatched from Atlanta are a treasure trove of information for students of both the siege and the Florida Brigade.[35]

On July 11, 1864, Vann departed Atlanta on foot, ambling northward toward the front burdened with a knapsack full of letters and food meant for the troops. After several wrong turns, he finally discovered the unit encamped near the Western and Atlantic Railroad. On the day Vann visited the brigade's bivouac, he found that the soldiers "congratulated themselves upon the quiet time they were having—no shells bursting near by, and no balls whistling." The brigade that Vann discovered in early July comprised six depreciated regiments numbering somewhere between 800 and 900 effectives. The historian Albert Castel has estimated that in July the average size for a Confederate brigade at this stage of campaign was 1,200 men; therefore, the Florida Brigade was significantly below the norm.[36]

Though Vann arrived on a Monday, at the 1st Florida Cavalry and 4th Florida's camp he witnessed Chaplain Wiggins delivering a sermon to an attentive congregation. Upon reaching the 1st and 3rd Florida, Vann found himself among his friends, family, and constituents. He distributed the mail from home and offered bread and ham slices to anyone who wished to partake. In his journal he described the physical condition of the men of the brigade as generally "hardy, fleshy, and strong—all O.K. They have had plenty to eat all the time, and all as well clothed as they wished to be. Only a few here and there barefooted, and some with very leaky shoes. Up until the time of falling back from Marietta they suffered from want of vegetables and often, were threatened with the scurvy."[37]

During his brief stay Vann gained introductions to the brigade's officers, remarking that he was "favorably impressed" with Lieutenant Colonel Edward Badger. He noted that the young Ocala lawyer "appears to be a perfect gentlemen [sic], intelligent and sober." Vann's meeting with Colonel Dilworth probably began awkwardly as the two had espoused conflicting political viewpoints before the war.

However, Vann noted that Dilworth "was very courteous and polite, invited me into his tent where we had a pleasant ½ hour's talk."[38]

At the time that Vann visited his fellow Floridians during July's third week, a lull had descended over the armies that faced each other just north of Atlanta. Sherman allowed his soldiers time to rest, and, likewise, the Army of Tennessee's veterans used the days to laze about and mend clothing and equipment. Then on July 17, Jefferson Davis, unsatisfied with General Johnston's handling of the campaign and at a loss as to what the general might do to halt Sherman's advance, removed "Old Joe" and replaced him with John Bell Hood.[39]

The youthful, crippled Hood was a relative newcomer to the Army of Tennessee, having arrived at Dalton only that spring to take command of one of the army's corps. An Old Army lieutenant, Hood had resigned his commission in 1861 to become one of Lee's hardest-hitting commanders. The Kentucky-born general first earned laurels at the head of the famed Texas Brigade at the Battle of Gaines Mill, then helped stave off disaster at Antietam. In 1864 Hood soldiered on regardless of the fact that his left arm hung uselessly and his right leg was gone just below the thigh. Once in the Western Theater, Hood maintained correspondence with Richmond, intent on undermining Johnston's command. Damning accusations from Hood in mid-July helped Jefferson Davis make the final decision to sack Johnston and bolstered "both his and [Braxton] Bragg's preference for the [corps commander] because they believed Hood would carry out their desired policy of being more aggressive."[40]

Historians of the campaign have depicted the common soldier's reaction to Johnston's departure as one of indignation and sorrow; several Floridians demonstrated their displeasure over the general's removal in letters home. The troops likely felt a bond with the Virginian after having suffered through the Mississippi summer with him the previous year. Like many troops in the Army of Tennessee, they felt "Johnston had done much to restore the army's shattered morale" in the wake of Missionary Ridge. William McLeod, a 7th Florida soldier, wrote in his diary on July 18, "[W]e hear that Gen. Johnston has quit the army and it seems to have a Bad effect among the troops." In August, Washington Ives confessed to his father, "Joe Johnston was dearly loved by the Army and his removal spread gloom over it which has not yet disappeared." Hugh Black recorded perhaps the most scathing response proffered by Florida Brigade members toward the removal: "The men are bitterly opposed to the Change and Swear that they Will not fight under Hood." Assessing the mood in Atlanta, Enoch Vann wrote home to Florida: "the dissatisfaction is universal and it is generally to be found that the army will become demoralized." The pragmatic Archie Livingston wrote that he did not mind the exchange of commanders as long as "the change may have an influence towards thwarting any advance nearer Atlanta by the enemy."[41]

Regardless of the soldiers' feelings about Davis's removal of Johnston, orders arrived at the brigade's headquarters early on the morning of July 20 to prepare for battle. On July 19 Hood had discovered that Sherman had moved two of his armies, those of McPherson and Schofield, east of Atlanta toward the Georgia Railroad; meanwhile, George Thomas's Army of the Cumberland had moved due south toward the city. Hood intended for Hardee's and Alexander P. Stewart's Corps (Polk's old unit) to strike Thomas's troops as they emerged onto high ground just south of Peachtree Creek. Hood envisioned an attack similar to Robert E. Lee's plan on the Second Day at Gettysburg, with the "assault divisions advancing 'en echelon' from his right." Hood intended to bottle Thomas's divisions between Peachtree Creek and the Chattahoochee and force them to surrender.[42]

On July 20 Bate's Division occupied the extreme right of the Confederate battle line. William McLeod wrote, "[A]bout 9 o'clock we were ordered to fill up our canteens and . . . to take 20 extra rounds of cartridges and then we all [k]new it was a charge and we were ordered to cross the Breast works and we done so and we were ordered to forward and we started in this time it was 10 or 11 o'clock." While the Confederates were formed in time for the planned 1:00 P.M. strike, the need to extend their lines to the right to cover Atlanta's eastward approaches against McPherson and Schofield caused delays. This movement made all the difference in terms of whether the Floridians would participate in a hotly contested fight or minor skirmishing; because of this adjustment, Bate's troops hardly became engaged at all that day.[43]

Though Bate's Division held a position where it could have landed a hammer blow on the Federal left flank, the overgrown terrain made it impossible for Bate to align his division for an attack. William McLeod recorded, "[T]he fighting was going on terrible on our left and it raged all day," but the Floridians' divisional commander never put his soldiers in contact with the enemy's main line. While Hugh Black claimed Bate held the Floridians in reserve that day, McLeod wrote that the 7th Florida provided skirmishers for the division; these men traded shots with the Federals and lost "one man killed out of the Regt. and 7 wounded."[44]

The Battle of Peachtree Creek brought Hood's Rebels no closer to halting Sherman's advance on Atlanta and cost the Army of Tennessee 2,500 casualties. On the night of July 20, the Florida Brigade withdrew to their breastworks, "the worst jaded men you ever saw." Not only had Bate failed to launch his brigades at the Yankees, but Colonel Dilworth was placed under arrest for drunkenness and Colonel Bullock once again commanded the brigade. Dilworth's preference for the bottle likely was not a recent development. Early in the conflict, Governor John Milton had accused Dilworth of frequent insobriety. A puzzling contradiction to Milton's statement is that Samuel Pasco, who served as Dilworth's clerk for two years, made no mention of the colonel's intemperance in his detailed diary. There is no evidence that points to a cause for Dilworth's sudden binge. Never brought before a court-martial to answer for his crime, Dilworth sought treatment for diarrhea in a military hospital in late July and then returned to Florida on extended sick leave. He would never return to the brigade, and his military career, which once held much promise, instead ended in shame.[45]

On the evening of July 21, Bate's Division formed ranks and prepared to march from their entrenchments. As lightning bugs flashed about them in the gathering twilight, the soldiers marched southward on Peachtree Road. General Hardee's entire corps passed through the city throughout the hot, humid night, as it marched toward a rendezvous with destiny the next day.[46]

Hardee's objective for July 22 was the Floridians' Dallas adversary, the Army of the Tennessee. General McPherson's force was positioned astride the Georgia Railroad, which led to Decatur, Augusta, and points beyond. The Yankee force's southern flank, unprotected by cavalry, lay ripe for a crushing assault. As he had days earlier, Hood chose Hardee's veterans for the task, ordering the old soldier to position his divisions southeast of the Union line so they might strike the rear of the unsuspecting bluecoats. Throughout the early morning hours of July 22, General Hardee's soldiers trekked south of Atlanta before turning east. As the night wore on, due to the heat and fatigue, "hundreds of Hardee's men fell behind their units or dropped exhausted alongside the road." Washington Ives estimated that the Florida Brigade marched twelve miles during the night and confessed, "I was compelled to rest as thousands did, though I did not straggle as many did."[47]

Though Hardee's attack was to have begun at dawn, because some of the general's troops had to disengage before redeploying, part of his corps was still in transit when daylight crept over Stone Mountain and the pine forests to the east. William McLeod recalled that while waiting for the other divisions to come up, the Floridians were able to eat and get several hours of sleep. When the troops finally formed for the attack shortly before 10:00 A.M., Bate's Division was located at the extreme right of the Confederate line. The Tennessean formed his unit with the Florida Brigade's 1st and 3rd Florida and 6th Florida regiments along with the Orphan Brigade in his front rank, while the 7th Florida and 1st Florida Cavalry and 4th Florida and Colonel Smith's Brigade formed a second line.[48]

While awaiting the order to advance, Colonel Bullock stood before his fellow Floridians and, according to McLeod, "made . . . a good speech in regards to going in a fight." Bate's men moved forward at 11:00 A.M. and quickly discovered that a millpond lay across their axis of advance. The soldiers plunged in and soon found themselves in "underbrush, muck, and knee-deep water." Private McLeod wrote of the uninviting terrain, "[W]e had creeks and Branches to wade and we pitched rite in like they were not their." In fact, General Bate described in his report of the battle that to take full advantage of surprise, he ordered his men "to move right on regardless of obstacles resisting every impediment and, if possible, overrun the enemy." Private McLeod observed that he and his comrades believed "the yankees knew nothing of our where a Bouts and was not expecting us their and we were in their rair on their left flank and that pleased us all."[49]

The enemy was closer than Bate and McLeod imagined that morning, and it was the Rebels who would, in fact, receive the surprise. The Army of the Tennessee's XVI Corps became the Floridians' foe that morning after McPherson, worried about his left flank, ordered them to take up a position to protect that vital section of the line. By 11:00 A.M. Major General Grenville Dodge's troops occupied a hill that overlooked swampy, brush-covered low ground, ready to meet any threat. As the Confederate soldiers struggled through the entangled millpond they came under fire from Dodge's artillery; Bate, stunned that the Federal left flank was not undefended, quickly threw his division at the newly discovered enemy. Washington Ives noted with chagrin, "[W]e tried to strike the enemy in the rear, but did not go quite far enough."[50]

Bate's assault was a disaster from the start. To begin with, the swampy, obstacle-laden ground just east of the Union line proved a major detriment to the progress of the attackers. Bate later confessed that in this area, "the line moved on through of necessity in fragments as only stout and athletic men were able to pass the morass in good time, while many were killed and wounded in struggling through its mire." Private McLeod believed the swamp "the worst place to go through" he ever beheld. In addition, the Federal troops placed a tremendous volume of fire into the Rebel ranks. After coming under attack from Yankee soldiers on their left, Bate's entire division drifted to the northeast to escape the horrible killing zone; McLeod noted that the right wing of his regiment "went farther on the right so that part never suffered as much as the left of the Regt." He continued, "[T]he yanks . . . pitched in with their cannon and small armes and we had to back rite off." In spite of the staunch Federal defense, the brigade "did charge within gun shot of the Yankees" before "they turned and run like scared turkeys," according to Hugh Black.[51]

Hardee's assault on the Army of the Tennessee failed to achieve the results that General Hood had imagined. Though the Confederates succeeded in killing General James B. McPherson, their attempt to destroy his army cost them nearly 5,500 casualties. In Hugh Black's words, "[T]his attack was as unsuccessful as the one made on the 20th." In addition, the Battle of Atlanta shattered any remaining faith that the Floridians had in General Bate. Many probably felt the general had led them into traps on both occasions, and they now felt no obligation to follow him into further attacks on Union fortifications. Hugh Black wrote home that many Florida soldiers "swear that they will not charge any more Yankee breastworks. They have told the General they will not charge breastworks." The Floridians were by no means alone in their feelings. According to the historian Albert Castel, "[T]he crucial truth is that the majority of Hood's troops resent what they perceive he has done to them and fear that he will continue doing it."[52]

The exact losses for the Florida Brigade are difficult to enumerate as neither

Bate's nor Bullock's official report of the engagement has survived. Captain Black wrote home that the 6th Florida suffered "six or seven killed and a great many wounded." He noted that his regiment "went into the fight on the 22nd with ten good large companies and they now . . . make but five very small companies." Washington Ives informed his father, "Bate's [Division] was badly cut up in the charge." However, it can only be assumed from an inspection report dated August 21, 1864, that counted 727 soldiers present that the brigade's casualties at the Battle of Atlanta exceeded 100.[53]

In the aftermath of a battle, soldiers who were only slightly wounded often returned to the ranks within days. Troops that sustained more serious injuries first received attention at aid stations established to the rear of the fighting and then endured a jolting ambulance ride to one of the brigade's infirmaries in Atlanta. Enoch Vann, who visited a hospital during the campaign, probably in the aftermath of the July 22 action, described the scene. Upon first arriving he witnessed "the surgeons under a tent where they operated on the wounded. . . . Near by, seated on benches were several wounded soldiers, awaiting their turn. . . . Outside there were at least an acre of men lying in rows, awaiting removal to hospitals further in the rear of the army. Several had died." As the campaign entered its third month, more than eight hundred Florida Brigade wounded and sick lay in a series of hospitals between Atlanta and Columbus and at their homes in Florida.[54]

On July 28, 1864, General Hood launched a third assault aimed at Sherman's troops; the Battle of Ezra Church, fought northwest of Atlanta, ended in Confederate defeat and cost several thousand more lives. Ezra Church signaled a shift in fighting for Atlanta, as in the following month Sherman's plans would focus on cutting the railroads that kept Hood's army provisioned. As the Union forces extended their line southward, General Hood stretched his own small army thinly to protect his supply lines. Hardee's Corps lay along the new line south of Atlanta; the Florida Brigade spent the last days of July and the first of August constructing fortifications.[55]

On August 3, 1864, after Colonel Bullock was wounded, command of the Florida Brigade passed to Colonel Lafayette Kenan of the 6th Florida. The thirty-nine-year-old slaveholder and former politician assumed command of the Florida Brigade at a critical moment, for General Sherman had recently ordered a move toward Atlanta's railroads.[56]

General Hood countered the Federals' early August movement by dispatching General Bate's Division to hold the southern end of the Confederate line. Washington Ives wrote that Bate's troops, reinforced following the Battle of Atlanta with General Henry R. Jackson's brigade of Georgians, looked to block the Federals' advance with a "line of fortifications perpendicularly to the front and at right angles with the main line." When one Federal brigade tested the strength of these entrenchments during the morning of August 6, Tyler's Brigade, commanded by

General Thomas Smith, inflicted a severe punishment on the attackers. Although General Hood praised the Florida Brigade in an official dispatch to Richmond, the Federals never made a serious attempt against the Floridians; as Washington Ives wrote, "[T]he enemy endeavored to charge us but the boys opened fire too soon, viz. 250 yards in woods, and they would not advance any further." That evening, Bate withdrew into a freshly constructed line of entrenchments that secured the railroad south to the important junction of East Point.[57]

By August 1864 the Florida Brigade's numbers had decreased to less than those of a full-strength regiment. When Lieutenant A. M. Harris inspected the brigade in its fortifications some six miles southwest of Atlanta on August 21, he counted only 727 effectives, which meant that the brigade's strength in battle equaled that of only a reinforced battalion. In addition, the three months of hard campaigning had worn out the soldiers' uniforms; they lacked nearly every item of necessary clothing. Without soap, the men reeked of foul odor, and their bodies, like the little clothing they possessed, bore a red hue from lying in the Georgia clay. A minority also did without knapsacks and canteens, and a few had even lost their cartridge boxes.[58]

Throughout the miserable days of August, the Florida Brigade's entrenchments lay just opposite those of the Federal XVII Corps; Washington Ives penned that until an informal cease-fire was declared by the pickets on August 14, "we did not know what minute a man would be killed." While the truce held, the young quartermaster sergeant wrote: "The Bands on both sides play every evening and as a band on either side plays, the partizans begin to yell. Three nights ago after the Fed. & Reb. Bands had played several times for each other the troops on both sides began yelling . . . during which a great many men picked up their guns and accoutrements and jumped into the fortifications thinking the enemy was going to charge us. Though the promise among the pickets not to fire at one another, the artillery did not heed the truce." Sergeant Archie Livingston wrote home on August 24 of a close call with cannon fire: "Yesterday my shoulder strap & cartridge box, straps to canteen and haversack were cut . . . by canister shot from a three inch rifle of the enemy fronting our breast works."[59]

On the day following Sergeant Livingston's brush with death, the first of General Sherman's armies designated to move out quietly slipped away from their trenches after dark. Two days later, the Army of the Tennessee reached the Atlanta and West Point Railroad south of Atlanta; a day later, the Army of the Cumberland also seized a section of the tracks. Sherman had ordered the overwhelming flanking maneuver meant to cut Atlanta's supply line after his cavalry failed to accomplish this same objective. In addition to cutting the Atlanta and West Point Railroad, the Federals would press eastward and take possession of the Macon and Western line at Jonesboro, fifteen miles south of Atlanta. With Sherman's soldiers astride these railroads, the Union forces severed Hood's last supply line.[60]

With the Federal entrenchments opposite Atlanta suddenly empty, Confederate soldiers and Atlanta civilians felt Joseph Wheeler, whose cavalry General Hood had dispatched to tear up the Western and Atlantic Railroad north of Atlanta, had succeeded in his task and forced Sherman to withdraw for lack of supplies. The historian Albert Castel, however, asserts that Hood believed instead that Sherman was attempting a flanking maneuver but was at a loss as to its destination. In fact, on August 28, General Bate's Division, commanded by Brigadier General John Calvin Brown since Bate's wounding on August 10, marched to and entrenched at Rough and Ready on the Macon and Western in preparation for an attack. Members of the 1st and 3rd Florida maintained fond memories of their old commander from the Kentucky Campaign and were glad to serve under him once again.[61]

On August 30, 1864, the Army of the Tennessee established a bridgehead over the Flint River only one mile from Jonesboro and the vital Macon and Western. To counter this threat, General Hood ordered General Hardee to hasten his own corps and that of Stephen D. Lee to Jonesboro and attack the Army of the Tennessee early the next morning. For the second time during the campaign the Floridians would complete a night march and then attack the enemy.[62]

William McLeod, elected second lieutenant in his 7th Florida company at the end of July, wrote hastily in his diary that the Floridians had only just completed their Rough and Ready fortifications when the order came to move yet again: "we started at sunset and marched all night." Lieutenant Francis P. Fleming of the 1st Florida Cavalry and 4th Florida informed his relatives on September 1: "Night before last we marched the whole night arriving here after sunrise." Washington Ives remembered that during the march early on the morning of August 31, Federal soldiers who had crossed the Macon and Western north of Jonesboro surprised Rebel cavalry riding just in front of the 1st Florida Cavalry and 4th Florida: "[W]e heard the enemy fire about 30 guns at the scouts, and as they never returned, I expect they were either killed or captured. . . . We then marched back 1 ½ miles on the road we had come and took a left hand road to Jonesboro, which we reached at sunrise."[63]

General Stephen Lee's Corps did not reach Jonesboro until early in the afternoon on August 31; while waiting for these reinforcements, Florida Brigade soldiers skirmished with their Union counterparts while improving rifle pits built by the Orphan Brigade. Once Lee's Corps arrived General Hardee arrayed his own divisions, temporarily commanded by General Patrick Cleburne, and Lee's troops for an afternoon assault; Hardee positioned General John C. Brown's Division in the southern portion of his own corps' line, and Lee's Corps extended the Rebel battle line farther to the north. Hardee planned for his troops to roll forward from south to north.[64]

The Army of the Tennessee awaited a Confederate attack upon a ridge crowned with breastworks, and the Yankees' harassed their foes throughout the morning with small-arms and artillery fire. William McLeod recalled that the Federals made the Floridians' line "as dangerous a place as could be for 3 cannon balls came through our ditch." While Federal pickets and artillery kept the Confederates at bay, infantry and pioneers made a strong position (since both flanks rested upon the Flint River's banks) even more defensible by further reinforcing their entrenchments against a possible frontal assault. By mid-afternoon the Federal line was "protected by abatis or palisades or both, and everywhere batteries . . . posted so that [they could] deliver cross fire as well as direct fire." Despite these formidable obstacles, just before 3:00 P.M. the Confederates shouldered their arms and started forward. General Finley, who had just returned from Florida, led the Florida Brigade into battle.[65]

Hardee's battle plan fell apart spectacularly as soon as the attack began. General Lee's troops on the right began their advance at the same moment as did General Cleburne's Division (commanded by Mark Lowrey) on the far left. To compound this failure, Lowrey angled his veteran soldiers to the southwest, thereby avoiding the main Union line entirely. In the middle of this chaos, Finley's Brigade surged ahead against the enemy's position in the face of thousands of rifled-muskets and dozens of cannon blazing away at their ranks. Lieutenant McLeod, who fell ill during the night march, claimed that as he lay resting near Jonesboro he could discern when the advance began because "the guns began to pop away and the cannons to a roaring."[66]

Lieutenant Fleming of the 1st Florida Cavalry and 4th Florida wrote that as the gray and butternut line surged northwest, "We advanced a mile through fields and woods before becoming opposed to a concentrated fire when we came upon the enemy strongly entrenched." Fleming continued: "We charged his works under a terrific fire of artillery and small arms but their works were too strong to be taken by a single line of battle." Captain Samuel Darwin McConnell, who led a company that numbered eleven soldiers that day, similarly described the assault in a letter to his sister: "We made a charge on the enemy and were repulsed as it was impossible for our lines of battle to take their lines of breastworks." William McLeod wrote in his diary, "[O]ur men went up pretty close [to] the yankee works and they began to pore in to our men so thick they have to fall back."[67]

Although it hardly saved the Union line from catastrophic defeat, "a dark gully, which intervened, brought a part of our line to a halt," according to Colonel Kenan. This was not entirely true; most soldiers simply refused to advance past the ravine's welcome protection in the face of such tremendous firepower. The Floridians also suffered a blow when General Finley fell wounded during the heat of the fight. A Federal projectile hit one of his feet and killed his mount. Colonel Kenan briefly assumed command of the unit but had to retire from the field after a minié bullet tore through his left hand, taking two fingers with it. Major Glover Ball, the brigade's new commander, realizing the futility of attempting another assault against the strong Federal line, ordered a withdrawal toward Jonesboro.[68]

During the Battle of Jonesboro, fought amid a scorching late summer afternoon, the Florida Brigade, according to Washington Ives's estimate, suffered 120 casualties. The 7th Florida alone had forty-six killed, wounded, and missing. William McLeod recorded that his 7th Florida company went into battle with nine men, and of these, "3 of our men were wounded and the Capt and 3 men surrendered and 2 come out unhurt." Captain McConnell wrote that his Company G "went into the charge with eleven officers and men and lost six, one killed, two wounded, and three captured." In addition to ravaging the Florida Brigade's ranks, the engagement that saw both Finley and Kenan fall victim to wounds served to punctuate the way in which the Atlanta Campaign devastated the Florida Brigade's officer corps. General Finley, who once more traveled to Florida to convalesce, never again commanded the brigade that bore his name.[69]

Finley remains the commander most associated with the Florida troops in the Army of Tennessee. During his tenure of command he demonstrated two qualities necessary in an effective leader: empathy for his troops and effective leadership on the battlefield. It is possible that his background in politics accounted for his desire to ensure that his soldierly constituents remained cheerful; it is also likely that his Christian principles influenced his actions as regimental and brigade commander. Finley lifted his pen many times during the war to demonstrate his desire to ensure his soldiers were clothed, shod, and well fed. On the battlefield, Finley's actions nearly reaped impressive dividends on the first day at Chickamauga and helped stem further disaster at Missionary Ridge. However, Finley demonstrated perhaps his finest example of courage at Jonesboro. An anecdote illustrating the general's actions in the aftermath of that battle found its way into a Florida newspaper several years after the general's death. The *Florida Times-Union* reported that after he was wounded on August 31, General Finley "declined being sent to the rear . . . until all his wounded men were embarked and narrowly escaped capture, being saved through the faithfulness of a driver who took him in a commissary wagon."[70]

Though more fighting took place at Jonesboro on September 1, for all practical purposes the August 31 engagement marked the final battle of the long and tiring campaign for the Floridians. On September 2, 1864, after the evacuation of the city by Hood's army, General Sherman's forces occupied Atlanta. For President Abraham Lincoln, Sherman's success meant a tremendous boost in his chances for reelection; Captain McConnell explained to his wife, "I am so afraid that their success will have a tendency to encourage the war party of the North, and thus prolong the war." For the Florida Brigade and the Army of Tennessee, Atlanta's fall meant thinned ranks, as more than six hundred Floridians had been killed or wounded in nearly four months' time. The campaign also ended in yet another retreat. Always the astute observer, the captain also wrote home, "[T]his army has always been unfortunate that [we] have never been able to stay long after our battles. I hope our luck will change after a while." The remaining months of 1864 would either grant or refuse the soldier's wish.[71]

16 This Is a Kind of Curious Management to Me

September 4, 1864–January 1, 1865

In the waning months of 1864, General John Bell Hood led the Army of Tennessee on a fateful crusade to liberate Tennessee and Kentucky from Federal occupation. The November and December 1864 campaign resulted in the battles of Franklin and Nashville and in actions fought on the outskirts of Murfreesboro. The Army of Tennessee was devastated by these engagements, and by the time the tired corps retreated south the ranks were severely depleted. The campaign exhausted the Florida Brigade and ruined its hard-fighting reputation. By January 1865 the brigade's strength would not even equal that of a battalion.

By 1864 General Sherman's intention was to destroy the Confederacy's will to continue the conflict. Images of the irascible general's armies leaving a path of desolation across both Mississippi and Georgia are often associated with Sherman. It is surprising, then, to discover an almost congenial correspondence between the Union commander and John Bell Hood that took place in September 1864 regarding a prisoner exchange.[1]

General Hood first proposed the return of combatants a week after Atlanta's fall, and Sherman assented to exchange two thousand soldiers captured during the Atlanta Campaign's final phase. The Confederate prisoners returned to the Army of Tennessee's encampment during September's third week, and the Florida Brigade's numbers received a considerable boost from this unexpected manpower trade. Though the Federals offered the captured Rebels an opportunity to take the Oath of Allegiance, Washington Ives recorded that "only six of Finley's Brigade could be induced to do so."[2]

Mid-September 1864 found the Florida Brigade encamped near Jonesboro, the scene of their recent defeat. When Lieutenant A. M. Harris inspected the brigade on September 18, only 657 soldiers were fit for combat, and of these, only 600 fielded weapons. Only twenty-eight days earlier this number had been 727. Though the killed and wounded figures for the Atlanta Campaign are difficult to determine, ascertaining the number of prisoners taken is easier: between August 21 and September 18, 1864, 49 Floridians surrendered. When the majority of these troops returned days later thanks to the exchange, the brigade's effective combat troop total increased. The release of the recovered sick and wounded from Georgia hospitals and the return of soldiers from special duty also contributed to the brigade's post–Atlanta Campaign strength. The Florida Brigade probably fielded close to 1,000 men for operations that fall.[3]

The Florida Brigade spent the days immediately following the surrender of Atlanta recovering from the rigors of the campaign. Captain Samuel McConnell noted that in the days following their victory, General Sherman's soldiers had destroyed "the Road from Lovejoy Station to this place burning the timbers and bending the iron. . . . Their actions . . . indicate that they do not expect to advance on this Road for some time at least." Lieutenant William McLeod enjoyed a "nights sleep for the firs time in several [days]" and finally "washed my clothes & come back & dried them by a fire." Washington Ives, like Captain McConnell, wandered on the Jonesboro battlefield. In the officer's words, "I have never seen a battlefield soon after a great battle and I have some curiosity to go over one." In walking behind the line held by the Federals on August 31, Ives miscalculated considerably when he claimed he "saw 400 graves of Michigan and Illinois troops. The Yankee loss is terrible." Of the respite at Jonesboro Captain McConnell said, "[W]e recuperated very rapidly for we were all much fatigued when we got there. The health of the Army is I think very good now."[4]

Though Hood had forsaken Atlanta, the soldiers viewed this only as a loss of more territory and another city: Had not the army continued to resist after the loss of Tennessee? Also, if the soldiers believed such high estimates of Federal casualties, they might have assumed that Sherman's armies were considerably reduced. Washington Ives claimed, "[T]he troops are in good spirits and considering everything a fine looking set of men." In this vein, Sergeant Archie Livingston wrote in early October that "my own heart is full of hope for victory and good results for our country."[5]

The only complaint that Ives voiced, as the first hint of fall appeared in the air, was the army's paucity of blankets. The young Columbia County soldier wrote that "we are very scarce of blankets and pieces of carpets are highly prized." He noted that most of the men lost their blankets when in order "to save themselves from capture they would throw away blankets in preference to clothing and many blankets were literally torn to pieces by shells and minie balls." Captain McConnell expressed grief over not having heard from his wife in some time, blaming it on the fact that "when Atlanta was evacuated. . . . the Army Post Office was burned to prevent its falling into the hands of the yankees."[6]

The brigade's officer corps suffered greatly from enemy projectiles and illness during the summer's hard fighting. In the early fall, Colonel Robert Bullock, recuperated from his Utoy Creek wound, once more commanded the brigade. Though combat veterans led the regiments, in some cases these men had never before commanded units larger than a company into battle. Major Glover A. Ball, of the 1st and 3rd Florida, first saw action at Perryville and commanded his regiment during the last month of the Atlanta Campaign. Though Ball's prior record seemed to establish his competence, Captain John Inglis questioned the major's courage, writing that he was "afflicted with a big scare when in a [small] place."[7]

In September the 7th Florida had finally rid itself of the enthusiastic yet inept Lieutenant Colonel Tillman Ingram. When he fell ill during the Atlanta Campaign's final days, command of the regiment passed to Major Nathan Snow Blount, whose family had pioneered the Peace River region of South Florida. When Blount fell ill in November, the senior captain, Robert Blair Smith, assumed leadership of the regiment. A thirty-year-old Pennsylvanian, Smith had taught school in Leon County prior to Florida's secession. A veteran of all of the 7th Florida's battles, Smith soldiered through the pain of a shoulder wound received at Missionary Ridge and carried the sword given to him by the sailors who transferred from his company the previous March.[8]

Because of Lafayette Kenan's and Robert H. M. Davidson's injuries and Angus McLean's untimely demise, Captain Steven Ashley Cawthon led the 6th Florida. A twenty-nine-year-old Walton County slave owner and Alabama native, Cawthon had enlisted in Company H in 1862 and became captain after McLean's promotion to lieutenant colonel. The former farmer failed to make a good impression on his soldiers at first. One wrote, "[T]he Capt. now is no military man nor any other sort of a man scarcely in my opinion. And the whole . . . have pretty much the same opinion." By 1864 Cawthon had captained his company for more than two years, but his greatest undertaking, that of leading the entire 6th Florida, was at hand.[9]

The 1st Florida Cavalry and 4th Florida possessed the most dependable field officers in the fall of 1864, as Lieutenant Colonel Edward Badger and Major Jacob Lash had led their regiment during Colonel W.L.L. Bowen's frequent absences. Their battlefield record was exceptional, and sources indicate that Badger's men held him in high esteem. In September 1864 Bowen commanded the post at Auburn, Alabama; he missed the Atlanta Campaign entirely, and he had no intention of returning to his regiment. During the fall months, Bowen attempted to gain a transfer to the Military Court in the Department of South Carolina, Georgia, and Florida with its coastal environs because he was not "able for Service any length of time in a cold climate during the winter season." It is not known whether the Confederate government approved Bowen's request, but he never returned to duty with the 4th Florida.[10]

Under this revamped command arrangement and with its soldiers refreshed, by September 29 the Florida Brigade was once more on the march. Still commanded by the one-legged General John Bell Hood, the Army of Tennessee slipped into the countryside west of Atlanta. Hood intended to sever the Western and Atlantic northwest of the recently fallen city, thereby causing Sherman to evacuate Georgia for lack of supplies. As the historian James Lee McDonough has written, "If Sherman followed Hood north, as fully expected, the Confederate commander might compel Sherman to attack him on favorable defensive terrain, thus negating much of the Federal numerical superiority."[11]

The Floridians began the fall campaign without their longtime corps commander, William J. Hardee. Jefferson Davis, who visited the beleaguered army once more in late September, noticed tension between Hardee and his commanding officer. To placate Hood, the president transferred General Hardee to the Department of South Carolina, Georgia, and Florida. Major General Benjamin Franklin Cheatham, a Mexican-American War veteran and commander of the Tennessee Division, assumed command of Hardee's old corps. Lieutenant William McLeod recalled in his diary on September 28, "Gen. Hardee made a speach [*sic*] for us & said he was going to leave us."[12]

During the first week of October the Army of Tennessee skirted west of Atlanta, headed for the Western and Atlantic; by October 5 the Florida Brigade reached Dallas, where in May the brigade had launched a tragic assault on a superior Federal force. Benjamin Glover of the 6th Florida explained the purpose of the campaign to his wife: "We left on the flank movement in a hurry and I did not have time to write to you. I think General Hoods object is to get the yanks out of Atlanta and he will do it. . . . I do not think that this campain will last long all we want is to get the yanks out of Atlanta and then we will go there ourselves and go into winter quarters." Sergeant Archie Livingston informed his mother, "[W]e are on a flanking expedition. . . . We are in Polk Co. Ga. Would you be surprised should we continue to Middle Tenn?"[13]

Livingston's words rang with a haunting truth, for General Sherman indeed moved north with the majority of his army, as he intended to halt Hood's assault on his supply line. Observing this success, Hood "hoped to entice Sherman to further detach and divide his forces by drawing him into rough country near the Tennessee River, where Hood might have an opportunity to offer battle from a strong defensive position." To accomplish this task, Hood's army struck the railroad north of Resaca. On October 13 General William Bate, having rejoined his division near Rome, led his troops toward Mill Creek Gap, which the Florida Brigade had defended against Sherman's advance in May. Presently, General Bate discovered a Federal blockhouse "constructed of earth and timber" guarding the pass.[14]

Though Bate at first surrounded the blockhouse with his entire division, he soon dispatched the Florida Brigade and General Henry R. Jackson's men to destroy the railroad near the fortification. As the infantry marched to tear up the rails, the ever-reliable Fifth Company of the Washington Artillery unlimbered two pieces within two hundred yards of the blockhouse. Though threatened by this artillery, the Union force within the small fort refused Bate's surrender demand. Henry Reddick recalled that with every shot sent at the blockhouse "splinters flew. After a few rounds another flag of truce was sent in and this time they surrendered." Archie

Livingston wrote that the Florida Brigade suffered one fatality during the rather one-sided affair.[15]

Fifty years later, Washington Ives informed a Federal veteran of the fight that those "who were in the blockhouse at Buzzard Roost" deserved a monument. He also described an interesting incident involving the 1st and 4th Florida. Ives remembered that "as we were surrounding the block house in Dalton (Mill Creek Gap) Col. Badger sent Major Lash and five men to follow eleven federals seen going up the mountain northward. They returned bringing the prisoners and . . . their arms. One had a large Navy revolver and it was presented to Col. B." Henry Reddick of the 1st and 3rd Florida also found a souvenir at Mill Creek Gap: "When a messmate and myself went in the house, which was quite dark inside to see if we could find anything to eat. I was feeling around on the ground and found something cold that felt like a piece of meat, and when I picked it up and took it to the light I found it to be an ear that had been shot off of some of the soldiers who had been in there. It was a big flat ear but I had no appetite."[16]

After neutralizing the Mill Creek Gap blockhouse, the Florida Brigade encountered a sight not before witnessed during the conflict. Up the railroad from Dalton marched more than six hundred African Americans wearing the blue uniform of the Union. These soldiers, who had surrendered on October 13 at Dalton and belonged to the 44th United States Colored Troops, were placed under General Bate's supervision.[17]

Although Colonel Lewis Johnson surrendered the Dalton garrison under the proviso that his soldiers be "treated humanely," he wrote that soon after "several men who were taken from the hospital and unable to travel were shot down in cold blood and left on the road." Though the Dalton episode did not devolve into another Fort Pillow, "there is no doubt that the Southerners took what they wanted from the blacks, particularly shoes." The Floridians, apparently at the orders of General Bate, participated in this humiliation of the African Americans, seizing not only shoes but overcoats as well. The day after the Dalton garrison's surrender, the Florida Brigade, along with General Henry R. Jackson's Georgia Brigade, "were sent forward destroying the R R from Mill Creek Gap to Tunnel Hill." The Rebels used their black prisoners to "tear up the track for a distance of nearly two miles."[18]

Near Dalton, General Hood altered his plans once again although, as the historian Thomas Connelly has pointed out, Hood's original plan was succeeding, for Sherman's force was in pursuit. Hood only had to place his army in an excellent defensive position and await the Federal attack. Now, Hood intended to "cross the Tennessee River northwest of Gadsden [Alabama] at Guntersville, destroy Sherman's rail communications in the Stevenson-Bridgeport area, rout any defending forces in Tennessee, capture Nashville, and invade Kentucky." Word of Hood's impending move traveled quickly through the ranks. Benjamin Glover assumed, "We may make a raid on the Nashvill [*sic*] road and then fall back to . . . blue mountain [Alabama] and go in winter quarters." After receiving some badly needed clothing and blankets at Gadsden, the army began its march toward the Tennessee River on October 22.[19]

Hood originally intended his army to cross the Tennessee River near Decatur, Alabama. Upon reaching the outskirts of the town, however, the Rebels found it strongly fortified. In addition, Federal riverine craft lay in the Tennessee ready to add the weight of their guns to any fight. Lieutenant McLeod recalled that while on picket duty near the town, he "could see lots of Yankees & their forts & they would shoot at us & we at them." Wiley Sword maintains that Hood, after viewing the strength of the Federal garrison, determined to "push the army further westward . . . so as to effect a crossing below Muscle Shoals. The shoals would prevent the gunboats from dropping down to interfere." Major Lash informed his wife, "[W]e left decatur the other day without taking the garrison I withdrew last pickets about four o'clock. [They] followed us out some distance but did not make any attack."[20]

November 1 found the Army of Tennessee at Tuscumbia, Alabama, and there, on the Tennessee River's south bank, the advance seemed to falter. For more than three weeks the army remained on the verge of invading Middle Tennessee, subsisting on little food. Major Lash told his wife that the men had dubbed Hood's offensive "a parched corn campaign," maintaining that while marching through northern Georgia the soldiers "had to subsist on parched corn for two days at a time. Yet we fare better most of the time than I expected we would when we started." Because the soldiers spent so much time trying to obtain food, of the Florida Brigade's soldiers whose letters survived, none found Abraham Lincoln's reelection important enough to mention.[21]

Tired of "poor beef and cornbread," Colonel Bullock and Captain McConnell proceeded with great tenacity to procure a good meal for themselves. Having heard rumor of "a wealthy family by the name of Abernathy," the two determined to take a ride in the country and arrive at the Abernathys' home when supper was on the table. McConnell wrote to his wife that upon arriving at their destination, "we introduced ourselves and were kindly received by the lady of the house, who soon invited us to remain for dinner. We did not require much urging on that part I assure you. We spent the day very pleasantly and got a very nice dinner. You ought to have seen me enjoying it."[22]

General Hood's hasty and arduous campaign through northwestern Georgia and into Alabama was very similar to Bragg's Kentucky invasion of 1862. Both offensives were undertaken to force the enemy to abandon captured territory, and both movements consisted of long tiring marches with little rest and saw the Confederate commanders vacillate as to what course of action to take once the campaign was underway. In October, Sergeant Livingston wrote of the offensive: "the marching has been rapid and long indeed." Major Lash described the campaign as "a very trying one. We have been marching regular for over 30 days and have traveled some five hundred miles without rest, going into bivouac sometimes at sun down and some times ten, eleven, and twelve o'clock at night, and starting at daylight and sometimes, two hours before day." Benjamin Glover informed his wife that the army had endured "some very hard marching." In spite of persistent camp rumors to the contrary, Glover did not believe they were headed for Tennessee: "[S]ome say that we are going to Tenn but I do not believe it. I think we are going to Corinth and then go into winter quarters."[23]

On November 10 orders arrived dispatching the Florida Brigade across the Tennessee River. However, Glover still believed that the army would not undertake a campaign into Middle Tennessee: "it is the opinnion of a good many that we will go across the river and then down in to Corrinth and go in to winter quarters." Though General Hood countermanded the brigade's orders to cross the river on November 11, two days later the soldiers formed ranks, shouldered arms, and marched across the pontoon bridge that spanned the Tennessee River's width. Sergeant Livingston wrote with pride that "the passage on the pontoons was a grand sight. Infantry long columns—Artillery, immense wagon trains, Cavalry, droves of beef cattle & c & c, all to be seen from a lofty rock over looking the river presented a picture truly interesting and imposing."[24]

For the first time in more than a year the Floridians stood on the Tennessee River's northern bank; they encamped near Florence, a quaint river city that in Major Lash's words "has been quite a pretty little town, but a considerable portion of it has been burnt down." Archie Livingston thought the city "a pretty place" that "seems to have been a manufacturing town, cotton mills & c . . . but like every point in this region has the mark of the presence of our un-merciful, unmanly, and destructive foe." While the army was at Florence, a cold front passed through the Confederacy's Heartland, bringing freezing rain. The Army of Tennessee's soldiers huddled around fledgling fires to stay warm as "hundreds were very indifferently clad and without good blankets." Despite the hardships the soldiers faced, Sergeant Livingston claimed that "they appear ready for any move that will increase our supplies enlarge the ranks or better our cause."[25]

Jacob Lash disagreed. When word arrived during the third week of November that Sherman was marching south rather than north, the news alarmed Lash. He expressed frustration with the Confederacy's strategy: "This is a kind of curious management to me. I can't fully understand it, Sherman is going south and we going north. We may damage the enemy sufficiently to pay for all the injury they may do us south, but I doubt it." With Sherman on the move through Georgia, Lash pondered the whether his letter would ever reach his wife.[26]

On November 21, with the permission of General P.G.T. Beauregard, Military Division of the West commander, the Army of Tennessee marched north. The next day, under a falling snow and with Colonel Bullock in the lead, the Florida Brigade returned to Tennessee; some may have hoped that this tenure in the Volunteer State would not end as embarrassingly as the previous year's endeavor had at Missionary Ridge. The men marched, confidently aware that the commanding general had promised them "'a fight with equal numbers and choice of the ground.'" The soldiers perhaps interpreted these remarks to mean that Hood would order no more attacks on a well-entrenched enemy. That notion, particularly after the slaughters at Dallas, the July battles around Atlanta, and Jonesboro, set well with the Florida Brigade. Washington Ives told his mother that at the state line someone had hung a large white banner inscribed "Tennessee, A Grave or a Free Home." For many Floridians, the rich Middle Tennessee soil would soon become their final resting place; they would never see their homes again.[27]

Hood's army followed different routes into Middle Tennessee, with the Florida Brigade's line of march taking its soldiers on a northwesterly bearing toward Waynesboro, a hamlet roughly twenty miles east of the old Shiloh battlefield. By November 23 the brigade faced northeastward toward Columbia. It was at this town, which sat astride the Duck River, that General Hood's columns were to converge. General Bate's Division reached their intended destination on November 26; skirmishers discovered Union soldiers entrenched before the town, and General Hood soon ordered his three corps to invest the Yankee fortifications. General Cheatham's Corps took position on the right, with his own right flank anchored on the Duck River and the left forming on General A. P. Stewart's troops.[28]

Lieutenant Colonel Badger's 1st Florida Cavalry and 4th Florida drew picket duty in Bate's front during the night of the twenty-sixth and throughout the next day. Washington Ives recalled that the soldiers were disgruntled because the day had been "cold and rainy," and the men had just begun their fires when the order arrived to move out. He penned that on the twenty-seventh, the pickets remained active, with the "boys having some very fair shots at the Yankees," and "kept firing all day."[29]

Ives wrote that at Columbia, the army's logistical system faltered and rations failed to arrive at the 1st Florida Cavalry and 4th Florida's bivouac. He noted that Floridians alleviated this shortage by subsisting off of Middle Tennessee farms. He explained, "[W]e gathered corn out of the fields and boiled it in camp kettles . . . until it is soft enough to grate . . . & by patiently grating it a man can get enough meal from an ear of corn to make him a mess of mush and although it is a tedious process, yet it is far preferable to going hungry." The 1st and 3rd Florida lived off the countryside as well; Archie Livingston informed his brother, "[A]lready we have feasted on some of the 'fat porkers' of this rich and beautiful Country. Bread rations are not abundant yet, I suppose owing to the difficulty of getting mills."[30]

Two Union corps, the IV and XXIII, comprised the threat that lay before the Army of Tennessee at Columbia. Led by Major General John Schofield (who had been one of John Bell Hood's West Point classmates), these veterans of the campaigns in Tennessee and Georgia numbered twenty-five thousand effectives. On the night of November 28, Schofield's force crossed over to the Duck River's north bank and prepared to "delay Hood's northward advance." In response to Schofield's movement, the Confederate commander decided to outflank Columbia with two corps to "[gain] the [Franklin] pike at Schofield's rear in order to outrace the Federals to Nashville." As Thomas Connelly has noted in his excellent study of the Army of Tennessee, Hood "knew little of" the Federal "strength at Nashville, and perhaps he even still considered Schofield's army the only real obstacle to the city's capture."[31]

On November 29, while General Stephen D. Lee's Corps demonstrated before Schofield's troops, Cheatham and Alexander P. Stewart's men crossed upriver and marched for the Franklin Pike at Spring Hill. To enable the flanking force to travel quickly, the bulk of Hood's artillery remained with Lee. Archie Livingston wrote to his brother as the plan developed: "Lee's Corps is now in motion and already the 'dogs of war' are let loose." When Bate's soldiers crossed the Duck River on pontoons at first light, only eleven miles separated the troops from their objective. However, due to the poor, winding road upon which the troops marched, the troops actually traversed sixteen miles of rough country, according to Ives.[32]

Historians have long acknowledged that Hood became aware of Federal soldiers on his left flank and that he deployed John C. Brown's (Cheatham's) Division to screen this vital sector in case of an assault. This threat, and the necessity of deploying Brown's troops, possibly helped account for the delay in Hood's march to Spring Hill. But Ives recalled that these Federal soldiers posed more of a menace to Hood's column than previously noted, as along the line of march "the enemy's sharpshooters were near" and "continually shooting at us." Surgeon Henry McCall Holmes endorsed Ives's claim when he wrote that the column "moved toward Springhill having marched 15 miles with skirmishing going on." With the Confederate columns under fire, the march probably slowed to a crawl, and this added considerably to the belated arrival at their destination.[33]

Reaching Spring Hill at three o'clock, General Hood's flanking column discovered General Nathan Bedford Forrest's Rebel cavalry engaged near the village. By mid-afternoon the "Wizard of the Saddle" had launched several assaults on the seven thousand Federals entrenched around the town and had met with defeat in these sharp fights. Hood's lead division, that of Patrick Cleburne, arrived on the field at three and immediately formed and assaulted the Union position unsuccessfully. Confusion reigned over the next few hours as Hood's plan disintegrated before the Federal defenders at Spring Hill.[34]

During the afternoon, "Hood and Cheatham were working at cross purposes, the former attempting to seize the pike while the latter planned an assault on Spring Hill." General Bate found himself caught between the conflicting orders of his army and corps commanders; he and his division acted first to achieve Hood's objective and moved within sight of the pike before General Cheatham ordered Bate to join Cleburne's troops for an assault on the Union line. However, Bate's attack on the Federal position at Spring Hill never materialized, and one historian has estimated that the general did not reach his assigned position until ten o'clock that evening. Contradictory instructions passed along during the day between Hood and his subordinates also kept General Stewart's soldiers from striking at the vital roadway north of the town. That evening, General John Schofield, who remained alert but unsure as to Hood's intentions until mid-afternoon, started his troops toward Spring Hill. By eight o'clock the first of Schofield's troops were on the march to Franklin, ten miles to the north.[35]

The Florida Brigade's soldiers built their fires that evening within several hundred yards of the Franklin Pike. Unfortunately, only one letter, that of Washington Ives to his mother, survives to provide a contemporary glimpse of the unit's experience at Spring Hill. Ives wrote only that his division "advanced, . . . before dark so near the pike that the Yanks were compelled to quit the pike and cut through the wood 7 miles, where they retook the pike." John Inglis recalled years later that during the night "they passed us, trains and troops, nearly the whole long night." Henry Reddick, also of the 1st and 3rd Florida, remembered in his memoirs that the soldiers "lay down to sleep in line of battle so near the road that we could hear the Yankee officers giving the commands to their men as they marched down the road."[36]

Not long after daylight on November 30, a day that "developed bright and warm—a good example of Indian summer," the Florida Brigade's soldiers were tramping northward along the Franklin Pike in pursuit of Schofield's small army. The soldiers perhaps saw General Hood ride by their ranks, his body strapped in the saddle and face flushed with indignation at the failure of the previous day. Henry McCall Holmes wrote that before the Army of Tennessee, "Forrest was passing thru & they were stampeding. About 2 o'c reached . . . hills 2 ½ miles from Franklin, country very hilly, the town is on Big Harper [sic] river, fordable. Our lines have formed for attack." When General Schofield's troops reached Franklin on the morning of November 30, they discovered the bridges over the Big Harpeth River unusable and the Federal commander immediately put his soldiers to work either improving existing entrenchments or digging fresh fortifications. By afternoon the Union Army manned strong entrenchments with both flanks anchored on the Big Harpeth.[37]

Arriving on the hills that overlooked the town, General Hood informed his subordinates of his decision to assault the Federal line. Following the Spring Hill bungle, the Kentuckian had decided, according to Thomas Connelly, "to discipline his army by means of a frontal assault." Hood aligned his two available corps so that they would converge at the Federal line between the Franklin Pike, which ran north-south, and the Big Harpeth River a half mile to the east. Hood ordered General Bate "to strike the Federal flank along the Carter's Creek pike at the far west of the battlefield." Bate positioned his division with Generals Smith and Jackson's brigades in the first line; Colonel Bullock's Floridians assumed a supporting role in the second line.[38]

Waiting in line of battle atop the ridges, the Floridians could see a "rolling country with few trees and almost no fences" and the town of Franklin in the distance. In the silence before the attack, General Bate rode before his division exhorting the men to duty, telling them "the Yankees had thrown up breastworks, but they were temporary and we could go right over them, and this done we would go right on to Nashville, and asked us if we would follow him. We gave the rebel yell and said that we would follow him." At 4:00 P.M. on November's last day "a flag was dropped at Cheatham's order. . . . It was the long-awaited signal to advance." Henry McCall Holmes recalled, "Our troops went up in Splendid Style, they became engaged just before night."[39]

As the battle commenced, according to Holmes, Cheatham's two divisions assigned to strike the Union center advanced, "[Patrick] Cleburn . . . on right of the pike, [John C.] Brown on the left & they sustained the brunt of the fight. The Yankee position here was extremely strong." These two units and those of General Stewart had long engaged the enemy before General Bate's Division became involved in the Battle of Franklin. The historian Wiley Sword has identified the cause of the delay as "the greater distance traveled—at least additional three-quarters of a mile considering the nearly thirty-degree divergent angle of advance and the recurved Federal line bending away to the north." In order to arrive at his appointed place of attack, Bate marched his soldiers "over a mile at right angles to the main attacking force to reach the vicinity of the Carter's Creek Pike." Once Bate's sapped infantry reached their assigned position, the general brought forward Bullock's unit to the main line. This extended his line's left so that the Florida Brigade's center rested on Carter's Creek Pike, a thoroughfare stretching away from the town toward the southwest.[40]

The Floridians' attack at Franklin, which angled northeastward up Carter Creek Pike, began as dusk fell. Colonel John E. Bennett, commanding the 75th Illinois, wrote of the Confederate attack, "He advanced in good order within good-musket range. I then ordered the men to fire. The first volley partially stopped his advance. A few more well-aimed volleys sent the enemy back in confusion." On the receiving end of the Illinois soldiers' fire, as well as volleys from several other midwestern units, Henry Reddick remembered: "the muskets began popping in all directions, coming and going hot from both sides . . . our boys began dropping like corn before a hailstorm, and we never did succeed in reaching their mainline, for about fifty yards in front of it they had cut down a lot of thorny locust bushes and it was impossible in face of the hot fire to get through them."[41]

Sometime during this assault, as Lieutenant Colonel Badger urged his men forward, a projectile killed his mount. As his horse collapsed to the ground, Badger hit the ground hard as well, breaking the revolver given to him at Mill Creek. The young lawyer pressed on afoot, encouraging his men. According to General Bate, the youthful colonel suffered three wounds before finally being carried from the field. Captain McConnell also fell after suffering a serious leg wound. Though doctors managed to save the leg, the injury ended McConnell's army service and caused him in later years to "go on crutches."[42]

Under the intense fire coming from the Federal line, Reddick wrote, "[T]he order was given to lie down. It was the only hope for us for we cold [sic] neither go forward or go back in such a fire and live. This was about seven o'clock in the evening, and we laid there under that terrific fire until 11." John Inglis wrote of lying on the ground as darkness gathered: "Nearly all the men so dear to me in the long, suffering years lay around me stark and stiff in the cold." Remembering the Franklin battle in the early 1900s, John L. McKinnon bitterly noted that the "boys called this battle 'Hoods Killing.'" By nine o'clock the Union line had withstood savage Confederate charges and inflicted serious losses on the Rebels.[43]

Daylight revealed carnage that even the battle-hardened Rebel veterans could hardly believe. No shots rang from the Union entrenchments, for during the early morning hours of December 1 General Schofield's army slipped unnoticed across the Big Harpeth River and moved toward Nashville. In Schofield's wake, more than 7,500 Confederates lay on the field and around the Union entrenchments; around 1,750 were dead, including Patrick Cleburne and several other generals. Washington Ives wrote upon glimpsing the Columbia and Franklin Pike area, where the most savage fighting occurred, that he "saw at 10 A.M. human blood 3 inches deep in the ditch at the main line & running like water."[44]

While A. P. Stewart's shattered corps and Stephen D. Lee's divisions marched in pursuit of General Schofield's men, Cheatham's troops remained around Franklin to bury the dead. Henry Reddick recalled: "Though it has been more than forty years since then, the scenes of the battlefield are as fresh in my mind as though it was yesterday. I think the hardest fighting must have been near the old gin house on pike road, for there bodies were so thick that we could have stepped from one to another." Henry Holmes, after working during the night of November 30 and throughout the next day to save the wounded, penned only "our loss very heavy."[45]

When Bate's Division finally marched on December 2, it left 47 dead on the battlefield. More than 250 wounded languished in field hospitals, and 19 had been taken prisoner. These losses represented only a fraction of the total Confederate losses. Although it is impossible to extract the Florida Brigade's casualties from this general list of divisional losses, a general estimate, given the number of soldiers remaining on December 10, would place the day's losses between 50 and 100.[46]

On December 2, 1864, as the Army of Tennessee moved north against Nashville, Bate's Division moved southeast toward Murfreesboro. It was just north of that quaint railroad town nearly two years earlier that Washington Ives and the 4th Florida passed through their baptism by fire. General Hood's reason for dispatching the Floridians back to the old battlefield was so that their division might destroy the Nashville and Chattanooga Railroad and thus "prevent the Murfreesboro garrison . . . from joining [General George] Thomas at Nashville." To accomplish this task, Bate's infantrymen joined General Nathan Bedford Forrest's Cavalry Corps in focusing their attention on the many blockhouses that guarded the tracks.[47]

While Forrest succeeded in seizing four of the fortifications, the blockhouse that guarded the Overall Creek bridge, seven miles from Murfreesboro, proved a tough nut to crack. General Bate, moving his division against this obstacle on the morning of December 4, hoped to achieve a success similar to that at Mill Creek. He thus deployed the Washington Artillery's guns to shell the blockhouse while General Henry R. Jackson's Brigade tore up the railroad in the vicinity. To protect the guns against any threat, Bate positioned the 1st and 3rd Florida, 1st Florida Cavalry and 4th Florida, and 7th Florida regiments on the northern bank of Overall Creek to guard against any approaching enemy.[48]

Lieutenant McLeod wrote in his diary of the day's activities: "struck the Rail Road & their was a block house & we began to shoot at it with the cannon & they reenforced it from murfreesborough." This relief force, dispatched by General Lovell Rosseau, was commanded by General Robert Milroy and marched from Fortress Rosecrans (near Murfreesboro) to investigate the gunfire coming from the north. Milroy moved with three infantry regiments and several artillery pieces. This brigade-sized unit arrived in the late afternoon, with the Union commander deploying the reduced 61st Illinois Veteran Volunteers into a skirmish formation to challenge the Floridians. McLeod wrote as the two sides became engaged, "[W]e went into them & they onto us & we began to fight." Nearing twilight, after a Federal cavalry charge failed to take the Washington Artillery's pieces, Milroy deployed the green 174th Ohio for battle. The advance of the six-hundred-strong unit proved too much for Colonel Bullock's Floridians, who held the north bank of the creek. The Buckeyes splashed through the stream and, in the words of their colonel, "advanced directly against the enemy, driving him steadily before us until we advanced from one-half to three-quarters of a mile, when we were ordered to withdraw."[49]

As the large Ohio regiment pressed the small Florida regiments away from Overall Creek, General Thomas Benton Smith's regiments failed to move to the Florida Brigade's aid. Washington Ives complained bitterly that the Florida Brigade "had no support and as it was to [sic] weak to contend against such odds . . . was compelled to fall back." Indeed, a Louisiana artillerist seconded Ives's assertion, writing that General Smith's Brigade advanced "no farther than my pieces."

Outnumbered, the Floridians soon were soon without a leader, as Colonel Bullock fell with an unspecified, though incapacitating, wound. Without Bullock's steadying influence, the small unsupported brigade was overwhelmed by Union soldiers. General Henry R. Jackson's men, coming up from the railroad, finally checked the Union advance, though not before the Floridians suffered fifty casualties, a majority of the eighty-six that Bate's Division lost that day.[50]

That evening, with his surgeons still working to prepare the wounded for transportation, Henry Holmes explained that Bate "fell back to . . . ten miles from Murf., leaving only a few cavalry, 12, to picket between hospital and the Yankees. Wounded not got off till near morning." Besides the wounded Colonel Bullock, the 7th Florida also lost the pious Reason Wilson Jerkins to a mortal wound. General Milroy admitted losing sixty-four men in the lopsided contest.[51]

Following the Battle of Overall Creek, as the skirmish around the blockhouse came to be known, the Washington Artillery's cannoneers expressed their disappointment to the Floridians with whom they had long served. One of the company's privates dubbed the Florida Brigade's conduct "shameful." Lieutenant Joseph Chalaron remembered that the Floridians stopped running once they reached the safety of the cannon but remained "disorganized." General Henry Rootes Jackson called Bullock's retreat a "rout." It was the first time during the war that the Floridians conducted themselves disgracefully on a battlefield; sadly this became the norm over the next two weeks.[52]

Led now by Major Jacob Lash, the brigade's survivors drifted away from the scene of their defeat in the gathering darkness. On December 5, the brigade was once again on the march toward Murfreesboro and the enemy. The Floridians moved under the orders of Lieutenant General Nathan Bedford Forrest; the cavalry commander had arrived with his divisions that morning and assumed command of Bate's infantry. Forrest hoped to deploy his strike force so as to cut off "Rousseau's supplies and force the enemy to come out and fight." To accomplish this, General Bate's infantry entrenched across the Nashville and Chattanooga Railroad; ironically, the Floridians occupied a position close to the Round Forest, overlooking the field where the 1st and 3rd Florida and 4th Florida regiments had charged nearly two years before. Henry Reddick recalled passing through a cemetery "where our boys were buried that had fallen in the first fight there."[53]

Long before December 7 became a day of infamy for Americans, the Florida Brigade's veterans remembered it as one of their most humiliating defeats of the entire war. Near midmorning, a Federal column of 3,300 soldiers, again commanded by General Milroy, departed Fortress Rosecrans to determine Forrest's strength and disposition. Forrest planned to counter this move by blocking the Federal advance with his infantry and then use his cavalry to strike the enemy's flank and rear. General Bate deployed his division, augmented by the brigades of Generals Claudius Sears and Joseph Palmer, just south of the Wilkinson Pike. The Florida Brigade's soldiers, along with General Henry R. Jackson's troops, held the right flank of this new line, with their front facing a broad cotton field. General Bate reported that as soon as the soldiers arrived at their new position, "temporary works were constructed of rails and logs."[54]

Rather than attack the Confederate position head-on, Milroy withdrew his soldiers behind one of the cedar groves so identified with the Murfreesboro area, "where they were lost to Confederate view." Choosing not to return to the safety of Fortress Rosecrans, Milroy instead deployed his two brigades across Wilkinson Pike and prepared to assault the Confederates' left flank. When Forrest ordered Bate to readjust his line to meet this new threat, Bate faltered. He claimed Forrest never provided him with the particulars of the enemy's new position. Yet the infantry commander still allowed his division to haphazardly redeploy. The Florida Brigade had but a short distance to travel, as Bate placed the unit and Palmer's Brigade in the entrenchments recently vacated by Generals Jackson and Sears's commands as they moved to extend the line to the left. General Thomas Benton Smith's Brigade had orders to occupy the space between Jackson's Brigade and Lash, but for some reason the youthful Smith was negligent in his duty once again, and his troops never made contact with the Floridians. Because of General Bate's failure to closely oversee his soldiers' movement, a "space of perhaps 75 or 100 yards" existed "between Smith's right and Finley's left."[55]

Before Bate could close this gap, the Federal advance fell like a hammer blow on Lash's men. The Floridians' outposts hardly provided any warning, for the 7th Florida's pickets were quickly routed by the 61st Illinois, and Lieutenant William McLeod admitted that the Floridians "had to run in" with the bluecoats on their heels. Holmes wrote: "the enemy . . . before our men reached point charged and drove in our men." As the Federal troops moved across the cotton field that fronted the Rebel lines, Forrest pleaded with the Floridians to maintain their position: "'Men, all I ask of you is to hold the enemy back for fifteen minutes, which will give me sufficient time to gain their rear with my cavalry, and I will capture the last one of them.'" It is unlikely that the Floridians held for even five minutes. Henry Reddick recalled, "[W]e fired a few vollies but soon had to give way."[56]

The troops that slammed into the Floridians' front and through the gap to their left belonged to the 174th Ohio, the regiment that caused so much trouble for Lash's infantry on December 4, and the 8th Minnesota. Between them, the two regiments totaled more than a thousand men. A member of the recently mustered 174th Ohio wrote home after the fight: "The rapid discharge of the 12 pounders and the roar of the muskets told us all was not play. Our men were charging, shouting, and the guns were filling the air with their reports." Once the Federal infantry reached the breastworks, "the fighting was in such close quarters" as the numerous Yankees swarmed around the Floridians. Though their officers tried to maintain order, the majority of Major Lash's men put up only a feeble resistance from behind their fortifications before beating a hasty retreat. In only a short time ninety-one Floridians either surrendered or were apprehended by Federal soldiers. To add insult to injury, after the Federal soldiers broke through the Floridians' position, a 174th Ohio soldier seized the 1st Florida Cavalry and 4th Florida's battle flag, making it the first regiment of the Florida Brigade to suffer that embarrassment during the war.[57]

With the Florida Brigade's line collapsed, General Palmer's troops, positioned on Lash's right, also gave way. Lieutenant McLeod wrote of the retreat, "the hole command run off & we could not rally under a mile." The Floridians, despite General Forrest's renown throughout the Confederacy, paid the officer little attention as he rode among the fleeing mass attempting to halt the rout. In the ensuing chaos, the Federals rushed the Washington Artillery's position and captured two of the company's cannons. Luckily for General Forrest, Henry R. Jackson's and Thomas Smith's soldiers curbed the Federal advance and halted the fighting for the evening.[58]

A Washington Artillery cannoneer recorded that as the brigade plodded north from the battlefield, his comrades let loose their fury at the Floridians and "cursed them without measure as they slouched along. Nay, heaped up execrations upon them until we were exhausted." The next day the Florida Brigade assembled, and in the words of McLeod, "Gen. Bate give us a talk about running from the Yanks." General Henry R. Jackson wrote, "General Bate, in a speech . . . to the Florida Brigade ascribed our discomfiture to the disgraceful conduct of that command in allowing the enemy to take our breastworks in which he declared he had purposely placed them."[59]

The two engagements fought near Murfreesboro cost the Florida Brigade more than 150 irreplaceable casualties, including Colonel Robert Bullock, and permanently damaged the unit's bright reputation they had earned earlier in the conflict. To be fair to the Floridians, Bate's poor management of his division's readjustment caused the brigade to occupy the section of the line where the Federals' heaviest assault fell during the Cedars fight. The Union regiments that advanced against the Florida Brigade totaled over 1,000, meaning the Rebels were outnumbered two to one. Despite these disadvantages, the veteran Floridians should have given a better account of themselves during the December 7 fight.[60]

Their service with General Forrest completed, Bate's Division began their march toward Nashville on December 11 in the midst of horrible weather. Lieutenant McLeod wrote of the first day's march, "[I]t was the coldest day ever I saw & the wind blew all the time in our faces." Of the next day Washington Ives remembered, "[M]any men were frostbitten and the ice was so thick the wagons did not disturb it." Arriving at the Confederate line near Tennessee's capital on December 12, the Floridians could view the city and its surrounding fortifications. They discovered that in the intervening twelve days that they had been at work destroying the railroad near Murfreesboro, the Army of Tennessee had marched to within a few miles of Nashville and then entrenched. Historians have pointed out that Hood's line, which stretched four miles from southwest to northeast, was terribly designed with "exterior lines of communication" and "highly vulnerable to an enemy development on either flank."[61]

The Florida Brigade, which on December 13 numbered 410 men capable of bearing arms and 350 soldiers on the sick and wounded list, was commanded at that point by Major Glover A. Ball. The brigade, along with Cheatham's Corps, was positioned on the northeastern portion of Hood's "siege" line. General Lee's Corps held the center of the line, while General Stewart's held the left, which included a series of redoubts constructed to protect that flank. The Floridians spent December 13 and 14 "in the ditches around Nashville" in relative quiet and encased in fog. It seemed as though December 15 would be similar, as in the morning a thick mist covered the two armies. However, that afternoon as the fog lifted, General George H. Thomas launched his fifty thousand Federal soldiers at the outnumbered Confederates.[62]

On the afternoon of December 15, the Federal blow fell on General Hood's left flank as General A. J. Smith's three divisions from the Army of the Tennessee and General James H. Wilson's Cavalry Corps, a total of twenty-four thousand troops, swept over the redoubts and into A. P. Stewart's flank. In addition to this flanking force, General Thomas Wood's IV Corps and Schofield's Army of the Ohio, yet another twenty-four thousand Union troops, stood ready to move against Stewart's center. As Stewart's Corps fought for its life, Hood ordered two divisions, those of Edward Johnson and Bate, to support his beleaguered left. While Johnson's Division was engaged that afternoon as Stewart's line crumbled, Bate's Division did little good, as it failed to even begin its march west until after sunset. McLeod remembered, "[We] went around & reenforced on the left & we got their after night & we commenced our breast works." Arriving on the left flank, Hood posted Bate's small division atop Compton's Hill, a knoll that guarded Granny White Pike, one of Hood's lines of retreat, which ran northeast to southwest. Hood's new line lay a few miles south of his previous entrenchments. Lee's Corps held Peach Orchard Hill on the right, where it protected the vital Franklin Pike, and Stewart's men saddled the valley between the two. The following day, Compton Hill served as the scene for the Florida Brigade's last stand.[63]

As December 16 dawned, the Floridians' tired eyes beheld a foggy, gloomy morning. The Florida Brigade's soldiers were exhausted, for, in the words of William McLeod, they had "worked all night" digging entrenchments on the slopes of the knoll. Despite this frantic pace, the soldiers "never got them finished tho we quit them." During the night, General Bate placed his division on the northwestern face of the hill, with the Florida Brigade occupying his center. General Mark Lowrey's troops connected with Bate's left, while General Edward Walthall's Division held the right slopes of the hill. Because Cheatham's Corps' line ran due south from the hill and Stewart's line jogged in an easterly direction from Compton's Hill, the position presented a protruding salient. Furthermore, the Confederate entrenchments mirrored those constructed on Missionary Ridge in that they "were constructed too far back, along the actual crown of the hill rather than on the forward slopes." To make matters even worse, Bate's three brigades' defensive lines were thinned considerably when his units were forced to extend to fill gaps caused by the withdrawal of other troops from the hill. As in the Battle of the Cedars fought a week earlier, the Floridians were, due to forces beyond their control, placed in a precarious position atop Compton's Hill from which their superiors expected the impossible.[64]

At first light the skirmishers began exchanging shots, with the Rebels receiving the worst of the duel. The Federals were reinforced by artillery that unlimbered within four hundred yards of Compton's Hill. That morning these cannon "played back and forth across the Southern position." Due to the exposed nature of their lines atop Compton's Hill, Confederate entrenchments were "pounded by a devastating barrage from every direction of the compass except the east, and even there, fire was coming from the northeast." McLeod penned in his diary, "[W]e had to lay low all day until evening the Yankee batteries was within 5 hundred yards of us & their was a good many of them & they shot our works all down . . . their was a shot come through our works and shot off our adjutants head and wounded 2 more men." John Love McKinnon remembered that this bombardment "lasted from early morning until well onto evening."[65]

During the bombardment, McLeod exposed himself enough to observe Union troops advancing "2 lines of battle upon us & they come up in 3 or 4 hundred yards of us & all lay down." These were undoubtedly Schofield's Army of the Ohio troops, yet it was John McArthur's Army of the Tennessee's soldiers that initiated the attack along the western end of the Confederate line. Thomas's intended attack on the fight's second day was to duplicate the battle plan of December 15, with the Federals exerting tremendous pressure on the Confederate left. When Thomas's generals failed to launch this attack by 3:00 P.M., McArthur took matters into his own hands. Witnessing McArthur's brigades advance, General Thomas commanded his other troops to converge upon Compton's Hill. Even before this assault began, one of General Wilson's cavalry brigades had gained the Granny White Pike south of the Confederate position, thus depriving the Confederates on Compton's Hill of their line of retreat.[66]

On Compton's Hill, Colonel William McMillan's Brigade of McArthur's Division was moving up under fire, but his men had difficulty ascending the steep knoll. However, "the steeper the ground, the greater the difficulty experienced by Confederate artillerists attempting to depress their few guns and fire accurately down the height. The steeper the ground, the more likely were the Southern in-

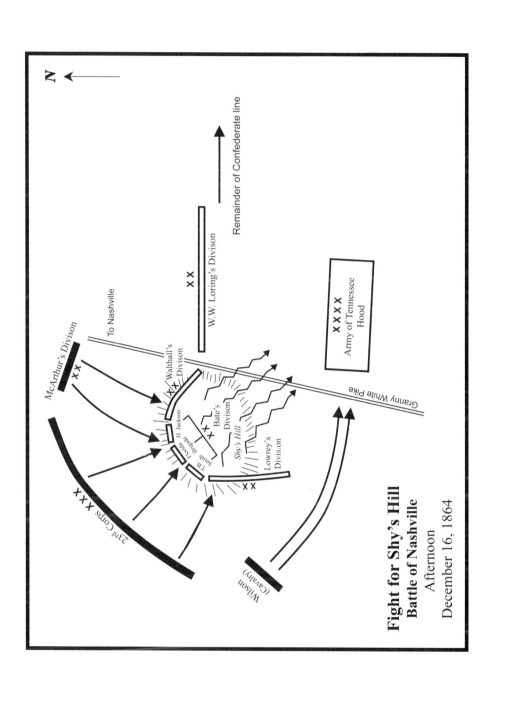

**Fight for Shy's Hill
Battle of Nashville**
Afternoon
December 16, 1864

N ←

Remainder of Confederate line

W.W. Loring's Divison
x x

Army of Tennessee
Hood
x x x x

To Nashville

McArthur's Divison
x x

Walthall's
Divison
x x

Granny White Pike

Bate's
Divison
x x

H. Jackson

T.B. Smith Brigade

Shy's Hill

Lowrey's
Divison
x x

23rd Corps
x x x

Wilson
(Cavalry)

fantry to overshoot." The Federal brigade, comprised of units raised in the old
Northwest, surged over General Thomas B. Smith's line of crumbled works and
caused the Rebels to flee. John McKinnon wrote in his memoirs that as the Florida
Brigade's soldiers took shots at the advancing enemy, "private Robt. Holley turned
his face toward me to reload, grabbed me by the right arm with a grasp I long felt,
and said 'Look at the U.S. flag on our breastworks!' I looked to my left and there
it was, our ditches empty, the men escaping through the mountain woodlands."[67]

With the enemy gaining their flank and now coming up in front, the Florida
Brigade gave way. General Bate reported that as soon as Smith's men fell back, "the
lines lifted from either side as far as I could see almost instantly and fled in confusion." Some Floridians held out until no hope remained; John L. McKinnon surrendered only when the "Federals jumped in the ditches with us, . . . an officer said
to me, 'Let me have your sword; let's all get out of the ditches and go to the rear.'"
Henry Reddick was one who did not hesitate. He sprinted down the opposite slope
of Compton's Hill even as "Col's and Gen's came dashing across the hills trying
to rally the men, with pistols and swords drawn." A Sergeant Roberts of the 3rd
Florida recalled that he tried to escape, but "I had a sore foot, and a whole crowd
of Yanks got in the road and told me that if I did not stop they would shoot. Well,
I stayed in Camp Chase till the 12th of June, 1865." J. W. Kellum, the 1st and 3rd
Florida's color-bearer, wrote, "We became surrounded by the enemy; and after we
were forced to lay down our arms, in order to prevent the enemy from getting our
flag, I tore it into strings."[68]

The 6th Florida's men were not so fortunate; Private Otis Smith of the 95th Illinois came away from the fight bearing the 6th's regimental flag as a souvenir. In
addition, at least 122 soldiers of the Florida Brigade were captured and a number
were also killed and wounded. Major Jacob Lash, who earlier questioned the necessity of a Tennessee invasion and was portrayed by General Bate as having displayed "coolness and gallantry" during the campaign, was taken prisoner, as were
John Inglis, his cousin Archie Livingston, and Angus Gillis, whose letters to his
aunt had informed Walton County citizens of the war's progress.[69]

Lieutenant William McLeod, who climbed "a tree in the rear" soon after the
7th Florida's adjutant lost his head, recalled, "their I staid until the Yanks come &
broke our lines & was coming over the hill & then we all had to run about 2 miles
to get away . . . & we rallied at [Brentwood] Station on the pike & RR about 4
miles from the place we started." Henry Reddick escaped the confusion on Compton's Hill only to become mired in the mud of the Franklin Pike. He wrote, "I
thought several times that I would have to fall out, I was completely broken down,
but when I would think of being captured I would come to a new life." Many did
fall by the wayside, their patriotism and spirit gone. The pursuing Federals seized
another thirty-seven Floridians in the days after the battle.[70]

With the Compton's Hill position in shambles, Cheatham's "corps melted into a disorganized rabble that tossed away small arms, abandoned artillery, and scurried for the Franklin Pike. Stewart's Corps was caught up in the rout as well." The Army of Tennessee, with the Florida Brigade under the command of Major Glover Ball, fled southward following the Nashville defeat. Washington Ives described the army's retreat from Middle Tennessee: "The weather was cold and it rained incessantly. There was much suffering, the men nearly naked and bare foot & I saw dozens of the men (who had been severely wounded at Franklin) marching day after day on crutches. It is scarcely worth my while to write some of the scenes I saw as they would not be believed."[71]

Lieutenant Colonel Edward Badger was counted among those whose wounds prohibited walking. Ives remembered seeing the officer on December 18, "riding a mule colt—his wounds were sore. He had put a quilt on the mule's back and had cotton rope for stirrups." The withdrawal finally ended on New Year's Day 1865, when the pitiful remnants of the Army of Tennessee reached Corinth where General Beauregard had organized supply caches. At the Mississippi railroad town, which was once so important to both Union and Confederate forces, the troops mustered for inspection. Early in the winter of 1865, the Florida Brigade numbered probably between 500 and 600, half of whom were sick or wounded and thus incapable of bearing arms. Surely the Florida Brigade had come full circle since that day nearly three years before when 250 raw, untested Floridians arrived at Corinth to participate in the Battle of Shiloh.[72]

The hard marching and tough fighting of General John Bell Hood's Tennessee Campaign of 1864 finally served to whittle the Florida Brigade to insignificance. The core that remained was barefoot and dressed in tatters, and many had no weapon. Two regiments had suffered the ignoble fate of having lost their flags, and the brigade's survivors shouldered the blame for breaking on Compton's Hill. The December 16 disaster, when added to the Florida Brigade's pitiful performances before Murfreesboro, provided the Floridians with a legacy of poor performance under fire. Sam Watkins remembered of the Nashville battle, "Finney's Florida brigade had broken before a mere skirmish line, and soon the whole army had caught the infection." In addition to damaging the Florida Brigade's reputation, the campaign also resulted in the death, incapacitation, or incarceration in Federal prison camps of hundreds of Floridians. Yet those who remained were soldiers for the war, and the war, despite the Confederacy's many great setbacks, was not yet over.[73]

EPILOGUE

It Is the Duty of Everyman to Obey the Powers That Be

January–May 1865

On February 1, 1865, the Florida Brigade undertook its fourth and final rail movement of the war when its small regiments embarked at West Point, Mississippi, for the journey east. During February's first ten days, the brigade, with the corps of Generals Benjamin Cheatham (led by General William Bate) and Alexander Stewart (commanded by William Loring), sped—at least as fast as trains could proceed along the Confederacy's decrepit rail system—through towns in Mississippi, Alabama, and Georgia that were now familiar to the Floridians. The Army of Tennessee, then led by Stewart and numbering only five thousand effectives, moved east to reinforce the Carolinas and attempt to defend those regions against Sherman. He had not rested on his laurels after reaching Savannah in December and instead turned north in January, determined to take his campaign of demoralization into the state that seceded first.[1]

Led by Lieutenant Colonel Edward Mashburn, the Florida Brigade crossed the Savannah River at Augusta, the men shouldering new Enfield rifles obtained from the arsenal there. At the head of Bate's old division rode the crippled Lafayette Kenan, who was the division's senior surviving officer. The men were in good spirits, their morale boosted by the fact that Jefferson Davis had reluctantly appointed Joe Johnston commander over most Confederate troops in the Carolinas. Lieutenant Albert Livingston applauded: "The great good & noble Johnston commands us again. The boys are delighted with this news."[2]

During February and early March the troops slogged through the western portions of South Carolina. Livingston wrote on March 5, "[U]ntil this morning we have had rain every day for the last Ten. The roads were in miserable condition—mud in some places over knee deep & in no place less than ankle." In their attempt to reach Johnston, the veteran infantry made long marches comparable to those completed in Kentucky and on Hood's recent campaign. In North Carolina, the cautious Johnston had decided to gather his scattered forces near Smithfield, intending to impede Sherman's progress north. "Once Sherman committed himself—either across Johnston's front toward Goldsboro or by his flank toward Raleigh—Johnston would attack." Upon discovering on March 18 that one wing of Sherman's army was near Bentonville, a hamlet just south of Smithfield on Goldsboro Road, Johnston committed his troops to the offensive.[3]

On the afternoon of March 19, color-bearers unfurled the brigade's surviving tattered banners. As 3:00 P.M. neared, the Army of Tennessee's small number of survivors formed ranks and lurched forward for one last charge. Livingston informed his parents that the soldiers seized "2 lines of their Breastworks & completely [routed] the Yanks for 2 miles. It was a glorious days work for the 'Tenn Army' as it was generally circulated & believed that our army was demoralized." Though their attack finally faltered, the Floridians perhaps felt vindicated, for afterward General Bate "came around to our brigade & said that he really felt proud of Little Florida."[4]

The Florida Brigade's exoneration did not come cheaply, though; after the fight Henry Holmes reported, "[O]ur brigade lost one fourth of its [numbers]." Benjamin Glover, who was in South Carolina at the time of the battle, wrote his wife with news: "Johnson has had a hard fight with Sherman and gave him a whipping. Our Brig suffered as useual [sic]." Albert Livingston, who fell during the battle with a shell fragment through his knee, explained, "[T]he loss of the brigade for the numbers engaged I am sorry to say is heavier than it has ever been before." One irreplaceable casualty was Colonel Kenan. While leading the remnants of Bate's Division into the fray, a Federal bullet shattered his right leg, and surgeons were forced to amputate. The Bentonville battlefield lay thirty miles northwest of Kenansville, the wounded colonel's birthplace.[5]

As Sherman's forces concentrated against Johnston's army, the outnumbered Confederates retreated from the Bentonville battlefield in the early morning hours of March 22. Camping between Smithfield and Raleigh, the Florida Brigade remained inactive—save for corps reviews—until April 9, 1865. On the day Robert E. Lee surrendered the Army of Northern Virginia to Ulysses S. Grant at Appomattox, General Johnston began a new phase of consolidation within the Army of Tennessee. With depleted brigades becoming regiments, the proud Florida Brigade, comprising fewer soldiers than a battalion, became the 1st Florida Infantry, Consolidated. This fused soldiers from all of Florida's regions into a single unit, symbolizing the unity of the state. On May 1, 1865, five days after Johnston surrendered the force under his command at Bennett's Place near Durham, the troops of the 1st Florida Infantry, Consolidated, were paroled.[6]

Just over four hundred Florida soldiers took the Oath of Allegiance on May 1. Washington Ives was counted among the number, as were Henry Holmes and Benjamin Glover. Roddie Shaw was not, and neither was James Hays or Michael Raysor; their bodies had long been interred in the Georgia and Florida soil. Jacob Yearty, who had painstakingly described the Chickamauga victory to his parents, lay near the spot where he fell on Missionary Ridge. Archie Livingston, Samuel Pasco, John Inglis, and Jacob Lash were all in Federal prison camps.[7]

In parting from Bennett's Place, General Johnston asked his men to "discharge the obligations of good and peaceful citizens at your homes as well as you have performed the duties of thorough soldiers." With these words fresh in their minds, the Florida Brigade's survivors drifted home in groups; they were joined in Florida later in the summer by parolees released from Federal prison camps. Theodore Livingston wrote Archie on May 22 from Madison regarding the general's request: "All the 3rd Fla and in fact all the Confederate Army are home now. . . . Now that we are overpowered, and no longer a confederacy, [it] is the duty of everyman to obey the powers that be." He emphasized the South's defeat by adding that General Quincy Gilmore, commanding the Federal department encompassing Florida, "has issued an order that all persons, black and white are on an equality. There is great excitement among both classes."[8]

Ferocious fighters, the Florida Brigade's units had given their all on the battlefields on which they fought. Over the course of the war, one in every three became a battlefield casualty, and hundreds more died of disease. Their disastrous performances late in the war during the engagements fought outside Murfreesboro and Nashville, however, caused their reputation to suffer. Today, these soldiers are mainly remembered for those disasters. Their rearguard action at Missionary Ridge, as well as their charges at Perryville, Murfreesboro, and Chickamauga, should not be overlooked. Truly, by the noble daring of her sons, Florida was not embarrassed in the war.[9]

In 1865 the Florida Brigade's survivors arrived in Florida, the beaten remnant of a once proud army. Their lives were forever changed by the war and its outcome; men coped with the loss of limbs and refought battles in their nightly dreams. Jaded by defeat, Daniel McLean perhaps chose the right words when he wrote, "[A]las a cruel war, waged by cruel men, has destroyed the happiness & blighted the hopeful aspirations of the youths of an intire [sic] nation." As civilians, these ex-soldiers fought to reverse the war's battlefield losses on the home front, as they emerged from the Reconstruction era defiant. Florida Brigade members helped draft and approve Florida's Constitution of 1885, which denied African Americans voting rights and legalized segregation. Yet these same men also worked to pass progressive legislation, such as the bill that created the State Board of Health.[10]

In 1864, on the eve of Sherman's Georgia Campaign, Roddie Shaw wrote that he was "so very confident of our success . . . that I will be unprepared for anything but a quiet home next year." By the late 1890s, Florida's Civil War generation's era had passed, and their children ushered the state into the twentieth century. One by one, the veterans, collecting state pensions for their Confederate service, retired to those serene surroundings that Roddie Shaw never experienced, and it was there that these players exited quietly from the stage that had witnessed one of the greatest dramas effected by men.[11]

The Generals

William George Mackey Davis

Following his resignation in 1863, Davis sponsored several blockade runners in an attempt to recoup his financial losses. After the war, Davis eventually settled in Alexandria, Virginia, where he practiced law; he lived until 1898.

Jesse Johnson Finley

In the war's waning days, General Finley was granted his parole at Quincy. Living in Lake City after the conflict, he wrote in 1866 that the war had "left him without a dollar in the world," yet he confessed he was "making a plain—very plain, but yet comfortable living by my profession." In 1874 he returned to the political arena he loved so well, ironically as a Democrat, and represented Florida's Second District for a single term in the House of Representatives. In the 1880s and 1890s he returned to the bench, serving as a circuit judge for six years. The old general died in 1904 at the age of ninety-one. Later in the twentieth century the Alachua County School Board honored Finley by naming an elementary school for him.[12]

Robert Bullock

Though promoted to brigadier general on November 29, 1864, Bullock's Overall Creek wound prevented him from rejoining his command. As Marion County's Freedman's Bureau agent during 1865–66, he became known "for his prudent and impartial administration of this difficult position." In 1867, however, Bullock refused to allow integrated juries to hear criminal cases, casting a pall over his previously respectable reputation. Entering politics in 1872, Bullock served in the state legislature in 1879 and was elected to the U.S. House of Representatives in 1888 and 1890. After he returned to private life, Bullock practiced law until his death in 1905, having survived his beloved wife by only days.[13]

William Miller

Although he was wounded at Murfreesboro, Miller gained his general's stars in August 1864 and succeeded James Patton Anderson as commander of the District of Florida. Settling in the panhandle, Miller engaged in various business interests and was elected to the Florida legislature in 1885; he also sat in the state senate. Miller was eighty-nine when he died in 1909.[14]

James Patton Anderson

After rising to the rank of major general during the conflict, Anderson commanded the District of Florida before surrendering at Bennett's Place. Soon after the war he removed to Memphis. Anderson's career options remained limited for "he refused to seek a pardon and therefore he could neither practice law nor hold public office." He died in Memphis in 1872 at age fifty; he was laid to rest there, instead of in the Kentucky soil he so cherished.[15]

The Officers

William Scott Dilworth

Returning to practice law in Jefferson County after the war, Dilworth focused on freedmen's rights. He died in 1869.[16]

Edward Hopkins

Resigning after failing to gain reelection to the 4th Florida's colonelcy, Hopkins enjoyed a resurgence in his public career after the war. He won two terms as mayor of Jacksonville in 1868–69, and during Rutherford B. Hayes presidency he was appointed the port's customs collector. He was again nominated to this position by President Grover Cleveland. The former Whig politician died in 1887.[17]

Madison Starke Perry

The governor who led Florida through secession returned to the state after his resignation. He succumbed to illness in early 1865.

Thaddeus A. McDonell

Until the day he died the 1st Florida's lieutenant colonel claimed that he was on detached service in the Confederacy's capital at the war's end and "was on the train with Jefferson Davis at the evacuation of Richmond." After the war McDonell practiced law and served as state attorney for both Alachua and Duval counties. He died in 1901, having just celebrated his seventieth birthday.[18]

George Troup Maxwell

Released from Johnson's Island, Ohio, in 1865, Maxwell returned to Florida in time to participate in Florida's Constitutional Convention held later that year. Removing to Delaware in 1871, Maxwell practiced medicine and invented an early laryngoscope. Maxwell returned to Florida in the late 1870s and taught at the State Agricultural College in Lake City. The author of numerous papers regarding health and hygiene, Maxwell survived until 1897.[19]

Wylde Lyde Latham Bowen

Bowen, like Colonel McDonell, claimed to have escaped from Richmond with Jefferson Davis. Marrying in 1877, Bowen removed to Jewell, Georgia, where he helped found the Bowen and Jewell Company. He died in 1905.[20]

William T. Stockton

The West Point graduate never recovered from illnesses contracted while in the service. He died in 1869.

Edward Nathaniel Badger

Following the war, Badger and his bride removed to Louisville, Kentucky, where he practiced law and gained election to both the Kentucky legislature and the local school board. Returning to Ocala in 1886, Badger died of Bright's Disease six years later at the age of forty-five.[21]

Jacob Alexander Lash

Captured at Nashville, Major Lash was imprisoned at Johnson's Island, Ohio. He contracted pneumonia and expired on May 21, 1865. He was buried in the prison's cemetery.[22]

Daniel Lafayette Kenan

Crippled from his Jonesboro and Bentonville wounds, Kenan returned to Gadsden County a broken man. The former colonel remarried after the war and served his county as tax assessor until his death in 1884. William Stockton called Kenan "the highest and biggest soldier of us all."[23]

Robert H. M. Davidson

Surviving the amputation of a foot following the Battle of Dallas, Davidson convalesced in Gadsden County and at the war's end again practiced law. Elected to Congress in 1877, he served seven consecutive terms before failing to gain renomination in 1891. He died in 1908.[24]

Edward Mashburn

Lieutenant Colonel Edward Mashburn, who commanded the remnants of the Florida Brigade at the Bennett Place surrender, remains an enigma. A contemporary described the officer as possessing "fine intellect, and varied information," which "united to an unaffected melody and purity of character." Mashburn became a farmer after the surrender but died in May 1866.[25]

Tillman Ingram

The devoted but ineffective 7th Florida officer migrated to Limestone County, Texas, soon after the war's end. He died in 1890.[26]

Walter Terry Saxon

One of the Florida Brigade's ablest and most beloved company officers, Saxon was an Alabama native and worked as a surveyor before the war. After the war he served in the Florida legislature for two terms. He left for Hamilton, Texas, in 1873, where he was a schoolteacher and then a county surveyor for forty-seven years. He died in 1925.[27]

David Ewell Maxwell

Badly wounded at the Battle of Atlanta on July 22, 1864, Maxwell convalesced in Tallahassee. Still in a weakened condition, he fought at the Battle of Natural Bridge in March 1865. After the war Maxwell played a significant role in Florida's economic development, as he became vice president of the Florida Central and Peninsular line and then superintendent of the Seaboard Air Line system in Florida. He died in 1908 at the age of sixty-five.[28]

Augustus O. McDonell

Captured during the Atlanta Campaign, McDonell spent nine months at Johnson's Island, Ohio. Gaining employment with the Florida Railroad in 1871, McDonell rose from chief clerk to assistant general passenger agent of the Seaboard Air Line system.[29]

S. Darwin McConnell

Incapacitated by his Franklin wound, McConnell returned home to Ocala. Following the war's conclusion he practiced law in both Marion County and Atlanta. After serving as Ocala's mayor, he lived out the remainder of his days in relative quiet.[30]

John Livingston Inglis

Returning to Florida in 1865, the Scotsman dabbled in several business ventures before becoming a leading figure in the state's phosphate industry. The old warrior founded the Dunnellon Phosphate Company in 1889, and in 1902 the company named its principal port Inglis in his honor. Inglis lived into the twentieth century, dying in 1917 as the Great War raged in Europe.[31]

Hugh Black

Retiring from active service in October 1864, Hugh Black lived the remainder of his life in Leon County. He was employed as a schoolteacher and served as a school board trustee and clerk of the state legislature. He died in 1915.[32]

Francis Philip Fleming

A Florida native, Fleming served in the 2nd Florida Infantry before transferring to the 1st Florida Cavalry, Dismounted, in 1863. Fleming practiced law in the years following the war and entered politics, earning a seat on the Florida Democratic Executive Committee in the early 1870s. Elected governor in 1888, Fleming initially followed a path of liberal reform during his term. Among his accomplishments were the establishment of the State Board of Health, the construction of a state prison, and the creation of the state Bureau of Immigration. He died in St. Augustine in 1908.[33]

William McLeod

The South Florida soldier surrendered at Bennett's Place and returned to his wife. He fathered ten children and died in 1925 at the age of eighty-seven.[34]

Robert Blair Smith

After surrendering with the 1st Florida Infantry, Consolidated, at Bennett's Place, the Pennsylvanian began the long trek to Florida rather than to his birthplace. Stranded in Social Circle, Georgia, due to lack of funds, Smith gained employment as a teacher and later served as Superintendent of Schools for Greene County. Returning to Florida upon his retirement, he died in 1920 on a visit to Georgia.[35]

The Enlisted Men

Thomas Benton Ellis

Transferring to Munnerlyn's Battalion in October 1863, Ellis remained in Florida until the war's end. He became a merchant in Alachua County and was elected Gainesville's city tax collector in 1897, a position he held for many years. Ellis died in February 1926.[36]

William D. Rogers

Rogers transferred to the 3rd Florida Cavalry Battalion in October 1863 and served near Pensacola and Mobile until his capture in November 1864. Incarcerated on Ship Island, Mississippi, he died there from disease on March 8, 1865.[37]

Charles C. Hemming

Hemming escaped from a Federal prison camp in September 1864 and, through a series of spectacular events, rejoined the Florida Brigade before its surrender at Bennett's Place. He moved to Texas in 1866 and became a bank cashier in Brenham. He later served as president of the Gainesville National Bank and was president of the Texas Bankers' Association. He died in Colorado Springs in 1916 and was interred there. He provided funds for the construction of a Confederate monument in Jacksonville in 1898.[38]

Archibald Livingston

Leaving Camp Chase in June 1865, Livingston returned to Madison, Florida, where he "resolved never to eat corn bread, never to walk when he could ride, and never to shoot a gun." He became a businessman and passed away in April 1916.[39]

Robert Watson

As a Confederate sailor, Watson survived the evacuation of Savannah and surrendered in Virginia on April 8, 1865. Returning to Key West, Watson earned a living as a carpenter before dying in April 1911.[40]

Washington M. Ives Jr.

The Florida Brigade soldier returned to Columbia County at war's end and, like his father, became an attorney. Ives served many terms as county judge before passing away in 1925. His extensive letter collection has survived.

Edward Clifford Brush

Despite being discharged in 1862 for being only seventeen, the Perryville veteran reenlisted in the 2nd Florida Battalion, which fought in Virginia in 1864–65. Captured near Petersburg in 1864, he was imprisoned at Camp Lookout, Maryland, until the war's end. He died in 1931 in Massachusetts at the age of eighty-six.[41]

Samuel Pasco

Following his parole from Camp Morton, Indiana, the Englishman returned to Jefferson County where he read law under Colonel Dilworth. He took over the practice upon the latter's death. Gaining recognition in the Democratic Party during Reconstruction, Pasco ascended to chair Florida's Democratic Party in 1876 and served as president of the 1885 Constitutional Convention. Seriously considered by the party as a gubernatorial candidate, he served as Florida's Speaker of the House before the Florida Senate chose him to represent the state in the U.S. Senate in 1887. After serving two consecutive terms, he was appointed by President Theodore Roosevelt to the Isthmian Canal Commission. He died in Tampa on March 13, 1917, at the age of eighty-three. In the 1880s the Florida legislature named a newly created county in his honor.[42]

Appendix

Organization of the Regiments of Jesse Johnson Finley's Florida Brigade

1st Florida Infantry Regiment (April 1861–April 1862)
Colonel: James Patton Anderson
Lieutenant Colonel: William Kelly Beard
Major: Thaddeus A. McDonell

Company	Nickname	Primary Commander	Origin
A	Leon Rifles	A. Perry Amaker	Leon
B		William E. Cropp	Franklin
C		Benjamin W. Powell	Alachua
D		Robert B. Hilton	Leon
E		Henry H. Baker	Walton
F		Richard Bradford	Madison
G	Young Guards	John H. Gee	Gadsden
H	Minute Men	T. J. Myers	Alachua
I		William Capers Bird	Jefferson
K	Pensacola Guards	Alexander H. Bright	Escambia

1st Florida Infantry Battalion (April 1862)
Major: Thaddeus A. McDonell

Company	Nickname	Primary Commander	Origin
A	Leon Rifles	William G. Poole	Leon
B		T. Sumpter Means	Alachua
C		William Capers Bird	Jefferson
D		Augustus O. McDonell	Alachua

1st Florida Infantry Regiment (August 1862)
Colonel: William Miller
Lieutenant Colonel: Thaddeus A. McDonell
Major: Glover A. Ball
This regiment was formed by the consolidation of Thaddeus A. McDonell's Battalion and William Miller's 3rd Florida Infantry Battalion.

Company	Nickname	Primary Commander	Origin
A	Leon Rifles	William G. Poole	Leon
B		T. Sumpter Means	Alachua

Company	Nickname	Primary Commander	Origin
C		William Capers Bird	Jefferson
D	Walton Guards	E. L. McKinnon	Walton
E		A. B. McLeod	Walton
F		John Walston	Santa Rosa
G		John D. Leigh	Conecuh County, Alabama
H	Conecuh Rebels	H. H. Malone	Conecuh County, Alabama
I		Daniel Coleman	Various
K		Augustus McDonell	Alachua

3rd Florida Infantry Regiment
Colonel: William Scott Dilworth
Lieutenant Colonels: Arthur J. T. Wright (1861–62), Lucius Church (1862–63), Edward Mashburn (1863–65)
Majors: Lucius Church (1861–62), Edward Mashburn (1862–63), John Lott Phillips (1863–64)

Company	Nickname	Primary Commander	Origin
A	Jacksonville Light Infantry	Holmes Steele	Duval
B	St. Augustine Blues	John Lott Phillip	St. Johns
C	Wildcats	Walter T. Saxon	Hernando
D	Wakulla Guards	Daniel Frierson	Wakulla
E	Jefferson Beauregards	Daniel B. Bird	Jefferson
F	Cowboys	Lucius Hardee	Duval
G	Grey Eagles	Thomas Langford	Madison
H	Jefferson Rifles	William Girardeau	Jefferson
I	Dixie Stars	Jesse S. Wood	Columbia
K	Columbia and Suwannee Guards	William G. Parker	Columbia/Suwannee

4th Florida Infantry Regiment
Colonels: Edward Hopkins (1861–62), James Hunt (1862), Wylde L. L. Bowen (1862–65)
Lieutenant Colonels: M. Whit Smith (1861–62), Wylde L. L. Bowen (1862), Edward Badger (1862–65)
Majors: Wylde L. L. Bowen (1861–62), Edward Badger (1862), John Thomas Lesley (1862–63), Jacob A. Lash (1863–65)

Company	Nickname	Primary Commander	Origin
A		Charles A. Gee	Gadsden
B	Beauregard Rifles	Adam W. Hunter	Franklin
C		William H. Dial	Madison
D	Perry Guards	William A. Sheffield	Columbia
E	Lafayette Rangers	Thomas J. McGehee	Columbia/Lafayette
F		James P. Hunt	New River
G		William L. Fletcher	Marion/Levy
H	Washington Invincibles	William F. Lane	Washington/Liberty
I	Dixie Boys	Joseph B. Barnes	Jackson
K		John T. Lesley	Hillsborough

6th Florida Infantry Regiment
Colonels: Jesse Johnson Finley (1862–63), Angus McLean (1863–64), Daniel L. Kenan (1864–65)
Lieutenant Colonels: Angus McLean (1862–63), Daniel L. Kenan (1863–64), R.H.M. Davidson (1864–65)
Majors: Daniel L. Kenan (1862–63), R.H.M. Davidson (1863–64)

Company	Nickname	Primary Commander	Origin
A	Florida Guards	Robert H. M. Davidson	Gadsden
B	Gadsden Greys	Samuel B. Love	Gadsden
C	Gulf State Infantry	James C. Evans	Gadsden
D	Jackson Co. Volunteers	John L. Hays	Jackson
E		Henry O. Bassett	Jackson
F	Magnolia State Guards	Lawrence Attaway	Jackson
G	Camillia Grays	Henry B. Grace	Jackson
H	Union Rebels	Stephen A. Cawthon	Walton
I	Choctawhatchie Volunteers	Harrison K. Hagan	Jackson
K		Angus McMillan	Washington

7th Florida Infantry Regiment
Colonels: Madison Starke Perry (1862–63), Robert Bullock (1862–65)
Lieutenant Colonels: Robert Bullock (1862–63), Tillman Ingram (1862–64)
Majors: Tillman Ingram (1862–63), Nathan S. Blount (1863–65)

Company	Nickname	Primary Commander	Origins
A		Roland Thomas	Columbia
B	South Florida Infantry	James Gettis	Hillsborough
C		Philip B. H. Dudley	Alachua
D	Alachua Rebels	Sion Vanlandingham	Alachua
E	South Florida Bulldogs	Nathan S. Blount	Polk
F		William W. Stone	Orange
G		Robert Bullock	Marion
H	Marion Hornets	Wade S. Eichelberger	Marion
I		A. S. Moseley	Putnam
K	Key West Avengers	Robert Blair Smith	Various

1st Florida Cavalry
Colonels: W.G.M. Davis (1861–62), George T. Maxwell (1862–63)
Lieutenant Colonels: George T. Maxwell (1861–62), William T. Stockton (1862–63)
Majors: William T. Stockton (1861–62), William Footman (1862–63)

Company	Primary Commander	Origin
A	Arthur Roberts	Columbia
B	John G. Haddock	Nassau
C	John A. Summerlin	Clay
D	John Harvey	Bradford/Baker
E	Charles F. Cone	Suwannnee
F	B. M. Burroughs	Leon

Company	Primary Commander	Origin
G	Nicholas Cobb	Levy
H	Noble Hull	Duval
I	W. D. Clarke	Alachua
K	David Hughes	Polk/Hillsborough

Notes

Chapter 1

1. William S. Coker and Susan R. Parker, "The Second Spanish Period in the Two Floridas," in *The New History of Florida,* ed. Michael Gannon (Gainesville: University Press of Florida, 1996), 161; Edward E. Baptist, *Creating an Old South: Middle Florida's Plantation Frontier before the Civil War* (Chapel Hill: University of North Carolina Press, 2002), 45.

2. Baptist, *Creating an Old South,* 45; Julia H. Smith, "The Plantation Belt in Middle Florida, 1850–1860" (Ph.D. diss., Florida State University, 1964), 18.

3. Baptist, *Creating an Old South,* 42–43; Robert A. Taylor, *Rebel Storehouse: Florida's Contribution to the Confederacy* (Tuscaloosa: The University of Alabama Press, 2003), 1; Chandra Manning, *What This Cruel War Was Over: Soldiers, Slavery, and the Civil War* (New York: Knopf, 2006), 33.

4. Baptist, *Creating an Old South,* 42–43; Taylor, *Rebel Storehouse,* 1; Manning, *What This Cruel War Was Over,* 33.

5. Baptist, *Creating an Old South,* 2; Emily Porter, "The Movement for the Admission of Florida into the Union" (Master's thesis, Florida State College for Women, 1938), 7; Daniel L. Schafer, "U.S. Territory and State," in Gannon, *The New History of Florida,* 212–14.

6. Smith, "The Plantation Belt in Middle Florida," 44, 214; Taylor, *Rebel Storehouse,* 2–4, 6; Clifton Paisley, *The Red Hills of Florida, 1528–1865* (Tuscaloosa: The University of Alabama Press, 1989), 124.

7. Charlton W. Tebeau, *The History of Florida,* 2nd ed. (Coral Gables, FL: University of Miami Press, 1971), 119.

8. Canter Brown Jr., *Florida's Peace River Frontier* (Orlando: University of Central Florida Press, 1991), 64–66.

9. Schafer, "U.S. Territory and State," 217; Everett W. Caudle, "Settlement Patterns in Alachua County, Florida, 1850–1860," *Florida Historical Quarterly* 67 (1989): 434.

10. Herbert J. Doherty Jr., *The Whigs of Florida, 1845–1854* (Gainesville: University of Florida Press, 1959), 56–57; William Watson Davis, *The Civil War and Reconstruction in Florida* (1913; reprint, Gainesville: University of Florida Press, 1964), 20.

11. Doherty, *The Whigs of Florida,* 56–57; Seth A. Weitz, "The Rise of Radicalism in Antebellum Florida Politics: 1845–1856" (Master's thesis, Florida State University, 2004), 37, 72.

12. Davis, *Civil War and Reconstruction in Florida,* 435; John F. Reiger, "Florida after Secession: Abandonment by the Confederacy and Its Consequences," *Florida Historical Quar-*

terly 50 (1971): 132; Larry Eugene Rivers, *Slavery in Florida: Territorial Days to Emancipation* (Gainesville: University Press of Florida, 2000), 34.

13. Paisley, *The Red Hills of Florida,* 147; Caudle, "Settlement Patterns," 439; William Warren Rogers, "A Great Stirring in the Land: Tallahassee and Leon County in 1860," *Florida Historical Quarterly* 62 (1985): 148.

14. Taylor, *Rebel Storehouse,* 22.

15. Weitz, "The Rise of Radicalism in Antebellum Florida Politics," 72, 76. For more on John C. McGehee's career, particularly his role during the Compromise of 1850 debates within the state, see pp. 63–65.

16. Doherty, *The Whigs of Florida,* 60; Weitz, "The Rise of Radicalism in Antebellum Florida Politics," 9–10. For more on the Union Bank and the rise of countrymen in Florida politics, see Baptist, *Creating an Old South,* 154–90.

17. Doherty, *The Whigs of Florida,* 49; Dorothy Dodd, "The Secession Movement in Florida, 1850–1861, Part 1," *Florida Historical Quarterly* 12 (1933): 15–16.

18. Weitz, "The Rise of Radicalism in Antebellum Florida Politics," 80.

19. Dodd, "The Secession Movement in Florida, 1850–1861, Part 1," 10–12.

20. John E. Johns, *Florida during the Civil War* (1963; reprint, Jacksonville, FL: Miller Press, 1989), 5; Dorothy Dodd, "The Secession Movement in Florida, 1850–1861, Part II," *Florida Historical Quarterly* 12 (1933): 46; Jon L. Urbach, "An Appraisal of the Florida Secession Movement, 1859–1861" (master's thesis, Florida State University, 1972), 15–16.

21. Davis, *The Civil War and Reconstruction in Florida,* 37; Weitz, "The Rise of Radicalism in Antebellum Florida Politics," 86.

22. Dodd, "The Secession Movement in Florida, 1850–1861, Part II," 46; Weitz, "The Rise of Radicalism in Antebellum Florida Politics," 86.

23. *Monticello Family Friend,* July 28, 1860; Johns, *Florida during the Civil War,* 9; Dodd, "The Secession Movement in Florida, 1850–1861, Part II," 47.

24. Johns, *Florida during the Civil War,* 9; *St. Augustine (FL) Examiner,* August 18, 1860.

25. Baptist, *Creating an Old South,* 269; Dodd, "The Secession Movement in Florida, 1850–1861, Part II," 49; Johns, *Florida during the Civil War,* 9; Doherty, *The Whigs of Florida,* 61.

26. Doherty, *The Whigs of Florida,* 61–62; Dodd, "The Secession Movement in Florida, 1850–1861, Part II," 50.

27. *Fernandina East Floridian,* July 12, 1860.

28. Dodd, "The Secession Movement in Florida, 1850–1861, Part II," 51.

29. Samuel Darwin McConnell to My Dear Eloise, November 12, 1860, Samuel Darwin McConnell Papers, 1859–1876, P. K. Yonge Library of Florida History, Gainesville (hereafter McConnell Papers).

30. Dodd, "The Secession Movement in Florida, 1850–1861, Part II," 51–52; Johns, *Florida during the Civil War,* 11–12. See also Western Circuit judge J. J. Finley's remarks in the *Tallahassee Floridian and Journal,* December 8, 1860, regarding state unity.

31. *St. Augustine (FL) Examiner,* November 17, 1860; *Fernandina East Floridian,* November 14, 1860.

32. *Monticello Family Friend,* November 24 and December 1, 1860.

33. Johns, *Florida during the Civil War,* 11; Dodd, "The Secession Movement in Florida, 1850–1861, Part II," 54–55; Reiger, "Secession of Florida," 362; *St. Augustine (FL) Examiner,* December 22, 1860.

34. *Tallahassee Floridian and Journal,* January 12, 1861; Dorothy Dodd, ed., "Edmund Ruffin's Account of the Florida Secession Convention, 1861," *Florida Historical Quarterly* 12 (1933): 71.

35. Johns, *Florida during the Civil War,* 15–21; Dodd, "The Secession Movement in Florida, 1850–1861, Part II," 61–62; *Tallahassee Floridian and Journal,* January 12, 1861. For a thorough examination of the convention delegates, see Ralph A. Wooster, "The Florida Secession Convention," *Florida Historical Quarterly* 36 (1958): 373–85.

36. Johns, *Florida during the Civil War,* 23–24; David J. Coles, "Ancient City Defenders: The St. Augustine Blues," *El Escribano* 23 (1986): 68; War Department, *The War of the Rebellion: A Compilation of the Official Records of the Union and Confederate Armies,* 128 vols. (Washington, DC: GPO, 1880–1901), series I, vol. I, 332–33.

Chapter 2

1. Johns, *Florida during the Civil War,* 26–27; George F. Pearce, *Pensacola during the Civil War: A Thorn in the Side of the Confederacy* (Gainesville: University Press of Florida, 2000), 11–14.

2. *Official Records,* series I, vol. I, 444; Pearce, *Pensacola during the Civil War,* 29.

3. *Official Records,* series I, vol. I, 445.

4. Ibid., 354–55.

5. James M. McPherson, *Battle Cry of Freedom: The Civil War Era* (New York: Ballantine Books, 1989), 267; Pearce, *Pensacola during the Civil War,* 48.

6. Richard S. Nichols, "Florida's Fighting Rebels: A Military History of Florida's Civil War Troops" (master's thesis, Florida State University, 1967).

7. Richard M. McMurry, "Patton Anderson: Major General, C.S.A.," *Blue and Gray Magazine* 1, no. 2 (1983): 10–11; "Sketch of General Anderson's Life," James Patton Anderson Papers, P. K. Yonge Library of Florida History, Gainesville. There is evidence that Anderson likely became acquainted with another future Confederate general, Nathan Bedford Forrest, during the time he lived in Hernando.

8. "Sketch of General Anderson's Life"; McMurry, "Patton Anderson," 11.

9. "Sketch of General Anderson's Life"; McMurry, "Patton Anderson," 12. In Mississippi, unlike Florida, the Conservatives gained power following the Compromise of 1850 debacle.

10. McMurry, "Patton Anderson," 12; "Sketch of General Anderson's Life"; Jefferson County, FL, Tax Rolls, 1839–1854, 1856–1864, Florida State Archives (FSA) Microcopy S28, Roll 33.

11. McMurry, "Patton Anderson," 12; Pearce, *Pensacola during the Civil War,* 34. Patton Anderson claims the companies were to embark at St. Marks, but see *Monticello Family Friend,* January 19, 1861.

12. *Monticello Family Friend,* March 30, 1861; George C. Bittle, "Florida Prepares for War, 1860–1861," *Florida Historical Quarterly* 51 (1972): 145. For more on the Florida

militia in the years before the war, see George C. Bittle, "In the Defense of Florida: The Organized Florida Militia from 1821 to 1920" (Ph.D. diss., Florida State University, 1965).

13. William Warren Rogers, "Florida on the Eve of the Civil War as Seen by a Southern Reporter," *Florida Historical Quarterly* 39 (1960): 155; *Madison (FL) Southern Messenger,* April 3, 1861, in "Regimental History to Z," History Vertical Files (copy), Florida State Library (FSL), Tallahassee; William H. Trimmer, "A Volunteer in Company B: 1st Florida Infantry from Apalachicola," United Daughters of the Confederacy Scrapbooks, 1900–1935, vol. 1, FSA, Tallahassee. The ritual of these ceremonies is described in Bell I. Wiley, *The Life of Johnny Reb: The Common Soldier of the Confederacy* (1943; reprint, Baton Rouge: Louisiana State University Press, 2000), 20–21.

14. Rogers, "Florida on the Eve of the Civil War," 153; John R. Blocker, "Company D, First Florida Infantry," *Confederate Veteran* 20 (1912): 156; "Col. George M. Edgar," *Confederate Veteran* 22 (1914): 85; Allen Johnson and Dumas Malone, eds., *Dictionary of American Biography* (New York: Charles Scribner's Sons, 1937), 440–41.

15. Nichols, "Florida's Fighting Rebels," 8; *Official Records,* series IV, vol. I, 128; J. Patton Anderson to Hon. T. B. Monroe, October 3, 1861, Letters Received, Confederate Secretary of War, National Archives (NA) Microcopy M437, Reel #14, Washington, DC (hereafter Letters Received, Confederate Secretary of War).

16. McPherson, *Battle Cry of Freedom,* 128; Wiley, *Life of Johnny Reb,* 19–20; Grady McWhiney, *Braxton Bragg and Confederate Defeat,* vol. 1, *Field Command* (New York: Columbia University Press, 1969), 162.

17. "Sketch of General Anderson's Life"; Weitz, "The Rise of Radicalism in Antebellum Florida Politics," 49; *Tallahassee Weekly Floridian,* August 15, 1882; David W. Hartman and David Coles, *Biographical Rosters of Florida's Confederate and Union Soldiers, 1861–1865,* 5 vols. and index (Wilmington, NC: Broadfoot Publishing, 1995), 1:2; 1860 U.S. Census (Slave Schedule), Leon County, FL, Reel #110.

18. *Jacksonville (FL) Times-Union,* March 6, 1901; McPherson, *Battle Cry of Freedom,* 105–6; For McDonell's participation during the secession crisis, see *Tallahassee Floridian and Journal,* December 8, 1860; "Col. George M. Edgar," 85.

19. Taylor, *Rebel Storehouse,* 18; Nichols, "Florida's Fighting Rebels," 7.

20. *Monticello Family Friend,* April 20, 1861; *Columbus (GA) Daily Sun,* April 7, 1861; *Columbus (GA) Daily Enquirer,* April 9, 1861.

21. *Monticello Family Friend,* April 20, 1861; Trimmer, "A Volunteer in Company B"; Pearce, *Pensacola during the Civil War,* 64. Pearce noted that Abraham Lincoln decided to reinforce Fort Pickens so as to maintain a foothold on southern soil in the likely event Fort Sumter fell. More reinforcements arrived at Fort Pickens on April 16.

22. McWhiney, *Braxton Bragg,* 1:165, 169, 180.

23. General Orders No. 22, April 19, 1861, General and Special Orders, 1861–1862, Army of Pensacola, NA, Washington, DC; Augustus Oswald McDonell to My Dear Mother, April 28, 1861, Augustus Oswald McDonell Papers, 1861–1864, P. K. Yonge Library of Florida History, Gainesville (hereafter McDonell Papers). Augustus O. McDonell was the nephew of Major Thaddeus A. McDonell.

24. Trimmer, "A Volunteer in Company B"; *Quincy (FL) Commonwealth* quoted in *Monticello Family Friend,* June 22, 1861.

25. Paddy Griffith, *Battle Tactics of the Civil War* (1987; reprint, New Haven: Yale University Press, 2001), 105; Grady McWhiney and Perry D. Jamison, *Attack and Die: Civil War Tactics and the Southern Heritage* (Tuscaloosa: The University of Alabama Press, 1982), 49–53.

26. Roderick G. Shaw to My Dear Sister, May 13, 1861, Roderick G. Shaw Letters, 1861–1864, FSA, Tallahassee (hereafter Shaw Letters). For mention of the construction of the batteries, see both Trimmer, "A Volunteer in Company B," and Augustus O. McDonell to My Dear Father, April 22, 1861, McDonell Papers.

27. Pearce, *Pensacola during the Civil War,* 76; McWhiney, *Braxton Bragg,* 1:175–77.

28. *Pensacola Weekly Observer,* June 9, 1861.

29. Thomas Eston Randolph to Dear Father, June 28, 1861, and W. D. Randolph to Dear Father, July 23, 1861, Randolph Family Papers, FSA, Tallahassee (hereafter Randolph Family Papers); S. H. Harris to Dear Angie, November 20, 1861, S. H. Harris Papers, Eleanor S. Brockenbrough Library, Museum of the Confederacy (MOC), Richmond, VA (hereafter Harris Papers). The "Sebastopol" in Thomas Randolph's letter refers to the Crimean War siege of Sevastopol.

30. Trimmer, "A Volunteer in Company B"; *Monticello Family Friend,* October 5, 1861; Patton Anderson to Hon. T. B. Monroe, October 3, 1861, Letters Received, Confederate Secretary of War, NA Microcopy M437, Reel #14. See also Jonathan C. Sheppard, "Everyday Soldiers: The Florida Brigade of the West, 1861–1862" (master's thesis, Florida State University, 2004), 18.

31. *Monticello Family Friend,* October 5, 1861; Bittle, "Florida Prepares for War," 144; Captain Alexander H. Bright to Missers Cambell, Louge, and Abercrombie, May 31, 1861, Captain A. H. Bright Letter, P. K. Yonge Library of Florida History, Gainesville.

32. Ridgeway Boyd Murphree, "Rebel Sovereigns: The Civil War Leadership of Governors John Milton of Florida and Joseph E. Brown of Georgia, 1861–1865" (Ph.D. diss., Florida State University, 2007), 34; *Official Record,* series I, vol. I, 466.

33. *Official Record,* series IV, vol. I, 211, 221, 412, and series I, vol. I, 469; Nichols, "Florida's Fighting Rebels," 10–12.

34. Nichols, "Florida's Fighting Rebels," 17–18.

35. Coles, "Ancient City Defenders," 65–66; Anthony Joseph Iacono, "So Far Away, So Close to Home: Florida and the Civil War Era" (Ph.D. diss., Mississippi State University, 2000), 53.

36. *Jacksonville (FL) Times-Union,* September 26, 1908, quoted in Richard A. Martin and Daniel L. Schafer, *Jacksonville's Ordeal by Fire* (Jacksonville: Florida Publishing Company, 1984), 24.

37. *Monticello Family Friend,* May 4 and 18, 1861; Jefferson County Tax Rolls, FSA; 1860 U.S. Census (Free Schedule), Columbia County, FL, p. 175, family 57, dwelling 57, lines 35–44, NA Microcopy M653, Reel #109.

38. *Monticello Family Friend,* April 20, 1861, June 29, 1861, and August 10, 1861; *Jacksonville (FL) Times-Union,* May 22, 1887. Because antebellum Florida had only a fledgling public school system, the majority of the education provided to the state's youths came from academies. These institutions used public examinations at the end of each term to allow students to demonstrate their knowledge. Students also recited speeches and sang popular

songs as part of these public ceremonies. For more on these examinations, see Robert C. Crandall, "Academy Education in Antebellum Florida, 1821–1860" (Ph.D. diss., Florida State University, 1987). For an example of the examinations, see *Monticello Family Friend,* July 28, 1860.

39. *Jacksonville (FL) Times-Union,* May 22, 1887.

40. Ibid.; Gen. B. W. Partridge, "Samuel Pasco," in Samuel Pasco, *Private Pasco: A Civil War Diary,* ed. William Pasco and William Gibbons (Oak Brook, IL: McAdams Multigraphics, 1990), 186.

41. *Jacksonville (FL) Times-Union,* May 22, 1887; Samuel Pasco Jr., "Samuel Pasco (1834–1917)," *Florida Historical Quarterly* 7 (1928): 135; *Monticello Family Friend,* August 3, 1861.

42. *Monticello Family Friend,* August 3 and 17, 1861; Lemuel Moody to My Dear Sister, July 23, 1861, Lemuel Moody Letters, Collection of Zack C. Waters, Rome, GA (hereafter Moody Letters).

43. *Monticello Family Friend,* August 17, 1861.

44. *Monticello Family Friend,* May 4 and August 17, 1861; Nichols, "Florida's Fighting Rebels," 17. See also William T. Stockton to Adjutant General Samuel Cooper, August 11, 1861, in Herman Ulmer Jr., transcriber, *The Correspondence of Will and Ju Stockton, 1845–1869* (privately published, 1989), 66-a.

45. Folks Huxford, comp., *Pioneers of Wiregrass Georgia,* 10 vols. (Waycross, GA: Herrin's Print Shop, 1967), 3:73; *Tallahassee Floridian and Journal,* March 8, 1851, and June 16, 1860.

46. Washington M. Ives Jr. Diary, 1860–1862, December 27, 1860, FSA, Tallahassee (hereafter Ives Diary); 1860 U.S. Census, (Free Schedule), Columbia County, FL, p. 175, family 57, dwelling 57, lines 35–44 NA Microcopy M653, Reel #109; A.J.T. Wright, Service Records—FL Seminole Wars, NA Microcopy S608, Reel #52. Wright served as captain for one month and as lieutenant colonel for two; U.S. Census (Free Schedule), Madison County, FL, p. 163, family 106, dwelling 106, lines 36–40, NA Microcopy M653, Reel #108; Ralph A. Wooster, "The Florida Secession Convention," *Florida Historical Quarterly* 36 (1958): 383; Larry Eugene Rivers, "Madison County, Florida—1830–1860: A Case Study in Land, Labor, and Prosperity," *Journal of Negro History* 78 (1993): 238; "Representatives by Session, 1858," Vertical Files, FSL, Tallahassee. See also C. S. Livingston Letter (copy), Lewis G. Schmidt Research Collection, FSA, Tallahassee (hereafter Lewis G. Schmidt Research Collection); *Tallahassee Florida Sentinel,* July 31, 1860.

47. *Monticello Family Friend,* July 20, 1861; Martin and Schafer, *Jacksonville's Ordeal by Fire,* 33–34; Janet Hewett, Noah Andre Trudeau, and Bryce A. Suderow, eds., *Supplement to the Official Records of the Union and Confederate Armies,* 100 vols. (Wilmington, DC: Broadfoot Publishing, 1995), 5:247–66; T. B. Ellis Sr., "A Short Record of T. B. Ellis, Sr.," 1, T. B. Ellis Sr., Biographical File, FSL, Tallahassee.

48. Ives Diary, June 11, 1861.

49. Nichols, "Florida's Fighting Rebels," 13; Fred Robertson, comp., *Soldiers of Florida* (Live Oak, FL: Democrat Book and Job Print, 1903), 118.

50. For Jackson County's strong Whig population, see Doherty, *The Whigs of Florida,*

16. See *St. Augustine (FL) Daily Examiner,* October 6, 1860, for election results with majorities for Hopkins and Milton; *Cedar Keys (FL) Telegraph,* September 15, 1860.

51. *Jacksonville (FL) Times-Union,* September 29, 1887, and January 10, 2004, http://jacksonville.com/tu-online/stories/011004/neR_14484892.shtml (accessed September 18, 2011).

52. Ibid.; Huxford, *Pioneers of Wiregrass Georgia,* 6:212–14; Edward Hopkins to Secretary of War, May 25, 1861, Letters Received, Confederate Secretary of War, M437, Reel #3.

53. *Tallahassee Semi-Weekly Floridian,* September 11, 1866; 1860 U.S. Census (Free Schedule), Columbia County, FL, p. 175, family 54, dwelling 54, lines 18–22, NA Microfilm M653, Reel #109; Ives Diary, December 22, 1860.

54. "Bowen Line," Bowen Genealogical File, Collection of Zack C. Waters, Rome, GA; 1860 U.S. Census (Free Schedule), Columbia County, FL, p. 175, family 54, dwelling 54, lines 18–22, NA Microfilm M653, Reel #109. See also M. Whit Smith letter in Wylde L. L. Bowen, *Compiled Service Records of Confederate Soldiers Who Served in Organizations from the State of Florida, 1861–1865,* RG 109, NA, Washington, DC, NA Microfilm M251, Reel #52 (hereafter *CSR,* with appropriate reel number).

Chapter 3

1. J. P. Anderson to Hon T. B. Monroe, October 3, 1861, Letters Received, Confederate Secretary of War, NA Microcopy M437, Reel #14.

2. J. P. Anderson and T. B. Lamar to S. Cooper, September 25, 1861, Letters Received, Confederate Secretary of War, NA Microcopy M437, Reel #11; *Monticello Family Friend,* November 21, 1861.

3. J. P. Anderson to Hon. T. B. Monroe, October 3, 1861; J. H. Randolph to My Dear Friend, August 16, 1861, Fairbanks Collection, 1817–1942, Special Collections, Robert Manning Strozier Library, Florida State University, Tallahassee (hereafter Fairbanks Collection).

4. Pearce, *Pensacola during the Civil War,* 110–17; McWhiney, *Braxton Bragg,* 1:192–93; *Official Records,* series I, vol. VI, 461; John Matthew Brackett, "The Naples of America: Pensacola during the Civil War and Reconstruction" (master's thesis, Florida State University, 2005), 14.

5. Brackett, "The Naples of America," 14; Pearce, *Pensacola during the Civil War,* 115. Three of the Confederate commanders in the Battle of Santa Rosa Island eventually commanded divisions: Richard Anderson in Longstreet and Hill's Corps, Army of Northern Virginia, James Patton Anderson in the Army of Tennessee, and James Chalmers in Nathan Bedford Forrest's cavalry. John K. Jackson later commanded a brigade in the Army of Tennessee.

6. W. H. Treinner [Trimmer], "Experiences at Fort Pickens, Fla., 1861," *Confederate Veteran* 19 (1911): 337; Roderick G. Shaw to My Dear Sister, October 9, 1861, Shaw Letters.

7. W. J. Milner, "Battle of Santa Rosa Island," *Confederate Veteran* 11 (1903): 20–21; Pearce, *Pensacola during the Civil War,* 115.

8. C. Pat Cates, "From Santa Rosa Island to Bentonville: The First Confederate Regi-

ment Georgia Volunteers," *Civil War Regiments* 1, no. 4 (1991): 48; *Official Records,* series I, vol. VI, 461.

9. *Official Records,* series I, vol. VI, 461; Roderick G. Shaw to My Dear Sister, October 9, 1861. Several Union accounts assert that the left column, that of James Chalmers, slipped by undetected and flanked the Union line and entered the camp.

10. Special Orders No. 224, September 7, 1861, General and Special Orders, 1861–1862, Army of Pensacola, NA, Washington, DC; Frank Moore, ed., *Rebellion Record: A Diary of American Events with Documents, Narratives, Illustrative Events, Poetry, Etc.,* 12 vols. (1861–68; reprint, New York: Arno Books, 1977), 2:89.

11. *Augusta Daily Constitutionalist,* October 12, 1861; Pearce, *Pensacola during the Civil War,* 116; *Washington, D.C., National Tribune,* December 13, 1883; Trimmer, "A Volunteer in Company B"; Roderick G. Shaw to My Dear Sister, October 9, 1861; Mrs. Townes Randolph Leigh, "The City of Pensacola, Fla.," *Confederate Veteran* 36 (1928): 253.

12. *Monticello Family Friend,* October 19, 1861; 1860 U.S. Census (Free Schedule), Leon County, FL, p. 6, M653 Reel #108, family 48, dwelling 48, lines 15–27; J. H. Randolph to My Dear Sir, October 17, 1861, Fairbanks Collection.

13. *Official Records,* series I, vol. VI, 462; Mrs. Townes Randolph Leigh, "The City of Pensacola, Fla.," 253.

14. Roderick G. Shaw to My Dear Sister, October 9, 1861; S. H. Harris to Dear Angie, November 20, 1861, Harris Papers.

15. *Tallahassee Floridian and Journal,* November 2, 1861; *Official Records,* series I, vol. VI, 751.

16. General Orders No. 128, November 14, 1861, General and Special Orders, 1861–1862, Army of Pensacola, NA, Washington, DC; *Atlanta Daily Intelligencer* quoted in *Monticello Family Friend,* December 7, 1861.

17. *Monticello Family Friend,* October 19, 1861; Thomas Eston Randolph to Dear Father, December 3, 1861, Randolph Family Papers.

18. "Section 103 Detailed Project Report and Environmental Assessment: Fort Clinch Nassau County, Florida," P. K. Yonge Library of Florida History, Gainesville; *Richmond Daily Dispatch,* March 18, 1862.

19. *Official Records,* series I, vol. I, 471.

20. *Monticello Family Friend,* October 19 and 26, 1861; Lemuel Moody to My Dear Sister, August 27, 1861, Moody Letters.

21. *Official Records,* series I, vol. VI, 276, 287–88. Fifty-four-year-old John B. Grayson, a Kentuckian, graduated from West Point in 1826 and served on Winfield Scott's staff during the Mexican-American War. In 1861 he held the position of chief commissary, from which he resigned. He reported to Florida in September and died of "disease of the lungs" in Tallahassee on October 21, 1861. Ezra J. Warner, *Generals in Gray* (1959; reprint, Baton Rouge: Louisiana State University Press, 1987), 115–16.

22. *Official Records,* series I, vol. VI, 301; Boyd Murphree, who compares the wartime administrations of Joe Brown and John Milton, writes that Milton "disdained those volunteer Confederate officers who neglected to respect his authority as Florida's commander in chief." See Murphree, "Rebel Sovereigns," 60.

23. *Monticello Family Friend,* October 19, 1861; Benjamin Waring Partridge to Dear

Mother, October 13, 1861 (copy), Lewis G. Schmidt Research Collection, originals in Benjamin Waring Partridge Papers, Special Collections Department, Duke University, Durham, NC.

24. *Richmond Daily Dispatch,* October 12, 1861.

25. *Monticello Family Friend,* October 19 and 26, 1861; Benjamin Waring Partridge to Dear Brother Billy, October 20, 1861 (copy), Lewis G. Schmidt Research Collection.

26. For more on the saga of the 1st Florida Special Battalion, see Don Hillhouse, *Heavy Artillery and Light Infantry: A History of the 1st Florida Special Battalion and 10th Infantry* (Jacksonville: published by the author, 1992). This fiasco was the result of political infighting between Governors Milton and Perry and the conservative Hopkins family.

27. *Official Records,* series I, vol. VI, 312; R. E. Lee to Col. Dilworth, November 12, 1861, Letters Sent and Endorsements, Department of South Carolina, Georgia, and Florida, 1861–1862, NA, Washington, DC; W. S. Dilworth to R. E. Lee, November 27, 1861, Letters, Telegrams, and Reports, November 1861–May 1862, Department of South Carolina, Georgia, and Florida, 1861–1862, NA, Washington, DC (hereafter Letters, Telegrams, and Reports).

28. W. S. Dilworth to Major Josiah Gorgas, November 15, 1861, Letters Received, Confederate Secretary of War, NA Microcopy M437, Reel #17; Benjamin Waring Partridge to Dear Mother, November 1861 (copy), Lewis G. Schmidt Research Collection; *Official Records,* series I, vol. VI, 317.

29. W.G.M. Davis to Honorable L. P. Walker, September 3, 1861, Letters Received, Confederate Secretary of War, NA Microcopy M437, Reel #8.

30. Nichols, "Florida's Fighting Rebels," 16; Ives Diary, May 25 and October 19, 21, and 22, 1861.

31. *Official Records,* series I, vol. LIII, 203; Warner, *Generals in Gray,* 69; Wooster, "The Florida Secession Convention," 384; *Chattanooga Daily Rebel,* November 22, 1862. See also "To the Voters of Leon," *Floridian and Journal,* December 22, 1860, for Davis's position on secession.

32. "Col. George Troup Maxwell," Maxwell Mss., Collection of Zack C. Waters, Rome, GA (hereafter Maxwell Mss.).

33. *Tallahassee Florida Sentinel,* July 31, 1860; Johnson and Malone, *Dictionary of American Biography,* 440–41.

34. *Official Records,* series I, vol. LIII, 206.

35. *Official Records,* series I, vol. LIII, 206–7, and series I, vol. VI, 290.

36. *Official Records,* series I, vol. LIII, 211; Brigadier General J. H. Trapier to Captain T. A. Washington, January 15, 1862, Letters Sent, Department of South Carolina, Georgia, and Florida, February–July 1862, NA, Washington, DC. James H. Trapier, an 1838 graduate of West Point, resigned from the army in 1848 and until secession lived in his native state of South Carolina. The Confederate War Department appointed Trapier to the Department of Middle and East Florida on October 21, 1861. Warner, *Generals in Gray,* 309–10.

37. Joseph D. Cushman Jr., "The Blockade and Fall of Apalachicola, 1861–1862," *Florida Historical Quarterly* 41 (1962): 39; Lynn Willoughby, "Apalachicola Aweigh: Shipping and Seamen at Florida's Premier Cotton Port," *Florida Historical Quarterly* 69 (1990): 184.

38. Cushman, "The Blockade and Fall of Apalachicola," 41.

39. Ibid., 39–40; *Official Records,* series I, vol. VI, 286; Murphree, "Rebel Sovereigns," 59.

40. *Official Records,* series I, vol. VI, 286, 291; Cushman, "The Blockade and Fall of Apalachicola," 41; Murphree, "Rebel Sovereigns," 59; Edward Hopkins to Secretary of War, October 24, 1861, Letters Received, Confederate Secretary of War, NA Microcopy M437, Reel #14.

41. Drysdale to Milton, October 31, 1861, quoted in Murphree, "Rebel Sovereigns," 61; *Official Records,* series I, vol. VI, 301–2.

42. *Official Records,* series I, vol. VI, 301–2; Franklin A. Doty, ed., "The Civil War Letters of Augustus Henry Mathers, Assistant Surgeon, Fourth Florida Infantry, C.S.A.," *Florida Historical Quarterly* 36 (1957): 105. One source often utilized when discussing Hopkins and Apalachicola is the manuscript of Reverend Mr. Richardson, who left a colorful account of the undisciplined soldiers garrisoning the town. Richardson mentions M. Whit Smith in his account, but Smith commanded at Cedar Keys during the fall and probably never visited Apalachicola. His other accusations are suspect as well.

43. *Official Records,* series I, vol. VI, 302, 304; Ives Diary, November 13–14, 1861. Milton placed state troops at Apalachicola under his friend and aide-de-camp Richard Floyd. "By letter," the governor wrote, "he is to defend the place, if attacked, to the last extremity."

Chapter 4

1. Steven E. Woodworth, *Nothing But Victory: The Army of Tennessee, 1861–1865* (New York: Knopf, 2005), 94. For the botched Confederate defense of Kentucky and East Tennessee, see Thomas Lawrence Connelly, *Army of the Heartland: The Army of Tennessee, 1861–1862* (1967; reprint, Baton Rouge: Louisiana State University Press, 2001).

2. Woodworth, *Nothing But Victory,* 106, 113. General Albert Sidney Johnston, who was commanding the Confederate Army in the Western Theater, ordered the breakout. See Connelly, *Army of the Heartland,* 121. For more on the failed breakout and poor Confederate leadership at Fort Donelson, see Steven E. Woodworth, *Jefferson Davis and His Generals: The Failure of Confederate Command in the West* (Lawrence: University of Kansas Press, 1990), 82–84.

3. J. J. Finley to Hon. J. P. Benjamin, February 12, 1862, Letters Received, Confederate Secretary of War, NA Microcopy M437, Reel #28. Finley was referring to the Battle of Fishing Creek, fought on January 19, 1862, which caused the loss of eastern Kentucky, and the fall of Roanoke Island, February 8, 1862, that cost the Confederates Hatteras Inlet.

4. "Jesse Johnson Finley Biographical Sketch," Finley Family Papers, MOC, Richmond, VA (hereafter Finley Family Papers); J. J. Finley to Much Revered Father, September 30, 1839, Finley Family Papers. See also Warner, *Generals in Gray,* 89.

5. "Jesse Johnson Finley Biographical Sketch"; James M. Denham, *Rogue's Paradise: Crime and Punishment in Antebellum Florida, 1821–1861* (Tuscaloosa: The University of Alabama Press, 1997), 29; *Tallahassee Floridian and Journal,* November 30, 1850; Jesse Johnson Finley to His Excellency, Andrew Johnson, June 14, 1865, "Case Files of Appli-

cations from Former Confederates for Presidential Pardons, 1865–1867," NA Microcopy M1003, Reel #15.

6. *Official Records,* series IV, vol. I, 902–3.

7. *Columbus (GA) Daily Sun,* June 17, 1862. For the voting habits of West Florida, see the *St. Augustine (FL) Examiner,* October 13, 1860, and *Tallahassee Floridian and Journal,* October 13, 1860. Besides Finley and Kenan, two company commanders, Whigs Samuel B. Love and Robert H. M. Davidson, served terms in the state legislature. Captain Henry O. Bassett was previously sheriff of Jackson County. See Denham, *Rogue's Paradise,* 221.

8. John L. McKinnon, *History of Walton County* (Atlanta: privately published, 1911), chapter 24. Angus McLean had an extensive family in Walton County, including the McKinnons.

9. Alvaretta Kenan Register, comp., *The Kenan Family and Some Allied Families of the Compiler and Publisher* (Statesboro, GA: Kenan Print Shop, 1967), 27–30; "The Memorial Resolution on the Life and Character of Daniel Lafayette Kenan," Washington Lodge No. 2, Quincy, FL, February 8, 1884, Kenan Biographical File, Collection of Zack C. Waters, Rome, GA.

10. Angus I. Gillis to Dear Aunt, May 1, 1862, and M. M. Gillis to Dear Aunt, February 7, 1862, McLean Family Papers, P. K. Yonge Library of Florida History, Gainesville (hereafter McLean Family Papers).

11. J. J. Finley to Brigadier General Joseph Finnegan, April 29, 1862, Letters Received, Confederate Secretary of War, NA Microcopy M410, Reel #18; A. G. McLeod to My Dear Aunt, April 27, 1862, McLean Family Papers; William A. Scott to Mr. J. C. McKenzie, April 10, 1862, in William Hugh Tucker, ed., *The McKenzie Correspondence, 1849–1901* (Elmira, NY: privately published, 2004), 76.

12. *Official Records,* series I, vol. VI, 770–71.

13. Wm. D. Randolph to Dear Father, December 18, 1861, Randolph Family Papers; S. H. Harris to Dear Angie, December 9, 1861, Harris Papers.

14. Wm. D. Randolph to Dear Father, December 18, 1861, and Thomas Eston Randolph to Dear Ma, January 23, 1862, Randolph Family Papers.

15. *Monticello Family Friend,* February 8, 1862.

16. Numbers taken from Special Order No. 1, April 1, 1862, Orders of Patton Anderson's Brigade, Army of Mississippi, 1862, NA; Patton Anderson to Hon. T. B. Monroe, October 3, 1861, Letters Received, Confederate Secretary of War, NA Microcopy M437, Reel #14; Thomas Eston Randolph to Dear Father, December 3, 1861, Randolph Family Papers.

17. *Official Records,* series I, vol. VI, 843–44, 848–50, 855–57.

18. Brigadier General Samuel Jones to Lt. Col. Beard, March 16, 1862, Brigadier General Samuel Jones to Captain T. J. Myers, March 25, 1862, and Brigadier General Samuel Jones to Maj. Gen. Braxton Bragg, March 26, 1862, Letterbook, Braxton Bragg Papers, 1833–1879, MSS 2000, Microfilm Edition, Western Reserve Historical Society, Cleveland, OH.

19. Special Orders No. 27, March 28, 1862, Orders and Circulars of the Army of the Mississippi, 1861–1865, NA, Washington, DC; Special Orders No. 1, April 1, 1862, Or-

ders of Patton Anderson's Brigade, Army of Mississippi, 1862, NA, Washington, DC. The battalion's companies were commanded by William G. Poole, a Tallahassee merchant, T. Sumpter Means and Oliver P. Hull, both Alachua County physicians, and Capers Bird, who owned a plantation in Jefferson County.

20. Larry J. Daniel, *Shiloh: The Battle That Changed the Civil War* (New York: Touchtone, 1998), 73–74; Woodworth, *Nothing But Victory,* 138. Henry Halleck's Department of Missouri also included Tennessee and Kentucky west of the Cumberland River. Ulysses S. Grant, due to Halleck's jealousy over the former's successes, did not command the initial move up the Tennessee River. Instead, Major General C. F. Smith led Grant's force until an injury and intervention by Abraham Lincoln placed Grant back in command.

21. Daniel, *Shiloh,* 119. See also Connelly, *Army of the Heartland,* 160–61.

22. Connelly, *Army of the Heartland,* 155–56; Daniel, *Shiloh,* 120, 127, 143–47. Larry J. Daniel and Steven E. Woodworth both point out in their respective works that the elements of the Federal Army were aware of activity in their front as a result of the lack of discipline of Confederate units, and some officers conducted patrols to investigate. As a result of this diligence, some regiments were in line ready to receive the attack rather than being caught by surprise.

23. William K. Beard to My Dearest Lettie, April 12, 1862, vol. 2, United Daughters of the Confederacy, Florida Division Scrapbooks, 1900–1935, 12 vols., FSA, Tallahassee (hereafter UDC Scrapbooks). The movements of Hardee and Bragg's troops indicate that the Confederate plan to drive Grant's army away from the river fell apart early due to how Johnston and Beauregard deployed their forces.

24. Beard to My Dearest Lettie, April 12, 1862; Daniel, *Shiloh,* 158–59; Woodworth, *Nothing But Victory,* 160; *Official Records,* series I, vol. X, 496–97.

25. Beard to My Dearest Lettie, April 12, 1862; *Jacksonville (FL) Times-Union,* March 6, 1901; 1860 U.S. Census (Free Schedule), Leon County, FL, p. 18, NA Microcopy M653, Reel #108, family 176, dwelling 176, line 28; *Tallahassee Floridian and Journal,* January 7 and October 6, 1860.

26. *Official Records,* series I, vol. X, 502–4; Beard to My Dearest Lettie, April 12, 1862; *Jacksonville (FL) Times-Union,* March 6, 1901.

27. Daniel, *Shiloh,* 178–83; Beard to My Dearest Lettie, April 12, 1862; *Official Records,* series I, vol. X, 504–5; 1860 U.S. Census (Free Schedule), Leon County, FL, p. 15, NA Microcopy M653, Reel #108, family 122, dwelling 122, lines 8–11; *New Orleans Daily Picayune,* April 23, 1862. Compare casualty list with Special Orders No. 1, April 1, 1862. The wounded included Captain T. Sumpter Means (Co. B), 1st Lt. John T. Miller (Co. B), 2nd Lt. W. W. Tucker (Co. C), 2nd Lt. E. C. Stevens (Co. B), and 1st Lt. Oliver P. Hull (Co. D), who later died of his wounds. Orders, Patton Anderson's Brigade, Army of Mississippi, 1862, NA, Washington, DC. As Daniel demonstrates in *Shiloh,* the fighting at Shiloh, influenced by both the terrain and the poor management by Confederate commanders, lost all tactical quality and devolved into blunt frontal attacks.

28. Daniel, *Shiloh,* 202–4; Connelly, *Army of the Heartland,* 163–64.

29. *Official Records,* series I, vol. X, 498. See Daniel, *Shiloh,* map 9, p. 205.

30. *Official Records,* series I, vol. X, 149–50; Daniel, *Shiloh,* 236–37.

31. Daniel, *Shiloh,* 226, 236–37. Daniel and Connelly both agree that Beauregard called

a halt to the fighting as a result of the fatigued and disorganized state of the Confederate Army. Daniel also writes that Beauregard believed fire from river gunboats would inflict terrible casualties on his soldiers. See Daniel, *Shiloh*, 251, and Connelly, *Army of the Heartland*, 169.

32. *Official Records*, series I, vol. X, 505; Beard to My Dearest Lettie, April 12, 1862, UDC Scrapbooks, vol. 2.

33. Daniel, *Shiloh*, 290.

34. Beard to My Dearest Lettie, April 12, 1862.

35. *New Orleans Daily Picayune*, April 23, 1862; *Tallahassee Florida Sentinel*, April 22 and 29, 1862; Mark M. Boatner III, *The Civil War Dictionary*, rev. ed. (New York: David McKay Company, 1988), 757.

36. Lawrence H. Matthews to Sir, July 1, 1862, Letters Received, Confederate Secretary of War, NA Microcopy M437, Reel #61; *Official Records*, series I, vol. X, 502; Beard to My Dearest Lettie, April 12, 1862.

37. Joseph H. Crute Jr., *Units of the Confederate States Army*, 2nd ed. (Gaithersburg, MD: Olde Soldier Books, 1987), 156–57; Special Orders No. 51, 2nd Corps, Army of the Mississippi, Special Orders No. 6, Brigadier General Patton Anderson, May 1, 1862, and Morning Reports, May–June 1862, Orders of Patton Anderson's Brigade, Army of Mississippi, 1862, NA, Washington, DC.

Chapter 5

1. McPherson, *Battle Cry of Freedom*, 370–73.

2. *Official Records*, series I, vol. VI, 220; Horatio G. Wright later commanded VI Corps in the Armies of the Potomac and Shenandoah.

3. *Official Records*, series I, vol. VI, 220, 380, 393, 399; Brigadier General J. H. Trapier to Captain W. H. Taylor, February 1862, Letters, Telegrams, and Reports.

4. Brigadier General J. H. Trapier to Captain T. A. Washington, January 22, 1862; Augustus Henry Mathers to My Dear Wife, January 27, 1862, in Doty, "The Civil War Letters of Augustus Henry Mathers," 118; Nichols, "Florida's Fighting Rebels," 18; Wiley, *Life of Johnny Reb*, 247, 251; Larry J. Daniel, *Soldiering in the Army of Tennessee* (Chapel Hill: University of North Carolina Press, 1991), 64.

5. Augustus Henry Mathers to Dear Wife, February 27, 1862, in Doty, "The Civil War Letters of Augustus Henry Mathers," 122–23; William T. Stockton to My Darling Wife, February 16, 1862, in Ulmer, *The Correspondence of Will and Ju Stockton*, 91; Lemuel Moody to Dear Sister, February 16, 1862, Moody Letters; Ives Diary, March 15, 1862; *Official Records*, series I, vol. VI, 417.

6. Augustus Henry Mathers to Dear Wife, February 27, 1862, in Doty, "The Civil War Letters of Augustus Henry Mathers," 123.

7. *New York Times*, March 11 and 15, 1862; *Official Records*, series I, vol. VI, 93–95.

8. *Savannah Republican* quoted in *Columbus (GA) Daily Sun*, March 15, 1862; Ives Diary, March 21, 1862; *Official Records*, series I, vol. VI, 413.

9. Brigadier General J. H. Trapier to Captain T. A. Washington, January 15, 1862, Letters, Telegrams, and Reports; *Supplement to the Official Records—Records of Events*, 5:137.

10. Bvt. Major General George W. Cullum, *Notices of the Biographical Register of Officers and Graduates of the U.S. Military Academy at West Point from 1802–1867,* vol. 1, rev. ed. (New York: James Miller, 1879), 447; M. S. Perry et al. to Hon. L. P. Walker, March 25, 1861, in Ulmer, *The Correspondence of Will and Ju Stockton,* 57-b. The Battle of Camp Izard was fought on February 28, 1836, near the Withlacoochee River. The Oloklikoha may refer to Peliklakaha, a Seminole village burned on March 31, 1836. Among Stockton's classmates at West Point were Gabriel Paul and Goode Bryan, who fought against each other in Virginia.

11. William T. Stockton to Ju Stockton, February 2 and 23, 1862, in Ulmer, *The Correspondence of Will and Ju Stockton,* 83, 93.

12. R. E. Lee to General J. H. Trapier, February 13, 1862, Letters Sent and Endorsements, Department of South Carolina, Georgia, and Florida, 1861–1862, NA, Washington, DC; *Official Records,* series I, vol. VI, 390. For an example of the actions W.G.M. Davis pursued against the Union forces on Amelia Island, see *Official Records,* series I, vol. VI, 132–33.

13. Noble Hull to Gov. Milton, March 14, 1862, and John Milton to Dear Sir, March 17, 1862, John Milton Letterbook, 1861–1863, Governor's Office Letterbooks, 1836–1909, vol. 6, RG 101, Series 32, FSA, Tallahassee (hereafter John Milton Letterbook).

14. Lemuel Moody to Dear Sister, March 1, 1862, Moody Letters; Major John G. Barnwell to Maj. R. A. Anderson, February 2, 1862, Letters, Telegrams, and Reports. For a manifest of *Kate's* cargo, see *Official Records,* series IV, vol. I, 895.

15. Major John G. Barnwell to Maj. R. A. Anderson, February 2, 1862.

16. *Official Records,* series I, vol. VI, 111–12.

17. *Official Records,* series I, vol. LIII, 240–41 and vol. VI, 417–18. According to A. B. Noyes, the munitions were transferred overland to Ocala and then to Gainesville to the Florida Railroad. From there, trains carried the cargo to Baldwin, where the shipment was placed on Florida Atlantic and Gulf line cars for movement to Madison. Here, the weapons and equipment were hauled overland to Georgia and other rails. Federal interdiction of the line at Baldwin meant a time-consuming overland journey from Ocala to Madison.

18. Martin and Schafer, *Jacksonville's Ordeal by Fire,* 84–85; Brig. Gen. J. H. Trapier to Major T. A. Washington, March 28, 1862, Letters, Telegrams, and Reports; *Official Records,* series I, vol. VI, 131–32; Ives Diary, March 20 and April 23, 1862.

19. Crute, *Units of the Confederate States Army,* 77. For more on South Florida and the Third Seminole Indian War, see Brown, *Peace River Frontier.*

20. "Florida Senators by District," Vertical Files, FSL, Tallahassee; Madison Starke Perry to My Dear Wife, July 15, 1862, Madison Starke Perry Papers, 1860–1862, P. K. Yonge Library of Florida History, Gainesville; "Madison Starke Perry," Biographical Packets, P. K. Yonge Library of Florida History, Gainesville; Zack C. Waters, "'In the Country of an Acknowledged Enemy': The 7th Florida Regiment in East Tennessee" (unpublished paper in author's possession). Perry's health declined during the war, and he died in the spring of 1865.

21. Zack C. Waters, "'Through Good and Evil Fortune': Robert Bullock in Civil War and Reconstruction," *Proceedings of the 90th Annual Meeting of the Florida Historical Society*

at St. Augustine, May 1992 (1993): 136–37; S. D. McConnell to My Dear Mamy, May 7, 1862, McConnell Papers.

22. "Florida Senators by District" and "Florida Representatives by Session," both in Vertical Files, FSL, Tallahassee; Sanchez Family Papers, P. K. Yonge Library of Florida History, Gainesville.

23. "S. D. McConnell," *Biographical Souvenir of the States of Georgia and Florida* (Chicago: F. A. Battery and Company, 1889), 533; Samuel D. McConnell to My Dear Mamy, April 3, 1862, McConnell Papers. See Robert Blair Smith to Rev. J. F. Crowe, September 5, 1858, Duggan Library, Archives of Hanover College, Hanover, IN.

24. R. Thomas Campbell, ed., *Southern Service on Land and Sea: The Wartime Journal of Robert Watson, CSA/CSN* (Knoxville: University of Tennessee Press, 2002), xi.

25. April 4, 10, and 29, 1862, in ibid., 30–33.

26. McPherson, *Battle Cry of Freedom,* 429–30; *Official Records,* series IV, vol. I, 1031.

27. *Official Records,* series IV, vol. I, 1095–96, 1098.

28. McPherson, *Battle Cry of Freedom,* 419–20.

29. Colonel William S. Dilworth to General Samuel Cooper, February 8, 1862, Letters Received, Confederate Secretary of War, NA Microcopy M437, Reel #42; Benjamin Waring Partridge to Dear Mother, February 15, 1862 (copy), Lewis G. Schmidt Research Collection; Seaborn D. Harris to Dear Bro, May 3, 1862, Harris Civil War Records, FSA, Tallahassee.

30. W.G.M. Davis to John Milton, April 24, 1862, John Milton Letterbook.

31. John Milton to Dear Sir, March 17, 1862, John Milton Letterbook; *Official Records,* series I, vol. XIV, 473; Nichols, "Florida's Fighting Rebels," 48.

32. *Tallahassee Floridian and Journal,* June 7, 1862; Edward Clifford Brush Diary, May 5–8, 1862, MOC, Richmond, VA (hereafter Brush Diary); Mrs. O. F. Wiley, "Edward Clifford Brush," *Confederate Veteran* 40 (1932): 144.

33. Brush Diary, May 12, 1862; *Columbus (GA) Daily Sun,* May 13, 1862; Ellis, "A Short Record of T. B. Ellis, Sr.," 2; W. C. Middleton Diary, May 26, 1862, UDC Scrapbooks, vol. 5 (hereafter Middleton Diary). The Army of the Mississippi, P.G.T. Beauregard commanding, evacuated Corinth on the night of May 29–30 owing to pressure by several Federal armies and the unhealthiness of the area. The army retreated fifty miles south to Tupelo, and Jefferson Davis, incensed over the retreat and holding old grudges against Beauregard, replaced him with Braxton Bragg. The soldiers en route to Corinth were diverted elsewhere.

34. Hartman and Coles, *Biographical Rosters,* 1:390; Ives Diary, May 3, 1861, and April 22, 24, and 28, 1862.

35. Edward Hopkins to the Hon. Sec. of War, [May] 15, 1862, Letters Received, Confederate Secretary of War, NA Microcopy M437, Reel #52; Nichols, "Florida's Fighting Rebels," 45.

36. Rowland H. Rerick, *Memoirs of Florida,* ed. Francis P. Fleming (Atlanta: Southern Historical Association, 1902), 1:421–22; Edward N. Badger, Service Records—FL Seminole Wars, NA Microcopy S608, Reel #57, FSA, Tallahassee; Emily Badger Green, *The Badger Family* (Ocala: privately published, 1945), 2–4.

37. "Transportation Receipt," in James P. Hunt, *CSR,* Reel #54; B. L. Rice to Mother, June 8, 1862, B. L. Rice Letters, FSL, Tallahassee (hereafter Rice Letters); *Columbus (GA) Daily Sun,* June 12 and 13, 1862; Washington M. Ives Jr. to Dear Mother, June 26, 1862, Washington M. Ives Papers, FSL, Tallahassee (hereafter Ives Papers).

Chapter 6

1. Manning, *What This Cruel War Was Over,* 4, 32; James M. McPherson, *For Cause and Comrades: Why Men Fought in the Civil War* (New York: Oxford University Press, 1997), 19–20.

2. Manning, *What This Cruel War Was Over,* 34, 38; J. J. Finley to Most Revered Father, September 30, 1839, Finley Family Papers; *St. Augustine (FL) Examiner,* December 22, 1860. Hinton R. Helper, in his *The Impending Crisis* published in 1857, argued the evils of this class system imposed by slavery. See McPherson, *Battle Cry of Freedom,* 199–200.

3. *Jacksonville Standard,* December 6, 1860; *St. Augustine (FL) Examiner,* November 3, 1860.

4. August 14, 1863, in Pasco, *Private Pasco,* 148; S. D. McConnell to My Dear Eloise, November 12, 1860, McConnell Papers.

5. *Tallahassee Floridian and Journal,* December 8, 1860; *Cedar Keys (FL) Telegraph,* December 11, 1860.

6. *St. Augustine (FL) Examiner,* November 17, 1860; *Tallahassee Floridian and Journal,* December 8 and 22, 1860.

7. *St. Augustine (FL) Examiner,* December 22, 1860; Joseph T. Glatthaar, *General Lee's Army: From Victory to Collapse* (New York: Free Press, 2008), 31.

8. McPherson, *For Cause and Comrades,* xi; Glatthaar, *General Lee's Army,* 20; Rivers, *Slavery in Florida,* 34; 1860 U.S. Census (Slave Schedule), Florida, NA Microcopy M653, Reel #110. Data on Florida Brigade slave owners abstracted from Hartman and Coles, *Biographical Rosters,* 1:25–31, 47–65, 273–84, 305–14, 337–48, 450–58, 2:580–89, 725–33, 743–51, 4:1330–39, 1386–92; 1860 U.S. Census (Free Schedule), Alachua, Putnam, Jackson, Hamilton, Leon, Jefferson, Suwannee, Lafayette, Columbia, Nassau, St. Johns, Marion, Sumter, Hillsborough, Gadsden, Manatee, New River, Duval, Santa Rosa, and Walton counties, FL, NA Microcopy M653, Reels #106, 107, 108, 109.

9. Occupation data abstracted from Hartman and Coles, *Biographical Rosters,* 1:25–31, 47–65, 273–84, 305–14, 337–48, 450–58, 2:580–89, 725–33, 743–51, 4:1330–39, 1386–92; 1860 U.S. Census (Free Schedule), Alachua, Putnam, Jackson, Hamilton, Leon, Duval, Jefferson, Manatee, Suwannee, New River, Lafayette, Columbia, Nassau, St. Johns, Marion, Sumter, Hillsborough, Gadsden, Santa Rosa, and Walton counties, FL, NA Microcopy M653, Reels #106, 107, 108, 109.

10. Wiley, *Life of Johnny Reb,* 331; McPherson, *For Cause and Comrades,* viii.

11. 1860 U.S. Census (Free Schedule), Gadsden, Hillsborough, Lafayette, Sumter, and St. Johns counties, FL, NA Microcopy M653, Reels #106, 107, 108, 109; Coles, "Ancient City Defenders," 73.

12. 1860 U.S. Census (Free Schedule), Santa Rosa, Hillsborough, Manatee, Gadsden,

Hamilton, Liberty, Jackson, Putnam, New River, Walton, Sumter, and Marion, FL, NA Microcopy M653, Reels #107, 108, 109. Richard Lowe, in *Walker's Texas Division C.S.A. Greyhounds of the TransMississippi* (Baton Rouge: Louisiana State University Press, 2004), has written that his research on the soldiers who joined after the conscription act's passage were "older than the typical Confederate or Union soldier" (21).

13. Glatthaar, *General Lee's Army*, 36; Lowe, *Walker's Texas Division*, 21.

14. Caudle, "Settlement Patterns," 435–36; 1860 U.S. Census (Free Schedule), Alachua, Suwannee, Santa Rosa, and Walton counties, FL, NA Microfilm M653, Reel #109.

15. U.S. Census (Free Schedule), Jefferson, St. Johns, Manatee, New River, Lafayette, and Hillsborough counties, FL, NA Microfilm M653, Reels #106, 107, 108, 109; Coles, "Ancient City Defenders," 65.

16. S. D. McConnell to My dear Eloise, January 12, 1861, McConnell Papers; Michael O. Raysor to My Dear Wife, August 4, 1861, Raysor Family Correspondence, P. K. Yonge Library of Florida History, Gainesville (hereafter Raysor Family Correspondence).

17. Glatthaar, *General Lee's Army*, 34; Archie Livingston to My Dr Father, March 23, 1864, in John M. Coski, ed., "'I Am in for Anything for Success': The Letters of Sergeant Archie Livingston 3rd Florida Infantry," *North and South* 6 (2003): 80; Roddie Shaw to My Dear Sister, December 16, 1862, Shaw Letters; John L. Inglis to My Dear Cousins, Wm & W Vann, January 16, 1864, Livingston/Inglis Letters, MOC, Richmond, VA (hereafter Livingston/Inglis Letters).

18. Theodore Livingston to Dear Sister Scotia, December 12, 1864, Livingston/Inglis Letters; Francis R. Nicks to Dear Mike, March 9, 1863, Francis R. Nicks Letters, FSA, Tallahassee (hereafter Nicks Letters); Charles S. Herring to Dear Mother & family, March 15, 1863, in Tucker, *McKenzie Correspondence*, 92.

Chapter 7

1. Boatner, *The Civil War Dictionary*, 176; Connelly, *Army of the Heartland*, 176–77; Woodworth, *Nothing But Victory*, 207.

2. William D. Rogers to unknown, undated, William D. Rogers Letters, 1862–1865, FSA, Tallahassee (hereafter Rogers Letters); "Morning Reports, Fla. and Confed. Guards Response Batt.," Orders of Patton Anderson's Brigade, Army of Mississippi, 1862, NA, Washington, DC. In *Soldiering in the Army of Tennessee*, Daniel argues that the suffering at Corinth appeared terrible to the soldiers because of its scale. He demonstrates that there were in fact more sick cases at Tupelo than at Corinth.

3. General Orders No. 6, June 13, 1862, Orders of Patton Anderson's Brigade, Army of Mississippi, 1862, NA, Washington, DC.

4. Jacob E. Mickler to My Darling Wife, July 19, 1862, in David J. Coles and Zack C. Waters, eds., "Indian Fighter, Confederate Soldier, Blockader Runner, and Scout: The Life and Letters of Jacob E. Mickler," *El Escribano* 34 (1997): 43; Middleton Diary, May 25–26, 1862.

5. Middleton Diary, May 26–29, 1862.

6. Special Orders No. 127, June 8, 1862, General and Special Orders, 1861–1862,

Department of Alabama and West Florida, NA, Washington, DC; Jacob E. Mickler to My dearest Wife, June 25, 1862, in Coles and Waters, "The Life and Letters of Jacob E. Mickler," 41.

7. Jacob E. Mickler to My dearest Wife, June 25, 1862; Michael O. Raysor to My Dear Wife, June 30, 1862, Raysor Family Correspondence; Willie Bryant to Dear Davis, June 15, 1862, in Arch Fredric Blakey, Ann Smith Lainhart, and Winston Bryant Stephens Jr., eds., *Rose Cottage Chronicles: Civil War Letters of the Bryant-Stephens Families of North Florida* (Gainesville: University Press of Florida, 1998), 122.

8. Washington M. Ives Jr. to Sisters Katie and Fanny, July 6, 1862, Ives Papers.

9. Ibid.; Michael O. Raysor to My Dear Wife, July 6, 1862, Raysor Family Correspondence.

10. Michael O. Raysor to My Dear Wife, June 30, 1862; Lemuel Moody to Dear Sister, July 16, 1862, Moody Letters; Washington M. Ives Jr. to Dear Mother, July 20, 1862, Ives Papers; *Tallahassee Floridian and Journal,* July 26, 1862.

11. Noel C. Fisher, *War at Every Door: Partisan Politics and Guerilla Warfare in East Tennessee, 1860–1869* (Chapel Hill: University of North Carolina Press, 1997), 20, 31–32.

12. McPherson, *Battle Cry of Freedom,* 283; Woodworth, *Nothing But Victory,* 65; Shelby Foote, *The Civil War: A Narrative,* 3 vols. (1958; reprint, New York: Vintage Books, 1986), 1:559; Kenneth W. Noe, *Perryville: The Grand Havoc of Battle* (Lexington: University Press of Kentucky, 2001), 28; Emory M. Thomas, *The Confederate Nation: 1861–1865* (New York: Harper and Row, 1979), 94. For more on Lincoln's policy toward Southern Unionists, see David M. Potter, *Lincoln and His Party in the Secession Crisis* (1942; reprint, New Haven: Yale University Press, 1962). As Woodworth notes in *Jefferson Davis and His Generals,* Cumberland Gap was easily outflanked by various mountain passes and was thus abandoned by the Confederates.

13. *Official Records,* series I, vol. XVI, 9; Connelly, *Army of the Heartland,* 188–89.

14. William T. Stockton to My dear wife, June 13, 1862, in Ulmer, *The Correspondence of Will and Ju Stockton,* 115; J. Leonard Raulston and James W. Livingood, *Sequatchie: A Story of the Lower Cumberlands* (Knoxville: University of Tennessee Press, 1974), 21.

15. *Richmond Daily Dispatch,* June 18 and 24, 1862; William T. Stockton to Dearest Ju, June 21, 1862, in Ulmer, *The Correspondence of Will and Ju Stockton,* 117.

16. Charles Herring to Dear Mother & family, June 11, 1862, in Tucker, *McKenzie Correspondence,* 81; Hugh Black to Dear Wife, June 13, 1862, in Elizabeth Caldwell Frano, comp., *Letters of Captain Hugh Black to His Family in Florida during the War between the States, 1862–1864* (Newbury, IN: privately published, 1998), 34.

17. James Hays to My dear wife, July [?] 1862, James Hays Letters, United Daughters of the Confederacy Bound Typescripts, vol. 4, pp. 9–42, Georgia Department of Archives and History, Atlanta (hereafter Hays Letters); Hugh Black to Dear Mary A. Black, June 22, 1862, in Frano, *Letters of Captain Hugh Black to His Family,* 34; Reid Mitchell, *Civil War Soldiers: Their Expectations and Their Experiences* (New York: Viking Penguin, 1988), 64–65.

18. *Columbus (GA) Daily Sun,* June 26, 1862; A. G. Morrison to Mrs. Margaret, July 1, 1862, in Tucker, *McKenzie Correspondence,* 80.

19. Samuel D. McConnell to My darling wife, June 12, 1862, McConnell Papers; *Ad-*

ventures of the Marion Hornets, Co. H, 7th Regt. Fla. Vols. (Knoxville: published for the author, 1863), 6, original held in the Eleanor S. Brockenbrough Library, MOC, Richmond, VA; June 13, 1862, in Campbell, *Southern Service on Land and Sea,* 43; Robert Bullock to Amanda Waterman Bullock, June 25, 1862, Robert Bullock and Amanda Waterman Bullock Papers, Georgia Department of Archives and History, Atlanta (hereafter Bullock Papers).

20. *Columbus (GA) Daily Sun,* June 26, 1862.

21. Samuel D. McConnell to My darling wife, June 23, 1862, McConnell Papers; Robert Bullock to Amanda Waterman Bullock, June 28, 1862, Bullock Papers; Madison Starke Perry to My Dear Wife, July 15, 1862, MS Perry Letters, 1860–62, P. K. Yonge Library of Florida History, Gainesville.

22. Robert Bullock to Amanda Waterman Bullock, June 28, 1862; Samuel D. McConnell to My darling wife, June 23, 1862; *Adventures of the Marion Hornets* (Knoxville: privately published, 1863), 8; August 2, 1862, in Campbell, *Southern Service on Land and Sea,* 45.

23. Connelly, *Army of the Heartland,* 192; Nichols, "Florida's Fighting Rebels," 49; Waters, "In the Presence of an Acknowledged Enemy," 6.

24. Larry J. Daniel, *Days of Glory: The Army of the Cumberland, 1861–1865* (Baton Rouge: Louisiana State University Press, 2004), 93; Stephen D. Engle, *Don Carlos Buell: Most Promising of All* (Chapel Hill: University of North Carolina Press, 1999), 258; *Official Records,* series I, vol. XVI, part II, 17.

25. Earl J. Hess, *Banners to the Breeze: The Kentucky Campaign, Corinth, and Stones River* (Lincoln: University of Nebraska Press, 2000), 11.

26. Foote, *The Civil War,* 1:561–62; Connelly, *Army of the Heartland,* 201–2.

27. Connelly, *Army of the Heartland,* 179–81; William D. Rogers to Dear Jimmy, July 12, 1862, Rogers Letters.

28. Woodworth, *Jefferson Davis and His Generals,* 131; McWhiney, *Braxton Bragg,* 1:261, 268; Connelly, *Army of the Heartland,* 196–97.

29. *Supplement to the Official Records,* 5:188; Augustus O. McDonell Diary, August 10, 1862, McDonell Papers (hereafter McDonell Diary).

30. Middleton Diary, July 20–25, 1862.

31. Washington M. Ives to Dear Father, August 10, 1862, Ives Papers.

32. Ibid.

33. Jacob E. Mickler to My Darling Wife, July [28], 1862, in Coles and Waters, "The Life and Letters of Jacob E. Mickler," 44; Washington M. Ives to Dear Father, August 10, 1862, and to Dear Sister Katie, August 17, 1862, Ives Papers; Willie Bryant to Dear Davis, August 16, 1862, in Blakey, Lainhart, and Stephens, *Rose Cottage Chronicles,* 138; McDonell Diary, August 17, 1862.

34. "T. A. McDonell," *Biographical Souvenir of the States of Georgia and Florida*, 545; *Tallahassee Floridian and Journal,* June 7, 1862.

35. John Milton to George W. Randolph, June 21, 1862, John Milton Letterbook; Nichols, "Florida's Fighting Rebels," 47.

36. Warner, *Generals in Gray,* 217; S. R. Mallory to Jefferson Davis, August 12, 1863, in William Miller, *Compiled Service Records of Confederate Generals and Staff Officers and*

Non Regimental Enlisted Men, RG 109, NA, Washington, DC, NA Microfilm M331, Reel #178 (hereafter *CSR of Generals,* with appropriate reel number); *Tallahassee Floridian and Journal,* June 16, 1860.

37. *Supplement to the Official Records,* 5:183–88; McKinnon, *History of Walton County,* chapter 37; D. G. McLean to Miss Maggie McKenzie, August 2 and October 14, 1861, in Tucker, *McKenzie Correspondence,* 71, 73. For more on immorality in camps, see Wiley, *Life of Johnny Reb,* 36–38, 50.

38. Henry W. Reddick, *Seventy-Seven Years in Dixie: The Boys in Gray of 61–65* (Santa Rosa, CA: published by the author, 1910), 12–13; Daniel G. McLean to Miss Maggie McKenzie, June 20, 1862, in Tucker, *McKenzie Correspondence,* 79.

39. *Supplement to the Official Records,* 5:183. For the regiment's numbers, see Washington M. Ives to Dear Father, August 24, 1862, Ives Papers, and Daniel G. McLean to Miss Maggie McKenzie, June 20, 1862. Glover A. Ball, *CSR,* Reel #24; 1860 US Census (Free Schedule), Leon County, FL, p. 26, M653, Reel #108, family 227, dwelling 227, lines 10–12.

40. Washington M. Ives to Dear Father, August 10, 1862, Ives Papers.

Chapter 8

1. McWhiney, *Braxton Bragg,* 1:272; Connelly, *Army of the Heartland,* 209; Noe, *Perryville,* 32; Woodworth, *Jefferson Davis and His Generals,* 137.

2. Connelly, *Army of the Heartland,* 197–98; McWhiney, *Braxton Bragg,* 1:273–74; Foote, *The Civil War,* 1:576.

3. McWhiney, *Braxton Bragg,* 1:273; Connelly, *Army of the Heartland,* 211.

4. Foote, *The Civil War,* 1:583; August 13, 1862, in Campbell, *Southern Service on Land and Sea,* 46; *Adventures of the Marion Hornets,* 11. A Virginian, Heth served in western Virginia in early 1862 and during the winter months of 1863 transferred to the Army of Northern Virginia. On the morning July 1, 1863, Heth's division, in the van of A. P. Hill's Corps, encountered John Buford's cavalry outside Gettysburg. The resulting skirmish became the first action in that pivotal battle.

5. Hugh Black to Dear Wife, August 15, 1862, in Frano, *Letters of Captain Hugh Black to His Family,* 37–38; Major George B. Davis, Leslie J. Perry, and Joseph W. Kirkley, *The Official Military Atlas of the Civil War,* comp. Capt. Calvin D. Cowles (1891–95; reprint, New York: Barnes and Noble Publishing, 2003), plate 95:3.

6. Robert Bullock to My Dear Wife, August 21, 1862, Bullock Papers; James Hays to My Dear Wife and Children, August 20, 1862, Hays Letters; Connelly, *Army of the Heartland,* 212.

7. Connelly, *Army of the Heartland,* 212.

8. James Hays to [?], [undated letter fragment], Hays Letters; Hugh Black to Dear Wife, August 17, 1862, in Frano, *Letters of Captain Hugh Black to His Family,* 39; Hugh Black's Reminiscences, in Frano, *Letters of Captain Hugh Black to His Family*; Alex McKenzie Jr. to Dear Pa, October 4, 1862, in Tucker, *McKenzie Correspondence,* 87.

9. Sunday, August 17–Sunday, September 7, 1862, in Campbell, *Southern Service on Land and Sea,* 47–48.

10. Ibid.; James Hays to My Dear Wife and Children, August 20, 1862, Hays Letters.

11. Connelly, *Army of the Heartland,* 200, 209.

12. Nichols, "Florida's Fighting Rebels," 51; Hugh Black's Reminiscences, in Frano, *Letters of Captain Hugh Black to His Family,* 30.

13. Boatner, *The Civil War Dictionary,* 697–98; C. O. Bailey to Dear Father, October 15, 1862, Bailey Family Papers, P. K. Yonge Library of Florida History, Gainesville (hereafter Bailey Family Papers).

14. *Adventures of the Marion Hornets,* 15; William T. Stockton to Darling Wife, September 5, 1862, in Ulmer, *The Correspondence of Will and Ju Stockton,* 133.

15. Connelly, *Army of Heartland,* 217–18; Noe, *Perryville,* 40–41; C. O. Bailey to Dear Mother, October 31, 1862, Bailey Family Papers; *Adventures of the Marion Hornets,* 17.

16. Boatner, *The Civil War Dictionary,* 91; Warner, *Generals in Gray,* 35–36.

17. Crute, *Units of the Confederate States Army,* 94, 187; William Raulston Talley, "William Raulston Talley Memoir," 41–42, Georgia Department of Archives and History (GDAH), Atlanta; *Monticello Family Friend,* November 8, 1862, Bird Biographical File, Keystone Genealogical Society, Monticello, FL (hereafter Bird Biographical File); Washington M. Ives to Dear Father, September 12, 1862, Ives Papers. Colonel William S. Dilworth did not return to the regiment until November 1862. I could not find any documentation regarding his arrest, but both Pasco (writing as INOE) and Washington Ives confirm this occurrence.

18. Middleton Diary, August 19, 1862; Washington M. Ives to Dear Father, August 24, 1862, Ives Papers.

19. Willie Bryant to My dear Mother, August 24, 1862, in Blakey, Lainhart, and Stephens, *Rose Cottage Chronicles,* 139; Middleton Diary, August 21, 1862; Ellis, "A Short Record of Thomas Benton Ellis, Sr.," 2.

20. Washington M. Ives to Dear Father, August 24, 1862, Ives Papers; *Official Records,* series I, vol. XVI, part II, 761–62; Connelly, *Army of the Heartland,* 223.

21. John Livingston Inglis Diary, August 29, 1862 (copy), Special Collections, Robert Manning Strozier Library, Florida State University, Tallahassee (hereafter Inglis Diary); Raulston and Livingood, *Sequatchie,* 16; Willie Bryant to My dear Mother, August 24, 1862.

22. Connelly, *Army of the Heartland,* 222; Noe, *Perryville,* 41; James Lee McDonough, *The War in Kentucky: From Shiloh to Perryville* (Knoxville: University of Tennessee Press, 1994), 82.

23. R. Don McLeon, "Capt. John L. Inglis," *Confederate Veteran* 25 (1917): 517. See also John Livingston Inglis, "Commander Florida Division, U.C.V.," *Confederate Veteran* 22 (1914): 159.

24. Inglis Diary, August 30, 1862; Talley, "William Raulston Talley Memoir," 44; Ellis, "A Short Record of Thomas Benton Ellis, Sr.," 2; Willie Bryant to My dear Bro., September 14, 1862, in Blakey, Lainhart, and Stephens, *Rose Cottage Chronicles,* 148.

25. Inglis Diary, September 9, 1862; Willie Bryant to My dear Mother, September 7, 1862, in Blakey, Lainhart, and Stephens, *Rose Cottage Chronicles,* 145.

26. September 7, 9, and 10, 1862, in Pasco, *Private Pasco,* 1, 2; Charles C. Hemming, "The War of 1861 and Its Causes," 57, Charles C. Hemming Papers, P. K. Yonge Library of

Florida History, Gainesville. See also Daniel G. McLean to Miss Maggie Kate McKenzie, January 30, 1863, in Tucker, *McKenzie Correspondence,* 91.

27. September 13, 1862, in Pasco, *Private Pasco,* 3; McDonell Diary, September 14, 1862.

28. Inglis Diary, September 16, 1862; McDonough, *The War in Kentucky,* 158, 172; Connelly, *Army of the Heartland,* 228. In 1861, while a colonel, Chalmers led one of the columns during the attack on Santa Rosa Island.

29. McDonell Diary, September 16, 1862; September 17, 1862, in Pasco, *Private Pasco,* 4.

30. McDonough, *The War in Kentucky,* 180.

31. Inglis Diary, September 17, 1862; September 17, 1862, in Pasco, *Private Pasco,* 4; Middleton Diary, September 17, 1862.

32. Connelly, *Army of the Heartland,* 228, 230; Daniel, *Days of Glory,* 119, 121; Noe, *Perryville,* 72.

33. Inglis Diary, September 18, 19, and 20, 1862; September 18, 1862, in Pasco, *Private Pasco,* 4.

34. McWhiney, *Braxton Bragg,* 1:288–90; Noe, *Perryville,* 73; Daniel, *Days of Glory,* 124. According to his biographer, Bragg made this decision because his army was low on rations and Buell maintained a supply depot at Bowling Green, south of Munfordville. Connelly writes that Bragg's intelligence failed him at a critical moment, causing him to believe Buell was indeed flanking his position.

35. Noe, *Perryville,* 99.

36. Inglis Diary, September 24, 1862; McDonell Diary, September 26, 1862; Reddick, *Seventy-Seven Years in Dixie,* 15.

37. Hemming, "The War of 1861 and Its Causes," 58; Reddick, *Seventy-Seven Years in Dixie, 15;* Michael O. Raysor to My Dear Wife, December 21, 1862, Raysor Family Correspondence; Theodore Livingston to Dear Parents, October 11, 1862, Livingston/Inglis Letters.

38. McWhiney, *Braxton Bragg,* 1:296–97; McDonough, *The War in Kentucky,* 199; Noe, *Perryville,* 104. Noe claims that Bragg began second-guessing himself following the Munfordville incident and, losing control over the campaign, became irascible.

39. McWhiney, *Braxton Bragg,* 1:300–301, 307. Bragg's biographer argues that had Polk moved north, even as late as October 4, the combined Armies of the Mississippi and East Tennessee might have succeeded in destroying a portion of Buell's force because it was badly divided in its march across Kentucky. In his masterful history of the Army of the Cumberland (known at this time as the Army of the Ohio), Larry Daniel acknowledges this possibility. See Daniel, *Days of Glory,* 141.

40. McKenzie to Dear Pa, October 4, 1862, in Tucker, *McKenzie Correspondence,* 87; *Adventures of the Marion Hornets,* 19.

41. Noe, *Perryville,* 130–32; McWhiney, *Braxton Bragg,* 1:308–11; McDonough, *The War in Kentucky,* 204.

42. Noe, *Perryville,* 132; Brush Diary, October 7, 1862; Inglis Diary, October 7, 1862. McPherson, *For Cause and Comrades,* 37, argues that this pre-battle revelry was simply a way to relieve nervousness.

43. Inglis Diary, October 6, 1862; McDonough, *The War in Kentucky,* 202–3; Brush Diary, October 7, 1862.

44. McDonough, *The War in Kentucky,* 221–22; Daniel, *Days of Glory,* 147–49; Noe, *Perryville,* 172.

45. Ellis, "A Short Record of T. B. Ellis., Sr.," 2; Talley, "William Raulston Talley Memoir," 47; Noe, *Perryville,* 172, 217, 238.

46. Sam R. Watkins, *"Co. Aytch": A Side Show of the Big Show* (New York: Macmillan, 1962), 63; Noe, *Perryville,* 238; *Monticello Family Friend,* November 8, 1862; Willie Bryant to My dear mother, October 11, 1862, in Blakey, Lainhart, and Stephens, *Rose Cottage Chronicles,* 158; General William Miller, "Report of General Miller to Anna Jackson Chapter United Daughters of the Confederacy," UDC Scrapbooks, vol. 1; Wiley, *Life of Johnny Reb,* 73.

47. Connelly, *Army of the Heartland,* 263–64; Inglis Diary, October 8, 1862; Holmes Steele, *"Battle of Perryville Oct. 8th 1862,"* in Maxwell Mss. Steele's memoir was probably based on the report describing the regiment's part in the battle. Though incomplete regarding some aspects of the battle, it remains an invaluable document because of the lack of a 3rd Florida report.

48. Miller, "Report of General Miller," 2; *Chattanooga Daily Rebel,* November 7, 1862; Wiley, *Life of Johnny Reb,* 88; McPherson, *For Cause and Comrades,* 44; Roy P. Grinker and John P. Spiegel, *Men under Stress* (Philadelphia: Blakiston, 1945), 44, quoted in McPherson, *For Cause and Comrades,* 32.

49. Inglis Diary, October 8, 1862; *Monticello Family Friend,* November 8, 1862.

50. Archie Livingston to My Dear Mother, October 27, 1862, in Coski, "'I Am in for Anything for Success,'" 77; Theodore Livingston to Dear Parents, October 11, 1862, Livingston/Inglis Letters; Hartman and Coles, *Biographical Rosters,* 1:39; 1860 U.S. Census (Free Schedule), Madison County, FL, p. 26, M653, Reel #108, family 59, dwelling 59, lines 17–24. Thomas Mosely, whose father was a Methodist minister, served as a lieutenant in the 1st Florida. He reenlisted in the 3rd Florida as a private.

51. *Official Records,* series I, vol. XVI, part I, 1033; Noe, *Perryville,* 218, 240.

52. The time of the beginning of the assault is surmised from Willie Bryant and Theodore Livingston's letters and the Holmes Steele report. Livingston and Bryant give the times for the attack as 1:00 and 2:00 P.M., respectively, while Steele gives 12:30. More than likely this is the time the brigade came under fire from the artillery. I base my account of the way in which the battle raged on the Livingston letter and Hemming memoir. While Livingston writes that several charges occurred, Hemming alludes to at least two. Steele also records that Brown's brigade was partially withdrawn to replenish its ammunition.

53. Hemming, "The War of 1861 and Its Causes"; Ellis, "A Short Record of Thomas Benton Ellis, Sr.," 3.

54. McKinnon, *History of Walton County,* chapter 39; *Monticello Family Friend,* November 8, 1862.

55. Willie Bryant to My dear mother, October 11, 1862, in Blakey, Lainhart, and Stephens, *Rose Cottage Chronicles,* 158; *Monticello Family Friend,* November 8, 1862.

56. Miller, "Report of General Miller," 3; *Tallahassee Florida Sentinel,* November 11, 1862.

57. Brush Diary, October 8, 1862; *Tallahassee Florida Sentinel,* November 11, 1862.

58. Noe, *Perryville,* 265–66; Steele, "*Battle of Perryville Oct. 8th 1862*"; Miller, "Report of General Miller," 3; Inglis Diary, October 8, 1862; Theodore Livingston to Dear Parents, October 11, 1862, MOC, Richmond, VA; Willie Bryant to My own dear Mother, November 1, 1862, Stephens Family Papers, 1850–1930, P. K. Yonge Library of Florida History, Gainesville, and in Blakey, Lainhart, and Stephens, *Rose Cottage Chronicles;* Wiley, *Life of Johnny Reb,* 339.

59. *Monticello Family Friend,* November 8, 1862; Inglis, "Commander Florida Division, U.C.V."; Miller, "Report of General Miller," 3; Theodore Livingston to Dear Parents, October 11, 1862, Livingston/Inglis Letters; Steele, "*Battle of Perryville Oct. 8th 1862.*" Daniel Bird's brother Pickens died at Cold Harbor in June 1864.

60. Theodore Livingston to Dear Parents, October 11, 1862.

61. Ibid.; Willie Bryant to My own dear mother, November 1, 1862, in Blakey, Lainhart, and Stephens, *Rose Cottage Chronicles,* 167; Noe, *Perryville,* 312.

62. Brush Diary, October 8, 1862; Theodore Livingston to Dear Parents, October 11, 1862; Inglis Diary, October 8, 1862.

63. Noe, *Perryville,* 312–13, 421; McWhiney, *Braxton Bragg,* 1:319–20.

64. Miller, "Report of General Miller," 4; Inglis Diary, October 8, 1862; Willie Bryant to My own dear Mother, November 1, 1862.

65. *Tallahassee Florida Sentinel,* November 11, 1862; *Monticello Family Friend,* November 8, 1862. The 41st Mississippi carried 427 soldiers into the fight and suffered 90 casualties; see Noe, *Perryville,* 371. In the 3rd Florida the lieutenant colonel and three captains were wounded, as well as six lieutenants. One captain was killed. The 1st lost its major, two captains, and four lieutenants, all to wounds.

66. Hartman and Coles, *Biographical Rosters,* 1:137, 260–458; Zack Waters, "'In the Country of an Acknowledged Enemy'": The 7th Florida Regiment in East Tennessee," 8 (unpublished manuscript in the author's possession); Charlie C. Carlson, *The First Florida Cavalry Regiment, CSA* (New Smyrna, FL: Luthers, 1999), 28–30.

67. *Supplement to the Official Records,* 5:249, 315.

68. Willie Bryant to My dear mother, October 11, 1862, in Blakey, Lainhart, and Stephens, *Rose Cottage Chronicles,* 160; Steele, "*Battle of Perryville Oct. 8th 1862.*"

Chapter 9

1. Inglis Diary, October 9, 1862; McKinnon, *History of Walton County,* chapter 39.

2. McWhiney, *Braxton Bragg,* 1:321; Daniel, *Days of Glory,* 167.

3. Inglis Diary, October 16, 1862; Brush Diary, October 17, 1862; October 16 and 24, 1862, in Pasco, *Private Pasco,* 9;

4. Archie Livingston to My Dear Mother, October 27, 1862, in Coski, "'I Am in for Anything for Success,'" 76; Willie Bryant to My own dear Mother, November 1, 1862, in Blakey, Lainhart, and Stephens, *Rose Cottage Chronicles,* 167; October 26, 1862, in Pasco, *Private Pasco,* 12.

5. General Order, October 18, 1862, Records of the Department of East Tennessee, Orders and Circulars, 1861–1864, NA, Washington, DC; Casmero O. Bailey to Dear

Mother, October 31, 1862, Bailey Family Papers; William T. Stockton to Ju Stockton, October 21 and 28, 1862, in Ulmer, *The Letters of Will and Ju Stockton,* 138; Samuel D. McConnell to My darling Wife, November 12, 1862, McConnell Papers; *Chattanooga Daily Rebel,* November 22, 1862.

6. Willie Bryant to My own dear Mother, November 1, 1862, in Blakey, Lainhart, and Stephens, *Rose Cottage Chronicles,* 168; November 2, 1862, in Pasco, *Private Pasco,* 14.

7. *Official Records,* series IV, vol. I, 1099; Lowe, *Walker's Texas Division,* 26; Wiley, *Life of Johnny Reb,* 331; Middleton Diary, July 16, 1862. Only the 3rd and 4th Florida and 1st Florida Cavalry discharged non-conscripts. The 1st Florida Cavalry and 6th and 7th Florida had enlisted for three years.

8. October 29 and November 17, 1862, in Pasco, *Private Pasco,* 13; Brush Diary, November 1 and 2, 1862.

9. Thomas Lawrence Connelly, *Autumn of Glory: The Army of Tennessee, 1862–1865* (1971; reprint, Baton Rouge: Louisiana State University Press, 2001), 14–15; Peter Cozzens, *No Better Place to Die: The Battle of Stones River* (Urbana: University of Illinois Press, 1990), 7–8.

10. November 15, 16, 23, and 27, 1862, in Pasco, *Private Pasco,* 17–19.

11. Cozzens, *No Better Place to Die,* 7; Connelly, *Autumn of Glory,* 14; James Lee McDonough, *Stones River: Bloody Winter in Tennessee* (Knoxville: University of Tennessee Press, 1980), 3; Washington M. Ives Jr. to Dear Father, October 27, 1862, Ives Papers. In June 1862 Forrest attacked and defeated Murfreesboro's Union garrison.

12. Boatner, *The Civil War Dictionary,* 82–83; Warner, *Generals in Gray,* 34; Connelly, *Autumn of Glory,* 14.

13. Cozzens, *No Better Place to Die,* 38–40; *Official Records,* series I, vol. XX, part II, 439, 447–48, 456.

14. Warner, *Generals in Gray,* 246.

15. *Official Records,* series I, vol. XX, part II, 456; Crute, *Units of the Confederate States Army,* 241, 294, 315.

16. T. A. McDonell to Braxton Bragg, December 5, 1862; Thaddeus A. McDonell, *CSR,* Reel #27.

17. William Miller to unknown, November 17, 1862, Letters Received, Confederate Adjutant General, NA Microcopy M474, Reel #36.

18. Though the specific order combining the 1st and 3rd Florida regiments has long since disappeared, I used Special Orders No. 132, June 6, 1863, Orders and Circulars of William J. Hardee's Command, February 1863–March 1865, NA, Washington, DC, to piece together the consolidation process. Special Orders No. 1, December 19, 1862, Orders and Circulars, Department of Tennessee, 1862–1865, NA, Washington, DC, contains the first mention of the consolidation of the regiments. For the consolidation of companies, see Pasco, *Private Pasco,* 32, 47.

19. Archie Livingston to My dear Mother, October 27, 1862, in Coski, "'I Am in for Anything for Success,'" 77; B. L. Rice to Mother, December 14, 1862, Rice Letters; Willie Bryant to My dear Mother, November 14, 1862, in Blakey, Lainhart, and Stephens, *Rose Cottage Chronicles,* 170; Washington Ives to Dear Father, November 29, 1862, Ives Papers.

20. Mitchell, *Civil War Soldiers,* 66; Tracy J. Revels, *Grander in Her Daughters: Florida's*

Women during the Civil War (Columbia: University of South Carolina Press, 2004), 20–22; Wiley, *Life of Johnny Reb,* 99, 113;

21. Connelly, *Autumn of Glory,* 42; Cozzens, *No Better Place to Die,* 31; Jacob A. Lash to Missouri Tyson Lash, letter fragment, undated, Jacob A. Lash Letters (photocopy), Collection of Zack C. Waters, Rome, GA (hereafter Lash Letters). Lash's letter probably described the Christmas Eve party hosted by Louisiana and Kentucky officers.

22. Daniel, *Soldiering in the Army of Tennessee,* 96; Washington M. Ives to Sisters Fannie and Florence, January 14, 1863, Ives Papers; Henry T. Wright to Dear Laura, January 22, 1863, Henry T. Wright Letters, Special Collections, Robert Manning Strozier Library, Florida State University, Tallahassee (hereafter Wright Letters).

23. William D. Rogers to Dear Father and Mother, January 22, 1863, Rogers Letters.

24. Ellis, "A Short Record of T. B. Ellis, Sr.," 3.

25. The numbers of captives from each regiment are as follows: 3rd Florida, 81; 1st Florida Infantry, 52; 7th Florida, 50; 1st Florida Cavalry, 60; and 6th Florida Infantry, 79. The source for the 1st Florida Infantry, 3rd Florida, and 6th Florida Infantry is Hartman and Coles, *Biographical Rosters,* 1:1–137, 260–365, 2:578–679. The 1st Florida Cavalry numbers are from Carlson, *The 1st Florida Cavalry Regiment, CSA,* 28–30, and the 7th Florida's from Waters, "'In the Country of an Acknowledged Enemy,'" 8.

26. Gerald K. Prokopowicz, "Word of Honor: The Paroles System in the Civil War," *North & South* 6, no. 4 (May 2003): 26; *Official Records,* series II, vol. IV, 267–68; Wednesday, October 4 and 16, 1862, in Campbell, *Southern Service,* 50. The Union also confined its paroled soldiers to camps; see Prokopowicz, "Word of Honor," 29.

27. Reddick, *Seventy-Seven Years in Dixie,* 18; Ellis, "A Short Record of T. B. Ellis, Sr.," 2.

28. McKinnon, *History of Walton County,* chapter 39; Ellis, "A Short Record of T. B. Ellis, Sr.," 2.

29. Hartman and Coles, *Biographical Rosters,* 1:51.

30. Ellis, "A Short Record of T. B. Ellis, Sr.," 3; Michael O. Raysor to My Dear Wife, December 21 and 29, 1862, Raysor Family Correspondence; *Official Records,* series I, vol. XX, part 2, 453. See also *Chattanooga Daily Rebel,* January 22, 1863, for the publication of Exchange Notice No. 4.

31. Connelly, *Autumn of Glory,* 44; Daniel, *Days of Glory,* 193–95; Cozzens, *No Better Place to Die,* 48; McDonough, *Stones River,* 65.

32. Connelly, *Autumn of Glory,* 44, 46; Cozzens, *No Better Place to Die,* 55; McWhiney, *Braxton Bragg,* 1:346; Henry T. Wright to Dear Laura, January 23, 1863, Wright Letters; William D. Rogers to Dear Father and Mother, January 22, 1863, Rogers Letters.

33. Cozzens, *No Better Place to Die,* 59, 76; McDonough, *Stones River,* 79; McWhiney, *Braxton Bragg,* 1:350; Connelly, *Autumn of Glory,* 52.

34. Cozzens, *No Better Place to Die,* 83, 150–51; Washington M. Ives Jr. to Dear Sisters F & F, January 14, 1863, Ives Papers; Foote, *The Civil War,* 2:89.

35. Foote, *The Civil War,* 2:92; McWhiney, *Braxton Bragg,* 1:360; Cozzens, *No Better Place to Die,* 151; Daniel, *Days of Glory,* 216; McDonough, *Stones River,* 132–36.

36. McDonough, *Stones River,* 136–40; McWhiney, *Braxton Bragg,* 1:358–60; Cozzens, *No Better Place to Die,* 160–61; Connelly, *Autumn of Glory,* 59–60. Breckinridge's error only increased the enmity between the two men, which had simmered since the Kentucky Campaign.

37. Connelly, *Autumn of Glory,* 59–60; William C. Davis, *Breckinridge: Statesman, Soldier, Symbol* (Baton Rouge: Louisiana State University Press, 1974), 338; *Official Records,* series I, vol. XX, part I, 681; Washington M. Ives Jr. to Dear Sisters F & F, January 14, 1863, Ives Papers; William D. Rogers to Dear Father and Mother, January 22, 1863, Rogers Letters.

38. Washington M. Ives Jr. to Dear Sisters F & F, January 14, 1863.

39. Cozzens, *No Better Place to Die,* 164; *Official Records,* series I, vol. XX, part I, 812, 815, 817; Washington M. Ives Jr. to Dear Sisters F & F, January 14, 1863.

40. *Official Records,* series I, vol. XX, part I, 814; William D. Rogers to Dear Father and Mother, January 22, 1863.

41. *Official Records,* series I, vol. XX, part I, 477, 818; James M. Ray, "The Flags of the 4th Florida regiment" (unpublished manuscript in the author's possession).

42. *Official Records,* series I, vol. XX, part I, 812, 816, 819; Washington M. Ives Jr. to Dear Sisters F & F, January 14, 1863; Cozzens, *No Better Place to Die,* 166. Three companies of the 60th North Carolina advanced past the Cowan House; seven did not.

43. *Official Records,* series I, vol. XX, part I, 477; Washington M. Ives Jr. to Dear Sisters F & F, January 14, 1863; "Breckinridge's Division Charges; 4th Fla. Receives Baptism of Fire," *Atlanta Journal,* September 28, 1901.

44. Cozzens, *No Better Place to Die,* 165; Washington M. Ives Jr. to Dear Sisters F & F, January 14, 1863; "Breckinridge's Division Charges."

45. *Official Records,* series I, part XX, vol. 1, 679; "Breckinridge's Division Charges."

46. McDonough, *Stones River,* 152; Washington M. Ives Jr. to Dear Sisters F & F, January 14, 1863; "Breckinridge's Division Charges"; William D. Rogers to Dear Father and Mother, January 22, 1863.

47. Cozzens, *No Better Place to Die,* 174; Connelly, *Autumn of Glory,* 62; Daniel, *Days of Glory,* 218; McDonough, *Stones River,* 166.

48. Washington M. Ives Jr. to Dear Sisters F & F, January 14, 1863; "Breckinridge's Division Charges." Harris was a twenty-four-year-old native of Merriwether County, Georgia. See 1850 U.S. Census (Free Schedule), Merriwether County, GA, p. 339, family 1330, dwelling 1330, lines 18–24, NA Microcopy M432, Reel #77.

49. Connelly, *Autumn of Glory,* 62–63; McDonough, *Stones River,* 175; McWhiney, *Braxton Bragg,* 1:366; Cozzens, *No Better Place to Die,* 177; Davis, *Breckinridge,* 340.

50. Davis, *Breckinridge,* 341; Connelly, *Autumn of Glory,* 63; McDonough, *Stones River,* 177–79; McWhiney and Jamieson, *Attack and Die,* 60.

51. Washington M. Ives Jr. to Dear Sisters F & F, January 14, 1863; Davis, *Breckinridge,* 342; Warner, *Generals in Gray,* 104–5, 123–24, 241. Cozzens gives the distance between the lines as 150 yards.

52. Foote, *The Civil War,* 2:99; Cozzens, *No Better Place to Die,* 175, 185–86; McDonough, *Stones River,* 182, 188–89; Daniel, *Days of Glory,* 221; Connelly, *Autumn of Glory,* 65.

53. William D. Rogers to Dear Father and Mother, January 22, 1863; Cozzens, *No Better Place to Die,* 187, 191, 194–95; *Official Records,* series I, vol. XX, part I, 815, 817; "Breckinridge's Division Charges"; Ellis, "A Short Record of T. B. Ellis, Sr.," 4.

54. Daniel, *Days of Glory,* 222; McDonough, *Stones River,* 198; "Breckinridge's Division Charges"; *Official Records,* series I, vol. XX, part I, 816–17.

55. Albert Livingston to My Dear Mother, January 12, 1863, Livingston/Inglis Let-

ters; Ellis, "A Short Record of T. B. Ellis, Sr.," 4; Hartman and Coles, *Biographical Rosters,* 1:441.

56. Washington M. Ives Jr. to Dear Sisters F & F, January 14, 1863, and Washington M. Ives Jr. to Dear Sister Kate, September 29, 1863, Ives Papers; "Breckinridge's Division Charges." In "The Flags of the 4th Florida Regiment," Ray writes that the 4th Florida's flag had two streamers attached at the top of the staff; one was inscribed "In God We Trust" and the other "4th Fla." The latter was severed by fire and captured by an Ohio regiment.

57. *Official Records,* series I, vol. XX, part II, 817; Cozzens, *No Better Place to Die,* 195; Washington M. Ives Jr. to Dear Parents, January 22, 1863, Ives Papers; "Breckinridge's Division Charges"; Albert Livingston to My Dear Mother, January 12, 1863, Livingston/Inglis Letters. Buck and Ball, a combination of a .69 round and three buckshot, was commonly used in smoothbore muskets during the Civil War.

58. Ellis, "A Short Record of T. B. Ellis, Sr.," 4; William D. Rogers to Dear Father and Mother, January 22, 1863, Rogers Letters.

59. *Official Records,* series I, vol. XX, part II, 817, 824; Washington M. Ives Jr. to Dear Parents, January 22, 1863, Ives Papers; "Breckinridge's Division Charges."

60. *Official Records,* series I, vol. XX, part II, 813, 818; Washington M. Ives Jr. to Dear Parents, January 22, 1863.

61. *Official Records,* series I, vol. XX, part II, 679, 815, 817; General William Preston to Hon. James Seddon, July 14, 1863, in Miller, *CSR of Generals,* Reel #178; William D. Rogers to Dear Father and Mother, January 22, 1863, Rogers Letters; Hartman and Coles, *Biographical Rosters,* 1:456. Crute writes that the 4th Florida lost 42 percent of its strength at Murfreesboro, while the 1st and 3rd suffered losses of 26 percent. See Crute, *Units of the Confederate States Army,* 74, 76. Colonel Miller gained promotion to brigadier general in August 1864 and commanded the District of Florida until the end of the war. See Warner, *Generals in Gray,* 218.

62. Cozzens, *No Better Place to Die,* 200; McDonell Diary, January 4, 1863; William D. Rogers to Dear Father and Mother, January 22, 1863, Rogers Letters; Washington M. Ives Jr. to Dear Parents, January 22, 1863, Ives Papers; Albert Livingston to My Dear Mother, January 12, 1863, Livingston/Inglis Letters; Connelly, *Autumn of Glory,* 69. Cozzens writes that Bragg, fearing Rosecrans had received reinforcements, decided to retreat.

63. Washington M. Ives Jr. to Dear Parents, January 22, 1863; Daniel G. McLean to Miss Maggie Kate McKenzie, January 30, 1863, in Tucker, *McKenzie Correspondence,* 91.

Chapter 10

1. Connelly, *Autumn of Glory,* 24, 113–15; D. G. McLean to My Dear Aunt, January 28, 1863, McLean Family Papers. Connelly argues that Confederate Commissary Bureau agents combed this region for Robert E. Lee's Army of Northern Virginia, leaving Bragg's force shorthanded.

2. *Official Records,* series I, vol. XX, part II, 503; Daniel G. McLean to Miss Maggie Kate McKenzie, January 30, 1863; Henry T. Wright to My Dear Laura, February 13, 1863, Wright Letters; Francis R. Nicks to Dear Mike, March 9, 1863, Nicks Letters; D. G. McLean to My Dear Aunt, January 28, 1863; Daniel, *Soldiering in the Army of Tennessee,* 87. For more on Civil War winter encampments, see Wiley, *Life of Johnny Reb,* 59–62.

3. D. G. McLean to My Dear Aunt, January 28, 1863; Washington M. Ives Jr. to Dear Parents, January 22, 1863.

4. Daniel, *Soldiering in the Army of Tennessee,* 73; D. G. McLean to My Dear Aunt, January 28, 1863; Daniel G. McLean to Miss Maggie McKenzie, January 30, 1863; Joseph Jones, *Medical and Surgical Memoirs* (New Orleans: printed for the author by Clark and Hofeline, 1876–90), 1:650–66, quoted in Wiley, *Life of Johnny Reb,* 255; McDonell Diary, February 10, 1863.

5. Daniel, *Soldiering in the Army of Tennessee,* 73; Daniel G. McLean to Miss Maggie McKenzie, January 30, 1863; Jones, *Medical and Surgical Memoirs,* 1:650–66, quoted in Wiley, *Life of Johnny Reb,* 255; Ellis, "A Short Record of T. B. Ellis, Sr.," 4; Washington M. Ives Jr. to Dear Pa, January 26, 1863, Ives Papers; "Travels of the 4th Fla.," Ives Diary. Madison County soldier Sam Sessions was twenty-two in January 1863 and became Washington Ives's closest friend in the 4th Florida. See Hartman and Coles, *Biographical Rosters,* 1:395.

6. Lucius A. Church to Genl. S. Cooper, February 5, 1863, Lucius A. Church, *CSR,* Reel #47. Lucius Church enlisted in the 11th Florida and died in Madison on June 30, 1864. Hartman and Coles, *Biographical Rosters,* 1:26.

7. *Official Records,* series I, vol. XX, part II, 412; A. G. McLeod to Dear Mother, November 1, 1862, McLean Family Papers; J. J. Finley to My dear Sir, November 13, 1862, in G. Troup Maxwell, *CSR,* Reel #3; William T. Stockton to Ju Stockton, undated, in Ulmer, *The Correspondence of Will and Ju Stockton,* 142; Robert Bullock to My own dear darling, December 8, 1862, Bullock Papers.

8. Robert Tracy McKenzie, *Lincolnites and Rebels: A Divided Town in the American Civil War* (Oxford: Oxford University Press, 2006), 7, 13, 19; *Adventures of the Marion Hornets,* 30; Lt. James Hays to My Dear Wife, December 8, 1862, Hays Letters; Robert Bullock to My own dear darling, December 8, 1862.

9. Jonathan M. Atkins, *Parties, Politics, and the Sectional Conflict in Tennessee, 1832–1861* (Knoxville: University of Tennessee Press, 1997), 250; McKenzie, *Lincolnites and Rebels,* 44.

10. McKenzie, *Lincolnites and Rebels,* 38–39, 60, 64.

11. Ibid., 70; Fisher, *War at Every Door,* 39, 41; Atkins, *Parties, Politics, and Sectional Conflict in Tennessee,* 253.

12. McKenzie, *Lincolnites and Rebels,* 88–89, 93, 98; Fisher, *War at Every Door,* 50, 54, 61.

13. Fisher, *War at Every Door,* 69; James Hays to My Dear Wife and Children, August 20, 1862, Hays Letters; Robert Bullock to My Dear Wife, August 21, 1862, Bullock Papers; William T. Stockton to My dearest wife, August 22, 1862, in Ulmer, *The Correspondence of Will and Ju Stockton,* 124.

14. For more on Colonel Samuel P. Carter's December raid and the Confederate reaction, see *Official Records,* series I, vol. XX, part I, 88–131. For the dispersal of Davis's Brigade, see Samuel Darwin McConnell to My darling wife, December 19, 1862, McConnell Papers, and William T. Stockton to Ju Stockton, January 23, 1863, in Ulmer, *The Correspondence of Will and Ju Stockton,* 175. Regarding the fortifications built by the Florida troops at various locations in East Tennessee, see *Official Records,* series I, vol. XXIII, part II, 742–43.

15. *Official Records,* series I, vol. XXIII, part I, 385; *Supplement to the Official Records,*

5:303–9, 311–15, 317–18; A. G. McLeod to Dear Aunt Nancy, January 19, 1863, McLean Family Papers.

16. *Supplement to the Official Records,* 5:322–32; C. O. Bailey to Dear Mother, February 1, 1862, Bailey Family Papers; S. Darwin McConnell to My darling wife, December 19, 1862, Samuel D. McConnell Letters, P. K. Yonge Library of Florida History, Gainesville (hereafter McConnell Letters); *Adventures of the Marion Hornets,* 30–31.

17. John C. Inscoe and Gordon B. McKinney, *The Heart of Confederate Appalachia: Western North Carolina in the Civil War* (Chapel Hill: University of North Carolina Press, 2000), 118; Phillip Shaw Paludan, *Victims: A True Story of the Civil War* (Knoxville: University of Tennessee Press, 1991), 81–83; Lt. James Hays to Miss Sally Ann Hays, January 20, 1863, Hays Letters.

18. Paludan, *Victims,* 27; W.G.M. Davis to His Excellency Zebulon B. Vance, January 1863, in *Official Records,* series I, vol. XVIII, 810–11, quoted in Paludan, *Victims,* 89; *Official Records,* series I, vol. XVIII, 810, 853, and series II, vol. V, 841.

19. Paludan, *Victims,* 88, 90, 93, 97.

20. Ibid., 118–19; *Official Records,* series II, vol. V, 858, and series I, vol. XVIII, 853. My analysis of Davis's innocence is derived from Paludan's excellent study of the Shelton Laurel Massacre and his conclusion that General Henry Heth ordered the harsh retaliation.

21. *Official Records,* series II, vol. V, 811; *Supplement to the Official Records,* 5:312. For a list of Jackson's men who participated in the raid, see *Official Records,* series I, vol. XXIII, part II, 711.

22. March 1, 1863, in Henry McCall Holmes, *Diary of Henry McCall Holmes Army of Tennessee Assistant Surgeon Florida Troops with Related Letters Documents, Etc.* (State College, MS, 1968), 16; Hugh Black to Dear Wife, March 16, 1863, in Frano, *Letters of Captain Hugh Black to His Family,* 44.

23. Holmes, *Diary of Henry McCall Holmes,* 16; Charles S. Herring to Dear mother & family, March 15, 1863, in Tucker, *McKenzie Correspondence,* 92; *Supplement to the Official Records,* 5:312; *Official Records,* series I, vol. XXIII, part II, 662.

24. *Official Records,* series I, vol. XXIII, part II, 617.

25. Francis R. Nicks to Dear Mike, March 9, 1863, Nicks Letters; McDonell Diary, February 23, 1863; William D. Rogers to Dear Papa and Mother, April 10, 1863, Rogers Letters. See also April 14 and April 23, 1863, in Pasco, *Private Pasco,* 28–29.

26. Daniel, *Soldiering in the Army of Tennessee,* 24; William D. Rogers to Dear Papa and Mother, April 10, 1863; April 18, 1863, in Pasco, *Private Pasco,* 28–29; Roderick G. Shaw to My Dear Sister, May 17, 1863, Shaw Letters.

27. William D. Rogers to Dear Papa and Mother, April 17, 1863, Rogers Letters; Daniel, *Soldiering in the Army of Tennessee,* 24.

28. April 26, 1863, in Pasco, *Private Pasco,* 30–31; Henry T. Wright to Dear Laura, May 9, 1863, Wright Letters; William D. Rogers to Dear Papa and Mother, April 17, 1863; Roderick G. Shaw to My Dear Sister, May 17, 1863, Shaw Letters. For the popularity of sports, hunting, and card games in the Confederate Army, see Wiley, *Life of Johnny Reb,* 159–61.

29. For more on the revivals in the Confederate armies, see Gorrell Clinton Prim Jr., "Born Again in the Trenches: Revivalism in the Confederate Army" (Ph.D. diss., Florida State University, 1982); Drew Gilpin Faust, "Christian Soldiers: The Meaning of Revival-

ism in the Confederate Army," *Journal of Southern History* 53, no. 1 (1987): 63–90; Steven E. Woodworth, *While God Is Marching On: The Religious World of Civil War Soldiers* (Lawrence: University of Kansas Press, 2001); Wiley, *Life of Johnny Reb,* 180–85. For religion in the Army of Tennessee, see Daniel, *Soldiering in the Army of Tennessee,* 115–25.

30. Faust, "Christian Soldiers," 64; William A. Bennett, *A Narrative of the Great Revival which Prevailed in the Southern Armies during the late Civil War between the States of the Federal Union* (Philadelphia: Claxton, Remson, and Haffelfinger, 1877), 262, quoted in Prim, "Born Again in the Trenches," 25; Woodworth, *While God Is Marching On,* 160, 204; Daniel, *Soldiering in the Army of Tennessee,* 119.

31. Daniel, *Soldiering in the Army of Tennessee,* 119; Washington M. Ives to Dear Pa, January 26, 1863, Ives Papers; April 12, 1863, in Pasco, *Private Pasco,* 28.

32. Daniel, *Soldiering in the Army of Tennessee,* 116; Michael O. Raysor to My Dear Wife, May 17, 1863, Raysor Family Correspondence. In 1863 the Florida regiments' chaplains were William J. Duval of the 1st and 3rd Florida and Robert L. Wiggins of the 4th Florida. See Robertson, *Soldiers of Florida,* 102, 120, 156, 171. The 6th and 7th both gained new chaplains during 1863 who would serve at least through the Atlanta Campaign.

33. Hugh Black to Dear Wife, March 16, 1863, in Frano, *Letters of Captain Hugh Black to His Family,* 44; Robert Bullock to Amanda Bullock, May 23, 1863, Bullock Papers; Woodworth, *While God Is Marching On,* 160–61, 163; James Hays to Mrs. S. A. Hays, June 17, 1863, Hays Letters.

34. Faust, "Christian Soldiers," 73; Woodworth, *While God Is Marching On,* 218; Saturday, August 8, and Thursday, August 20, 1863, in Campbell, *Southern Service,* 65.

35. Wiley, *Life of Johnny Reb,* 191; Prim, "Born Again in the Trenches," 36.

36. Samuel D. McConnell to My darling Wife, November 12, 1862, McConnell Papers; Madison Starke Perry to Gen. S. Cooper, May 1, 1863, in Madison Starke Perry, *CSR,* Reel #79.

37. Madison Starke Perry to Gen. S. Cooper, May 1, 1863, in Madison Starke Perry, *CSR,* Reel #79; Casmero O. Bailey to Dear Father, May 9, 1863, Bailey Family Papers.

38. Robert Bullock to My darling wife, November 1, 1863, Bullock Papers; Casmero O. Bailey to Dear Father, May 9, 1863; Thursday, December 3, 1863, in Campbell, *Southern Service on Land and Sea,* 90.

39. W.G.M. Davis to Adjutant General Samuel Cooper, April 24, 1863, *CSR of Generals,* Reel #73; *Official Records,* series I, vol. XXIII, part II, 747; Connelly, *Autumn of Glory,* 107.

40. *Official Records,* series I, vol. XXIII, part II, 809; "Col. Robert C. Trigg, of Virginia," *Confederate Veteran* 17 (1909): 65.

41. Boatner, *The Civil War Dictionary,* 719–20; *Official Records,* series I, vol. XXIII, part II, 431; McKenzie, *Lincolnites and Rebels,* 146.

42. *Official Records,* series I, vol. XXIII, part I, 387, 392; *Atlanta Southern Confederacy,* July 3, 1863; June 20, 1863, in Campbell, *Southern Service,* 59; McKenzie, *Lincolnites and Rebels,* 146–47; Hugh Black to Dear Wife, June 24, 1863, in Frano, *Letters of Captain Hugh Black to His Family,* 54.

43. *Official Records,* series I, vol. XXIII, part I, 387, 391–92; *Atlanta Southern Confederacy,* July 3, 1863; June 20, 1863, in Campbell, *Southern Service,* 59.

44. Hugh Black to Dear Wife, June 24, 1863, in Frano, *Letters of Captain Hugh Black to*

His Family, 54; Benjamin Glover to Dear Betty, June 9, 1863, Benjamin R. Glover Letters, Alabama Department of Archives and History, Montgomery (hereafter Glover Letters).

45. Hugh Black to Dear Wife, June 24, 1863, in Frano, *Letters of Captain Hugh Black to His Family,* 54; James Hays to Mrs. S. A. Hays, June 24, 1863, Hays Letters.

46. *Official Records,* series I, vol. XXIII, part I, 388.

Chapter 11

1. *Official Records,* series I, vol. XXIII, part II, 849; May 23, 1863, in Pasco, *Private Pasco,* 35.

2. Connelly, *Autumn of Glory,* 81; Stanley Horn, *The Army of Tennessee* (1941; reprint, Norman: University of Oklahoma Press, 1993), 189.

3. May 1, 1863, in Pasco, *Private Pasco,* 31–32.

4. Boatner, *The Civil War Dictionary,* 668. For more on the Preston-Breckinridge-Bragg feud, see Connelly, *Autumn of Glory.*

5. May 25, 1863, in Pasco, *Private Pasco,* 36.

6. May 25–26, 1863, in Pasco, *Private Pasco,* 36.

7. May 25–26, 1863, in Pasco, *Private Pasco,* 36–37; Theodore Livingston to My Dear Mother, May 26, 1863, Livingston/Inglis Letters; May 26–27, 1863, in Pasco, *Private Pasco,* 36–37. Washington Ives wrote of Tennessee, "You dont have any idea what a state of destruction pervades the whole state. I cant see what the Women and children live on . . . the last harvest time they had nothing to eat." See Washington Ives to Dear Parents, January 22, 1863, Ives Papers.

8. May 28, 1863, in Pasco, *Private Pasco,* 37.

9. *Official Records,* series I, vol. XXIV, part I, 56. For an in-depth study on the campaign to seize Vicksburg, see Michael B. Ballard, *Vicksburg: The Campaign That Opened the Mississippi* (Chapel Hill: University of North Carolina Press, 2004).

10. *Official Records,* series I, vol. XXIV, part I, 242; Benjamin R. Wynne, *A Hard Trip: A History of the 15th Mississippi* (Macon, GA: Mercer University Press, 2003), 107.

11. Michael O. Raysor to My Dear Wife, May 31, 1863, Raysor Family Correspondence.

12. Boatner, *The Civil War Dictionary,* 810; June 5, 1863, in Pasco, *Private Pasco,* 39.

13. June 5, 1863, in Pasco, *Private Pasco,* 39; *Official Records,* series I, vol. XXIV, part III, 942; Michael O. Raysor to My Dear Wife, June 25, 1863, Raysor Family Correspondence.

14. Michael O. Raysor to My Dear Wife, June 25, 1863; William L. Shea and Terrence J. Winschel, *Vicksburg Is the Key: The Struggle for the Mississippi River* (Lincoln: University of Nebraska Press, 2003), 156; William D. Rogers to Father and Mother, June 23, 1863, Rogers Letters; June 5 and 7, 1863, in Pasco, *Private Pasco,* 39–40.

15. Horn, *The Army of Tennessee,* 217–18; Shea and Winschel, *Vicksburg Is the Key,* 168; Terrence J. Winschel, "A Tragedy of Errors: The Failure of the Confederate High Command in the Defense of Vicksburg," *North and South* 8, no. 7 (2006): 47. For two works on the Jefferson Davis–Joseph Johnston feud, which had a great impact on the Civil War in the Western Theater, see William C. Davis, *Jefferson Davis: The Man and His Hour* (New

York: HarperCollins, 1991) and Craig L. Symonds, *Joseph E. Johnston: A Civil War Biography* (New York: W. W. Norton, 1992).

16. Symonds, *Joseph E. Johnston,* 215; Michael O. Raysor to My Dear Wife, June 25, 1863. The feud between Johnston and Davis continued long after the war ended.

17. William D. Rogers to Father and Mother, June 23, 1863, Rogers Letters.

18. June 23 and July 1, 1863, in Pasco, *Private Pasco,* 42–43; *Official Records,* series I, vol. XXIV, part I, 985.

19. Hemming, "The War of 1861 and Its Causes."

20. Michael O. Raysor to My Dear Wife, July 3, 1863, Raysor Family Correspondence; July 1, 1863, in Pasco, *Private Pasco,* 44.

21. Nathaniel Cheairs Hughes Jr., *The Pride of the Confederate Artillery: The Washington Artillery in the Army of Tennessee* (Baton Rouge: Louisiana State University Press, 1997), 107; Edwin C. Bearss, *The Siege of Jackson, July 10–17, 1863* (Baltimore: Gateway Press, 1981), 55.

22. July 7, 1863, in Pasco, *Private Pasco,* 45; Bearss, *The Siege of Jackson,* 63.

23. Bearss, *The Siege of Jackson,* 57–58.

24. July 7, 1863, in Pasco, *Private Pasco,* 45.

25. July 9, 1863, in Pasco, *Private Pasco,* 46.

26. Hughes, *The Pride of the Confederate Artillery,* 108; Crute, *Units of the Confederate States Army,* 136–37.

27. July 10, 1863, in Pasco, *Private Pasco,* 46–47; Michael B. Dougan, "Herrmann Hirsch and the Siege of Jackson," *Journal of Mississippi History* 53, no. 3 (1991): 25.

28. Hemming, "The War of 1861 and Its Causes," 60, 62.

29. *Official Records,* series I, vol. XXIV, part III, 496, 502–3.

30. July 12, 1863, in Pasco, *Private Pasco,* 47.

31. Dougan, "Herrmann Hirsch and the Siege of Jackson," 19.

32. Hemming, "The War of 1861 and Its Causes," 61; July 12, 1863, in Pasco, *Private Pasco,* 47.

33. Boatner, *The Civil War Dictionary,* 674; Bearss, *The Siege of Jackson,* 84–85; *Official Records,* series I, vol. XXIV, part II, 604.

34. *Official Records,* series I, vol. XXIV, part III, 503–4; Boatner, *The Civil War Dictionary,* 472. For more on the activities of Jacob Lauman and Isaac Pugh during the war, see Woodworth, *Nothing But Victory.*

35. *Official Records,* series I, vol. XXIV, part II, 603–4.

36. Ellis, "A Short Record of Thomas Benton Ellis, Sr.," 6; Hemming, "The War of 1861 and Its Causes"; Rinaldo Pugh to My dear Mother, July 26, 1863, Isaac Pugh Papers (mss. 104), Special Collections, University of California, Riverside.

37. July 12, 1863, in Pasco, *Private Pasco,* 47; Ellis, "A Short Record of Thomas Benton Ellis, Sr.," 6; Hughes, *The Pride of the Confederate Artillery,* 114–15.

38. July 12, 1863, in Pasco, *Private Pasco,* 47; Hemming, "The War of 1861 and Its Causes," 63; Ellis, "A Short Record of Thomas Benton Ellis, Sr.," 6–7.

39. *Official Records,* series I, vol. XXIV, part II, 547, 604, and part III, 1001; *Richmond Daily Dispatch,* July 25, 1863; Bearss, *The Siege of Jackson,* 87. See also the *Mobile Register and Advertiser,* July 15, 1863.

40. *Official Records,* series I, vol. XXIV, part II, 654 and part III, 506; Clarence W. Smith, "Private Pasco," *Private Pasco,* 184, reprinted from Ben LaBree, ed., *Camp Fires of the Confederacy: A Volume of Humerous Anecdotes, Reminiscences, Deeds of Heroism, Etc.* (Louisville: Courier Journal Printing Company, 1898), 199–202.

41. Samuel Pasco, "Untitled Handwritten Manuscript, 1909," UDC Scrapbooks, vol. 1; July 13, 1863, in Pasco, *Private Pasco,* 48.

42. July 13, 1863, in Pasco, *Private Pasco,* 48; Pasco, "Untitled Handwritten Manuscript, 1909."

43. Smith, "Private Pasco," 185; Pasco, "Untitled Handwritten Manuscript, 1909."

44. *Official Records,* series I, vol. XXIV, part III, 1002; July 14, 1863, in Pasco, *Private Pasco,* 48–49. During the truce, Pasco became friendly with C. T. Lee of the 25th Illinois and asked the Yankee to forward a letter to *his* parents in Massachusetts. The two became reacquainted at a National Democratic Committee meeting in 1888 and began a long-lasting friendship. See *Jacksonville (FL) Times-Union,* June 16, 1888.

45. July 16 and August 26, 1863, in Pasco, *Private Pasco,* 49, 57.

46. Michael O. Raysor to My Dear Wife, July 22, 1863, Raysor Family Correspondence.

47. Mrs. Edward Badger to Judge Ives, March 28, 1906, Ives Papers.

48. Howard Michael Madaus and Robert D. Needham, illus., *The Battle Flags of the Confederate Army of Tennessee* (Milwaukee: Milwaukee Public Museum, 1976), 120, compliments of Bruce Graetz, curator and historian, Florida Museum of History, Tallahassee. The flag of the 1st and 3rd Florida, Consolidated, is in possession of the MOC, Richmond, VA.

Chapter 12

1. *Official Records,* series I, vol. XXIV, part I, 208, 246; Connelly, *Autumn of Glory,* 147.

2. *Official Records,* series I, vol. XXIV, part III, 1008; July 16, 1863, in Pasco, *Private Pasco,* 49. Thomas Connelly writes that Johnston took up this position so as to block Federal incursions into the important food-producing and industrial area of central Alabama. See *Autumn of Glory,* 147.

3. July 23, 1863, in Pasco, *Private Pasco,* 51; *Official Records,* series I, vol. XXIV, part II, 528–30. Washington Ives claims that Camp Hurricane was south of Morton. However, Samuel Pasco's description and the actual position of Hurricane Creek place the encampment between Morton and Canton.

4. Washington M. Ives Jr. to Dear Father, August 1, 1863, Ives Papers; July 28, 1863, in Pasco, *Private Pasco,* 53.

5. Washington M. Ives Jr. to Dear Father, August 1, 1863, and to Dear M[other], August 8, 1863, Ives Papers; Thomas W. Patton to My Dear Mother, July 29, 1863, in Christopher M. Watford, ed., *The Civil War in North Carolina: Soldiers' and Civilians' Letters and Diaries, 1861–1865,* vol. 2, *The Mountains* (Jefferson, NC: McFarland and Company, 2003), 117.

6. *Official Records,* series I, vol. XXIV, part II, 1027–28; July 26, 1863, in Pasco, *Private Pasco,* 52; Washington M. Ives Jr. to Dear M[other], August 8, 1863, and to Dear Sis-

ters, August 11, 1863, Ives Papers; M. O. Raysor to My Dear Wife, August 19, 1863, Raysor Family Correspondence.

7. Washington M. Ives Jr. to Dear Mother, August 12, 1863, Ives Papers; August 22, 1863, in Pasco, *Private Pasco,* 56.

8. *Tallahassee Florida Sentinel,* September 8, 1863.

9. August 24, 1863, in Pasco, *Private Pasco,* 57; *Official Records,* series I, vol. XXX, part IV, 507; Washington M. Ives Jr. to Dear Father, August 19, 1863, Ives Papers.

10. Daniel, *Days of Glory,* 287–88, 290–91; Steven E. Woodworth, *Six Armies in Tennessee: The Chickamauga and Chattanooga Campaigns* (Lincoln: University of Nebraska Press, 1998), 53–54, 62. For the Confederates' botched reaction to Rosecrans's offensive, see chapter 8 in Connelly, *Autumn of Glory.*

11. *Official Records,* series I, vol. XXX, part IV, 529, 541, 547; Connelly, *Autumn of Glory,* 149.

12. August 26–September 1, 1863, in Pasco, *Private Pasco,* 57–59; Washington M. Ives Jr. to Dear Father, September 4, 1863, Ives Papers.

13. Connelly, *Autumn of Glory,* 149. For the East Tennessee troops' movement to Tullahoma, see Saturday, June 27, 1863–Sunday, July 5, 1863, in Campbell, *Southern Service,* 60–62, and Hardy Herring to Dear Pa, Ma & Family, June 29, 1863, in Tucker, *McKenzie Correspondence,* 96–97.

14. Connelly, *Autumn of Glory,* 149–50, 168; Hugh Black to Dear Mary, August 27, 1863, in Frano, *The Civil War Letters of Captain Hugh Black to His Family,* 58; William T. Stockton to My Dearest Wife, September 3, 1863, in Ulmer, *The Letters of Will and Ju Stockton,* 220. By September 1863, the 1st Florida Cavalry's companies that initially retained their mounts joined their regiment as infantrymen.

15. Connelly, *Autumn of Glory,* 164, 169, 173; Daniel, *Days of Glory,* 290; Woodworth, *Six Armies in Tennessee,* 56–57, 66–67; Peter Cozzens, *This Terrible Sound: The Battle of Chickamauga* (Urbana: University of Illinois Press, 1992), 55–56.

16. Connelly, *Autumn of Glory,* 159; September 11, 1863, in Holmes, *Diary of Henry McCall Holmes,* 17.

17. Connelly, *Autumn of Glory,* 189, 198–99; Cozzens, *This Terrible Sound,* 97. For the McLemore's Cove debacle, see Connelly, *Autumn of Glory,* 177–85; Cozzens, *This Terrible Sound,* 65–75. For a Federal perspective, see Daniel, *Days of Glory,* 301–3.

18. *Official Records,* series I, vol. XXX, part I, 721, and part II, 429, 435; Cozzens, *This Terrible Sound,* 119; Saturday, September 19, 1863, in Campbell, *Southern Service,* 70; September 19, 1863, in Holmes, *Diary of Henry McCall Holmes,* 18.

19. *Official Records,* series I, vol. XXX, part II, 429, 435; Benjamin R. Glover to Dear Betty, September 22, 1863, Glover Letters; James Hays to Mrs. S. A. Hays, August 22, 1863, Hays Letters.

20. Connelly, *Autumn of Glory,* 206–7; Cozzens, *This Terrible Sound,* 205; William T. Stockton to My own darling Wife, September 21, 1863, in Ulmer, *The Correspondence of Will and Ju Stockton,* 225.

21. Steven E. Woodworth, *Chickamauga: A Battlefield Guide* (Lincoln: University of Nebraska Press, 1999), 25; Cozzens, *This Terrible Sound,* 198. A year earlier John T. Wilder had surrendered the Mumfordsville garrison to Braxton Bragg's army.

22. William T. Stockton to My own darling Wife, September 21, 1863; *Official Records,* series I, vol. XXX, part II, 433.

23. William T. Stockton to My own darling Wife, September 21, 1863; *Official Records,* series I, vol. XXX, part II, 433; Cozzens, *This Terrible Sound,* 205.

24. Connelly, *Autumn of Glory,* 193–94, 205–6; Foote, *The Civil War,* 2:717.

25. Connelly, *Autumn of Glory,* 151, 203, 205–6; Daniel, *Days of Glory,* 320; Cozzens, *This Terrible Sound,* 200; Woodworth, *Chickamauga,* 25.

26. Cozzens, *This Terrible Sound,* 202, 205, 207, 208; Casmero Bailey to Dear Father, September 27, 1863, Bailey Family Papers; *Official Records,* series I, vol. XXX, part II, 430.

27. *Official Records,* series I, vol. XXX, part II, 430, 435; Casmero Bailey to Dear Father, September 27, 1863; Cozzens, *This Terrible Sound,* 215–16, 218; *Tallahassee Florida Sentinel,* October 6, 1863.

28. *Tallahassee Florida Sentinel,* October 6, 1863; Saturday, September 19, 1863, in Campbell, *Southern Service,* 70; Casmero Bailey to Dear Father, September 27, 1863; Cozzens, *This Terrible Sound,* 218–19.

29. Cozzens, *This Terrible Sound,* 218–19; *Official Records,* series I, vol. XXX, part II, 435; Hugh Black to Dear wife, September 24, 1863, in Frano, *The Civil War Letter of Captain Hugh Black to His Family,* 58; *Tallahassee Florida Sentinel,* October 6, 1863; Benjamin R. Glover to Dear Betty, September 22, 1863, Glover Letters.

30. Saturday, September 19, 1863, in Campbell, *Southern Service,* 72; Casmero Bailey to Dear Father, September 27, 1863.

31. *Official Records,* series I, vol. XXX, part II, 436; *Tallahassee Florida Sentinel,* October 6, 1863; Jacob Yearty to Dear Father and Mother, September 22, 1863, Jacob Yearty Letter, P. K. Yonge Library of Florida History, Gainesville (hereafter Yearty Letter); Casmero Bailey to Dear Mother, September 21, 1863, Bailey Family Papers. While the 6th Florida lost 165 soldiers on September 19, it is impossible to determine how many troops the regiments carried into battle. Evidently, the 6th Florida had not suffered from disease to the extent the 1st Florida Cavalry or 7th Florida Infantry had, for the regiment drew rations for 320 men on November 21. See T. J. Robertson to Benjamin R. Glover, November 21, 1863, Glover Letters.

32. Hughes, *The Pride of the Confederate Artillery,* 122–27; September 19 and 20, 1863, in Pasco, *Private Pasco,* 64; McKinnon, *History of Walton County,* chapter 41.

33. Cozzens, *This Terrible Sound,* 300, 303; Connelly, *Autumn of Glory,* 208–9; Woodworth, *Six Armies in Tennessee,* 105; Davis, *Breckinridge,* 370.

34. Connelly, *Autumn of Glory,* 220–21; Cozzens, *This Terrible Sound,* 320; September 20, 1863, in Pasco, *Private Pasco,* 64.

35. *Official Records,* series I, vol. XXX, part II, 232, 235.

36. September 20, 1863, in Pasco, *Private Pasco,* 64; Cozzens, *This Terrible Sound,* 325.

37. Cozzens, *This Terrible Sound,* 332.

38. *Official Records,* series I, vol. XXX, part II, 233–34; Cozzens, *This Terrible Sound,* 332.

39. Woodworth, *Six Armies in Tennessee,* 108; Cozzens, *This Terrible Sound,* 332–35; September 20, 1863, in Pasco, *Private Pasco,* 65; *Official Records,* series I, vol. XXX, part II, 234–35; *Official Records,* series I, vol. XXX, part I, 570, quoted in Cozzens, *This Terrible Sound,* 335.

40. Woodworth, *Six Armies in Tennessee,* 110–11; September 20, 1863, in Pasco, *Private Pasco,* 65; *Official Records,* series I, vol. XXX, part II, 205, 219, 234, 235, 238, 239.

41. Davis, *Breckinridge,* 376; Daniel, *Days of Glory,* 326; Woodworth, *Six Armies in Tennessee,* 114; Foote, *The Civil War,* 2:736.

42. Connelly, *Autumn of Glory,* 224; Woodworth, *Six Armies in Tennessee,* 122; Daniel, *Days of Glory,* 331.

43. September 20, 1863, in Campbell, *Southern Service,* 73; Cozzens, *This Terrible Sound,* 471, 483; *Official Records,* series I, vol. XXX, part II, 436.

44. *Official Records,* series I, vol. XXX, part II, 437; Daniel, *Days of Glory,* 335; Mrs. J. B. Tutwiler, "Lieut. John Wilson on Snodgrass Hill," *Confederate Veteran* 21 (1913): 62.

45. Casmero Bailey to Dear Father, September 27, 1863.

46. William T. Stockton to My own darling Wife, September 21, 1863; *Official Records,* series I, vol. XXX, part II, 434.

47. Cozzens, *This Terrible Sound,* 503; Sunday, September 20, 1863, in Campbell, *Southern Service,* 73–74.

48. Casmero Bailey to Dear Father, September 27, 1863; Woodworth, *Six Armies in Tennessee,* 128; *Official Records,* series I, vol. XXX, part II, 432. Jacob Yearty listed the number of prisoners as 465, while Benjamin Glover claimed the two regiments seized 800 captives. Both Colonel Finley and Lieutenant Colonel Wade of the 54th Virginia estimated 500 taken by their regiments, and Bullock reported that the 7th Florida seized 150.

49. Woodworth, *Six Armies in Tennessee,* 127; Connelly, *Autumn of Glory,* 225; McKinnon, *History of Walton County,* chapter 41; September 20, 1863, in Pasco, *Private Pasco,* 65. See also Roddie Shaw to My Dear Sister, October 8, 1863, Shaw Letters. Colonel Dilworth obviously used Pasco's diary as a reference when writing his official report of the battle.

50. September 20, 1863, in Pasco, *Private Pasco,* 65; September 20, 1863, in Campbell, *Southern Service,* 73; Washington M. Ives Jr. to Dear Parents, September 27, 1863, Ives Papers; Jacob Yearty to Dear father and mother, September 22, 1863, Yearty Letter; Michael O. Raysor Obituary, Raysor Family Correspondence.

51. Cozzens, *This Terrible Sound,* 534; Michael O. Raysor Obituary, Raysor Family Correspondence.

52. J.S.M. Davidson to My Dear Madam, December 7, 1863, in Ulmer, *The Correspondence of Will and Ju Stockton,* 241.

53. Connelly, *Autumn of Glory,* 143.

Chapter 13

1. September 21 and 22, 1863, in Pasco, *Private Pasco,* 65. In the weeks prior to Chickamauga, Braxton Bragg ordered that details perform the cooking for each regiment. Quartermaster Sergeant Washington Ives commanded the 4th Florida's detachment. See Daniel, *Soldiering in the Army of Tennessee,* 61–62, Washington M. Ives to Dear Parents, September 27, 1863, Ives Papers, and Roderick G. Shaw to My Dear Sister, October 8, 1863, Shaw Letters, for this new system.

2. Jacob Yearty to Dear father and mother, September 22, 1863; Monday, September 21 and Wednesday, September 23, 1863, in Campbell, *Southern Service,* 73; Septem-

ber 21 and 23, 1863, in Holmes, *Diary of Henry McCall Holmes,* 18; September 23, 1863, in Pasco, *Private Pasco,* 66.

3. Wiley Sword, *Mountains Touched with Fire: Chattanooga Besieged, 1863* (New York: St. Martin's Press, 1993), 39, 42; Daniel, *Days of Glory,* 342; Connelly, *Autumn of Glory,* 233, 234; Horn, *The Army of Tennessee,* 281–82; Peter Cozzens, *The Shipwreck of Their Hopes: The Battles for Chattanooga* (Urbana: University of Illinois Press, 1994), 16–18. Sword reasoned that Bragg was indeed serious about either threatening the Federal depot at Bridgeport, Alabama, or driving Ambrose Burnside from East Tennessee. Eventually he decided to send James Longstreet's I Corps toward Knoxville. See Sword, *Mountains Touched with Fire,* 75–80.

4. Hughes, *The Pride of the Confederate Artillery,* 151; Sword, *Mountains Touched with Fire,* 91; September 24–26, 1863, in Pasco, *Private Pasco,* 66; Roderick G. Shaw to My Dear Sister, October 10, 1863, Shaw Letters; Jacob A. Lash to My Dear Wife, September 29, 1863, Lash Letters; September 25, 1863, in Holmes, *Diary of Henry McCall Holmes,* 18. In 1863 the 1st and 3rd, 4th, and 7th Florida infantry regiments all maintained regimental bands and after its creation that November, the Florida Brigade also had a band. See Washington M. Ives to Dear Father, August 10, 1863, Ives Papers, and Robert Bullock to Sweetness, June 9, 1863, Bullock Papers.

5. October 10, 1863, in Pasco, *Private Pasco,* 69; Roderick G. Shaw to My Dear Sister, October 10, 1863, Shaw Letters; Robert Bullock to My dear little wife, October 11, 1863, Bullock Papers; Saturday, October 10, 1863, in Campbell, *Southern Service,* 76; Washington M. Ives Jr. to Dear Mother, November 5, 1863, Ives Papers.

6. Judith Lee Hallock, *Braxton Bragg and Confederate Defeat: Volume II* (Tuscaloosa: The University of Alabama Press, 1991), 89–91, 98; Connelly, *Autumn of Glory,* 237; Sword, *Mountains Touched with Fire,* 31. Chief among these detractors was Lieutenant General James Longstreet, who hoped to gain command of the Army of Tennessee.

7. Connelly, *Autumn of Glory,* 245; Hallock, *Braxton Bragg and Confederate Defeat,* 98; James Lee McDonough, *Chattanooga: A Death Grip on the Confederacy* (Knoxville: University of Tennessee Press, 1984), 36; Sword, *Mountains Touched with Fire,* 64.

8. Sword, *Mountains Touched with Fire,* 64; Hallock, *Braxton Bragg and Confederate Defeat,* 109; Connelly, *Autumn of Glory,* 247–48, 251; McDonough, *Chattanooga,* 32; Cozzens, *The Shipwreck of Their Hopes,* 25; Davis, *Breckinridge,* 380, 384.

9. Connelly, *Autumn of Glory,* 126–27; Zack C. Waters, *Death Was Feasting in Our Midst: Major General William B. Bate and the Battle of Dallas, Georgia* (Hiram, GA: Friends of Civil War Paulding County, Georgia, 2003), 4; Steven E. Woodworth, *This Grand Spectacle: The Battle of Chattanooga* (Abilene, KS: McWhiney Foundation Press, 1999), 86; Cozzens, *The Shipwreck of Their Hopes,* 26; Warner, *Generals in Gray,* 19; Boatner, *The Civil War Dictionary,* 49–50.

10. Washington M. Ives Jr. to Dear Sister Kate, September 29, 1863, Ives Papers; *Tallahassee Florida Sentinel,* November 17, 1863; Roderick G. Shaw to Dear Sister, October 8, 1863, Shaw Letters. By October 1863 the 4th Florida fielded fewer than two hundred soldiers while the 7th still mustered more than four hundred.

11. Robert Bullock to My dear little wife, October 11, 1863, Bullock Papers.

12. Amanda Waterman Bullock to My own Dear Husband, November 17, 1863, and Robert Bullock to My dear little wife, October 11, 1863, Bullock Papers.

13. Hallock, *Braxton Bragg and Confederate Defeat,* 118; Connelly, *Autumn of Glory,*

251; Special Orders No. 294, Headquarters, Army of Tennessee, Braxton Bragg Papers, 1833–1879, MSS 2000 Microfilm Edition, Western Reserve Historical Society, Cleveland, OH; October 14 and November 13, 1863, in Pasco, *Private Pasco,* 70–71.

14. S. B. Buckner to Samuel Cooper, August 11, 1863, in G. Troup Maxwell, *CSR,* Reel #3; J.S.M. Davidson to Mrs. W. T. Stockton, December 7, 1863, in Ulmer, *The Correspondence of Will and Ju Stockton,* 241–42.

15. John C. Breckinridge to Samuel Cooper, August 17, 1863, in William Scott Dilworth, *CSR,* Reel #47; John Milton to Jefferson Davis, October 5, 1863, in Haskell M. Monroe et al., eds., *The Papers of Jefferson Davis,* 11 vols. (Baton Rouge: Louisiana State University Press, 1971–2004), 10:10.

16. Ronald A. Mosocco, *The Chronological Tracking of the Civil War per the Official Records of the War of the Rebellion* (Williamsburg: James River Publishing, 1994), 184; J.S.M. Davidson to Mrs. W. T. Stockton, December 7, 1863; Washington M. Ives Jr. to Dear Sister Kate, January 24, 1864, Ives Papers.

17. Sword, *Mountains Touched with Fire,* 109–10; McDonough, *Chattanooga,* 63; Cozzens, *The Shipwreck of Their Hopes,* 29–30.

18. Sword, *Mountains Touched with Fire,* 97; Archie Livingston to Dear Enoch, November 6, 1863, in Coski, "'I Am in for Anything for Success,'" 79; Willie Bryant to Dear Davis, October 26, 1863, in Blakey, Lainhart, and Stephens, *Rose Cottage Chronicles,* 277; Henry T. Wright to Dear Laura, October 3, 1863, Wright Letters.

19. Sword, *Mountains Touched with Fire,* 91–93; unknown to Miss Maggie McKenzie, October 23, 1863, in Tucker, *McKenzie Correspondence,* 106; Washington M. Ives Jr. to Dear Mother, November 5, 1863, Ives Papers; Robert Bullock to My dearest darling, November 6, 1863, Bullock Papers.

20. Sword, *Mountains Touched with Fire,* 108–9; McDonough, *Chattanooga,* 63; Cozzens, *The Shipwreck of Their Hopes,* 29; Daniel, *Soldiering in the Army of Tennessee,* 58–59; T. J. Robertson to Much Esteemed Friend, November 21, 1863, Glover Letters; Willie Bryant to Dear Davis, October 26, 1863, in Blakey, Lainhart, and Stephens, *Rose Cottage Chronicles,* 278; R. W. Jerkins to Dear Wife & Children, November 17, 1863, in Zonira Hunter Tolles, *Bonnie Melrose: The Early History of Melrose, Florida* (Keystone Heights, FL: privately published, 1982), 245–46; Washington M. Ives Jr. to Dear Father, November 10, 1863, Ives Papers. Sutlers were camp followers who sold merchandise and foodstuffs to the soldiers at inflated prices.

21. Washington M. Ives Jr. to Dear Father, November 10, 1863; unknown to Miss Maggie McKenzie, October 23, 1863, in Tucker, *McKenzie Correspondence,* 106; October 8, 1863, in Campbell, *Southern Service,* 76; October 21 and 29, 1863, in Pasco, *Private Pasco,* 72. In October 1862 the Confederate government voted to provide its soldiers with uniforms. Each soldier could, theoretically, draw a certain number of items from government stores each year. If a soldier took in excess of his allotted amount, the price of the clothing was deducted from his pay; likewise, a soldier who took fewer items was reimbursed. See Wiley, *Life of Johnny Reb,* 110–11.

22. October 16, 1863, in Holmes, *Diary of Henry McCall Holmes,* 19; Tuesday, October 27, 1863, in Campbell, *Southern Service,* 80; R. W. Jerkins to Dear Wife & Children, November 17, 1863, in Tolles, *Bonnie Melrose,* 245–46; November 23, 1863, in Pasco, *Private Pasco,* 80.

23. Bruce Catton, *Grant Takes Command* (Boston: Little, Brown and Company, 1969), 34; Sword, *Mountains Touched with Fire,* 114; Daniel, *Days of Glory,* 363–67.

24. Connelly, *Autumn of Glory,* 262–63; Sword, *Mountains Touched with Fire,* 77–78; McDonough, *Chattanooga,* 100.

25. McDonough, *Chattanooga,* 109–10.

26. November 22 and 24, 1863, in Pasco, *Private Pasco,* 79–80; November 23, 1863, in Campbell, *Southern Service,* 86; Catton, *Grant Takes Command,* 70–71; Cozzens, *The Shipwreck of Their Hopes,* 159–60.

27. Cozzens, *The Shipwreck of Their Hopes,* 250–51; Woodworth, *Six Armies in Tennessee,* 190; McDonough, *Chattanooga,* 183; Arthur M. Mannigault, *A Carolinian Goes to War: The Civil War Narrative of Arthur Middleton Mannigault, Brigadier General, C.S.A.* (Columbia: University of South Carolina Press, 1983), quoted in Cozzens, *The Shipwreck of Their Hopes,* 252; Connelly, *Autumn of Glory,* 271–73; Sword, *Mountains Touched with Fire,* 283, map. It is possible that General Finley temporarily commanded Bate's Division until November 24; some sources assert that he did not take command of his brigade until that date. See Herbert U. Feibelman, "Floridians Distinguished at the Bar and on the Field of Battle," *Florida Law Journal* 23, no. 4 (1949): 135; *Jacksonville (FL) Times-Union,* June 8, 1888; *New York Times,* July 28, 1878; Washington M. Ives Jr. to Dear Sister Kate, November 20, 1863, Ives Papers. For more evidence of Finley's unfamiliarity with the 1st and 3rd Florida and 4th Florida regiments, see Washington M. Ives Jr. to Dear Father, December 4, 1863, Ives Papers.

28. McDonough, *Chattanooga,* 162; Woodworth, *Six Armies in Tennessee,* 189, 191–93; Daniel, *Days of Glory,* 369.

29. *Official Records,* series I, vol. XXXI, part II, 740; Cozzens, *The Shipwreck of Their Hopes,* 255; Woodworth, *Six Armies in Tennessee,* 197; Davis, *Breckinridge,* 387; *Jacksonville (FL) Times-Union,* June 8, 1888; Sword, *Mountains Touched with Fire,* 298; November 25, 1863, in Pasco, *Private Pasco,* 82; Sam Davis Elliott, *Soldier of Tennessee: General Alexander P. Stewart and the Civil War in the West* (Baton Rouge: Louisiana State University Press, 1999), 150.

30. Sword, *Mountains Touched with Fire,* 270; Woodworth, *This Grand Spectacle,* 87; Reason W. Jerkins to Dear Wife and children, November 29, 1863, transcribed by Lee White from original at the Dalton, GA, Relics Show, February 14–15, 1998.

31. *Jacksonville (FL) Times-Union,* June 8, 1888; Wednesday, November 25, 1863, in Campbell, *Southern Service,* 87; Washington M. Ives Jr. to Dear Father, December 4, 1863, Ives Papers. Elliott, in *Soldier of Tennessee,* incorrectly accuses Finley's advanced regiments of retreating "without firing a shot." See pages 151–52.

32. Wednesday, November 25, 1863, in Campbell, *Southern Service,* 87; Cozzens, *The Shipwreck of Their Hopes,* 273; William T. Stockton to My dearest wife, December 11, 1863, in Ulmer, *The Correspondence of Will and Ju Stockton,* 243; Waters, "'Through Good and Evil Fortune,'" 139; E. B. McLean to Mrs. Amanda Waterman Bullock, December 8, 1863, Bullock Papers; Reason W. Jerkins to Dear Wife and children, November 29, 1863.

33. Cozzens, *The Shipwreck of Their Hopes,* 273, 283–85; Daniel, *Days of Glory,* 375; Wednesday, November 25, 1863, in Pasco, *Private Pasco,* 82.

34. Kenneth Flint, "The Battle of Missionary Ridge" (master's thesis, The University

of Alabama, 1960), 132, 137; *Memphis (Atlanta) Daily Appeal,* December 2, 1863; Sword, *Mountains Touched with Fire,* 287–89; Cozzens, *The Shipwreck of Their Hopes,* 296–99; General J. J. Finley to Archibald Gracie Jr., December 25, 1863 (typescript), "Eyewitness Accounts" File, Chickamauga-Chattanooga NMP, Fort Oglethorpe, GA. Hughes, *The Pride of the Confederate Artillery,* writes that the second section of the Washington Artillery lost its guns on Missionary Ridge because Finley's troops abandoned the ridge in disorder. It appears, however, that the loss of these pieces came as a result of the retreat of Tyler's men as the Floridians supported Havis's Georgia Battery. See Cozzens, *The Shipwreck of Their Hopes,* 298–99.

35. Sword, *Mountains Touched with Fire,* 298; Cozzens, *The Shipwreck of Their Hopes,* 287, 299, 301; *Official Records,* series I, vol. XXXI, part II, 741; Talley, "William Raulston Talley Memoir," 66; Washington M. Ives Jr. to Dear Father, December 4, 1863, Ives Papers; Charles Hemming, "A Confederate Odyssey," *American Heritage* 36 (December 1984): 71. There is no evidence that these skirmishers were from the 1st and 3rd Florida, as Cozzens states.

36. *Official Records,* series I, vol. XXXI, part II, 742; Sword, *Mountains Touched with Fire,* 301; Cozzens, *The Shipwreck of Their Hopes,* 291; Elliott, *Soldier of Tennessee,* 156; November 25, 1863, in Pasco, *Private Pasco,* 82.

37. *Atlanta Intelligencer,* December 9, 1863; Washington M. Ives Jr. to unknown, undated letter, Ives Papers.

38. Talley, "William Raulston Talley Memoir," 66; Reddick, *Seventy-Seven Years in Dixie,* 22; *Memphis (Atlanta) Daily Appeal,* December 18, 1863; J. J. Finley to His Excellency Governor Milton, December 16, 1863, Governor's Office Letterbooks, 1836–1909, vol. 7, FSA, Tallahassee (hereafter Governor's Office Letterbooks); Hemming, "A Confederate Odyssey," 72.

39. Wednesday, November 25, 1863, in Campbell, *Southern Service,* 87; November 25, 1863, in Pasco, *Private Pasco,* 82; Hemming, "A Confederate Odyssey," 72; John L. Inglis to My dear Cousins, Wm & W Vann, January 14, 1864, Livingston/Inglis Papers.

40. Sword, *Mountains Touched with Fire,* 315–16; Cozzens, *The Shipwreck of Their Hopes,* 339–41; *Official Records,* series I, vol. XXXI, part II, 742–43; *Atlanta Intelligencer,* December 9, 1863; *Memphis (Atlanta) Daily Appeal,* December 4, 1863; Hallock, *Braxton Bragg and Confederate Defeat,* 150–51; Davis, *Breckinridge,* 391.

41. Washington M. Ives Jr. to Dear Father, December 3 and 4, 1863, Ives Papers; Reason W. Jerkins to Dear Wife and children, November 29, 1863; *Supplement to the Official Records,* 5:303–19. It is possible that the 1st and 3rd Florida lost more than 100 soldiers during the battle. Compare unknown to Miss Maggie McKenzie, October 23, 1863, in Tucker, *McKenzie Correspondence,* 106, to Crute, *Units of the Confederate States Army,* 75. While many Florida soldiers allude to the casualty lists that appeared in many of the state's newspapers, these have yet to be located and might not exist anymore. Furthermore, because none of the Florida officers' reports survived, one might arrive at only an estimated casualty figure.

42. Daniel Hall to My Dear Father and Mother, December 9, 1863, Stone Family Papers, FSA, Tallahassee; J. J. Finley to His Excellency Governor Milton, December 16, 1863, Governor's Office Letterbooks; Washington M. Ives Jr. to unknown, undated, Ives

Papers; John L. Inglis to My dear Cousins, Wm & W Vann, January 14, 1863, Livingston/
Inglis Papers; *Richmond Daily Dispatch,* December 8, 1863; Nathaniel Cheairs Hughes Jr.,
General William J. Hardee: Old Reliable (Baton Rouge: Louisiana State University Press,
1965), 174.

Chapter 14

1. John Livingston Inglis to My Dear Cousin, Wm & W Vann, January 14, 1864,
Livingston/Inglis Letters; Benjamin R. Glover to Dear Betty, December 13, 1863, Glover
Letters; J. J. Finley to His Excellency Gov. Milton, December 16, 1863, Governor's Office
Letterbooks; Edward Mashburn to Dear Enoch, January 15, 1864, Enoch J. Vann Papers,
MOC, Richmond, VA (hereafter Vann Papers); Friday, December 25, 1863, in Campbell,
Southern Service, 91; Washington M. Ives Jr. to unknown, undated, Ives Papers; Daniel,
Soldiering in the Army of Tennessee, 33.

2. J. J. Finley to His Excellency Gov. Milton, December 16, 1863; Washington M.
Ives Jr. to Dear Father, December 19, 1863, Ives Papers.

3. E. B. McLean to Mrs. Amanda Bullock, December 8, 1863, Bullock Papers; Washington M. Ives Jr. to Dear Mother, December 9, 1863, Ives Papers; J.S.M. Davidson to Mrs.
W. T. Stockton, December 7, 1863, in Ulmer, *The Correspondence of Will and Ju Stockton,*
241; W. M. Ives, "Captured and Escaped Three Times," *Confederate Veteran* 12 (1904):
228; Crute, *Units of the Confederate States Army,* 73, 75, 77.

4. Washington M. Ives Jr. to Dear Father, December 4, 1863, and to Dear Mother,
December 12, 1863, Ives Papers; Friday, November 27, 1863, in Campbell, *Southern Service,* 91; Robertson, *Soldiers of Florida,* 247; Benjamin R. Glover to Dear Betty, January 4,
1863, Glover Letters.

5. *Official Records,* series II, vol. VI, 647–48; Catton, *Grant Takes Command,* 371–72;
McPherson, *Battle Cry of Freedom,* 567; Manning, *What This Cruel War Was Over,* 160–
61. There were exceptions to the cessation of prisoner swapping; in 1864 officers were exchanged for those of the same rank.

6. Dallas Wood to Dear Sister, December 25, 1863, Dallas Wood Letter, FSU, Tallahassee; Friday, December 25, 1863, in Campbell, *Southern Service,* 91; Washington M.
Ives Jr. to Dear Sister Fannie, December 25, 1863, Ives Papers.

7. Washington M. Ives Jr. to Dear Sister Fannie, December 25, 1863; Archie Livingston to My Dear Sister, December 26, 1863, in Coski, "'I Am in for Anything for Success,'"
79; Dallas Wood to Dear Sister, December 25, 1863.

8. Gary Gallagher, *The Confederate War* (Cambridge, MA: Harvard University Press,
1997), 36, 74–75; John L. Inglis to My dear Cousins, Wm & W Vann, January 14, 1864,
Livingston/Inglis Letters; Daniel, *Soldiering in the Army of Tennessee,* 137–38; Washington
M. Ives Jr. to Dear Father, December 19, 1863, Ives Papers; Benjamin R. Glover to Dear
Betty, December 13, 1863, Glover Letters. A rumor, espoused by both Ives and Inglis, evi-
dently ran through the camps proclaiming that soldiers were to receive a sixty-day furlough.
See John L. Inglis to My dear Cousins, Wm & W Vann, January 14, 1864, and Washington
M. Ives Jr. to Dear Father, January 5, 1864, Ives Papers.

9. Warner, *Generals in Gray,* 161–62; Connelly, *Autumn of Glory,* 34, 289; Richard M.

McMurry, *Two Great Rebel Armies: An Essay in Confederate Military History* (Chapel Hill: University of North Carolina Press, 1989), 127–28; Daniel, *Soldiering in the Army of Tennessee,* 139; Washington M. Ives Jr. to Dear Sister Kate, January 24, 1864, Ives Papers.

10. *Official Records,* series I, vol. XXXI, part III, 855 and vol. XXXII, part II, 558; Wiley, *Life of Johnny Reb,* 132; Washington M. Ives Jr. to Dear Father, January 5, 1864, and Dear Sister Fannie, January 18, 1864, Ives Papers; Daniel, *Soldiering in the Army of Tennessee,* 138; John L. Inglis to My Dear Cousin, March 4, 1864, Livingston/Inglis Letters.

11. *Official Records,* series IV, vol. II, 1041–42. See also vol. III, 114–15 for Davis's February plea for new draft laws.

12. Ibid., series IV, vol. III, 178–81; Wiley, *Life of Johnny Reb,* 132; Roderick G. Shaw to My Dear Sister, January 28, 1864, Shaw Letters; Albert Castel, *Decision in the West: The Atlanta Campaign of 1864* (Lawrence: University of Kansas Press, 1992), 27.

13. *Macon Daily Telegraph,* January 15, 1864; *Official Records,* series IV, vol. II, 948–49, 1000–1001; *Richmond Daily Dispatch,* December 30, 1863; Washington M. Ives Jr. to Dear Father, December 31, 1863, Ives Letters.

14. Roderick G. Shaw to My Dear Sister, January 28, 1864, Shaw Letters; Monday, February 8, 1864, in Campbell, *Southern Service,* 93; J. J. Finley to His Excellency Governor Milton, February 7, 1864, Governor's Office Letterbooks.

15. J. J. Finley to His Excellency Governor Milton, February 7, 1864, and J. J. Finley to My dear Governor, April 16, 1864; *Tallahassee Floridian and Journal,* March 12, 1864; Washington M. Ives Jr. to Dear Father, February 22 and March 29, 1864, Ives Papers.

16. *Memphis (Atlanta) Daily Appeal,* February 2, 1864; Ray, "The Flags of the 4th Florida Regiment." The large crimson flag carried by the 4th Florida at Murfreesboro was lost en route to Mississippi; at Chickamauga and Missionary Ridge the regiment bore a Hardee pattern flag. This banner was retired and sent to Tallahassee following the arrival of the flag from McNaught, Ormond, & Company.

17. Connelly, *Autumn of Glory,* 277, 313; Washington M. Ives Jr. to Dear Father, February 13, 1864, Ives Papers; Saturday, February 13, 1864, in Campbell, *Southern Service,* 94.

18. Thursday, March 3, and Wednesday, March 9, 1864, in Campbell, *Southern Service,* 97, 101; Lt. A. M. McLaughlin to Commander J. K. Mitchell, CSN, January, 30, 1864, Your Obedient Servants to Hon S. R. Mallory, January 28, 1864, and Jno K. Mitchell to Hon James Seddon, February 15, 1864, Letters Received, Adjutant and Inspector General's Office, NA Microcopy M474, Roll #11, NA, Washington, DC.

19. *Atlanta Southern Confederacy,* March 11, 1864; *Official Records,* series II, vol. VI, 978–79.

20. Daniel, *Soldiering in the Army of Tennessee,* 26; Tuesday, December 1, Tuesday, December 8, and Thursday, December 9, 1863, in Campbell, *Southern Service,* 89–91; Gillis to Dear Aunt, March 23, 1864, McLean Family Papers; Castel, *Decision in the West,* 33; W. B. Bate to My Dear General, March 17, 1864, Braxton Bragg Papers, 1833–1879, MSS 2000 Microfilm Edition, Western Reserve Historical Society, Cleveland, OH.

21. Archie Livingston to My Dr Father, March 23, 1864, in Coski, "'I Am in for Anything for Success,'" 80; Washington M. Ives Jr. to Sister Florence, January 30, 1864, Ives Papers; Roddie Shaw to Dear Sister, January 28, 1864, Shaw Letters.

22. Archie Livingston to My Dear Sister, April 24, 1864, Livingston/Inglis Letters;

Washington M. Ives Jr. to Dear Father, April 8, 1864, Ives Papers; Daniel, *Soldiering in the Army of Tennessee,* 27–28.

23. Washington M. Ives Jr. to Dear Father, March 25, 1864, Ives Papers; John L. Inglis to My dear Cousin, March 4, 1864, Livingston/Inglis Letters (this letter is obviously misdated; Inglis probably wrote it in April 1864); Sunday, February 21, 1864, in Campbell, *Southern Service,* 95.

24. George Fairbanks to Lt. General John Bell Hood, March 5, 1864, Fairbanks Collection (microfilm); *Gainesville Cotton States,* April 16, 1864; Sunday, February 21, 1864, in Campbell, *Southern Service,* 95.

25. Ella Lonn, *Desertion during the Civil War* (New York: Century Company, 1928), 18, 231; General Orders of Hardee's/D. H. Hill's/Breckinridge's/Hindman's Corps, Army of Tennessee, February 20, 1863–February 29, 1864, and General Orders of Hood's/S. D. Lee's Corps, Army of Tennessee, March 1, 1864–April 10, 1865 (transcripts), originals held in the Eleanor S. Brockenbrough Library, MOC, Richmond, VA; Hartman and Coles, *Biographical Rosters,* 1:1–137, 261–458, 2:579–778, 4:1317–1406.

26. Lonn, *Desertion during the Civil War,* 231; *Official Records,* series IV, vol. III, 687–88; General Orders of Hardee's Corps, Army of Tennessee, February 20, 1863–February 29, 1864, and General Orders of Hood's/S. D. Lee's Corps, Army of Tennessee, March 1, 1864–April 10, 1865; Jack A. Bunch, *Roster of the Courts-Martial in the Confederate States Army* (Shippensburg, PA: White Mane Books, 2001).

27. McLean Family Letters. G. A. Ball to Major H. Hampton, Inspector General, Hardee's Corps, March 16, 1864, and General J. J. Finley to Major George Fairbanks, March 20, 1864, Fairbanks Collection (microfilm). A. G. McLeod to Dear Aunt, March 25, 1864.

28. Washington M. Ives Jr. to Dear Father, March 25, 1864, Ives Papers; John L. Inglis to My dear Cousin, March 4, 1864, Livingston/Inglis Letters.

29. Gillis to My Dear Aunt, March 23, 1864, McLean Family Papers; *Macon (GA) Daily Telegraph,* March 31, 1864; Washington M. Ives Jr. to Dear Father, March 23, 1864, Ives Papers; Captain John L. Inglis to My Dear Cousins, March [April] 4, 1864, Livingston/Inglis Letters.

30. Captain John L. Inglis to My Dear Cousins, March [April] 4, 1864, Livingston/Inglis Letters; Archie Livingston to My Dr Father, March 23, 1864, in Coski, "'I Am in for Anything for Success,'" 80; Duncan G. McLeod to Miss Nancy Gillis, March 23, 1864, McLean Family Papers; *Macon (GA) Daily Telegraph,* March 31, 1864; Ray, "The Flags of the 4th Florida Regiments"; Washington M. Ives Jr. to Dear Father, March 23, 1864.

31. Washington M. Ives to Dear Father, April 14 and 17, May 3 and 7, 1864, Ives Papers; Archie Livingston to My Dear Sister, April 24, 1864, in Coski, "'I Am in for Anything for Success,'" 80.

32. Washington M. Ives Jr. to Dear Sister Kate, March 13, 1864, Ives Papers; Daniel, *Soldiering in the Army of Tennessee,* 119; Woodworth, *While God Is Marching On,* 236; *Gainesville Cotton States,* May 21, 1864.

33. *Milledgeville (GA) Confederate Union*, May 24, 1864; *Gainesville Cotton States,* May 21, 1864; Reason Jerkins to My Dear Daughter, March 27 and 28, 1864, in Tolles, *Bonnie Melrose,* 247; John L. Inglis to My Dear Cousins, March [April] 4, 1864, Livingston/Inglis Letters.

34. Archie Livingston to My dear Mother, May 3, 1864, in Coski, "'I Am in for Any-

thing for Success,'" 81; *Gainesville Cotton States,* May 21, 1864. General Finley's 1840s letters demonstrate a strong Christian faith not witnessed in his earlier writings.

35. *Gainesville Cotton States,* May 21, 1864; Angus I. Gillis to Dear Aunt, May 5, 1864, McLean Family Papers.

36. Washington M. Ives Jr. to Dear Father, May 7, 1864, Ives Papers; Benjamin R. Glover to Dear Betty, May 5, 1864, Glover Letters.

37. Roderick G. Shaw to My Dear Sister, January 28, 1864, Shaw Letters.

Chapter 15

1. Castel, *Decision in the West,* 68; David Herbert Donald, *Lincoln* (New York: Simon and Schuster, 1995), 477–78; Francis P. Fleming to My dear Aunt Tilly, May 4, 1864, in Edward C. Williamson, ed., "Francis P. Fleming in the War for Southern Independence: Letters from the Front, Part II," *Florida Historical Quarterly* 28, no. 2 (1949): 150.

2. Journal of Washington M. Ives, 1863–1864, May 7, 1864, Ives Papers; Castel, *Decision in the West,* 123; Richard M. McMurry, *Atlanta 1864: Last Chance for the Confederacy* (Lincoln: University of Nebraska Press, 2000), 42–43, 48, 57; John F. Marszalek, *Sherman: A Soldier's Passion for Order* (New York: Vintage Books, 1994), 264–65; Zack C. Waters, ed., "Lines of Battle: Major General William B. Bate's Partial Reports of the Atlanta Campaign," in Theodore Savas and David A. Woodbury, eds., *The Campaign for Atlanta & Sherman's March to the Sea* (El Dorado Hills, CA: Savas Woodbury Publishers, 1992), 1:177; Holmes, *Diary of Henry McCall Holmes,* 19–20.

3. Holmes, *Diary of Henry McCall Holmes,* 19–20; John L. Inglis to My Dear Cousin, May 28, 1864, Livingston/Inglis Letters; David E. Maxwell, "Some Letters to His Parents by a Floridian in the Confederate Army," transcribed by Gilbert Wright, *Florida Historical Quarterly* 36, no. 4 (1958): 370; "Captain David Ewell Maxwell," Maxwell Mss.

4. J. J. Finley to Major A. P. Mason, March 29, 1864, Finley, *CSR,* Reel #93. The Florida Brigade's strength at the outset of the campaign is derived from the "Inspection Report of Finley's Brigade, August 21, 1864," Inspection Reports and Related Records Received by the Inspection Branch in the Confederate Adjutant and Inspector General's Office, NA Microcopy M935, Reel #5, NA, Washington, DC.

5. Woodworth, *Nothing But Victory,* 495–96; Connelly, *Autumn of Glory,* 341.

6. Connelly, *Autumn of Glory,* 341; Castel, *Decision in the West,* 153; John H. Hill, "The Battle of Resaca," *Atlanta Journal,* February 9, 1901; Waters, "Lines of Battle," 1:177.

7. Castel, *Decision in the West,* 161; John L. Inglis to My dear Cousin, May 28, 1864, Livingston/Inglis Letters; Archie Livingston to My Dear Sisters, May 29, 1864, in Coski, "'I Am in for Anything for Success,'" 81; Journal of Washington M. Ives, 1863–1864, May 14, 1864, Ives Papers; May 14, 1864, in Holmes, *Diary of Henry McCall Holmes,* 20. Captain David E. Maxwell wrote that the 1st and 4th Florida lost thirty to forty soldiers and noted "the other parts of the Brigade losing in about the same proportion." See David E. Maxwell to Dear Father, May 29, 1864, in Maxwell, "Some Letters to His Parents," 371. These numbers contradict the rather low casualty figures given in the *Official Records,* series I, vol. XXXVIII, part III, 645. See also *Gainesville Cotton States,* May 28, 1864, for a partial list of casualties suffered at Resaca.

8. Hill, "The Battle of Resaca"; W. M. Ives, "Gen. Jesse J. Finley's Wounds," *Jackson-*

ville (FL) Times-Union, July 29, 1907; *Macon Daily Telegraph,* May 21, 1864; David E. Maxwell to Dear Father, May 29, 1864, in Maxwell, "Some Letters to His Parents," 371; May 15, 1864, in Holmes, *Diary of Henry McCall Holmes,* 20. Castel, in *Decision in the West,* 188, writes that the trees near the Rebel works were "scarred, splintered, and sometimes shattered by shells and bullets."

9. *Gainesville Cotton States,* June 4, 1864.

10. Castel, *Decision in the West,* 178–79, 192, 195, 201; Waters, "Lines of Battle," 1:178–79; McMurry, *Atlanta 1864,* 77, 81; Connelly, *Autumn of Glory,* 345–47.

11. Connelly, *Autumn of Glory,* 348–49; McMurry, *Atlanta 1864,* 82–83, 85.

12. David E. Maxwell to Dear Father, May 29, 1864, in Maxwell, "Some Letters to His Parents," 371; Francis P. Fleming to My dear Aunt Tilly, May 30, 1864, in Williamson, "Francis P. Fleming in the War for Southern Independence," 151; John L. Inglis to My Dear Cousin, May 28, 1864, Livingston/Inglis Letters. See Richard M. McMurry, "Confederate Morale in the Atlanta Campaign of 1864," *Georgia Historical Quarterly* 54 (1970): 226–43, and William J. McNeil, "A Survey of Confederate Soldier Morale during Sherman's Campaign through Georgia and the Carolinas," *Georgia Historical Quarterly* 45 (1971): 1–25.

13. Archie Livingston to My dear Sisters, May 29, 1864, in Coski, "'I Am in for Anything for Success,'" 81.

14. Connelly, *Autumn of Glory,* 354; McMurry, *Atlanta 1864,* 85–86; Castel, *Decision in the West,* 219; Waters, "Lines of Battle," 1:179.

15. Castel, *Decision in the West,* 242; Waters, *Death Was Feasting in Our Midst,* 3; Waters, "Lines of Battle," 1:180.

16. James P. Jones, *Black Jack: John A. Logan and Southern Illinois in the Civil War Era* (1967; reprint, Carbondale: Southern Illinois University Press, 1995), 203; Roddie Shaw to My Dear Uncle, May 27, 1864, Roderick and James Kirkpatrick Shaw Letters, Special Collections, Robert Manning Strozier Library, Florida State University, Tallahassee; Washington M. Ives Journal, 1863–1864, May 28, 1864, Ives Papers; A. M. Harris to Mr. T. R. Smith, June 14, 1864, Shaw Letters; Patrick Augustus McGriff to My Dear Susan, June 13, 1864, Patrick Augustus McGriff Letters, FSA, Tallahassee (hereafter McGriff Letters).

17. Castel, *Decision in the West,* 244; Waters, "Lines of Battle," 1:181; Waters, *Death Was Feasting in Our Midst,* 7–8.

18. J. C. McLean to D. G. McLean, May 29, 1864, McLean Family Papers; McKinnon, *History of Walton County,* chapter 42; Reddick, *Seventy-Seven Years in Dixie,* 24.

19. Waters, "Lines of Battle," 1:182; Waters, *Death Was Feasting in Our Midst,* 9–10; Castel, *Decision in the West,* 246; Connelly, *Autumn of Glory,* 256. Colonel Thomas Smith's Brigade received Bate's cancellation order and therefore did not participate in the attack.

20. *Memphis (Atlanta) Daily Appeal,* June 9, 1864; Woodworth, *Nothing But Victory,* 509.

21. *Memphis (Atlanta) Daily Appeal,* June 9, 1864; J. C. McLean to D. G. McLean, May 29, 1864, McLean Family Papers.

22. John K. Duke, *History of the Fifty-Third Regiment, Ohio Volunteer Infantry during the War of the Rebellion, 1861–1865* (Portsmouth, OH: Blade Printing Company, 1900), 137–38; McKinnon, *History of Walton County,* chapter 42, quoted in Waters, *Death Was Feasting in Our Midst,* 11; Reddick, *Seventy-Seven Years in Dixie,* 24–25; Patrick Augustus

McGriff to My Dear Susan, June 13, 1864, McGriff Letters; *Memphis (Atlanta) Daily Appeal,* June 9, 1864.

23. *Memphis (Atlanta) Daily Appeal,* June 9, 1864.

24. *Gainesville Cotton States,* June 11, 1864; Archie Livingston to Theodore Livingston, May 31, 1863[64], Livingston/Inglis Letters; Waters, *Death Was Feasting in Our Midst,* 13–14; Jones, *Black Jack,* 204. The Florida Brigade's casualty numbers at Dallas, like those of the Texan force at the Alamo, may truly never be known; however, the number published in the *Cotton States* is probably closer to the accurate count. The contemporary estimate is confirmed by Willie Bryant in a letter to his sister, where he claimed the regiments suffered a total of 219 casualties. See Willie Bryant to Dear Tivie, May 31, 1864, in Blakey, Lainhart, and Stephens, *Rose Cottage Chronicles,* 339. Numbers given in J. C. McLean to D. G. McLean, May 29, 1864, McLean Family Papers, could raise the total to 250. *Richmond Daily Dispatch,* June 7, 1864, gives the two brigades' losses as 478. A. M. Harris wrote in mid-June that the brigade had suffered 360 casualties since the beginning of the campaign, including both Dallas and Resaca and the skirmishing in mid-June. See A. M. Harris to Mr. T. R. Smith, June 14, 1864, Shaw Letters.

25. *Gainesville Cotton States,* June 11, 1864; Waters, *Death Was Feasting in Our Midst,* 14–15; Washington M. Ives Jr. to Dear Sister Kate, August 21, 1864, Ives Papers. See also Governor A. K. Allison to Jefferson Davis, April 12, 1865, Governor's Office Letterbooks. By early 1865 the Florida Brigade's poor opinion of Bate was probably mutual due to the brigade's poor showing at the Battle of Overall Creek and Nashville.

26. Castel, *Decision in the West,* 264–69; Connelly, *Autumn of Glory,* 357; Waters, "Lines of Battle," 1:184–85; Journal of Washington M. Ives, 1863–1864, June 2, 7, and 10, 1864, Ives Papers.

27. Journal of Washington M. Ives, 1863–1864, June 14, 1864, Ives Papers.

28. Ibid.; Castel, *Decision in the West,* 275–76; W. S. Dilworth, "A Correct Statement of the Death of Gen. Polk," *Memphis (Atlanta) Daily Appeal,* June 29, 1864.

29. Hugh Black to Dear Wife, June 21, 1864, in Frano, *Letters of Captain Hugh Black to His Family,* 65; Jacob A. Lash to My Dear Wife, June 26, 1864, Lash Letters; Albert Livingston to My Dear Parents, June 20, 1864, Livingston/Inglis Letters.

30. Connelly, *Autumn of Glory,* 357–58; Castel, *Decision in the West,* 285. See Journal of Washington M. Ives, 1863–1864, June 17–26, 1864, Ives Papers.

31. Castel, *Decision in the West,* 300–301; Connelly, *Autumn of Glory,* 359.

32. W. M. Ives, "The Finality of June 27th, 1864" (unpublished manuscript in author's possession). See also W. M. Ives, "A Florida Veteran Tells of the Battle of Chattanooga, Tenn.," *Atlanta Journal,* October 25, 1902. Although the title of this article indicates otherwise, the topic discussed is Kennesaw Mountain.

33. Ives, "The Finality of June 27th, 1864."

34. Ibid.; Castel, *Decision in the West,* 324–25; J. A. Campbell to My Ever Dear Sister, July 1, 1864, McLean Family Papers.

35. Castel, *Decision in the West,* 339–41; Enoch J. Vann Diary (typescript), 4, Vann Papers (hereafter Vann Diary).

36. Vann Diary, 4–5; Castel, *Decision in the West,* 350.

37. Vann Diary, 16–17.

38. Ibid.

39. Castel, *Decision in the West,* 345, 349, 361; McMurry, *Atlanta 1864,* 135–39. For a more thorough discussion of Johnston's removal, see Connelly, *Autumn of Glory,* 391–421.

40. Wiley Sword, *The Confederacy's Last Hurrah: Spring Hill, Franklin, and Nashville* (Lawrence: University of Kansas Press, 1993), 8; Connelly, *Autumn of Glory,* 322–23, 419–20.

41. Castel, *Decision in the West,* 364; Connelly, *Autumn of Glory,* 423; William McLeod Diary, 1864–1865, July 18, 1864, FSA, Tallahassee (hereafter McLeod Diary); Washington M. Ives Jr. to Dear Father, August 16, 1864, Ives Papers; Hugh Black to Dear Wife, July 20, 1864, in Frano, *Letters of Captain Hugh Black to His Family,* 66; Enoch Vann to My Dear Wife, July 19, 1864, Vann Papers; Archie Livingston to Dear Enoch, July 19, 1864, in Coski, "'I Am in for Anything for Success,'" 82. Hood's biographer, Richard McMurry, has countered the assertion that morale plummeted after Johnston's removal. See Richard C. McMurry, "Confederate Morale in the Atlanta Campaign of 1864," *Georgia Historical Quarterly* 54 (1970): 226–43.

42. Castel, *Decision in the West,* 366–68; McMurry, *Atlanta 1864,* 149.

43. McLeod Diary, July 20, 1864; Castel, *Decision in the West,* 371–72.

44. Castel, *Decision in the West,* 375–76; Hugh Black to Dear Wife, July 26, 1864, in Frano, *Letters of Captain Hugh Black to His Family,* 66; McLeod Diary, July 20, 1864.

45. McMurry, *Atlanta 1864,* 152; McLeod Diary, July 20, 1864; Hugh Black to Dear Jim, July 2[?], 1864, in Frano, *Letters of Captain Hugh Black to His Family,* 67. A possible eyewitness account of Colonel Dilworth's arrest may be located in the memoir of John Angus Campbell, published in Tampa's *Sunday Tribune,* June 14, 1953. Samuel Pasco, incarcerated in Camp Morton, Indiana, wrote in his diary after obtaining secondhand information: "Col. D. I am sorry to hear has tendered his resignation and is now in Florida." See August 24, 1864, in Pasco, *Private Pasco,* 153. Despite this statement, there is no evidence that Dilworth ever tendered his resignation, as he was paroled in Tallahassee in May 1865.

46. McLeod Diary, July 21, 1864.

47. Castel, *Decision in the West,* 387, 391; McMurry, *Atlanta 1864,* 153; Hugh Black to Dear Wife, July 26, 1864, in Frano, *Letters of Captain Hugh Black to His Family,* 67; Washington M. Ives Jr. to Dear Father, August 16, 1864, Ives Papers.

48. Foote, *The Civil War,* 3:477; McLeod Diary, July 22, 1864.

49. Castel, *Decision in the West,* 393; McLeod Diary, July 22, 1864; Waters, "Lines of Battle," 1:186–87.

50. Woodworth, *Nothing But Victory,* 542–43; Waters, "Lines of Battle," 1:187; Washington M. Ives Jr. to Dear Father, August 16, 1864, Ives Papers.

51. Waters, "Lines of Battle," 1:187; McLeod Diary, July 22, 1864; Woodworth, *Nothing But Victory,* 547–49; McMurry, *Atlanta 1864,* 153; Hugh Black to Dear Wife, July 26, 1864, in Frano, *Letters of Captain Hugh Black to His Family,* 68.

52. Gary Ecelbarger, *The Day Dixie Died: The Battle of Atlanta* (New York: Thomas Dunne Books, 2010), 83–84; Hugh Black to Dear Wife, July 26, 1864, in Frano, *Letters of Captain Hugh Black to His Family,* 68; McMurry, *Atlanta 1864,* 155; Castel, *Decision in the West,* 450–51.

53. Hugh Black to Dear Wife, July 26, 1864, and Hugh Black to Dear Jim, July 2[?], 1864; Washington M. Ives Jr. to Dear Father, August 16, 1864, and Journal of Washington M. Ives, 1863–1864, July 22, 1864, Ives Papers; "Inspection Report of Finley's Brigade, August 21, 1864."

54. Vann Diary, 8–9. For a discussion of the Army of Tennessee's medical facilities and the treatment of Confederate battlefield wounded in general, see Daniel, *Soldiering in the Army of Tennessee,* 74–79; Wiley, *Life of Johnny Reb,* 262–67; "Inspection Report of Finley's Brigade, August 21, 1864."

55. McLeod Diary, July 24–August 1, 1864.

56. "Inspection Report of Finley's Brigade, August 21, 1864"; McLeod Diary, August 3, 1864; Castel, *Decision in the West,* 453; D. Lafayette Kenan was appointed colonel on May 28, 1864, and the Confederate Congress approved his promotion on July 19, 1864. See Kenan, *CSR,* Reel #70.

57. McMurry, *Atlanta 1864,* 162; *Richmond Daily Dispatch,* August 8, 1864; Washington M. Ives Jr. to Dear Friend, August 16, 1864, Ives Papers; Castel, *Decision in the West,* 458–59.

58. "Inspection Report of Finley's Brigade, August 21, 1864"; Wiley, *Life of Johnny Reb,* 118.

59. Washington M. Ives Jr. to Dear Friend, August 16, 1864, and to Sister Katie, August 24, 1864, Ives Papers; Archie Livingston to My Dr Father, August 24, 1864, in Coski, "'I Am in for Anything for Success,'" 82. For a general description of life in the trenches during the Atlanta Campaign, see Castel, *Decision in the West,* 480–85.

60. Castel, *Decision in the West,* 292–93, 297, 461, 489, 492; McMurry, *Atlanta 1864,* 170–71.

61. Castel, *Decision in the West,* 483, 487, 491; McKinnon, *History of Walton County,* 137.

62. Castel, *Decision in the West,* 496–97.

63. McLeod Diary, August 30, 1864; Francis P. Fleming to My dear Mother, September 1, 1864, in Williamson, "Francis P. Fleming in the Southern War for Independence, Part II," 153; McMurry, *Atlanta 1864,* 172; Washington M. Ives Jr. to Dear Father, September 7, 1864, Ives Papers.

64. Castel, *Decision in the West,* 499–500.

65. Ibid., 502; McLeod Diary, August 31, 1864; Jones, *Black Jack,* 227; Foote, *The Civil War,* 3:526.

66. Castel, *Decision in the West,* 502–3; McLeod Diary, August 31, 1864.

67. Francis P. Fleming to My dear Mother, September 1, 1864, in Williamson, "Francis P. Fleming in the Southern War for Independence, Part II," 154; S. D. McConnell to My dear sister, September 23, 1864, http://www.soldierstudies.org/ (accessed January 20, 2010); McLeod Diary, August 31, 1864. For a postwar account of the battle, see J. W. Grantham, "Death of Gen. Cleburne on Federal Breastworks," *Atlanta Journal,* September 21, 1901

68. *Macon Daily Telegraph,* September 5, 1864; Castel, *Decision in the West,* 503; James R. Ferqueron, "The Finest Opportunity Lost: The Battle of Jonesborough, August 31–September 1, 1864," *North & South* 6, no. 6 (2003): 58; *Jacksonville (FL) Times-Union,* July 29, 1907; C.A.H., "Brig. Gen. Jesse J. Finley," *Jacksonville (FL) Times-Union,* July 28, 1907; Register, *The Kenan Family,* 30.

69. Washington M. Ives Jr. to Dear Father, September 7, 1864, Ives Papers; McLeod Diary, August 31, 1864; S. D. McConnell to My dear sister, September 23, 1864; Feibelman, "Floridians Distinguished," 135.

70. C.A.H., "Brig. Gen. Jesse J. Finley."

71. Castel, *Decision in the West,* 543–44; S. Darwin McConnell to My darling wife, September 8, 1864, McConnell Letters.

Chapter 16

1. Marszalek, *Sherman,* 234–36, 251, 290.

2. *Official Records,* series II, vol. VII, 784, 791–92, 822; S. D. McConnell to My Dear Sister, September 23, 1864; Washington M. Ives Jr. to Dear Father, September 23, 1864, Ives Papers.

3. Sword, *The Confederacy's Last Hurrah,* 37; "Inspection of Finley's Brigade, September 18, 1864."

4. S. D. McConnell to My darling wife, September 8, 1864, McConnell Letters; McLeod Diary, September 2 and 7, 1864; Washington M. Ives Jr. to Dear Col., September 11, 1864, Ives Papers; S. D. McConnell to My Dear Sister, September 23, 1864.

5. Washington M. Ives Jr. to Dear Sister Florence, September 17, 1864; Archie Livingston to My dear Mother, October 9, 1864, in Coski, "'I Am in for Anything for Success,'" 82.

6. Washington M. Ives Jr. to Dear Sister Florence, September 17, 1864; S. D. McConnell to My darling wife, September 8, 1864.

7. John L. Inglis to My Dear Cousin, May 28, 1864, Livingston/Inglis Letters.

8. "Inspection of Finley's Brigade, September 18, 1864"; Brown, *Peace River Frontier,* 91; *Gainesville Cotton States,* March 12, 1864; Robert Blair Smith to Hon. E. Amos, May 12, 1917, Robert Blair Smith Soldier's Pension Claim, Florida Confederate Pension Claims, FSA, Tallahassee.

9. 1860 U.S. Census (Free Schedule), Walton County, FL, p. 982b, family 375, dwelling 375, lines 4–8 NA Microcopy M653, Reel #109; *Supplement to the Official Records,* 5:299; Angus McIntosh Gillis to Dear Aunt, May 1, 1862, McLean Family Papers.

10. W.L.L. Bowen to Honorable James A. Seddon, November 13, 1864, and December 12, 1864, Letters Received, Confederate Adjutant and Inspector Generals Office, NA Microcopy M474, Reels #60 and 154, NA, Washington, DC.

11. Sword, *The Confederacy's Last Hurrah,* 46; Connelly, *Autumn of Glory,* 477–78; James Lee McDonough, *Nashville: The Western Confederacy's Final Gamble* (Knoxville: University of Tennessee Press, 2004), 30.

12. Connelly, *Autumn of Glory,* 471; Sword, *The Confederacy's Last Hurrah,* 47; Boatner, *The Civil War Dictionary,* 147; McLeod Diary, September 28, 1864. Hood blamed Hardee for the losses at the various battles around Atlanta. For an in-depth look at the Hood-Hardee controversy, see Hughes, *General William J. Hardee,* 233–49. For more on General Benjamin Cheatham, see Christopher Losson, *Tennessee's Forgotten Warriors: Frank Cheatham and His Tennessee Division* (Knoxville: University of Tennessee Press, 1989).

13. Benjamin R. Glover to Dear Betty, October 5, 1864, Glover Letters; Archie Livingston to My dear Mother, October 9, 1864, in Coski, "'I Am in for Anything for Success,'" 82.

14. Sword, *The Confederacy's Last Hurrah,* 56; James Lee McDonough and Thomas L. Connelly, *Five Tragic Hours: The Battle of Franklin* (Knoxville: University of Tennessee Press, 1988), 13; *Official Records,* series I, vol. XXXIX, 827.

15. Hughes, *Pride of the Confederate Artillery,* 224; Reddick, *Seventy-Seven Years in Dixie,* 28; *Official Records,* series I, vol. XXXIX, 827; Archie Livingston to My Dear Brother, October 15, 1864, in Coski, "'I Am in for Anything for Success,'" 83.

16. *Washington National Tribune,* December 12, 1912; Washington M. Ives Jr. to Mrs. Edward Badger, November 1, 1915 (photocopy), Collection of Zack C. Waters, Rome, GA; Reddick, *Seventy-Seven Years in Dixie,* 28.

17. Sword, *The Confederacy's Last Hurrah,* 56; McDonough and Connelly, *Five Tragic Hours,* 13; McDonough, *Nashville,* 36.

18. McDonough, *Nashville,* 37; Benjamin R. Glover to Dear Betty, October 15, 1864, Glover Letters; Sword, *The Confederacy's Last Hurrah,* 57; Reddick, *Seventy-Seven Years in Dixie,* 27; *Official Records,* series I, vol. XXXIX, pt. 1, 720–21; Archie Livingston to My Dear Brother, October 15, 1864.

19. Connelly, *Autumn of Glory,* 482–83; Benjamin R. Glover to Dear Betty, October 21, 1864, Glover Letters; McDonough, *Nashville,* 40; Sword, *The Confederacy's Last Hurrah,* 65; James C. McLean to Aunt Nancy, November 4, 1864, McLean Family Papers.

20. McLeod Diary, October 29, 1864; Sword, *The Confederacy's Last Hurrah,* 64–65; Jacob A. Lash to My Dear Wife, November 2, 1864, Lash Letters.

21. Jacob A. Lash to My Dear Wife, November 2, 1864; Sword, *The Confederacy's Last Hurrah,* 68.

22. S. D. McConnell to My darling wife, November 8, 1864, McConnell Papers.

23. Archie Livingston to My Dear Brother, October 15, 1864; Jacob A. Lash to My Dear Wife, November 2, 1864; Benjamin Glover to Dear Betty, October 31, 1864, Glover Letters.

24. Benjamin R. Glover to Dear Betty, November 10, 1864, Glover Letters; Sword, *The Confederacy's Last Hurrah,* 68; Archie Livingston to My dear Sisters, November 13, 1864, in Coski, "'I Am in for Anything for Success,'" 84.

25. Jacob A. Lash to My Dear Wife, November 19, 1864, Lash Letters; Archie Livingston to My dear Sisters, November 13, 1864, and Archie Livingston to My dear Brother, October [November] 29, 1864, in Coski, "'I Am in for Anything for Success,'" 83; Sword, *The Confederacy's Last Hurrah,* 69.

26. Connelly, *Autumn of Glory,* 488–89; Jacob A. Lash to My Dear Wife, November 19, 1864. For Sherman's decision to make the March to the Sea, see Marszalek, *Sherman,* 293–97.

27. Connelly, *Autumn of Glory,* 489; Sword, *The Confederacy's Last Hurrah,* 72; McDonough, *Nashville,* 40; Norman D. Brown, ed., *One of Cleburne's Command: The Civil War Reminiscences and Diary of Capt. Samuel T. Foster, Granbury's Brigade, CSA* (Austin: University of Texas Press, 1980), 150–51, quoted in McDonough, *Nashville,* 111; Washington M. Ives Jr. to Dear Mother, February 13, 1865, Ives Papers.

28. McDonough and Connelly, *Five Tragic Hours,* 31; Sword, *The Confederacy's Last Hurrah,* 91.

29. Washington M. Ives Jr. to Dear Mother, February 13, 1865, Ives Papers; McLeod Diary, November 27, 1864.

30. Washington M. Ives Jr. to Dear Mother, February 13, 1865; Archie Livingston to My dear Brother, October [November] 29, 1864; Sword, *The Confederacy's Last Hurrah,* 95–96; McDonough, *Nashville,* 47. Surgeon Henry McCall Holmes proclaimed Maury County, of which Columbia is the seat, "one of the richest in the state, fine land & good crops." See November 26, 1864, in Holmes, *Diary of Henry McCall Holmes,* 22.

31. Sword, *The Confederacy's Last Hurrah,* 83; McDonough and Connelly, *Five Tragic Hours,* 22–23, 34; Connelly, *Autumn of Glory,* 491–92.

32. Foote, *The Civil War,* 3:656; McLeod Diary, November 29, 1864; Archie Livingston to My dear Brother, October [November] 29, 1864; Sword, *The Confederacy's Last Hurrah,* 114–15; Washington M. Ives Jr. to Dear Mother, February 13, 1865.

33. Sword, *The Confederacy's Last Hurrah,* 115; Washington M. Ives Jr. to Dear Mother, February 13, 1865; November 29, 1864, in Holmes, *Diary of Henry McCall Holmes,* 23. Interestingly, writing nearly twenty years later, General Cheatham wrote that the march to Spring Hill was "without occurrence of note." See B. F. Cheatham, "General Cheatham at Spring Hill," in Clarence C. Buel and Robert U. Johnson, eds., *Battles and Leaders of the Civil War,* 4 vols. (New York: Century Company, 1887–89), 4:438–39.

34. Connelly, *Autumn of Glory,* 494; McDonough and Connelly, *Five Tragic Hours,* 44–46, 53; Sword, *The Confederacy's Last Hurrah,* 126–27.

35. *Official Records,* series I, vol. LXV, part I, 742; McDonough, *Nashville,* 59.

36. Connelly, *Autumn of Glory,* 500; Washington M. Ives Jr. to Dear Mother, February 13, 1865; Inglis, "Commander Florida Division, U.C.V."; Reddick, *Seventy-Seven Years in Dixie,* 28. Unfortunately, the historian must rely on memoirs written decades after the war to piece together the Florida Brigade's role at Spring Hill. It is possible that these veterans' memories were influenced by other memoirs and secondary sources published after the conflict and by stories told at United Confederate Veteran camp meetings.

37. McDonough, *Nashville,* 80, 85, 88–90; Connelly, *Autumn of Glory,* 502; November 30, 1864, in Holmes, *Diary of Henry McCall Holmes,* 23; Washington M. Ives Jr. to Dear Mother, February 13, 1865.

38. Connelly, *Autumn of Glory,* 502–3; *Official Records,* series I, vol. LXV, part II, 743; Connelly, *Autumn of Glory,* 503–4; Sword, *The Confederacy's Last Hurrah,* 177–78; McDonough and Connelly, *Five Tragic Hours,* 88–89.

39. McDonough and Connelly, *Five Tragic Hours,* 91, 96; Reddick, *Seventy-Seven Years in Dixie,* 29; Sword, *The Confederacy's Last Hurrah,* 184; November 30, 1864, in Holmes, *Diary of Henry McCall Holmes,* 23.

40. Holmes, *Diary of Henry McCall Holmes,* 23; Sword, *The Confederacy's Last Hurrah,* 238; McDonough and Connelly, *Five Tragic Hours,* 141.

41. Sword, *The Confederacy's Last Hurrah,* 238; *Official Records,* series I, vol. LXV, part I, 214; Reddick, *Seventy-Seven Years in Dixie,* 29.

42. Washington M. Ives Jr. to Mrs. Edward Badger, November 1, 1915 (photocopy), Collection of Zack C. Waters, Rome, GA; *Biographical Souvenir of the States of Georgia and Florida,* 538.

43. Reddick, *Seventy-Seven Years in Dixie,* 29; Inglis, "Commander Florida Division, U.C.V."; McKinnon, *History of Walton County,* 303.

44. McDonough, *Nashville,* 109, 111–12; Washington M. Ives Jr. to Dear Mother, February 13, 1865.

45. McDonough, *Nashville,* 109, 111–12; Reddick, *Seventy-Seven Years in Dixie,* 30; December 1, 1864, in Holmes, *Diary of Henry McCall Holmes,* 23.

46. *Official Records,* series I, vol. XLV, part II, 745. The casualty figures are derived from assuming that by the time the Florida Brigade marched into Tennessee it numbered between 800 and 900 able to bear arms and knowing that on December 13 it totaled 410 effectives. See *Official Records,* series I, vol. XLV, part II, 682. With at least 50 casualties at the Battle of Stewart's Creek on December 4 and more than 100 at the Battle of the Cedars on December 7, a loss of around 50 at Franklin seems most logical. Four of these casualties are buried at the McGavock Confederate cemetery in Franklin.

47. McDonough, *Nashville,* 143; Sword, *The Confederacy's Last Hurrah,* 296.

48. Edwin Bearss and Charles Spearman, "The Battle of the Cedars," 2, unpublished account in the Stones River National Military Park files, Murfreesboro, TN; Hughes, *The Pride of the Confederate Artillery,* 232; McDonough, *Nashville,* 144; Sword, *The Confederacy's Last Hurrah,* 295; December 4, 1864, in Holmes, *Diary of Henry McCall Holmes,* 23–24. The 6th Florida guarded the division's wagon train during the battle.

49. Sword, *The Confederacy's Last Hurrah,* 293; McLeod Diary, December 4, 1864; *Official Records,* series I, vol. XLV, part I, 615, 624; Bearss and Spearman, "The Battle of the Cedars," 5. Washington Ives wrote that the Florida Brigade had but two hundred soldiers in the fight. The number, when compared with the December 13 report, is likely inaccurate. See Washington M. Ives Jr. to Dear Mother, February 13, 1865.

50. Washington M. Ives Jr. to Dear Mother, February 13, 1865; *Official Records,* series I, vol. XLV, part I, 616, 745; J. Adolphe Chalaron, "Hood's Campaign at Murfeesboro," *Confederate Veteran* 11 (1903): 439–40, quoted in Hughes, *The Pride of the Confederate Artillery,* 234–35; "Report of Henry Rootes Jackson of the Atlanta Campaign," Benjamin Franklin Cheatham Papers, Tennessee State Library and Archives, Nashville. Colonel John Jones of the 174th Ohio claimed to have captured twenty Floridians, which would increase Confederate casualty numbers. See *Official Records,* series I, vol. XLV, part I, 624. See also the letter of an excited Ohio soldier in the *Ohio State Journal,* January 4, 1865.

51. December 4, 1864, in Holmes, *Diary of Henry McCall Holmes,* 24; McLeod Diary, December 4, 1864.

52. Philip D. Stephenson, *Civil War Memoir,* ed. Nathaniel C. Hughes Jr. (Conway, AK, 1995), 299, and Chalaron, "Hood's Campaign at Murfeesboro," quoted in Hughes, *The Pride of the Confederate Artillery,* 234–35; "Report of Henry Rootes Jackson of the Atlanta Campaign."

53. Bearss and Spearman, "The Battle of the Cedars," 2–3; Sword, *The Confederacy's Last Hurrah,* 296; Reddick, *Seventy-Seven Years in Dixie,* 31.

54. Sword, *The Confederacy's Last Hurrah,* 296; McDonough, *Nashville,* 145; *Official Records,* series I, vol. LXV, part I, 746.

55. McDonough, *Nashville,* 146; Sword, *The Confederacy's Last Hurrah,* 297; Bearss and Spearman, "The Battle of the Cedars," 6; *Official Records,* series I, vol. LXV, part I, 746.

56. McLeod Diary, December 7, 1864; December 7, 1864, in Holmes, *Diary of Henry*

McCall Holmes, 24; Bearss and Spearman, "The Battle of the Cedars," 6; John Allen Wyeth, *Life of Nathan Bedford Forrest* (1901; reprint, Dayton, OH: Morningside Bookshop, 1988), 551, quoted in Sword, *The Confederacy's Last Hurrah,* 297; Reddick, *Seventy-Seven Years in Dixie,* 31.

57. A. N. McGinnis to Mr. Wash M. Ives, December 17, 1912, Ives Papers; *Ohio State Journal,* January 4, 1865; Hartman and Coles, *Biographical Rosters,* 1:1–137, 260–368, 2:579–778, 4:1317–1406. For an excellent account of the capture and return of the 1st and 4th Florida's battle flag, see Don Hillhouse, "The Colors Twice Lost," *Confederate Veteran* (September–October 1988): 16–21.

58. Hughes, *The Pride of the Confederate Artillery,* 244–45; McLeod Diary, December 7, 1864; Sword, *The Confederacy's Last Hurrah,* 298.

59. Stephenson, *Civil War Memoir,* 511, quoted in Hughes, *The Pride of the Confederate Artillery,* 245; McLeod Diary, December 7, 1864; "Report of Brigadier-General Henry Rootes Jackson of the Atlanta, Georgia Campaign."

60. *Official Records,* series I, vol. XLV, part I, 623, 626.

61. McLeod Diary, December 11, 1864; Washington M. Ives Jr. to Dear Mother, February 13, 1865; Connelly, *Autumn of Glory,* 507–8; McDonough, *Nashville,* 142; Sword, *The Confederacy's Last Hurrah,* 316.

62. *Official Records,* series I, vol. XLV, part I, 680; Connelly, *Autumn of Glory,* 508; McDonough, *Nashville,* 155, 180–81. General Bate mentions in his Tennessee Campaign report that Major Glover Ball had arrived and "assumed command and conducted it at Nashville." As Ball's commission outdated Lash's, the Tallahassee painter maintained seniority.

63. Sword, *The Confederacy's Last Hurrah,* 320, 342, 365; McLeod Diary, December 15, 1864; Foote, *The Civil War,* 3:691; McDonough, *Nashville,* 207–8; Connelly, *Autumn of Glory,* 510. Following the Battle of Nashville, Compton's Hill was renamed Shy's Hill in memory of the 20th Tennessee's William Shy, who was killed on its slopes.

64. Sword, *The Confederacy's Last Hurrah,* 370, 372; *Official Records,* series I, vol. XLV, part I, 748; McLeod Diary, December 15, 1864; McDonough, *Nashville,* 239, 243–44.

65. McDonough, *Nashville,* 241; McLeod Diary, December 15, 1864; McKinnon, *History of Walton County,* 303; Foote, *The Civil War,* 3:701.

66. Sword, *The Confederacy's Last Hurrah,* 366–67; McDonough, *Nashville,* 246, 368; Foote, *The Civil War,* 3:700–701.

67. McDonough, *Nashville,* 248; Sword, *The Confederacy's Last Hurrah,* 373; December 16, 1864, in Holmes, *Diary of Henry McCall Holmes,* 25; McKinnon, *History of Walton County,* 303; Connelly, *Autumn of Glory,* 511–12.

68. *Official Records,* series I, vol. XLV, part I, 750; McKinnon, *History of Walton County,* 303–4; Reddick, *Seventy-Seven Years in Dixie,* 32; M. Roberts, "Third Florida Regiment," *Confederate Veteran* 10 (1902): 355; J. W. Kellum, "Third Florida Regiment-Personal," *Confederate Veteran* 14 (1906): 554.

69. Howard Michael Madaus and Robert D. Needham, illus., "The Battle Flags of the Confederate Army of Tennessee" (Milwaukee: Milwaukee Public Museum, 1976), 65; "Jacob Alexander Lash (1829–1865) Background," Lash Letters; Inglis, "Commander Florida Division, U.C.V.," 159; Hartman and Coles, *Biographical Rosters,* 2:659.

70. McLeod Diary, December 16, 1864; Reddick, *Seventy-Seven Years in Dixie,* 33; Hart-

man and Coles, *Biographical Rosters,* 1:25–31, 47–65, 273–84, 305–14, 337–48, 450–58, 2:580–89, 725–33, 743–51, 4:1330–39, 1386–92.

71. Connelly, *Autumn of Glory,* 511–12; December 16, 1864, in Holmes, *Diary of Henry McCall Holmes,* 25; Washington M. Ives Jr. to Dear Mother, February 13, 1865, Ives Papers.

72. Washington M. Ives Jr. to Dear Mrs. Badger, November 1, 1915, Ives Papers. For the Florida Brigade's retreat from Tennessee, see Holmes, *Diary of Henry McCall Holmes,* 25–27, and McLeod Diary, December 16, 1864–January 1, 1865.

73. Washington M. Ives to Dear Mother, February 13, 1865; Watkins, *Company Aytch,* 240.

Epilogue

1. Washington M. Ives to Dear Mother, February 13, 1865; Connelly, *Autumn of Glory,* 514; Nathaniel Cheairs Hughes Jr., *Bentonville: The Final Battle of Sherman and Johnston* (Chapel Hill: University of North Carolina Press, 1996), 25, 42; Marszalek, *Sherman,* 317.

2. February 11, 1865, in Holmes, *Diary of Henry McCall Holmes,* 30; Hughes, *Bentonville,* 43; Albert Livingston to My dear Parents, March 5, 1865, Livingston/Inglis Letters.

3. Albert Livingston to My dear Parents, March 5, 1865; Hughes, *Bentonville,* 29, 30.

4. Albert Livingston to My Dear Parents, March 24, 1865, Livingston/Inglis Letters; March 19, 1865, in Holmes, *Diary of Henry McCall Holmes,* 32.

5. March 19, 1865, in Holmes, *Diary of Henry McCall Holmes,* 32; Benjamin R. Glover to Betty, March 30, 1865, Glover Letters; Albert Livingston to My Dear Parents, March 24, 1865.

6. April 10, 1865, in Holmes, *Diary of Henry McCall Holmes,* 34.

7. Abstracted from 1st Florida Infantry, Consolidated, *Muster Rolls and Lists of Confederate Troops Paroled in North Carolina,* NA Microcopy M1781, Roll #2, NA, Washingon, DC.

8. *Official Records,* series I, vol. XLVII, part I, 1061; Theodore Livingston to Dear Archie, May 22, 1865, Livingston/Inglis Letters.

9. From Santa Rosa Island through Bentonville, more than two thousand Florida Brigade soldiers were killed, wounded, or captured.

10. Daniel G. McLean to Miss Maggie McKenzie, March 21, 1863, in Tucker, *McKenzie Correspondence,* 94. For more on the Constitutional Convention of 1885, see Edward Williamson, "The Constitutional Convention of 1885," *Florida Historical Quarterly* 41, no. 2 (1962): 116–26.

11. Roderick G. Shaw to My Dear Sister, April 16, 1864, Shaw Letters.

12. J. J. Finley to My Dear Father, February 28, 1866, and General J. J. Finley Biographical Sketch, Finley Family Papers; Warner, *Generals in Gray,* 89; Jerrell H. Shofner, *Nor Is It Over Yet: Florida in the Era of Reconstruction, 1863–1877* (Gainesville: University Presses of Florida, 1974), 304.

13. Schofner, *Nor Is It Over Yet,* 304, 63; Waters, "Through Good and Evil Fortune," 142–44; Warner, *Generals in Gray,* 39–40.

14. Warner, *Generals in Gray,* 39–40, 217–18.

15. Ibid., 7–8; McMurry, "Patton Anderson," 17.

16. Shofner, *Nor Is It Over Yet,* 90, 103.

17. *Jacksonville (FL) Times-Union,* September 29, 1887.

18. Ibid., March 6, 1901; "Thaddeus MacDonell," *Biographical Souvenir of the States of Georgia and Florida,* 545–46.

19. James M. Phalen, "George Troup Maxwell," *Dictionary of American Biography* Base Set (American Council of Learned Societies, 1928–36).

20. "Bowen Line."

21. "Col. Edward Badger," *Biographical Souvenir of the States of Georgia and Florida,* 33–34; *Jacksonville (FL) Times-Union,* November 22, 1892; Green, *The Badger Family,* 5–6.

22. "Jacob Alexander Lash (1829–1865) Background."

23. *Quincy Herald,* February 9, 1884; *Jacksonville (FL) Times-Union,* February 9, 1884; Register, *The Kenan Family,* 30.

24. *Biographical Dictionary of the US Congress 1774 to Present,* http://bioguide.congress .gov/ (accessed January 6, 2010).

25. *Jacksonville (FL) Times-Union,* June 2, 1866.

26. Kosse Cemetery Survey, http://ftp.rootsweb.ancestry.com/pub/usgenweb/tx/limestone/ cemeteries/kosse.txt (accessed January 6, 2010).

27. "Capt. W. T. Saxon," *Confederate Veteran* 33 (1925): 62.

28. "David Ewell Maxwell," Maxwell Mss.; Maxwell, "Some Letters to His Parents," 353.

29. Rerick, "Augustus O. McDonell," *Memoirs of Florida,* 1:610.

30. "S. D. McConnell," *Biographical Souvenir of the States of Georgia and Florida,* 533–34.

31. McLeon, "Capt. John L. Inglis"; *Jacksonville (FL) Times-Union,* June 4, 1917.

32. Hartman and Coles, *Biographical Rosters,* 2:580.

33. "In Memoriam: Francis Philip Fleming," *Florida Historical Quarterly* 2, no. 1 (1909): 3–8.

34. William McLeod Soldier's Pension Claim, Florida Confederate Pension Claims, FSA, Tallahassee; Florida State Archives Civil War Guide, http://www.floridamemory.com/ collections/civilwarguide.cfm (accessed January 5, 2010).

35. Robert Blair Smith to Hon. E. Amos, May 12, 1917, Robert Blair Smith Soldier's Pension Claim, Florida Confederate Pension Claims, FSA, Tallahassee; Geer Ancestry, http://wc.rootsweb.ancestry.com (accessed October 13, 2011).

36. Ellis, "Short Record of T. B. Ellis, Sr.," 11.

37. Hartman and Coles, *Biographical Rosters,* 1:80.

38. "Official Souvenir Programme of the Unveiling Ceremonies of the Confederate Monument at St. James Park, Jacksonville, Florida, June 16, 1898" (Jacksonville: Conkling and Dudley, 1898); Mary C. Dixon, "Charles C. Hemming," *Confederate Veteran* 24 (1916): 364–65.

39. Coski, "'I Am in for Anything for Success,'" 85–86; "Archibald Livingston," *Confederate Veteran* 24 (1916): 323.

40. Campbell, *Southern Service,* xiii–xiv.

41. Mrs. O. F. Wiley, "Edward Clifford Brush," *Confederate Veteran* 40 (1932): 145.

42. *New York Times,* March 14, 1917.

Bibliography

Primary Sources

Published Government Documents

Davis, Major George B., Leslie J. Perry, and Joseph W. Kirkland. Comp. Captain Calvin D. Cowles. *The Official Military Atlas of the Civil War.* 1891–95. Reprint, New York: Barnes and Noble Publishing, 2003.

Hewett, Janet, Noah Andre Trudeau, and Bryce A. Suderow, eds. *Supplement to the Official Records of the Union and Confederate Armies.* 100 vols. Wilmington, NC: Broadfoot Publishing, 1995.

War Department. *War of the Rebellion: A Compilation of the Official Records the Union and the Confederate Armies.* 128 vols. Washington, DC, 1880–1901.

Manuscript Government Documents

Compiled Service Records of Confederate Generals and Staff Officers and Non Regimental Enlisted Men. War Department Collection of Confederate Records, Record Group 109, Microfilm 331. Washington, DC.

Compiled Service Records of Confederate Soldiers Who Served in Organizations from the State of Florida. War Department Collection of Confederate Records, Record Group 109, Microfilm 251. Washington, DC.

Eighth Census of the United States, 1860. Records of the Census, Record Group 29, Microfilm M653. Washington, DC.

Florida Tax Rolls, 1839–1854, 1856–1864. Florida State Archives, Tallahassee, Microcopy, S28.

General and Special Orders, 1861–1862. Army of Pensacola. Records of Military Commands. War Department Collection of Confederate Records, Record Group 109. Washington, DC.

General and Special Orders, 1861–1862. Department of Alabama and West Florida. Records of Military Commands. War Department Collection of Confederate Records, Record Group 109. Washington, DC.

Inspection Records and Related Records Received by the Inspection Branch in the Confederate Adjutant and Inspector General's Office. War Department Collection of Confederate Records, Record Group 109, Microfilm M935. Washington, DC.

Letters Received by the Confederate Adjutant General, 1861–1865. War Department Collection of Confederate Records, Record Group 109, Microfilm M474. Washington, DC.

Letters Received by the Confederate Secretary of War, 1861–1865. War Department Collection of Confederate Records, Record Group 109, Microfilm M437. Washington, DC.

Letters Sent, February to July 1862. Department of South Carolina, Georgia, and Florida, 1861–1862. Records of Military Commands. War Department Collection of Confederate Records, Record Group 109. Washington, DC.

Letters Sent and Endorsements, Department of South Carolina, Georgia, and Florida, 1861–1862. Records of Military Commands. War Department Collection of Confederate Records, Record Group 109. Washington, DC.

Letters, Telegrams, and Orders Received and Sent, General John C. Breckinridge's Command, 1861–1865. Records of Military Commands. War Department Collection of Confederate Records, Record Group 109. Washington, DC.

Letters, Telegrams, and Reports, November 1861–May 1862. Department of South Carolina, Georgia, and Florida, 1861–1862. Records of Military Commands. War Department Collection of Confederate Records, Record Group 109. Washington, DC.

Muster Rolls and Lists of Confederate Troops Paroled in North Carolina. National Archives Microcopy M1781. War Department Collection of Confederate Records, Record Group 109. Washington, DC.

Orders and Circulars, Department of Tennessee, 1862–1865. Records of Military Commands. War Department Collection of Confederate Records, Record Group 109. Washington, DC.

Orders and Circulars of the Army of the Mississippi, 1861–1865. Records of Military Commands. War Department Collection of Confederate Records, Record Group 109. Washington, DC.

Orders and Circulars of William J. Hardee's Command, February 1863–March 1865. Records of Military Commands. War Department Collection of Confederate Records, Record Group 109. Washington, DC.

Orders of Patton Anderson's Brigade. Army of the Mississippi, 1862. Records of Military Commands. War Department Collection of Confederate Records, Record Group 109. Washington, DC.

Records of the Confederate Department of East Tennessee, 1861–1864. Records of Military Commands. War Department Collection of Confederate Records, Record Group 109. Washington, DC.

Manuscript Collections

Badger, Mrs. Edward to "Gov. Fleming." December 8, 1905. Typescript. Collection of Zack C. Waters, Rome, GA.

Bailey Family Papers. P. K. Yonge Library of Florida History, Gainesville.

Bird Biographical File. Keystone Genealogical Society, Monticello, FL.

Bowen, W.L.L. H. A. Clinch Camp Confederate Veterans Questionnaire, May 8, 1900. Typescript. Collection of Zack C. Waters, Rome, GA.

"Bowen Line." Bowen Genealogical File. Collection of Zack C. Waters, Rome, GA.

Bragg, Braxton. Papers. William P. Palmer Collection, Western Reserve, Cleveland, OH.

Bright, Captain Alexander H. Letter. P. K. Yonge Library of Florida History, Gainesville.

Brush, Edward Clifford. Diary. Museum of the Confederacy, Richmond, VA.

Bullock, Robert. Letters. Georgia Department of Archives and History, Atlanta.

Cheatham, Benjamin Franklin. Papers. Tennessee State Library and Archives, Nashville.

Fairbanks Collection, 1817–1942. Special Collections, Robert M. Strozier Library, Florida State University, Tallahassee.

Finley, J. J. Letter. "Eyewitness Account File." Chickamauga-Chattanooga National Military Park, Fort Oglethorpe, GA.

Finley Family Papers. Museum of the Confederacy, Richmond, VA.

Florida Confederate Pension Claims. Florida State Archives, Tallahassee.

"Florida House Members by District." Florida Biographical Files. Florida State Library, Tallahassee.

"Florida Senators by District." Florida Biographical Files. Florida State Library, Tallahassee.

Glover, Benjamin. Letters. Alabama State Department of Archives and History, Montgomery.

Gospero, Roderick, and James Kilpatrick Shaw. Letters. Special Collections, Robert M. Strozier Library, Florida State University, Tallahassee.

Harris, Seaborn. Civil War records, 1861–1862. N2002-4. Florida State Archives, Tallahassee.

Harris, S. H. Letters. Museum of the Confederacy, Richmond, VA.

Hays, James. Letters. United Daughters of the Confederacy Bound Transcripts. Vol. 4. Georgia Department of Archives and History, Atlanta.

Hemming, Charles C. Papers. P. K. Yonge Library of Florida History, Gainesville.

Inglis, John Livingston. Diary. Special Collections, Robert M. Strozier Library, Florida State University, Tallahassee.

Ives, Washington M. Diary, 1860–1862. M88-45. Florida State Archives, Tallahassee.

———. "The Finality of June 27th, 1864." Typescript. Collection of Zack C. Waters, Rome, GA.

———. Letter to "Dear Mrs. Badger." November 1, 1915. Typescript. Collection of Zack C. Waters, Rome, GA.

———. Papers. M44. Florida State Library, Tallahassee.

Jerkins, Reason W. Letter. Typescript. Collection of Zack C. Waters, Rome, GA.

Lash, Jacob A. Letters. Photocopy. Collection of Zack C. Waters, Rome, GA.

Livingston/Inglis Letters. Museum of the Confederacy, Richmond, VA.

"Madison Starke Perry." Biographical Packets. P. K. Yonge Library of Florida History, Gainesville.

Maxwell Mss. Photocopy. Collection of Zack C. Waters, Rome, GA.

McConnell, Samuel D. Papers, 1859–1876. P. K. Yonge Library of Florida History, Gainesville.

McDonell, Augustus O. Papers, 1861–1864. P. K. Yonge Library of Florida History, Gainesville.

McGriff, Patrick Augustus. Letters. M87-19. Florida State Archives, Tallahassee.

McLean Family Papers. P. K. Yonge Library of Florida History, Gainesville.

McLeod, William. Civil War pocket diary, 1864–1865. M97-20. Florida State Archives, Tallahassee.

Milton, John. Letterbook, 1861–1863. S32-6. Florida State Archives, Tallahassee.

———. Letterbook, 1863–1865. S32-7. Florida State Archives, Tallahassee.

Moody, Lemuel. Letters. Collection of Zack C. Waters, Rome, GA.

Nicks, Francis Rinaldo. Letters, 1863–1864. M88-3. Florida State Archives, Tallahassee.

Ottinger, Daniel L. et al. Kenan Epitaph by Washington Lodge No. 2. Photocopy. Collection of Zack C. Waters, Rome, GA.

Palmer Family Letters. M87-36. Florida State Archives, Tallahassee.

Partridge, Benjamin Waring. Letters. Perkins Library, Duke University, Durham, NC.

Perry, Madison Starke. Letters, 1860–1862. P. K. Yonge Library of Florida History, Gainesville.

Pugh, Isaac. Papers. Special Collections Library, University of California, Riverside.

Randolph Family Papers, 1814–1978. M75-86 (typescript). Florida State Archives, Tallahassee.

Raysor Family Correspondence. P. K. Yonge Library of Florida History, Gainesville.

Rice, B. L. Letters. MS 7. Florida State Library, Tallahassee.

Rogers, William D. Letters, 1862–1865. M89-22. Florida State Archives, Tallahassee.

Shaw, Roderick G. Letters. M87-6. Florida State Archives, Tallahassee.

Stone Family Letters. M88-1. Florida State Archives, Tallahassee.

Talley, William Raulston. Memoir. Georgia Department of Archives and History, Atlanta.

Tippins-Wild Family Papers. Howard-Tilton Memorial Library, Tulane University, New Orleans, LA.

United Daughters of the Confederacy. Florida Division Scrapbooks, 1900–1935. M96-18. Florida State Archives, Tallahassee.

Vann, Enoch J. Papers. Museum of the Confederacy, Richmond, VA.

Wood, Dallas. Letter. Special Collections, Robert M. Strozier Library, Florida State University, Tallahassee.

Wright, Henry T. Letters. Special Collections, Robert M. Strozier Library, Florida State University, Tallahassee.

Collected Works, Letters, Diaries, Memoirs, and Reminiscences

Adventures of the Marion Hornets, Co. H, 7th Regt. Fla. Vols. Knoxville: privately published, 1863.

Blakey, Arch Fredric, Ann Smith Lainhart, and Winston Bryant Stephens Jr., eds. *Rose Cottage Chronicles: Civil War Letters of the Bryant-Stephens Families of North Florida.* Gainesville: University Press of Florida, 1998.

Campbell, R. Thomas, ed. *Southern Service on Land & Sea: The Wartime Journal of Robert Watson, CSA/CSN.* Knoxville: University of Tennessee Press, 2002.

Coles, David, and Zack C. Waters, eds. "Indian Fighter, Confederate Soldier, Blockade Runner, and Scout: The Life and Letters of Jacob E. Mickler." *El Escribano* 34 (1997): 34–69.

Coski, John M., ed. "'I Am in for Anything for Success': The Letters of Sergeant Archie Livingston 3rd Florida Infantry." *North and South* 6 (2003): 76–86.

Dodd, Dorothy, ed. "Edmund Ruffin's Account of the Florida Secession Convention, 1861." *Florida Historical Quarterly* 12 (1933): 67–76.

Doty, Franklin A., ed. "The Civil War Letters of Augustus Henry Mathers, Assistant Surgeon, Fourth Florida Regiment, C.S.A." *Florida Historical Quarterly* 36 (1957): 94–124.

Duke, John K. *History of the Fifty-Third Regiment, Ohio Volunteer Infantry during the War of the Rebellion, 1861 to 1865.* Portsmouth, OH: Blade Printing Company, 1900.

Ellis, Thomas Benton, Sr. "Short Record of T. B. Ellis, Sr." T. B. Ellis Biographical File. Florida State Library, Tallahassee.

Frano, Elizabeth Caldwell, comp. *Letters of Captain Hugh Black to His Family in Florida during the War between the States, 1862–1864.* Newburgh, IN: privately published, 1998.

Hemming, Charles. "A Confederate Odyssey." *American Heritage* 36 (December 1984): 69–84.

Holmes, Henry McCall. *Diary of Henry McCall Holmes Army of Tennessee, Assistant Surgeon Florida Troops with Related Letters Documents, Etc.* State College, MS, 1968.

Inglis, John Livingston. "Commander Florida Division, U.C.V." *Confederate Veteran* 22 (1914): 159.

Ives, W. M. "Captured and Escaped Three Times." *Confederate Veteran* 12 (1904): 228.

———. *Civil War Journal and Diary of Serg. Washington Ives, 4th Florida, C.S.A.* Transcribed by Jim R. Cabaniss. N.p., 1987.

———. "Friends and Comrades." *Confederate Veteran* 24 (1916): 427.

———. "Gen. Jesse J. Finley's Wounds." *Jacksonville Florida Times-Union,* July 29, 1907.

Johnson, Robert U., and Clarence C. Buel, eds. *Battles and Leaders of the Civil War.* 4 vols. New York: Century Company, 1887–89.

Maxwell, David E. "Some Letters to His Parents by a Floridian in the Confederate Army." Transcribed by Gilbert Wright. *Florida Historical Quarterly* 36, no. 4 (1958): 353–72.

McConnell, Samuel D. Letter. http://www.soldierstudies.org/ (accessed January 20, 2010).

McKinnon, John L. *History of Walton County.* Atlanta: privately published, 1911.

Milner, W. J. "Battle of Santa Rosa Island." *Confederate Veteran* 11 (1903): 20–21.

Moore, Frank, ed. *Rebellion Record: A Diary of American Events with Documents, Narratives, Illustrative Events, Poetry, Etc.* 12 vols. 1861–68. Reprint, New York: Arno Books, 1977.

Murray, Dr. W. J. "Concerning the Twentieth Tennessee." *Confederate Veteran* 6 (1898): 123–24.

Pasco, Samuel. *Private Pasco: A Civil War Diary.* Ed. William Pasco and William Gibbons. Oak Brook, IL: McAdams Multigraphics, 1990.

Perry, W. L. "Departure of the Volunteers." *Southern Messenger,* April 3, 1861.

Reddick, Henry W. *Seventy-Seven Years in Dixie: The Boys in Gray of 61–65.* Santa Rosa, FL: published by the author, 1910.

Roberts, M. "Third Florida Regiment." *Confederate Veteran* 10 (1902): 355.

Rogers, William Warren, ed. "Florida on the Eve of the Civil War as Seen by a Southern Reporter." *Florida Historical Quarterly* 39 (1960): 145–58.

Savas, Theodore, and David A. Woodbury, eds. *The Campaign for Atlanta & Sherman's March to the Sea*. El Dorado Hills, CA: Savas Woodbury Publishers, 1992.

Stockton, William T., and Ju Stockton. *The Correspondence of Will and Ju Stockton, 1845–1869*. Transcribed by Herman Ulmer, Jr. Privately published, 1989.

Tolles, Zonira Hunter. *Bonnie Melrose: The Early History of Melrose, Florida*. Keystone Heights, FL: privately published, 1982.

Treinner [Trimmer], William H. "Experiences at Fort Pickens, Fla., 1861." *Confederate Veteran* 19 (1911): 337–38.

Tucker, William Hugh, ed. *The McKenzie Correspondence, 1849–1901*. Elmira, NY: privately published, 2004.

Tutwiler, Mrs. J. B. "Lieut. John Wilson on Snodgrass Hill." *Confederate Veteran* 21 (1913): 62.

Watford, Christopher M., ed. *The Civil War in North Carolina: Soldiers' and Civilians' Letters and Diaries, 1861–1865*. Vol. 2, *The Mountains* Jefferson, NC: McFarland and Company, 2003.

Williamson, Edward C., ed. "Francis P. Fleming in the War for Southern Independence: Letters from the Front, Part II." *Florida Historical Quarterly* 28 (1949): 144–55.

———. "Francis P. Fleming in the War for Southern Independence: Letters from the Front, Part III." *Florida Historical Quarterly* 28 (1950): 205–10.

Newspapers

Atlanta Daily Intelligencer
Atlanta Journal
Atlanta Southern Confederacy
Augusta (GA) Daily Constitutionalist
Cedar Keys (FL) Telegraph
Chattanooga Daily Rebel
Columbus (GA) Daily Enquirer
Columbus (GA) Daily Sun
Fernandina (FL) East Floridian
Gainesville Cotton States
Jacksonville (FL) Times-Union
Jacksonville St. John's Mirror
Jacksonville Standard
Macon (GA) Daily Telegraph
Memphis Daily Appeal
Mobile Register and Advertiser
Monticello Family Friend
New Orleans Daily Picayune
New York Times
Pensacola Weekly Observer
Quincy (FL) Herald

Richmond Daily Dispatch
Tallahassee Florida Sentinel
Tallahassee Floridian and Journal
Tallahassee Weekly Floridian
Tampa Florida Peninsular
Washington, D.C., National Tribune

Secondary Sources

Books

Atkins, Jonathan M. *Parties, Politics, and the Sectional Conflict in Tennessee, 1832–1861.* Knoxville: University of Tennessee Press, 1997.

Baptist, Edward E. *Creating an Old South: Middle Florida's Plantation Frontier before the Civil War.* Chapel Hill, NC: University of North Carolina Press, 2002.

Bearss, Edwin C. *The Siege of Jackson, July 10–17, 1863.* Baltimore: Gateway Press, 1981.

Biographical Souvenir of the States of Georgia and Florida. Chicago: F. A. Battery and Company, 1889.

Boatner, Mark M., III. *The Civil War Dictionary.* Rev. ed. New York: David McKay Company, 1988.

Brown, Canter, Jr. *Florida's Peace River Frontier.* Orlando: University of Central Florida Press, 1991.

Bunch, Jack. *Roster of the Courts-Martial in the Confederate States Army.* Shippensburg, PA: White Mane Books, 2001.

Carlson, Charlie. *The First Florida Cavalry Regiment, CSA.* New Smyrna, FL: Luthers, 1999.

Castel, Albert. *Decision in the West: The Atlanta Campaign of 1864.* Lawrence: University of Kansas Press, 1992.

Catton, Bruce. *Grant Takes Command.* Boston: Little, Brown and Company, 1969.

Connelly, Thomas L. *Army of the Heartland: The Army of Tennessee, 1861–1862.* 1967. Reprint, Baton Rouge: Louisiana State University Press, 2001.

———. *Autumn of Glory: The Army of Tennessee, 1862–1865.* 1971. Reprint, Baton Rouge: Louisiana State University Press, 2001.

Cozzens, Peter. *No Better Place to Die: The Battle of Stones River.* Urbana: University of Illinois Press, 1990.

———. *The Shipwreck of Their Hopes: The Battles for Chattanooga.* Urbana: University of Illinois Press, 1994.

———. *This Terrible Sound: The Battle of Chickamauga.* Urbana: University of Illinois Press, 1992.

Crute, Joseph J., Jr. *Units of the Confederate States Army.* 2nd ed. Gaithersburg, MD: Olde Soldier Books, 1987.

Cullum, George W. *Notices of the Biographical Register of Officers and Graduates of the U.S. Military Academy at West Point from 1802–1867.* Vol. 1. Rev. ed. New York, 1879.

Daniel, Larry J. *Days of Glory: The Army of the Cumberland, 1861–1865.* Baton Rouge: Louisiana State University Press, 2004.

———. *Shiloh: The Battle That Changed the Civil War.* New York: Touchtone, 1998.

——. *Soldiering in the Army of Tennessee.* Chapel Hill: University of North Carolina Press, 1991.

Davis, William C. *Breckinridge: Statesman, Soldier, Symbol.* Baton Rouge, LA: Louisiana State University Press, 1974.

Davis, William Watson. *The Civil War and Reconstruction in Florida.* 1913. Reprint, Gainesville, FL, 1964.

Denham, James M. *Rouge's Paradise: Crime and Punishment in Antebellum Florida, 1821–1861.* Tuscaloosa: The University of Alabama Press, 1997.

Dickison, J. J. *Confederate Military History.* Vol. XVI, *Florida.* 1899. Reprint, Wilmington, NC: Broadfoot Publishing, 1989.

Doherty, Herbert J., Jr. *The Whigs of Florida, 1845–1854.* Gainesville: University of Florida Press, 1959.

Donald, David Herbert. *Lincoln.* New York: Simon and Schuster, 1995.

Ecelbarger, Gary. *The Day Dixie Died: The Battle of Atlanta.* New York: Thomas Dunne Books, 2010.

Elliott, Sam Davis. *Soldier of Tennessee: General Alexander P. Stewart and the Civil War in the West.* Baton Rouge: Louisiana State University Press, 1999.

Engle, Stephen D. *Don Carlos Buell: Most Promising of All.* Chapel Hill: University of North Carolina Press, 1996.

Fisher, Noel C. *War at Every Door: Partisan Politics and Guerilla Warfare in East Tennessee, 1860–1869.* Chapel Hill: University of North Carolina Press, 1997.

Foote, Shelby. *The Civil War: A Narrative.* 3 vols. 1958. Reprint, New York: Vintage Books, 1986.

Gallagher, Gary W. *The Confederate War.* Cambridge, MA: Harvard University Press, 1997.

Gannon, Michael, ed. *The New History of Florida.* Gainesville, FL: University Press of Florida, 1996.

Glatthaar, Joseph T. *General Lee's Army: From Victory to Collapse.* New York: Free Press, 2008.

Green, Emily Badger. *The Badger Family.* Ocala: privately published, 1945.

Griffith, Paddy. *Battle Tactics of the Civil War.* 1987. Reprint. New Haven: Yale University Press, 2001.

Hallock, Judith. *Braxton Bragg and Confederate Defeat.* Vol. II. Tuscaloosa: The University of Alabama Press, 1991.

Hartman, David W., and David J. Coles, comps. *Biographical Rosters of Florida's Confederate and Union Soldiers, 1861–1865.* 5 vols. Wilmington, NC: Broadfoot Publishing, 1995.

Hess, Earl J. *Banners to the Breeze: The Kentucky Campaign, Corinth, and Stones River.* Lincoln: University of Nebraska Press, 2000.

Horn, Stanley F. *The Army of Tennessee.* 1941. Reprint, Norman: University of Oklahoma Press, 1993.

Hughes, Nathaniel Cheairs, Jr. *Bentonville: The Final Battle of Sherman and Johnston.* Chapel Hill: University of North Carolina Press, 1996.

——. *General William J. Hardee: Old Reliable.* Baton Rouge: Louisiana State University Press, 1965.

——. *The Pride of the Confederate Artillery: The Washington Artillery in the Army of Tennessee.* Baton Rouge: Louisiana State University Press, 1997.

Huxford, Folks. *Pioneers of Wiregrass Georgia.* 10 vols. Waycross, GA: Herrin's Print Shop, 1951.

Inscoe, John C., and Gordon B. McKinney. *The Heart of Confederate Appalachia: Western North Carolina in the Civil War.* Chapel Hill: University of North Carolina Press, 2000.

Johns, John E. *Florida during the Civil War.* 1963. Reprint. Jacksonville, FL: Miller Press, 1989.

Johnson, Allen, and Dumas Malone, eds. *Dictionary of American Biography.* New York: Charles Scribner's Sons, 1937.

Jones, James P. *Black Jack: John A. Logan and Southern Illinois in the Civil War Era.* 1967. Reprint, Carbondale: Southern Illinois University Press, 1995.

Jones, Joseph. *Medical and Surgical Memoirs.* New Orleans: printed for the author by Clark and Hofeline, 1876–90.

Kellum, J. W. "Third Florida Regiment-Personal." *Confederate Veteran* 14 (1906): 554.

Lonn, Ella. *Desertion during the Civil War.* New York: Century Company, 1928.

Lowe, Richard. *Walker's Texas Division C.S.A. Greyhounds of the TransMississippi.* Baton Rouge: Louisiana State University Press, 2004.

Madaus, Howard Michael, and Robert D. Needham, illus. "The Battle Flags of the Confederate Army of Tennessee." Milwaukee, WI: Milwaukee Public Museum, 1976.

Manning, Chandra. *What This Cruel War Was Over: Soldiers, Slavery, and the Civil War.* New York: Knopf, 2007.

Marszalek, John F. *Sherman: A Soldier's Passion for Order.* 1992. New York: Vintage Books, 1994.

Martin, Richard A., and Daniel S. Schafer. *Jacksonville's Ordeal by Fire.* Jacksonville: Florida Publishing Company, 1984.

McDonough, James Lee. *Chattanooga: A Death Grip on the Confederacy.* Knoxville: University of Tennessee Press, 1984.

———. *Nashville: The Western Confederacy's Final Gamble.* Knoxville: University of Tennessee Press, 2004.

———. *Stones River: Bloody Winter in Tennessee.* Knoxville: University of Tennessee Press, 1980.

———. *The War in Kentucky: From Shiloh to Perryville.* Knoxville: University of Tennessee Press, 1994.

McDonough, James Lee, and Thomas L. Connelly. *Five Tragic Hours: The Battle of Franklin.* Knoxville: University of Tennessee Press, 1988.

McDonough, James Lee, and James Pickett Jones. *War So Terrible: Sherman and Atlanta.* New York: W. W. Norton, 1987.

McKenzie, Robert Tracy. *Lincolnites and Rebels: A Divided Town in the American Civil War.* Oxford: Oxford University Press, 2006.

McMurry, Richard M. *Atlanta 1864: Last Chance for the Confederacy.* Lincoln: University of Nebraska Press, 2000.

———. *Two Great Rebel Armies: An Essay in Confederate Military History.* Chapel Hill: University of North Carolina Press, 1989.

McPherson, James M. *Battle Cry of Freedom: The Civil War Era.* New York: Ballantine Books, 1989.

———. *For Cause and Comrades: Why Men Fought the Civil War.* New York: Oxford University Press, 1997.

McWhiney, Grady. *Braxton Bragg and Confederate Defeat.* Vol. 1, *Field Command.* New York: Columbia University Press, 1969.

McWhiney, Grady, and Perry D. Jamison. *Attack and Die: Civil War Tactics and the Southern Heritage.* Tuscaloosa: The University of Alabama Press, 1982.

Mitchell, Reid. *Civil War Soldiers: Their Expectations and Their Experiences.* New York: Viking Penguin, 1988.

Noe, Kenneth W. *Perryville: The Grand Havoc of Battle.* Lexington: University Press of Kentucky, 2001.

Nulty, William H. *Confederate Florida: The Road to Olustee.* Tuscaloosa: The University of Alabama Press, 1990.

Paisley, Clifton. *The Red Hills of Florida, 1528–1865.* Tuscaloosa: The University of Alabama Press, 1989.

Paludan, Phillip Shaw. *Victims: A True Story of the Civil War.* Knoxville: University of Tennessee Press, 1991.

Pearce, George. *Pensacola during the Civil War: A Thorn in the Side of the Confederacy.* Gainesville: University Press of Florida, 2000.

Raulston, J. Leonard, and James W. Livingood. *Sequatchie: A Story of the Lower Cumberlands.* Knoxville: University of Tennessee Press, 1974.

Register, Alvaretta Kenan, comp. *The Kenan Family and Some Allied Families of the Compiler and Publisher.* Statesboro, GA: Kenan Print Shop, 1967.

Rerick, Rowland H. *Memoirs of Florida.* Ed. Francis P. Fleming. 2 vols. Atlanta: Southern Historical Association, 1902.

Revels, Tracy J. *Grander in Her Daughters: Florida's Women during the Civil War.* Columbia, SC: University of South Carolina Press, 2004.

Rivers, Larry Eugene. *Slavery in Florida: Territorial Days to Emancipation.* Gainesville: University Press of Florida, 2000.

Robertson, Fred, comp. *Soldiers of Florida.* Live Oak, FL: Democrat Book and Job Print, 1903.

Shea, William, and Terrence J. Winschel. *Vicksburg Is the Key: The Struggle for the Mississippi River.* Lincoln: University of Nebraska Press, 2003.

Shofner, Jerrell H. *Nor Is It Over Yet: Florida in the Era of Reconstruction, 1863–1877.* Gainesville: University Presses of Florida, 1974.

Smith, Julia Floyd. *Slavery and Plantation Growth in Middle Florida.* Gainesville, FL: University of Florida Press, 1973.

Sword, Wiley. *The Confederacy's Last Hurrah: Spring Hill, Franklin, and Nashville.* Lawrence: University of Kansas Press, 1993.

———. *Mountains Touched with Fire: Chattanooga Besieged, 1863.* New York: St. Martin's Press, 1995.

Symonds, Craig L. *Joseph E. Johnston: A Civil War Biography.* New York: W. W. Norton, 1992.

Taylor, Robert A. *Rebel Storehouse: Florida's Contribution to the Confederacy.* 1995. Reprint, Tuscaloosa: The University of Alabama Press, 2003.

Tebeau, Charlton W. *The History of Florida.* 2nd ed. Coral Gables, FL: University of Miami Press, 1971.

Thomas, Emory M. *The Confederate Nation: 1861–1865.* New York: Harper and Row, 1979.

Warner, Ezra. *Generals in Gray.* 1959. Reprint, Baton Rouge: Louisiana State University Press, 1987.

Waters, Zack C. *Death Was Feasting in Our Midst: Major General William B. Bate and the Battle of Dallas, Georgia.* Hiram, GA: Friends of Civil War Paulding County, Georgia, 2003.

Watkins, Sam R. *"Co. Aytch": A Side Show of the Big Show.* New York: Macmillan, 1962.

Weber, David J. *The Spanish Frontier in North America.* New Haven: Yale University Press, 1992.

Wiley, Bell I. *The Life of Johnny Reb: The Common Soldier of the Confederacy.* 1943. Reprint, Baton Rouge: Louisiana State University Press, 2000.

Woodworth, Steven E. *Chickamauga: A Battlefield Guide.* Lincoln: University of Nebraska Press, 1999.

———. *Jefferson Davis and His Generals: The Failure of Confederate Command in the West.* Lawrence: University of Kansas Press, 1990.

———. *Nothing But Victory: The Army of Tennessee, 1861–1865.* New York: Knopf, 2005.

———. *Six Armies in Tennessee: The Chickamauga and Chattanooga Campaigns.* Lincoln: University of Nebraska Press, 1998.

———. *This Grand Spectacle: The Battle of Chattanooga.* Abilene, KS: McWhiney Foundation Press, 1999.

———. *While God Is Marching On: The Religious World of Civil War Soldiers.* Lawrence: University of Kansas Press, 2001.

Wynne, Benjamin R. *A Hard Trip: A History of the 15th Mississippi.* Macon, GA: Mercer University Press, 2003.

Articles

"Archibald Livingston." *Confederate Veteran* 24 (1916): 323.

Bearss, Edwin, and Charles Spearman. "The Battle of the Cedars." Unpublished manuscript in the Stones River National Military Park files, Stones River National Military Park, Murfreesboro, TN.

Bittle, George C. "Fighting Men View the Western War." *Florida Historical Quarterly* 47 (1968): 26–34.

———. "Florida Prepares for War, 1860–1861." *Florida Historical Quarterly* 51 (1972): 144–55.

Blocker, John R. "Company D, First Florida Infantry." *Confederate Veteran* 20 (1912): 156.

"Capt. W. T. Saxon." *Confederate Veteran* 33 (1925): 62.

Cates, C. Pat. "From Santa Rosa Island to Chickamauga: The First Confederate Regiment Georgia Volunteers." *Civil War Regiments* 1, no. 4 (1991): 42–73.

Caudle, Everett W. "Settlement Patterns in Alachua County, Florida, 1850–1860." *Florida Historical Quarterly* 67 (1989): 428–40.

"Col. George M. Edgar." *Confederate Veteran* 22 (1914): 85.

"Col. Robert C. Trigg, of Virginia." *Confederate Veteran* 17 (1909): 65.

Coles, David James. "Ancient City Defenders: The St. Augustine Blues." *El Escribano* 23 (1986): 65–89.

Cushman, Joseph D., Jr. "The Blockade and Fall of Apalachicola, 1861–1862." *Florida Historical Quarterly* 41 (1962): 38–46.

Dixon, Mary C. "Charles C. Hemming." *Confederate Veteran* 24 (1916): 364–65.

Dodd, Dorothy. "The Secession Movement in Florida, 1850–1861, Part I." *Florida Historical Quarterly* 12 (1933): 3–24.

———. "The Secession Movement in Florida, 1850–1861, Part II." *Florida Historical Quarterly* 12 (1933): 45–66.

Dougan, Michael B. "Herrmann Hirsch and the Siege of Jackson." *Journal of Mississippi History* 53 (1991): 19–33.

Faust, Drew Gilpin. "Christian Soldiers: The Meaning of Revivalism in the Confederate Army." *Journal of Southern History* 53, no. 1 (1987): 63–90.

Feibelman, Herbert U. "Floridians Distinguished at the Bar and on the Field of Battle." *Florida Law Journal* 23, no. 4 (1949): 133–37.

Hadd, Donald R. "The Irony of Secession." *Florida Historical Quarterly* 41 (1962): 22–28.

Hill, John H. "The Battle of Resaca." *Atlanta Journal,* February 9, 1901.

"In Memoriam: Francis Philip Fleming." *Florida Historical Quarterly* 2, no. 1 (1909): 3–8.

Leigh, Mrs. Townes Randolph. "The City of Pensacola, Fla." *Confederate Veteran* 36 (1928): 253.

Martin, Walter. "The Proposed Division of the Territory of Florida." *Florida Historical Quarterly* 20 (1942): 260–76.

McLeon, R. Don. "Capt. John L. Inglis." *Confederate Veteran* 25 (1917): 517.

McMurry, Richard M. "Patton Anderson: Major General, C.S.A." *Blue and Gray Magazine* 1, no. 2 (1983): 10–17.

"Official Souvenir Programme of the Unveiling Ceremonies of the Confederate Monument at St. James Park, Jacksonville, Florida, June 16, 1898." Jacksonville, FL, 1898.

Partridge, B. W. "Capt. David Ewell Maxwell." *Confederate Veteran* 17 (1909): 417.

Pasco, Samuel, Jr. "Samuel Pasco (1834–1917)." *Florida Historical Quarterly* 7 (1928): 135–39.

Prokopowicz, Gerald K. "Word of Honor: The Parole System in the Civil War." *North and South* 6 (2004): 24–33.

Reiger, John F. "Florida after Secession: Abandonment by the Confederacy and Its Consequences." *Florida Historical Quarterly* 50 (1971): 128–42.

Rivers, Larry Eugene. "Madison County, Florida—1830–1860: A Case Study in Land, Labor, and Prosperity." *Journal of Negro History* 78 (1993): 233–44.

Rogers, William Warren. "A Great Stirring in the Land: Tallahassee and Leon County in 1860." *Florida Historical Quarterly* 64 (1985): 148–60.

Sheppard, Jonathan C. "'This Seems to Be Our Darkest Times': The Florida Brigade in Mississippi, June–July, 1863." *Florida Historical Quarterly* 85 (2006): 64–90.

———. "'Through Good and Evil Fortune': Robert Bullock in Civil War and Reconstruction." *Proceedings of the 90th Annual Meeting of the Florida Historical Society at St. Augustine, May 1992* (1993): 135–49.

Wiley, Mrs. O. F. "Edward Clifford Brush." *Confederate Veteran* 40 (1932): 145.

Williamson, Edward. "The Constitutional Convention of 1885." *Florida Historical Quarterly* 41, no. 2 (1962): 116–26.

Willoughby, Lynn. "Apalachicola Aweigh: Shipping and Seamen at Florida's Premier Cotton Port." *Florida Historical Quarterly* 69 (1990): 178–94.

Winschel, Terrence J. "A Tragedy of Errors: The Failure of the Confederate High Command in the Defense of Vicksburg." *North and South* 8 (2006): 40–49.

Wooster, Ralph A. "The Florida Secession Convention." *Florida Historical Quarterly* 36 (1958): 373–85.

Dissertations and Theses

Bittle, George Cassel. "In the Defense of Florida: The Organized Florida Militia from 1821–1920." Ph.D. diss., Florida State University, 1965.

Brackett, John Matthew. "The Naples of America: Pensacola during the Civil War and Reconstruction." Master's thesis, Florida State University, 2005.

Flint, Kenneth. "The Battle of Missionary Ridge." Master's thesis, The University of Alabama, 1960.

Guinn, Gilbert S. "Coastal Defense of the Confederate Atlantic Seaboard States, 1861–1862." Ph.D. diss., University of South Carolina, 1973.

Iacono, Anthony Joseph. "So Far Away, So Close to Home: Florida and the Civil War Era." Ph.D. diss., Mississippi State University, 2000.

Murphree, Boyd R. "Rebel Sovereigns: The Civil War Leadership of Governors John Milton of Florida and Joseph E. Brown of Georgia, 1861–1865." Ph.D. diss., Florida State University, 2007.

Nichols, Richard S. "Florida's Fighting Rebels: A Military History of Florida's Civil War Troops." Master's thesis, Florida State University, 1967.

Porter, Emily. "The Movement for the Admission of Florida into the Union." Master's thesis, Florida State College for Women, 1938.

Prim, Gorrell Clinton, Jr. "Born Again in the Trenches: Revivalism in the Confederate Army." Ph.D. diss., Florida State University, 1982.

Smith, Julia H. "The Plantation Belt in Middle Florida, 1850–1860." Ph.D. diss., Florida State University, 1964.

Stein, Leslie Reicin. "David Levy and Florida Territorial Politics." Master's thesis, University of South Florida, 1973.

Urbach, Jon L. "An Appraisal of the Florida Secession Movement, 1859–1861." Master's thesis, Florida State University, 1972.

Weitz, Seth A. "The Rise of Radicalism in Antebellum Florida Politics: 1845–1856." Master's thesis, Florida State University, 2002.

Index

trenchments, 130; casualties of brigade at
    Jackson, 131
Pugh, Rinaldo, and description of the
    Jackson battlefield, 130

Quincy, Fl., 16, 48, 54, 223; location of
    Constitutional Union Party state conven-
    tion, 7

R. B. Taney, 70
Raleigh, N.C., 221
Randolph, Thomas E., 16–17, 39–40
Randolph, William, 17, 39–40
Raysor, Michael O., 61, 64–65, 83, 125–
    126, 132, 149, 221; exchanged at Vicks-
    burg, 99; and revivals of 1863, 117; on
    furloughs and morale, 135; wounding
    and death of, 147–148
Reddick, Henry, 83, 98, 212; at Battle of
    Dallas, 184; describes Mill Creek Block-
    house fight, 202–203; at Spring Hill,
    208; describe Battle of Franklin, 209–
    210; at Battle of the Cedars, 213; at
    Battle of Nashville, 218
Resaca, Battle of, 179–180
Reynolds, Alexander, retreat of brigade from
    Missionary Ridge's base, 163
Rice, B. L., 96; death of, 107
Richmond, Battle of, 77
Richmond Daily Dispatch, 131, 166
Robertson, Jerome, commands Texas Brigade
    at Battle of Chickamauga, 140, 142, 148
Robertson, T. J., on rations issued at Mis-
    sionary Ridge, 159
Rocky Face Ridge, Ga., Confederate fortifi-
    cations on, 178
Rogers, William D., 101, 107–108, 117,
    125–126; opinion of Corinth and Tu-
    pelo, 63; and Christmas, 1862, 97; and
    January 2, 1863 battle, 105–106; on
    drill and instruction in camp, 116; death
    of, 227
Rosecrans, William Starke, 134, 137–138;
    replaces Buell as Army of the Ohio's com-
    mander, 99; decides to remain at Mur-
    freesboro, 104; characteristics of army
    movement, 136; and retreat from Battle
    of Chickamauga, 155
Rosseau, Lovell, 87, 211–212
Rough and Ready, GA., 195

"Round Forest," 100; occupied by Confeder-
    ates, 104; at Battle of the Cedars, 212
Routh, William, 27
Ruggles, Daniel, 41

Sanders, William P., and East Tennessee raid,
    120–121
Santa Rosa Island, Fl., 10–11, 15, 17, 144;
    and Battle of Santa Rosa Island, 25–27
Savannah Republican, 48
Savannah River, 220
Saxon, Walter Terry, 131; postwar career of,
    225
Schofield, John, 181, 190, 208, 210, 216;
    commands Army of the Ohio, 206–207
Sears, Claudius, 212–213
XVII Corps at Atlanta, 194
17th Louisiana Infantry Regiment, 41
7th Florida Infantry Regiment, 117, 142,
    146, 148, 168, 172, 201, 211, 213; or-
    ganization of, 51; ordered to Tennes-
    see, 66–67; encamped at the "Canyon of
    the Tennessee," 68; ordered to Cumber-
    land Gap, 93; and bushwacker attacks,
    112; and defense of Knoxville, 120; ca-
    sualties suffered on September 19, 1863,
    143; position at the base of Missionary
    Ridge, 162, casualties suffered at Battle of
    Missionary Ridge, 166; and reenlistment
    declaration, 171; and baseball at Dalton,
    175; at Battle of Resaca, 180; casualties
    suffered at Jonesboro, 197
7th Iowa Infantry Regiment, 43
75th Illinois Infantry Regiment, 204
Shaw, Roderick G., 16, 25–27, 39–40, 61,
    173, 183, 221–222; describes Jefferson
    Davis, 155; and disgruntlement re-
    garding lack of regimental reelections in
    1864, 170; on regimental reenlistments,
    171; attitude of, on eve of Atlanta Cam-
    paign, 176; death of, 182
Shelton Laurel Massacre, 113–115
Sheridan, Philip, division overruns rifle pits
    at Missionary Ridge's base, 163
Sherman, William T., 132–134, 137, 176,
    185–186, 190, 201–202, 205; launches
    expedition against Jackson, 127; army in-
    vests Jackson, 129; at Battle of Mission-
    ary Ridge, 160–162; and 1864 offensive,
    178; at Battle of Resaca, 180; changes